The Holy Spirit
of
My Uncle's Cojones

A Novel

Marcos McPeek Villatoro

Arte Público Press
Houston, Texas
1999

Fic
VIL

This volume is made possible through grants from the City of Houston through The Cultural Arts Council of Houston, Harris County.

Recovering the past, creating the future

Arte Público Press
University of Houston
452 Cullen Performance Hall
Houston, Texas 77204-2004

Cover design by Giovanni Mora
Cover illustration by Giovanni Mora and Efrain Quijada
Text design by Sandra Villagomez

Villatoro, Marcos McPeek.
   The Holy Spirit of my uncle's Cojones / by Marcos McPeek Villatoro.
   p.   cm.
   ISBN 1-55885-283-2 (pbk. : alk. paper)
   1. Mexican Americans--California--San Francisco--Fiction.
I. Title.
PS3572.I386H65   1999
813'.54—dc21   99-22554
                                                                       CIP

Four lines by Pablo Neruda are quoted from "I Ask for Silence," in *Extravagaria,* by Pablo Neruda (translated by Alastair Reid); published by the University of Texas Press-Farrar Straus Giroux.

⊕ The paper used in this publication meets the requirements of the American National Standard for Information Sciences—Permanence of Paper for Printed Library Materials, ANSI Z39.48-1984.

1 2 3 4 5 6 7 8 9 0   11 10 9 8 7 6 5 4 3 2

Other Books by Marcos McPeek Villatoro

A Fire in the Earth

Walking to La Milpa: Living in Guatemala
with Armies, Demons, *Abrazos,* and Death

They Say That I Am Two

To Michelle

Tanto que te quiero que quiero quererte otro tanto.

He vivido tanto que un día
tendrán que olvidarme por fuerza,
borrándome de la pizarra:
mi corazón fue interminable.

Pablo Neruda

I have lived so much that some day
they will have to forget me forcibly,
rubbing me off the blackboard.
My heart was inexhaustible.

(Translation: Alastair Reid)

Part One

I said nothing once Mamá told me that Uncle Jack had died of natural causes.

"Tony? Are you there? *Hijo*, talk back to me. Are you all right?"

I lifted the receiver back toward my mouth. "Yes, Mamá, I'm fine."

She whimpered. She had been crying while telling me the news. "Your uncle. He is dead. My brother, he is dead."

She wept. I shivered while listening to her sobs.

She turned the sobs off like a spigot. "Hey. What's the matter? Didn't you hear me?"

"Yeah . . . Yes, I heard you, Mamá. What . . . what did he die of?"

"They don't know. No gunshot wound. He wasn't beaten. No signs of poisoning. No one ran over him. Nothing. Absolutely nothing! He's just there, dead."

"Where?"

"In his bedroom here on Capp Street."

"But, was anybody with him when he died? Like, you know . . ."

"No hookers. No pimps. No *cholos*. Not one *pachuco* or *marijuano*. Nobody. Chucho wasn't there, of course. They haven't spoken in years."

I had not heard Chucho's name in years; it was a Guatemalan nickname that meant "doggie."

"So there's absolutely no sign of an attack?" I asked.

"I'm telling you, *hijo*. He just died. I suppose I should see that as a blessing . . ."

"My gosh, he wasn't that old, was he?"

"He would have been sixty-nine next year, I think. Yes, he was young!"

Sixty-nine, I thought. Appropriate.

"So," my mother asked, "will you go?"

"Go? To the funeral? I don't know, Mamá. San Francisco's a long trip. I've got my classes to teach. I don't have the money for the plane flight."

Though that was a half-truth, and my mother knew it, she did not contradict me, choosing not to comment upon what I did with my savings. Still, she was not the champion of poignant silence. She allowed for half a second before speaking: "I know it's been almost twenty years. But you haven't forgotten everything, have you?"

Ours was a coded form of communication, not one that hid anything, but rather relied easily upon mutually understood references. I knew exactly what she meant. I didn't want to believe I had forgotten.

"Mamá, you know I've got to teach."

"He died yesterday. They won't bury him until Saturday, or maybe even Sunday. Can't you miss just one or two days of class?"

Hers was a more logical voice. Yes, I could easily afford to miss a few classes, especially for a funeral. I had not missed any classes in my one-year career as adjunct professor at three separate colleges. In eight months I had put thirty thousand miles on my little Honda, zipping between the University of Tennessee in Knoxville, Jameson County College, and Wallace State in Morristown. I taught five classes each semester, all divided up among the three institutions. Each college saw me as a part-time employee, and thus didn't worry about trifles such as health insurance, benefits, retirement, or a parking space. In response to their forced asceticism, I had always arrived on time, sometimes sprinting through each campus in order to appear, sweating, before my class. Of course, I told myself, the reason I did not mind receiving three pauper's salaries that added up to one big pauper salary was because the students made the self-abnegation all worth it. I had never missed a class, not even when I had the flu.

"I can loan you some money," Mamá said, interrupting my thoughts. This was no altruism; it was a verbal slap of shame: poor Carmen McCaugh had to *pay* her son to go to her brother's funeral.

"No. I've got money. If I decide to go." Though it meant to be adamant, my voice trembled under those final words.

"Do you think Julie will come?" she asked.

I paused, too long for her not to notice. "No. I don't think so."

"What's wrong?"

"Nothing's wrong."

"Antonio, you can tell your mother."

She called me by my formal name, and not "Tony." I was trapped.

Then I was saved. The woman in question shoved her keys into the doorknob. I heard Julie open the door, jiggle the keys, then slam it behind her, no doubt with her thin hip. I could not see her from where I stood in the kitchen of our one-bedroom apartment. I clicked my teeth seven times, then tapped my forehead with the knuckle of my left index finger. Then I fell into the original language, *"Ya viene, Mamá. Debo irme."*

"Oh. She's there. And you want to speak Spanish. Well, that says it all, doesn't it?"

"Hablo más tarde."

"Vaya, pues. You call me if you need me."

"All right," I almost whispered.

"You're not happy, are you?"

Jesus, I would be happy if I could hang up this fucking phone. *"Oh, estoy bien, Mamá."* I smiled, hoping she could feel her boy's grin over the telephone lines.

"I've not wanted to say anything, but I was never sure. She seems like a nice enough girl. And you know I have nothing against living together. But you all did seem to rush into it."

"I'll call you later."

"You don't want to talk to me about it, do you?"

"How did you guess?"

A pause, then, *"Vaya pues. Te quiero, hijo."*

"A usted también."

We hung up. I sighed.

The Holy Spirit of My Uncle's Cojones

Julie walked around the corner. She carried a small plastic sack of groceries from Kroger in one hand and her red purse in the other. She wore jean shorts and an old Sandinista shirt of mine, one that displayed a red and black painted heart (the color of that Nicaraguan party), with the words *"Vamos adelante en la revolución"* scrawled wildly over the front, resting upon her breasts. I used to wear that shirt quite often before I had met Julie. Somehow it had migrated, during trips to the laundrymat, from my dresser to hers.

Actually, both dressers were mine. She had taken the larger one six months ago, when we decided to have her move in with me. It had been a mutual agreement, one done out of both necessity and desire. Rent in Knoxville had become almost competitive with housing in such cities as Nashville and some parts of Atlanta. We both saved money, splitting the costs. That soon changed, however, once the summer months came on and her work-study job at the university ended. Julie could no longer pay her part. I had told her not to fret about it, that I could assume full payment. I remember the day we had talked about that: she had quickly taken me up on the deal, including not fretting at all. My landlady never found out about my live-in lover. Julie and I chose not to get the outside world involved in our private affairs.

As a graduate student in Political Science, Julie had few possessions such as furniture. It had taken little time to get her moved in with me. It had taken less time for items such as my Sandinista shirt to get folded into her clothes. The shirt seemed strange on her. I remember seeing numerous shirts such as those ten years ago on the shoulders of Nicaraguans back in Managua or out in the mountains of Nueva Segovia and Estelí. Darker skinned young people—some of them almost ebony—led marches and held rifles and books and, smiling, shouted out rhymed slogans concerning their hard-won revolution. It was beyond an anomoly to see the same shirt on the back of this white skinned, North American woman.

She was beautiful. Julie had dark brown hair that, in summers such as this one, she haphazardly tied up with a pinched bow. The strings of hair that hung to the sides of her face heightened the sexiness, giving her a slight whisp of wildness. Though Caucasian, she risked the dangers of melanoma just to acquire an even tan that now made the deadly sunbathing all worthwhile. Though I once jokingly told her that she didn't need to sunbathe just to please me, I was glad she did. The sun had yet to create wrinkles around her eyes, which were much darker than her hair or her skin. And her bikini line, I knew (though I had not seen it in two weeks) barely covered her nipples and pubis. She had begun work on that tan long before summer. I believe that was one of the prime reasons she had come south from her home in Minneapolis: it gets hot earlier here.

Tennis was her game. She played every day during the spring, summer, and fall. She was good. Everyone knew how good she was. Having played on her college team, she had never given it up. A group of her friends gathered together every week and chose who would play whom. She was so good that she had been picked to play against the top seated men in the group. No other woman could keep up with her.

I wondered if she had played tennis in my Sandinista shirt. I thought to ask her, though I did not want to sound offensive. I decided to wait.

"Who was that?" she asked.

"My mother."

"Oh. How is Doña Carmen doing since yesterday?" Julie nasalized the tilde "ñ" of "doña." I don't know why she did this. It sounded blatantly sarcastic.

"She's fine." I walked toward the kitchen to find a beer in the refrigerator. After opening the door and grabbing the can, I glanced at it, then placed it back in the doorshelf. "My uncle died."

"Uncle? I didn't know you had an uncle." Julie walked by me and placed groceries away: peanut butter in the shelves, fruit in a basket, yogurt in the refrigerator. She grabbed the beer that I decided not to drink and tore the top open. "What was his name?"

"Jack. Juan. Most everybody called him Jack. Except Grandmamá, of course." I glanced over at the Sandinista shirt. The apartment's loud air conditioning had worked on her. I could see her nipples through the cloth. Revolution never looked so good.

"Were you close to him?"

"When I was a kid. I spent a summer with him once. I was sixteen." I was about to tell her that I had a photo of him on my dresser, one that she had never paid any attention to. My lips opened, then my breath hesitated and fell back into the recesses of my throat.

"Did he ever come out here to visit you?"

"No. Mamá and I spent the summer in San Francisco."

"Oh. That's neat. So are you thinking of going?" She raised the beer to her lips and looked at me for the first time since entering the apartment.

"I'm . . . I'm not sure."

"Could be a good chance to be with family, don't you know." She walked by me and toward the bedroom.

"Yeah. Hey . . . isn't that my shirt?"

She looked down at the Spanish words. "Oh. Yeah. I guess it is. You want to wear it?"

"Well, no. But if you were going out to play tennis now, I didn't know if you were going to use it. It's kind of a keepsake from old times."

"No problem." She whipped it off her shoulders and above her head, then tossed it on the bed. "I was going to change for tennis anyway." She flipped off her bra, then turned toward a drawer. Her breasts moved with her, jiggling only slightly, yet the movement through the apartment's cool air puckered their tips more, as if an invisible baby sucked upon them. Then she turned and looked at me and spoke about other things: her summer classes, how she hated being cooped up in a classroom when all this beautiful weather was beckoning her outside; her tennis game last night with Bill, how it sucked to high heaven. I did not hear these things (except for Bill's name). I only saw the full of her figure from her navel to her shoulders. The thin muscles of her twenty-three-year old hips curved upward in light brown swirls, all the way to her breasts that just stood there, erect and cool. I could not help but look at them, and not look at her face as she spoke. She stood, half-naked, working on the strap of her bra before putting it away and snatching up her exercise bra. For a moment the analogy of a wife came to mind: a wife who, through time, has become comfortable with flinging off clothes before her husband. But I had been married before and knew that this was different. It was not to be confused with the ordinariness of a marriage. Julie and I had not touched each other in two weeks. I had taught both night and day, as the summer schedule was more demanding, my classes filling with older, working students who had to read Faulkner's *Light in August* in three nights so as to cover all the other material on the syllabus within the short semester. Then we spent one poorly constructed class on T. S. Eliot's *The Wasteland* and *The Love Song of J. Alfred Prufrock*. I knew I was doing damage to one of my favorite poet's works, forcing a fast, cryptic lecture over two of the more profound poems of the century, not to mention not allowing my students to explore the poems themselves in some meditative, Buddhist posture. But hey, who was going to complain? I got a shrivelled paycheck. My students were getting a required class out of the way.

Whenever I came home from one of the three colleges, Julie was never there. She either was at the library studying for her own classes or out on the tennis courts. Two weeks had passed without so much as a peck on the cheek. I knew it was a sign; and recently I had learned what the sign stood for. Now she stood before me, naked and distant. My hands could not push through the gap to touch those perfect nipples.

The Holy Spirit of My Uncle's Cojones

Our sex had been rational. Actually, it had gone from passionate to rational once she realized that I was nothing like the characters in my novel. She had read my first book before attending a signing of mine at a local bookstore on the west end of Knoxville. She, like most fans, knew nothing about the literary marketplace. She did not know that my publisher, though very prestigious, was literary, a term which, while meaning many things, does not always signify revenue. She also had never read Borges' perspective on how the audience makes a fiction out of the writer: the audience reads a work and expects the writer to be some sort of carnal symbol of the characters in the book. My novel, *Ashes from the Fire,* was based loosely upon my Salvadoran family's history. It had been the culmination of a seven-year obsession I had with the 1932 massacre, which my mother had survived. *Ashes in the Fire* had been one of the fundamental reasons why I, at twenty-three (Julie's present age) had moved to Central America and had stayed there throughout most of the eighties. I had found my roots and had written about them. Publication created a transient notion of success. The book had done fairly well in the world of reviews. Yet it was a first novel and had opened only a small nitch in the market-place. I had yet to see one royalty check.

The excitement of having sex with a published novelist kept us going for the first few weeks. Julie had invited me out for a drink after the reading. We had talked in the quiet bar until closing. I learned that she was over a decade younger than I. She learned bits and pieces of my past, my life in Nicaragua during the revolution years of the eighties (this also added to the excitement: living in war zones can seem downright sexy to one who has never had the experience), my desire to write, and the recent beginning of my publishing career. As she was a graduate student in political science, she was able to refer to Central America and its history, though she always confused Nicaragua with Guatemala, and the Nicaraguan Contras with the Salvadoran Death Squads. I gave her some slack on that. Especially when she rolled her index finger into her loose lock of hair.

We had made love that first time at three o'clock in the morning. The following day I had received word from U.T. that they wanted me to be an adjunct professor. I was to return to Knoxville, the town of my youth. At first Julie did not understand my excitement over teaching; why would an established author need to work in the academic system? She soon learned that my excitement stemmed also from a need to eat and pay rent. Thus another chunk of Borges' fictitious image of the author came tumbling down: My financial concerns were not to be confused with those of Steven King.

Not that our sex was unsatisfying. There was a certain joy in making love with a woman so much younger than myself. Still, our movements were orthodox. Why, I do not know. Sometimes she would crawl on top of me, which made for a nice change of pace. That made me orgasm more quickly, which made her happy; she could jump off me earlier and fetch from the fridge a cup of frozen coconut yogurt with sprinkles, her after-fucking snack of choice. Whenever I was on top, it took longer. I have no idea why, except for *that* reason: age. Here I was, after having lived a fairly exciting life of tromping around Central America through my twenties and finally publishing in my thirties, now having the opportunity to lay out my first groupie who was just four years out of her teens. That should have been exciting enough to maintain a decent, perpetual erection. Yet after the first few months, I don't think the feelings over age difference were reciprocated; perhaps that was what kept me on the brink of flaccidity. I rarely considered using new moves or positions to lather up any excitement. I'm still not sure why. Living in Knoxville had its drawbacks, as it was my old stomping grounds. My Salvadoran mother and Appalachian father had left their East Tennessee home of Rakertown to spend the past half year with our Latino family in San Francisco. Yet Mamá called me as if she lived down the block. She always seemed to catch us in bed. Like most normal sons, my hard-earned, barely stable erection usually desiccated the moment I heard her voice over the phone. Like most disappointed fans, Julie started to see that I was more than a novelist, I was more than my books: I had three jobs, rent to pay, and a mother.

After the first few months we fell into schedules. She took classes at U.T. I taught and tried to work on another novel. The publication of my first book had created a dark, enigmatic writer's block. That was as difficult to explain as the lack of gumption in my underwear. I did a lot of staring at the computer screen. Though the screen was blank, I could see things: my rent bill, the books I needed to read for class, the last credit card statement showing how many times I had put gas on the Visa. I didn't see much of a story.

Julie and I made love at first four times a week, then three, twice, then once. Then passed the two weeks up to my uncle's death. We did not touch. She did not seem bothered by this. I learned why the night that I gave my literature class an exam that they all finished long before the two-hour time limit. I came home before sunset. I heard Julie making noises that I always associated with her backswing: she always let out a certain grunt whenever smashing the ball over the net after playing for an hour or two. It was exhausted yet complete, as guttural as those thin lungs behind those perfect breasts could get. So guttural were they that neither she nor Bill heard my key as I pushed it into the door and turned the knob. I did not have to look far down the short hallway toward the bedroom door to see Bill's long, loosened blonde hair, which was usually tied in a ponytail, falling over Julie's face as she opened her mouth wide.

That happened just two nights before my mother called, telling me of Uncle Jack's death. I had left the apartment and walked to a nearby bar. I drank two scotches. I ate nuts and watched reruns of "Mork and Mindy" and "Happy Days" on a television that loomed above the bartender. I paid and returned to my apartment. When I entered, I heard no grunting noises. I only saw Julie's face as she smiled at me. "How was class?"

That night, as she took a shower, I looked about the room, hoping to find a condom. I did not. Then I knew that they would not have been so stupid. It obviously ended up somewhere in the bottom of the trash or in my toilet. Julie's preferred prophylactic was a rubber; it was all that we used the past several months, even during the exciting first days. I figured I was safe.

I lay next to her and listened to her snore. I remembered what I had seen earlier, before the two scotches: Bill had been on top. His hair had fallen all over her face. She opened her mouth to it, as if wanting the hair to choke her. My hair was short. It had been short since my days in Nicaragua. I had no facial hair, while Bill sported a thick moustache. Other than that, I was not sure what the difference between Bill and me was, except that he was a decade younger. He played tennis. I abhorred the game. My daily exercise was three miles of running and a few sets of pushups and situps. The reps had diminished this past year with my busy schedule. Bill was white with a tan, while I was light olive with a tendency to stay out of the sun. His hair was blonde, mine black. He with piercing blue eyes the color of crudely cut gems; I the eyes of a shit-laden texture. But all he did was mount her, and yet she still grunted and sucked air. The evening I caught them, her tennis grunt metamorphosed into a wide mouth moan, as if in stretching her jaw, she could make for more room below. That was when the comparisons needed to end. I did not see what size member he had and did not care to compare.

The night of that discovery I rose from the bed, poured cheap scotch into a tall glass, and drank it down like medicine. I slept on the couch.

Two days had passed since realizing I was a true, practically card-carrying *cabrón*. Now I had just learned that my uncle had died. It all felt oooh so symbolic.

"So," Julie said, pulling the sports bra over her mounds, snapping them into place, "are you thinking of going to the funeral?"

"Yeah. I might. I'm not sure."

"I think it's a good idea. It's almost the weekend. You can be with family. They may need you." Then, as if an afterthought, she looked at me and her eyes turned deeper, an understanding that went beyond all comprehension. She held the counselor-like smile for three seconds, then snapped out of it. "You should call the airport as soon as you can." She walked by me and through the kitchen to the living room. She glanced over at the corner of the room where my computer's screen saver danced about, creating perfect images of flying books, pencils, and cute little terminals.

"Nothing to write about, huh?"

I drove to the airport the week that Flight 800 to France exploded just outside of New York and a crude shrapnel bomb blew up in the Olympic Park of Atlanta. I decided not to stop at a McDonalds, not wanting to be late for the flight. At the same time I did not want to board the plane. A deadly fate surely awaited me. I was a brand new published novelist. My claim to fame had yet to be reached. I stood before a writer's block the size of Bill's dick. I wondered if, these days, I could blame Bill for the lack of inspiration. Then again, could the writer's block be the source of my impotence? Or was that, too, Bill's fault? Whosever fault it was, my fate still hung in the balance: I knew an explosive device was going to be packed onto my flight from Knoxville to Chicago to San Francisco. I was never to publish again.

The Atlanta bombing did not come to mind until a white pickup truck approached me. At first I did not notice; I was thinking about the two tiny plastic bottles of scotch that I had purchased at a liquor store in my neighborhood, and whether or not I had packed them in the side pocket of my carry-on. I planned to suck both of them down just before boarding the plane, which would have lubricated my intestines enough before consuming the two drinks that I planned to purchase while in flight. Though my mother was always so good to share her expired Prozac with me or the old Valium that relatives in El Salvador bought on the street and mailed to her, I preferred to go under naturally.

It was then that the white pickup truck pulled up from behind. It was wider and taller than most trucks. I could see most of its grill hovering over the trunk of my little Honda. It drove up behind me, flashed its lights in broad daylight, revved and lowered and revved its engine again and hunkered up to my fender as close as it could. I looked down. I had to speed up to keep him from touching me, reaching eighty-five miles an hour. I was in the left lane, also trying to pass an eighteen wheeler that was having a hard time climbing the hill. I had yet to pass the truck. The pickup demanded that I get over in the right lane.

When I finally got around the eighteen wheeler, I swerved quickly to avoid the hot breath of the pickup. This left little room between me and the eighteen wheeler. The pickup lunged forward. The driver honked his horn. I barely caught his laughing face inside a scruffy red beard. He adjusted his green baseball cap. While trying to keep ahead of the eighteen wheeler, an enraged curiosity made me turn to get a good look at His Asshole-ness.

I threw him a middle finger.

My first mistake of the day. He saw it. He pulled up in front of me, then slowed down. I moved to the left lane. He jerked up ahead of me and slowed down again. I tried for the right. He followed. I could not get around him. He kept his tail against my hood. The eighteen wheeler pulled around us and drove on. Other cars drove by. The red-head and I moved at fifty miles per hour. I was forced to stare at all four back wheels of his truck sticking out from under the bed, the gun rack in the back window with a large rifle resting in it, and his bright red hair sticking out of his green cap. Then he punched the gas and left me.

I crawled back up to sixty five. I kept in the right lane. My heart had migrated to my throat. "Jesus, what a nutcase." I could not see him in the traffic. Breaths left me as if fleeing an intense heat in my lungs. My legs took on that inevitable cliché of noodles. My thighs ached with molten adrenaline. "It's idiots like that who hide bombs in garbage cans," I muttered, thinking about the recent Olympic news. Perhaps, I pondered, this *was* the guy. Theories had broken over the recent bombing, one being that it was an ur-Nazi lunatic who didn't want so many internationals invading his beloved South. I thought about all this, placing a tremulous, yet somewhat calming analysis upon the incident. It helped somewhat, until I saw the white pickup once again slow in the left lane, letting me pass him in the right. I saw his face. It was originally pale white, but according to the red splotches on his cheeks, had seen too much sun. The face first smiled, then contorted into a strange rage, one that spat out words, slapping spittle on his passenger seat window. Seeing that the window was an obstacle, he leaned over, cranked the glass down, and let the words fly again. I could hear them. They were not in any syntactical order. "Fuck" was used a lot, as was "faggot," "queer," "white skinned nigger," "pink-blooded dickless bitch," "pussy-face cunt." No real verbs came out until he yelped "kill."

Then he slowed down, pulled up behind me, revved his engine, hunkered his fender up to mine, pulled back, pulled up again, back and up again and again, as if wishing to shove a projectile up into my trunk.

My hands and face dropped into a ritual that would have been saved for the moment my jet left the ground: I clicked my teeth seven times, then tapped my forehead seven times with my knuckle. I clicked my teeth again, tapped my forehead, again and again.

I sought out a police car. There was not one anywhere. I kept driving. He followed me, pulling up and away from me, all the way through Knoxville. I tried not to look into the mirror. My breath turned shallow against my tongue.

Finally a cop appeared, giving a ticket to a motorist one mile before my exit to the airport. I turned on my right signal, slowed and moved toward the officer.

The white pickup turned to the left lane, hit the accelerator and drove on ahead. It moved away from me, beyond my exit ramp, toward some distant mountain of east Tennessee.

I almost pulled up behind the officer, but suddenly changed my mind. I could see the puzzled look of the policeman as he watched me drive away.

After turning off Interstate 40 and taking the Airport Road south through Knoxville, I reached over in my carry-on case and pulled at the side zipper. In front of me the tarnished golden ball barely stuck up through Knoxville's skyline, the remnant of a dinky world's fair from the previous decade. I ignored it, drinking and driving while heading toward the airport, thinking too much of exploding planes and bombs hidden in garbage cans.

I glanced about at Knoxville, the little city that I was leaving behind for a few days. The scotch was enough to bring about a philosophical thought or two regarding the region. Some poignant words that collected around the philosophies: backward, fascist, white supremacist, incestuous hillbilly *Deliverance*-driven primates. Spanish tremulously kicked in: *pendejos, cabrones, hijos de la puta de la madre de la gran chingada*. Then again, I'm from here. Part of my blood is this place, the place I so quickly cursed.

After parking the car I sucked on the second bottle. Some of the scotch did not make it to my mouth, but fell from the tiny plastic lip and splashed against my shirt. I looked at my hand as if it were someone else's. It moved as if it were not mine; no, this could not have been mine, this hand without bones, with its wobble, its lack of grip.

By the time the plane was halfway to Chicago I was quite drunk. Once I had almost forgotten to click my teeth and tap my forehead with my knuckles. Then I remembered to do it, though I may not have gotten the count right. In Chicago I got refills at a couple of bars, then wettened them up on the flight to the west coast.

I slept in a dreamless state of thick, brown-liquored catatonia for the last half of the trip. The captain woke me, telling us all to prepare for landing. The alcohol still pumped over my eyes as I looked out at the foggy sky that blanketed the city. The off-red towers of the Golden Gate barely poked through the low clouds. The Translatlantic Pyramid Tower was nowhere to be found.

It had been eighteen years since I first returned to the city of my birth. I had been sixteen at the time. The alcohol did not allow for much reminiscing at the moment. Nor did the fear of landings.

I buckled up and did not breathe well until the plane came safely to its stop. A legion of seat buckles unsnapping told me that I had survived. I cursed God for superstitions while crossing myself.

My mother met me at the terminal. She wore some of her sister's clothes: long black and gold leotard pants that clung to her skinny, seventy-one-year-old legs; a thin leopard skin jacket tossed over her shoulders; at least three bracelets upon each wrist, some of them gold, others silver, one that held blue rhinestones; and large gold rimmed sunglasses that shielded her eyes, even here, inside the terminal.

We embraced.

"You look peaked," were the first words she said. "That girl Julie, is she feeding you well?"

I said nothing about the pizza boxes, empty Chinese food tubs, cans of beer and soda, salads from the grocery store.

"Are you hungry? You want a drink or something?" she asked me.

"No. I'm fine. We can go."

"Vaya pues," she smiled for the first time, not able to control the delight over seeing her son.

"Where's Dad?"

"He's with your Auntie Felícita. Trying to hold her together. You know how delicate she can be."

Delicate like a bulldozer. But I didn't say that.

Mamá drove a fifteen-year-old darkly silvered Mercedes Benz convertible. She moved adroitly out of the parking ramp and pulled into the heaviest part of traffic. "Your auntie gave me this car. I don't know why. I never put the top down like she does. She loves to feel the wind in her hair. Me, it just makes my sinuses get worse."

She talked about her sinuses for two or three more minutes as I studied the traffic around us and her ability to weave into it. A couple of times I closed my eyes, unsure as to how a seventy-one-year-old woman dressed like a panther could make it between the trucks and cars.

"You seem to have accustomed yourself to the big city life again," I said.

"What? This traffic? This is nothing. You've just got to be aggressive. That's the key: Don't let them push you around."

The final waves of alcohol washed through my brain, trying to knock over the image of the crazed white man who I had left in Knoxville.

"So what made you decide to come?" she asked.

"I'm not sure. I had the weekend. And Julie thought it would be a good idea . . ."

"I see. Julie thought it was a good idea."

"Well, I wanted to come too."

"I'm glad of that. Your *tío* would be happy. He asked for you just a couple of weeks before we found him dead."

I tried to ignore that, remembering the last time I had written him. It had not been that long ago, perhaps six months. I counted that up as a reason not to feel too guilty.

Mamá filled me in on other facts of local life. Aunt Felícita had moved to Daly City, into a huge two-storey house that Mamá suspected cost over a million. Mamá and Dad were still living on Capp Street, where Felícita had also been residing before buying her new house. Uncle Jack had been living in one room on the first floor of the house on Capp Street, where they had found his body. The business, as usual, was doing well; the Doña Roselia Fine Latin Cuisine Company Inc. had brought in record figures the past year.

We drove into the city. Mamá took us right into the Mission District, where Aunt Felícita was waiting for us.

I looked around. The neighborhood had changed, most definitely. There were not that many Latin faces around. Not like in my childhood, when I could look out the window of my grandmother Doña Roselia's Victorian house and see two Mexican young men sticking their heads under the hood of a 1964 Chevrolet or boys playing stickball in the empty field across the street. That field was no longer there. High rise apartments had been built since my departure. New cars now drove by us. My mother's grey Mercedes was the oldest car on the block. At least it was a Mercedes. I saw more white people than I ever remember seeing in my childhood, or even during my summer here eighteen years ago. I also caught more Asian faces.

"It's not the same neighborhood at all," my mother said, as if reading my thoughts. "I miss the old days. But those were some tough times too. Gangs were forming all over the city. Felícita tells me they had two gangs always fighting it out right here, or over on Market. Then the Asians began buying up property. That raised the value of the land and the buildings. They've really done some good work renovating the places. You won't believe how much 77B is now worth!" Mamá smiled behind her gold sunglasses as she pulled into the numbered home, clicked a button behind the visor, and pulled into the garage. "But your father and I won't sell. Not now, at least. Oh, he's missing the hills in East Tennessee. But he's pretty happy here, with my sister spoiling him."

In the garage I glanced ahead at a tiny half-built airplane. The wings hung from hooks in the ceiling. The fuselage faced the grille of the Mercedes. I did not need to question, knowing it was Dad's. To one side was parked a black 1967 Mustang. I stared longer at the Mustang than I did at the small airplane. Then, while Mamá closed her door, I reached over and touched the cold, thick steel of its hood. No doubt its motor had not been turned over in at least two days.

We walked out of the garage and to the first floor. I carried my bags. Mamá walked behind me, warning me to watch my step in the dark. I turned the corner after passing the door of the first floor and looked up the eighteen steps to the second floor. There, standing on the top landing, was my Aunt Felícita.

She wore a white suit, with white lace that covered her wrists. She wore a diamond necklace that sparkled like hard water over her chest. Though her hair was still long and thick, I could see the matching diamond earrings as they shattered light through the black shafts. She wore white shoes that hugged her tiny feet and pushed her up in the air upon two-inch spiked heels. No doubt about it, she was still well-built. She was less brown than my mother, though brown nonetheless. Hers had been a body that men had sought like a Latin grail.

I walked carefully up the steps, pushing a smile out of my mouth as I ascended. It seemed to take a full minute to climb the stairs. Then she embraced me as I murmured *"Tía Felícita, que alegre es verla a usted . . ."*

"Oh Tony, Tony, Tony," and she hugged me, repeating my name like a personal mantra.

Once on top of the steps, I stood taller than she. She had the look of a woman who had been crying an hour earlier, but had dried her face and had put on fresh mascara. "Look at you," she said, pulling back to stare at my body. "Are you still running? You look like you run two miles too many."

"I try to run every day," I murmured somewhat proudly.

"Do you still do your exercises? Your pushups and situps, just like your uncle taught you?"

"Every morning."

"You still look peaked."

"That's what I told him," my mother said as she passed us. She turned and kissed Felícita on the cheek. The younger sister reciprocated.

"What, he's not eating right?" my aunt turned and asked my mother, as if forgetting that I was in the room. "What is it, that girlfriend of his does not feed him anything?" She then turned to me. "What is her name? Jill, Janie . . ."

"Julie."

"*Ya*. Julie. She's a *chela*, right?"

"Well, yeah. She's a white woman . . ."

"'Yeah?' 'Yeah?' Tony, Tony, where have your manners gone? You know that 'yeah' is such a weak word, used by people *sin educación*. You say 'yes.' 'Yes' is strong, it speaks. It is virile." Aunt Felícita held her fist up as she spoke the words. "So she's white. That has its advantages and disadvantages, you know." She stopped, pausing in a thought as one arm crossed under her taut bosom and the other propped itself on the first's elbow. "White women like to be independent, which is very good. But they also think they can do it without a man, which is stupid. I don't know where such thoughts come from, do you, *hermana*?" she called back into Mamá's bedroom.

Mamá answered that no, she did not. I could tell she had not heard what her sister had said.

"So you've come, you've come, Tony! For your uncle, you've come . . ."

She began to weep. My head bounced in the air twice, as if trying to make a silent decision, before I took her into my arms. I held her carefully, wanting to show her correct signals of giving her some space while at the same time letting her know I was there for her. I was what you would call a politically correct Latino.

"Jesus, Tony. You hug like a doped *maricón*." She pulled away to clean her nose. "Oh, it's been so difficult. I cannot believe he is gone. Do you know where we found him? Right in there." She pointed to a front room that faced Capp Street. It was a bedroom that I had stayed in that summer eighteen years ago. "He had been sleeping in there for the past several months. Your mother walked out the other morning and found him dead. Right there, dead on the floor. No blood stains, no signs of a struggle, nothing. He had just fallen right where his last breath of life had held him. Now he's dead. Dead! That's your bedroom, by the way. You can put your bags in there."

I could not argue. I moved my luggage into the room. Though familiar, many things had changed. The bed was relatively new, as were the desk and chairs. The carpeting had been taken up. You could see the wood floor. There was no chalk drawing on the floor, its absence yet another reminder of the amazing way in which Jack had died.

I hung my clothes in the closet and placed the small suitcase on the desk. My mother informed me that we would leave in a couple of hours for the funeral home. "You should lie down awhile and rest, *hijo.*"

I took her advice. The alcohol had made its way through my body and out my bladder, washing out with it the remnants of tied nerves that had balled up during the flight. Now my body shivered slightly in desiccation. I needed to drink water to keep the impending headache from coming on. Either that or more scotch.

I barely glanced out the window while lying down. My eyes closed slightly, opening from time to time as if to check the reality, to see if it were true, that I had returned to San Francisco. I did not feel it yet. I still felt Knoxville in my blood, pumping slowly, the residue of the eighty-five mile an hour shock of having a neo-Nazi southerner knock me off the road. I turned my head and looked at the room, barely remembering what it looked like eighteen years ago. They had not taken as good care of it in those days. Grandmother had been slowing down, so most attention was paid to taking care of her. She had been the one who had started Doña Roselia's Fine Latin Cuisine Company, Inc. She began fifty years ago making tortillas by hand and selling them to working wives who came home to hungry men who didn't give a damn how many hours the women had worked on the docks, riveting ships together for the war effort; a pile of fresh tortillas had better be waiting for them. Business had always been good. Even twenty years ago there had been plenty of money in the corporation to take care of Grandmamá Rosie. Money, it seemed, had never been an issue. Caring for the matriarch had been the priority.

This was the room where Uncle Jack and I had begun our summer together eighteen years ago. I had been staying in here at the time. He had barged in. An hour later I smoked my first reefer while sitting with him in the black Mustang. I was only sixteen and never had smoked, so I choked and spat on my first sucked breaths. Jack had chuckled at my endeavors, until he realized I was wasting good fumes. "No man, come on, *sobrino*, suck it in, shit, that stuff is the best Mexican gold you can get . . ."

Now smiling while drifting off to sleep, I barely remembered Jack talking in that gravel, stone-cutting voice about his first sexual encounter. "It was just down the street here, man. I was fifteen. She was, oh I don't know, twice my age, maybe thirty-one. Mexican-Guatemalan woman, her name was Nancy. Nancy Osegueda. Damn, what a snatch. Her son Chucho was a friend of mine who had invited me over for a Coke. Chucho's dad was an old drunk who had forgotten how beautiful his wife was. No wonder she was in such hot shape, married to him. She sent Chucho off on an errand to his daddy's garage. Next thing I know she's showing me her tits. I didn't know what to do. I had never done it before. So she taught me. Damn, she taught me." Uncle Jack had chuckled, sucking on his homemade fag.

"She grabbed my head like a basketball and pushed it down under her legs. I had never been in a place like that before. Then she screamed and grabbed me up like I was her little boy and put me on her. She was hot. Too hot. But she broke me in."

I could not remember all the details that he had told me that night. The remaining whiskey still in my veins was heavier than the libido down under. I slept for an hour. Then someone knocked on my door.

"What's going on, son?"

My father barely touched the door with one knuckle. I looked over and glanced at his elderly face. Pete McCaugh pushed his bald head through the door. He smiled at me.

"Hey Dad. Come on in." I lifted up from the bed to greet him. We shook hands.

"You're looking pretty good," he said, barely glancing at me. "How's it going over in Knoxville?"

"Oh, all right. Teaching a lot. Paying bills." I noticed my own voice as it slid away from Latino lilts into the groove of Appalachia.

"I know what you're talking about," he said.

"Yeah. You?"

"Oh, your mother keeps busy all the time. Seems like she's always running somewhere. So I'm downstairs mostly, in the old shop. You remember the shop? Where I used to have the welding business when you were just a kid? Your grandmother never did anything with it. Said it was my room, and that no one should touch it, even after she died. So now I'm in there, building another airplane."

This was no surprise. Wherever they lived, no matter if it was East Tennessee, El Salvador, or here, Dad would always be building a plane. An Ultralight, to be exact. He never really finished the aircrafts. Dad had been a pilot most of his life. He had owned a 1946 Luscombe, the first airplane made out of metal—thin aluminum— and not cloth. After retiring from the coal mines, he became enamored with the Ultralight. He started building the tiny, two hundred and fifty-pound planes that one could construct in a carport and fly without a license. But he never flew them. He just built them. He would spend years on each plane, without ever having any of them completely ready for flight. Whenever they visited El Salvador, he would have the project waiting for him, one in which he would pick up right where he had left off three years earlier. The one in Tennessee was the most intricate, as that was his home base. Instead of finishing it, however, he kept adding to it: changing the propeller, tinkering with the motor, repainting the entire fuselage. He even had Mamá paint the image of one of our dogs upon the tail section. Chica had passed away years earlier. She was a cross between a Chihuahua, a tiny Doberman, and a miniature gnu (at least, those three animals came to mind whenever you looked at her). No more than seven inches tall, her hair looked as if someone had tried to blow dry it with an electric cattle prod. Try as we might, we never could brush the black and gray tufts down flat. Once, when I was eight, I took an entire jar of petroleum jelly and combed it through her back, legs, and face. When it dried, she had a difficult time walking. Her jaw wouldn't open very wide either. "She was my favorite dog," Dad said years after she had passed away from old age, years after I had gone away to college. Mamá immortalized her, painting her frazzled body on Dad's tail section. They christened the Ultralight "Chica," with the name, in quotation marks, under her paws.

Now Dad had a plane here, on Capp Street. Except for the wings hanging off of ceiling hooks, it looked ready to fly. Yet I wondered how long it would take before he ever got around to christening it. Sometimes we wondered why Dad took so much time in the detailed construction, a certain meticulousness that kept him from finishing. "*Va construyendo su ataúd con alas,*" Mamá once said—He's building his own flying coffin. Perhaps that was true. He always had loved to fly. His preference, no doubt, was to die doing what he loved most. But not quite yet. He didn't need to make that final flight as long as he kept building.

"You want to see the plane? I'll show it to you tonight, when we come back from the wake."

"Sure." I didn't tell him that I had noticed it when Mamá and I arrived from the airport.

"Hey, I hear you're dating somebody again. That's good. What's her name?"

"Julie."

"Yeah. That's what your mother told me. Is she nice? Pretty?"

I answered positively to both.

"She good in bed?" he asked, grinning as he lowered his voice.

I chortled appropriately, raised my eyebrows and grinned widely, almost snorting, giving all male signals—ones that fit well into either the Appalachian or the Latino heritages—that most definitely she was a good roll in the sack. I believe that I shielded any concerns over not really knowing the answer to my father's question anymore, considering I had not rolled with her in several days, that the only thing rolling through her was Bill's Florida-sized cock. *Cabrón*, though a Spanish word, had a deep, hot sting in both my cultures.

"Well I should let you rest a bit. I bet you're whipped from the trip." Dad's voice gently moved away as he walked to the door. So different, I thought, from the voice of the other southern man who had, just a few hours previous, screamed promising threats at me. Though the same accent, the voices were as distinct as two languages. "I know how those plane rides affect me across country. I sleep for two days straight afterward."

Dad walked out of the room. I watched him move down the hallway. He was seventy-six years old. Though he did not wish to slow any, his body could not do what it had done just a decade ago. Though he once was my same size—five feet nine inches—he seemed to have shortened in these final years. Decades of alcohol also created slight impediments, though drink had not been an issue in our family's life for the past fifteen years. He had given up the bottle—be it whiskey, vodka, or real, honest-to-goodness moonshine—the year I entered college. We all remembered that year. After amazing the world with his ability to suck down a half litre of vodka in one afternoon, for him to quit like that cleft our family history into two parts: pre-drink and post-drink. I wondered how long Dad would live. Had he not been an alcoholic nor smoked cigarettes, it seemed that he would have survived to one hundred and fifty. His was a body of resistance.

"You just take it easy, son," he said. He turned slightly. I watched him roll a cigarette. He was a master. Within a few leisurely seconds Dad had the papers out, had Prince Albert tossed evenly across one sheet, rolled, licked and smoothed before lighting the perfect fag. I wondered if it had been he who had taught a very young Uncle Jack this adroit habit. "We'll get you up before the wake."

He walked down the hallway, then took the stairs down to the second floor. I had no doubts that he would be heading toward his plane, ready to take some quiet moments upon the fuselage, the hanging wings, the motor that stood upon planks in one corner of the shop. Some called his work "piddling." Yet he held all his planes in his rough hands with the same delicacy as he used to create the perfectly rolled legal joint.

"Jesus, Tony! Get in front of that guy. This Menchez has more power than that!"

My aunt called the Mercedes by its rightful nickname: Any woman in Central America given that name will undoubtedly be referred to as Menchez. Thus the car received the same intimate respect.

I had not wanted to drive to the funeral home. Even the fact that I had the opportunity to sit behind the wheel of a 1978 Mercedes 450 SLC Automatic did not, at the moment, excite me. The only thing I could think of were the sluggish nerves that tried to jump about on my whiskey-soaked muscles. They jumped because of the traffic. Though San Francisco has its aura of a western Mecca living upon a different, tranquil dimension of existence from the rest of the country, heavy traffic broke that image. An older man in a new Pontiac yelled at me for going too slow. "Hey! Move out of the way *please!*" I jumped in the seat upon hearing his curseless, articulate yelp, nothing like the foaming complaints of my rabid "Hee Haw" friend back in Knoxville.

"You're in San Francisco now, *hijo,*" said my mother from the back seat. "You've got to be more aggressive on the road."

Aunt Felícita, sitting to my right, calmly smoked a cigarette. She never adjusted her sunglasses. Once they were on, they were perfect. She never adjusted anything about her: not her clothes, nor her hair, nor her makeup.

It was a natural expectation that I drive. Dad was the elder, who had driven all his life. The women could not drive, not with a man in the car (though Mamá had said nothing about this *faux pas* to her sister, when she drove me home from the airport). It was up to me—the young man—to take the wheel.

The Funeraria Colón was just about one mile from our Capp Street house. It stood on the other side of Misión Dolores, on a small road called Chula. As we passed the white stucco walls of La Misión, both the women in the car crossed themselves.

I left my family off at the front door of the funeral home and drove off to find a parking space. It took awhile. Cars lined the avenues and streets. Ten minutes later a van drove off, leaving a large gap between two other vehicles, one which I could fit the Menchez into comfortably. I was glad of this; the thought of putting a scratch on this automobile made me nervous.

I walked back alone to the funeral home under the shade of trees that grew over the sidewalk, smoothing down my gold guayabera with my palms and placing my sunglasses into one of the shirt's lower pockets. Other people entered the funeral home, most all of them Latinos. They all dressed well. A number of them were older, obviously well established. Their teenage children who wore earrings and who were all hunched over in a perpetual state of nonchalance spoke lowly to each other—whenever they did speak—in English.

Walking through the door, I heard wailing. *"¿Quién será?"* I muttered, asking myself who would be crying so hard for Uncle Jack. I turned to my right. The family that had just walked in before me made their way toward the casket, shaking others' hands as they walked. I could barely see the casket, as numerous mourners stood between the box and me. The crowd parted slightly, allowing my eyes passage. A woman knelt upon the kneeler just in front of the coffin. She wept openly. A few middle-aged men stood just behind her, waiting their turn to kneel before the dead. Yet they did not wait to kneel before showing their emotions: the men cried as well. They fought not to show such sadness, but the tears proved too heavy. They wept loudly. I felt something rend itself through me. To see Latino men gathering around a coffin and demonstrate what was obviously boiling within, a sense of loss, of dread, knowing that the world was no longer to have this man's presence, was an inspiration to my own sense of manhood. If Latino men cried, we could all weep. I walked into the crowded room, taking in a breath while glancing at the casket. The corpse's nose and a lock of black hair protruded slightly from the rim. His stomach also pushed upward. This confused me, as Jack had always been careful about his weight. Then again, that was a long time ago, when I last saw his well-toned body. My own youth and that summer eighteen years ago drenched my memory, which would have allowed for more tears to flow had not one of the funeral home assistants touched my shoulder.

"Excuse me, sir," he said. "You look a little lost. Are you part of the González family?"

"What? No, no I'm not. I'm with the Villalobos family."

"Oh. Well then, you will want to go over there," he smiled, pointing toward another room on the opposite side of the hall.

"Oh."

Stumbling slightly, I thanked him and walked away from the crowded parlor, then turned to the half empty parlor. A casket stood up front, easily seen. The name placed upon the plaque next to the door said Juan Villalobos. My mother, aunt, and father sat in three chairs up front. A dozen other people either sat behind them or stood, waiting to approach the casket. No one wept. If anything, a sense of surprise and curiosity was upon most people's faces. Only one older gentleman allowed for a mixture of satisfied anger to cross over his resolute face. He looked about the room, his eyes open wide. I recognized him immediately as Uncle Jack's old friend (and enemy of the past eighteen years) Chucho. I could not remember his last name.

After moving around the empty chairs, I sat down to my mother's right. Dad was sitting next to her. Aunt Felícita was sitting next to Dad, but she quickly jumped up, passed us, and grabbed the seat to my right.

"What took you so long?" she whispered.

"I went to the wrong funeral."

"Oh. Over there?" Aunt Felícita pointed toward the other parlor. "Those are the Gonzálezes. Mexican family. Couldn't you tell?"

I wasn't sure what to say to that, so I didn't say anything. Aunt Felícita had yet to take off her sunglasses. She lowered them slightly to glance around the room. "Not many people so far. It's still early. We have the room until nine o'clock. Oh shit," she said, "There's Chucho."

"What's Chucho doing here?" my mother asked, barely hiding her panic.

"Chucho?" Dad echoed. "I know that word . . ." He stared down a moment at the thin carpeting just in front of his feet. This had been a common gesture all his married life. He had never learned Spanish, though he prided himself on knowing a few words. He turned toward us, looking mostly at me, "Ain't that a word for 'dog?' What the hell's a dog doing in here?"

I was about to explain, but my mother cut me off with words aimed at her sister: *"Y ¿por qué quiere estar aquí después de toda aquella bulla?"*

"Saber, hermana," answered Aunt Felícita, "They haven't spoken in years, *sabés vos?* And I rarely see him. *Bien gordo ya, ¿verdád?"*

I remembered Chucho from when I had stayed in San Francisco. My aunt was right, he had gained a good deal of weight.

"Where's the dog?" my dad asked again. "What is he, a beagle? Or just one of those damn useless couch yippers? It's just like being in El Salvador, with dogs and pigs running around in church."

"There's no dog, Pete," Mother said, scolding him with quick words.

"But you all said Chew-chough, I remember, that means 'dog,' don't it?"

As Mamá and Dad bickered lowly, I turned to Aunt Felícita. "May I ask, what was it between them that caused so much animosity?"

"What? You don't remember?" she looked at me incredulously. *"Sobrino*, you were right in the middle of it."

"Oh, the . . . yeah, all that, the money, and the grass . . ." I commented carefully, not wanting to say details with the few individuals around us. "But I thought that was all, you know, worked out."

"Oh it was. The money and all . . ." My aunt glanced back over at Chucho. "But you know that money can't be the real issue with your Uncle Jack around."

"Then what was the issue?"

Aunt Felícita turned and smiled at me. Her eyes closed slightly. Her voice lowered, not to hide, but to purr, "You know. Sex will always be the real reason behind everything." She laughed lowly, touching my knee. "Especially with your *Tío* Jack."

Something shot from her fingertips through my knee and up my thigh. I glanced down from her eyes, as if shy. But my eyes did not fail to scrape down the front of her body, her breasts that filled the white suit, the V that plunged down wide from her light brown neck and narrowed into the still perfect valley of her cleavage. She was in her late fifties, I calculated, and she still carried that air, that pungency, of sex. Though she did not exercise nor did she watch her diet, her thighs and her hips still hugged well beneath her clothes, with only the slight bulges of a woman who has aged. She had never had children; I wondered if this were one of the reasons that her shape had not been debilitated.

My scraping vision also tore into a quick memory. Fifteen years earlier we had all spent a Christmas together in Mexico City. Aunt Felícita had invited us all out to a very expensive restaurant. Afterwards we went to a bar that had a pianist playing both Spanish and English popular songs. Aunt Felícita had a couple of drinks too many, a rare occurrence in her tightly controlled corporate life. For whatever reason, she refused to leave the bar. All the other clientele had left. The pianist had closed his instrument and had said goodnight to his audience of four. The owner walked by and informed us that it was closing time. Aunt Felícita refused to leave.

"The newspaper said there was a band here tonight to dance to," she growled in English. "Not some fucking queer pianist. I'm not leaving until I get my band."

My mother first tried to speak logically with her, but that didn't last long. "Sister, get your tight little ass off that chair!" Mamá's ire did not help matters any.

Then my dad used an old, sweet-talking voice from when Felícita was a little girl and Dad was the young man courting her older sister. "Come on, honey, let's you and me find a bar in the hotel. Maybe they got a juke box there."

"Peter, I am not moving from this chair until the band that they promised shows up." Her voice had a way of diving under, staying there like a shark ready to leap from the water and clamp your head.

The owner asked us to leave. Mamá and Dad left me to persuade her to come back to the hotel. The owner said he was locking up the place. She refused to budge. Two men had to lift her and the chair up, carry the chair out of the bar, and place it just outside the door. I walked out. They locked the door, but not before smiling at me with b*uena suerte* grins on their faces.

I do not remember how, but I finally persuaded her to leave the premises. We got on the elevator. During the long trip down, Aunt Felícita became more *cariñosa*.

"You are a good nephew, aren't you, Tony?" she said to me, gently grabbing my arm and hugging it while looking up into my eyes. She had said it in English. She could have been my mother; I certainly felt at times like her son. The elevator assistant, a young Mexican man who stood in one corner of the elevator, smirked. That was his last mistake for the night.

My aunt turned to him and heaped Spanish on him. I was nineteen. After having lived all my teenage years in Tennessee, my Spanish was still quite torpid. Two phrases I could scarcely snatch: the first was a question, *"Entonces, pendejo, ¿piensas que ése es mi puto?"* and the explanation, *"Es mi sobrino, cabrón."* The assistant did not respond to the two worst insults anyone could give a man in Spanish. He only smirked again, unable to control it. So Aunt Felícita took her tiny foot and planted it in his groin.

When the door opened, Aunt Felícita took a fifty dollar bill from her purse and dropped it down to the kneeling assistant.

"Can you believe that man?" she calmly explained to me as we left the building and caught a cab. "He actually thought you were my gigolo. I tried to explain to him that you were my nephew. But he just wouldn't listen."

I could say nothing at the moment, as if choked with surprise or fear that the de-nutted elevator assistant would come running out of the building after us. He did not. The encounter had a strange effect upon my aunt. She no longer seemed intoxicated nor angry. Rather, she appeared refreshed from the surge of rage that she had been able to plant into the man's genitals. Now she spoke to me gently about the cuisine business back in San Francisco, about Mexico City, how it seemed so lovely at night. She pulled out a cigarette. I lit it, as was expected. I half listened to her. I could not help but look at her, that forty-four year old body of perfect, large breasts, her hourglass waist, her legs underneath the tight pants. I was nineteen at the time. Shame became a secondary consideration as my thoughts wrapped around an incestuous imagination. I had also been a seminarian at the time, studying at a Catholic college for the priesthood. Even more reason to let sexual mindgames play away.

That was almost fifteen years ago. I had left the seminary. I had lived in Central America, had married, gotten divorced, had written and published. I had grown. I was now thirty-four, and sometimes I could actually control my sex drive, a dubious power indeed. Now, at my uncle's funeral, with her fingertips barely touching my knee, my aunt could strike a lonely rock inside me and make the night light up with shattering sparks.

"So that man's name is Dog?" Dad said to Mamá. "Damn. What nicknames you all give to each other . . ."

"Tony," my aunt said, "go find out what Chucho's doing here."

"What? Why? Why me?"

"I want to make sure he doesn't desecrate the body or anything."

"What do you think he'll do?" I asked.

"Antonio, knowing the way he felt about Jack, he could do anything . . . piss on Jack's face, maybe cut him up. He may even slice off another finger, just to keep for old time's sake."

My face tightened at that thought, that memory.

"Go on. Get over there. He may not remember you. Talk with him. Get in line. Go."

Reluctantly, I stood up, walking away from my family while glancing over at Uncle Jack. I still hadn't had the chance to go up and pay my respects.

"You think there's any coffee around here?" my father asked Mamá as I walked away from them.

I got in the small line, right behind Chucho. More visitors had entered the parlor. They were mostly all women. They were different ages: some of the women were perhaps in their fifties, others in their forties, still others closer to my age. A few of them actually wept. They were not all Latinas. A few were whiter than Julie. One stood near the door, her thick blonde hair falling over her shoulders. She wore a short blue dress and stockings. She wore spiked heels. Her eyes were large, her lips thick. Her breasts were really, really nice. Aunt Felícita's fingertip-sparks still spat about inside me. I heard the Gringa speaking to one of the funeral home assistants; her English gave her away as most undoubtedly monolingual, "Gosh. I can't believe it. He seemed so young."

Only a handful of men entered the parlor. None were dressed in ties. Most of them wore jeans. One fellow about my age wore a T-shirt, sunglasses, several rings in both ears. His entire skin was a tattoo. He walked into the parlor, straight up the small aisle between the chairs, looked down into the casket, stared for five seconds, nodded his head affirmatively, then left. "*Bien*," he muttered on his way out, no doubt confirming rumors. "*Muy bien.*"

In front of me, Chucho took a handkerchief from his pocket and wiped his face of slight sweat. He turned toward me and nodded his head to recognize my presence. I lurched at the moment.

"*¿Qué tal?*" I said, asking him how he was.

"*Bien*," he said, "Fine. Actually, doing better than ever." He smiled, then quickly let the grin go.

"Were you a friend of the deceased?" I asked.

"Friend?" Chucho turned to me. "A long time ago, yeah. We were *compas*. We both lived on Capp Street as kids. That's when we were friends, man. But not as men. No. That no good motherfucking bastard of a *pendejo* has no reason to have any friends in this world, nor in the next."

"Oh. Then, why are you here?"

"I want to make sure he's good and dead. I won't believe it until I see him up close. He had a way of escaping things like death."

"I see."

Chucho calmed slightly, though not much. "I'm sorry. My name's Enrique Osegueda. They call me Chucho."

I introduced myself.

"Antonio . . . Tony McCaugh?" Chucho looked straight at me. A number of reactions crossed over his face: memory of a few days in a summer eighteen years ago; surprise at the man who I was, coming from the teen of back then; and a slight embarrassment that lasted very little time, wrapped under a sense of righteousness over the use of insults concerning my dead relative. "Man, Tony, you've grown. But that was a long time ago, wasn't it?"

We shook hands. The ring finger and pinky of my right hand wrapped around his right middle finger. I could feel the knubs of his open knuckles. He did not have two of his fingers. I remembered. I remembered that there were supposedly other things he did not have, not completely.

We moved closer to the casket, following the line of women. "Listen, in one way I'm sorry for the words I use about your uncle. I wish to respect the blood of your family, your mother, your aunt, and that wonderful gringo father of yours." Chucho actually smiled. The smile split downward. "But you know I got my reasons, don't you, *joven*?"

"Oh, sure. Sure. Don't worry about me, Chucho."

We turned silent. Then Chucho spoke more, a lilt of sadness pushing his words forward. "You were around for some of the things that happened between your uncle and me, Tony. Those were terrible days. You know I have enough reason to hate that cadaver," he pointed with his lips toward the casket. "I lost too much that summer," he held up his hand, showing the absence of the two fingers as proof of his losses. "But as time went on, I learned more and more about your uncle. Fuck, no way I could forgive him." He barely lowered his voice, "I mean, not only was he dealing in a lot of shit, the drugs, the fucking mushrooms . . . I don't got problems with that, man. That was his business. But his fucking dick never found one home!"

I looked around the room at all the women, proof of the homelessness of my Uncle's penis. Nowhere to lay one's head. Or perhaps everywhere.

Chucho whipped around and looked at me, his eyes glistening with tears. He still managed to whisper. "Do you know how he made me a *cabrón*?"

Considering my own recent situation in life, I could not believe that Chucho would say that, expressing to someone publicly that he had been cuckolded. Yet his rage over my uncle seemed to supersede any shame. Perhaps, I thought, he had joined a group, like *Cabrones Anónimos*.

"He fucked my wife. Yeah. He fucked her good for two years. Me working my ass off in the factory, and he was making good money in his drug dealings, so he never had to work. He humped my wife during the day. Then you remember what Gato did to me, when he, he . . ." Chucho's stutter slumped into dead silence.

Gato was another nickname I had not thought about in years.

After a moment Chucho gained his composure, "Then, to make it worse, Jack fucks my daughter Elisa on her eighteenth birthday! Damn, that bastard had enough sense to wait until she was eighteen. One day earlier and I could have hauled his ass to jail. But no, he waited until she was a legal woman. And she, well shit, I expect her to stop by here before the night's over and get in line to cry over his body. I'm surprised he never fucked my mother, God rest her soul."

I stopped taking the small steps toward the casket, pausing to make family connections. "By the way, what was your mother's name?"

Chucho glanced at me, "Nancy." Then he added, "Why?"

"Oh, I think she was a friend of my grandmother's," I lied. And then I thought: Nancy Osegueda. Then I remembered the image Uncle Jack had planted long ago in my youth while sharing our first grass together: *she grabbed my head like a basketball and pushed it down under her legs*. For no reason in particular, I almost said, yes, Chucho, Uncle Jack *did* fuck your mother.

We made it to the edge of the casket. A woman in her forties finished saying her prayers at the kneeler, crossed herself, touched Uncle Jack's forehead, then his lips, with her fingertips. She did not cry; she smiled, a smile of thanksgiving, not for death, but for living memories, most undoubtedly about those lips. She walked away. Chucho and I moved together to the head of the casket.

"There he is," Chucho grumbled. "Right there, where he needs to be."

We both looked down. I stared at his face, the closed eyes, the brown skin, the small yet well-groomed moustache. I barely paid attention to the suit that they had wrapped him in. I could still imagine the magnificence of his chest, one which he made do three hundred pushups a day, along with situps. His hair whipped back over his head; a few streaks of white had woven into the thick mane. I wished to see his eyes; I would need to rely upon memory, old photos, family movies, to see them. His hands were clasped perfectly over his abdomen. Though the funeral workers had tried to cover the mutilation, I could still see the open knub on his right hand, where his pinky had once been.

That had not escaped Chucho's attention either. "Yeah. Him and his one lost pinky. Nothing more . . ." He stared a long time at the body; I heard the words mumbling from Chucho's lips like a prayer: "*Ese buey pendejo con la mierda de suerte,* fucking prick-sucking cock who stole everything from me, may he perpetually rot inside the Devil's tight ass . . ."

After finishing the words, I half-expected Chucho to cross himself. He shut his eyes tight, then opened them and looked at me. He asked, "By the way, what brings you all the way here? You wanted to make sure he was dead too?" He chuckled slightly, as if knowing that it was not beyond Jack Villalobo's grasp to ruin even the lives of his own kin. "What in the world did he do to you to make you come all this way?"

I stared down at the corpse of my uncle. I muttered, as if it were the last of my strength seeping out with the words, "He once saved my life."

Part Two

Though I don't remember the initial pain, I can still see the peach-colored sink that filled with blood. I held the knife in my left hand. It was a large pocketknife. Dad had shown me in my childhood how to keep such a blade honed. I knew how to spit upon a whetstone and pull the blade over the lowering belly of the stone back and forth, incessantly, collecting a fine mix of spittle and grain with the blade's edge before stropping it with a leather belt or a piece of cardboard. This knife, given to me years ago by my father, was well taken care of. It could slice through paper, barely leaving a sound.

It had no problem with skin. I could see that from the mess collected in the sink. I could also tell from the gap in my wrist that appeared to grow, like rubber pulled tight over a ball. It took two quick inches of blood to fill the closed sink before a distant, yet somewhat familiar voice pulsed through that distance.

You don't want this . . .

I stared at the new wound on my right wrist. I had not cut downward, from my hand to my elbow, but across, leaving one slash, like an opening mouth, upon my flesh. In that mouth, behind the pumping blood, lay a white, wet strip. A tendon? I thought, momentarily fascinated with that wriggling ribbon hidden underneath the outer layer of what I called my self. I could also see a nicked artery; the blood dribbled thick from it. It did dribble. It did not spurt, as I had thought would happen. Still, the flow was enough to force my lungs to fill. The air pushed through me, flowing through my skull like a thick white wave. I fell into a corner of the bathroom. A cough shoved through a heave of tears. Then that distant voice *No* to the possibility of fainting. It was a practical voice, saying to me that to faint meant to slip into the gap upon my wrist, one that was now wet but that, with fainting, would turn dry, and such desiccation could mean only one thing.

"Get up, get up . . ." I muttered to myself, taking on the voice's commands. I pushed away from the corner and leaned over the sink. The bathroom was a mess. Crimson stains trailed from the pool in the peach sink over the edge of the cabinet, down upon the tile floor to the corner where I had fallen. I thanked God and the family of this house that there were no rugs on the floor, as rugs would absorb clues. I placed my left palm over the wound and held it there, applying pressure, just as we sophomores had all been taught in the recent high school first aid training. I panted. A small chuckle tripped through the panting from time to time, along with words, "You want to live . . . isn't that crazy, how you want to live . . ."

My chest sucked in the chuckles once I saw and felt the wet, greasy crimson that seeped between the fingers of my left hand. I lifted my hand away. An adolescent moan slipped out of me.

Jesus, God, Jesus almighty, please, don't let me die, don't let me die.

I used half a roll of toilet paper to daub the cut. Wet paper clotted up everywhere: upon the cabinet, over the floor. Some fell into the sink, floating in the thick pool like a horrible defecation gone awry.

I dared not use any towels. The woman of this house would later know immediately if I had touched my cut with her fabrics. I unrolled more and more paper and pushed it against the wrist. My breath quickened. The voice had gone, taken over by my own, "Please, please, forgive me, I don't want to die, I don't want this." Then I heard a door above me open. I silenced my own voice.

"Tony? You all right?"

I hesitated barely a second to gather up another voice. I smiled, as if smiling would help form my words, shape them into a believable lie. "Yes, Mrs. Hartland, I'm fine."

"I thought I heard you yell."

"Oh yeah. I dropped my dictionary on my foot. Hurts like the dickens. But I'm fine." I was almost proud of myself, saying "dictionary" instead of "book," giving the woman a detailed image instead of a generic one.

"Oh. Okay. I've got some hot spiced cider up here, if you want to take a break from studying soon."

"Thanks, Mrs. Hartland. I'll be up after I finish this chapter."

I could imagine her own smile as she closed the door.

I turned back to the sink. The blood had taken on a smell, much like the odor that wafted from squirrels and rabbits that Dad and I had gutted and cleaned. I wondered if that, too, was going to be a problematic clue. I would need to clean the blood from everything, flush it all down the toilet, then take a cleaning rag and pine cleaner disinfectant to the entire bathroom.

I pulled this last ball of toilet paper from my wrist. The artery had stopped dripping. Blood had coagulated around the cut, leaving a crust. "Oh, thank God." I stretched my hand and fingers outward to test whether or not they still worked. The movement pulled apart the clot upon the vein, tearing it open again.

"Fuck," I muttered, using the word saved for such drastic occasions. Now I was getting angry as well as frightened. More toilet paper. In ten minutes I helped form another clot. I wrapped paper completely around my wrist, used scotch tape to keep it bound, and began cleaning.

It took time. I worked the bathroom like a panicking murderer. I flushed it all down the toilet, then found cleaning materials. The bathroom had never been so disinfected.

With one last swipe of a rag over the counter, I looked up in the mirror at my sixteen-year-old face. My black hair sat upon my skull like a used mop. My olive skin, which always turned a pale, sickly color during the long winters away from the sun, had turned even more pasty. This was the problem with being from two different cultures: sometimes the skin just never seemed able to make up its mind. In the spring, summer, and fall, I looked like a regular little Latino guy. Come winter in the East Tennessee Mountains, I appeared like the smiling, walking dead. Now, with (I estimated) a pint less of blood in my body, I was the melancholic walking dead. "Jesus," I said, "how the hell do you get rid of a clue like that?" I thought about surreptitiously borrowing some rouge from the girl upstairs; yet Janice Lee Hartland, I told myself, was the reason for all this. I had to stay as clear away from her as possible. I used an old trick taught me by my Aunt Felícita in San Francisco: I pinched my cheeks. Red splotches appeared haphazardly upon my skin.

"Shit on this." A thick wave of malaise passed through me. I moved from the bathroom to my bedroom and fell upon the bed, then glanced over at the large picture window. There the Hartland family's driveway butt up against the house. Janice Lee's Volkswagon was not parked there. No doubt she had left the house within the past hour, since our encounter upstairs, the encounter that I would, for a while, blame for my actions.

I stared at the few posters on the wall in front of me. John Travolta, twenty-four years old and dressed in a white, open collar suit and black boots, stood in his pelvic-strutting, finger-piercing-the-sky position, staring down at me with the look of disco perfection. He stood upon a multicolored dance floor. A strobe ball dangled above him. The words to the title of the undoubtedly most wrenching, point-turning, most magnificent film ever created by humankind, *Saturday Night Fever,* were slashed across the top of the poster. I had little strength to appreciate flashbacks to scenes from the movie that I had sneaked in three times that winter to see. Nor did I have any strength to glance over toward another poster to admire Farrah Fawcett's nipple that protruded from a red bathing suit while her perfectly tanned thigh lifted up for her to rest her elbow upon. Even Farrah could not get me to tear off a wad of toilet paper and thicken it with a quick ejaculation. The thought of clean toilet paper, for the first time in my teenage life, did not rouse excitement but disgust. I could only see the clods of clotted paper that were previously floating in the now clean sink.

The Holy Spirit of My Uncle's Cojones

Over to my left I had taped a movie poster from *Close Encounters of the Third Kind*. Over a black horizon, a glowing light moved my way. A road lay before me. If I could not read the explanatory words of what a third kind of encounter meant, I would have thought it was a picture of a car coming over a hill. Instead, the young Mr. Spielberg had succeeded in making me and everyone else in the United States believe in extra terrestrials, and that they liked playing five-note electric organ music. I had little thought or imagination for that poster either. I had spent much of the past school year's nights pretending to be one of those people who, along with Amelia Earhart, planes in the Bermuda Triangle, and Dorothy, had been sucked up by the spaceship and taken away from this world. Of course, I changed the script of the movie. Instead of waiting years to return, I had become one of the few entrusted earthlings to help steer the ship. I had flown the ship right over this house and had shot a teleporter beam into Janice Lee's bedroom at three o'clock in the morning. I stood before the lovely Janice Lee as she slept. I stared at her beauty for a good long while before speaking to her. "Janice, Janice Lee, it's me. Tony." With that she bolted up from the bed, her thin pajamas barely covering her eighteen-year-old breasts. Then she leapt up and embraced me in my skin-tight purple space suit. We did not make love, of course. I was in love with her. Nor had I ever even dreamed of masturbating with Janice's face in mind, though I had masturbated imagining the face of every girl from my sophomore class, along with most of the senior girls and a few of the teachers. For example, the history teacher Miss Hartentson who, though she had a mouthful of teeth not unlike a horse's, had round, filled tits where I could hide my sight from her smile. That was nice. Then there was Miss Donnelson. And Sister McCartney . . .

Janice was beyond masturbation; she was beyond the Virgin Mary; she was Janice Lee, perfection and savior to my battled body and soul. I could not make love to her until we beamed up into Spielburg's ship and flew toward a higher existence, where she and I would become the sacramental purity of human/universal copulation, far away from this earth, from the place of my memory.

These were all old, reused fantasies. My absent blood, which had by now slipped into the sewers of Knoxville, did not allow for much creative thought. "I'm alive, damn, I'm alive." I started praying to God, everything from Hail Marys to Our Fathers to a legion of promises concerning not only living, but living right.

I shut up, then turned on the radio next to my bed. Though five o'clock on a Thursday afternoon, it was already dark outside. Mrs. Hartland would have supper on the table at precisely six-thirty. I had an hour and a half to collect some energy. The disc jockey on the pop radio played, probably for the seventh time that day, the Bee Gee's "How Deep Is Your Love?" I listened to the words. For the first time in a month, the song did not make me weep. For the first time after a strange winter of much snow in East Tennessee, I did not feel a thickening sadness fill me with the Brothers Gibb's lilting slow disco song. "What do I feel?" Nothing, really, said a thought. I remembered a lesson from history class, how they believed in George Washington's time that bleeding oneself was a way to get rid of certain diseases. Had I bled a certain melancholy from my body? I closed my eyes, listening to the three singers as they tried, with all their romantic might, to penetrate my skull with a wash of tears. It did not happen. I slept, dry-eyed, for the first time in a long winter of a sophomore year.

My mother called later that evening. "How many days has there been no school?" she asked.

"Three. We may go back tomorrow."

"Oh. That's good. Are you enjoying your days off?" I imagined her smile.

"Oh, yes. Well, it's getting a little boring. But I'm fine."

"That's good. Your father is home, you know. It's about to drive him crazy."

"Is the snow that bad, that he can't drive back to Kentucky?"

"No, Tony. Haven't you heard the news? The miners are still on strike. Nobody's working. If you dare move any equipment or pick up a shovel, the strikers will kill you. Your father hates that. He prefers to be home now."

I had seen parts of the news, where Jimmy Carter was trying to negotiate with the mining unions. It meant little to me, even with my father working as a mechanic in the coal shafts of Turkey Creek, Kentucky. This job had come later in our family's life. Dad had been a mechanic for every auto shop in Rakertown, Tennessee, my Appalachian home town. Yet auto repair had never brought in much money. Then one of his friends invited him to work in the coal fields of neighboring Kentucky. Suddenly my parents saw more money than ever. Somewhere in the ebullience of the new work and the grand salary (around $18,000 a year), they decided that it was best for me to leave the trapping confines of Rakertown—where young boys my age ended up dropping out and going to local jails for shoplifting—and attend a Catholic high school. The only such school in the area was Tennessee Catholic High in Knoxville. In my thirteenth year all the arrangements were made: I was to live with families who had children in the school. My parents paid a modest sum for room and board. I went home once a month.

The Hartlands were the second family I had lived with. The very roots of pulling a knife over my wrist were buried in my freshman year, long before I knew the Hartlands. Then I had boarded with the Giltens, whose eighteen year old son Barry—their only child—was to graduate that spring from Tennessee Catholic. The fact that he was an only child seemed, in all the adults' mind, a perfect boarding match. I had a brother almost ten years older than myself. He left home when I was still a kid. People saw me as a lone child. Everyone thought Barry and I would hit it off. I am not sure where this logic came from.

Considering we both were used to having our lives and our parents to ourselves, with no other siblings to compete with, it seemed the adults would have seen some inevitable pattern of conflict.

Freshman year had proved to be a difficult one, though no one would ever learn that. Barry, a shorter senior who was only slightly taller than I, and as stout as a football player, had a tendency to take underwear from my dresser and stretch it between the bedposts. He also, on occasion, walked into my room and pulled down his shorts to show me his buttocks, ordering me to kiss them. I did not. This seemed to anger him, as he would always slap my skull with his class ring and grumble a whisper, "Watch it boy, I'll have you kissing my dick some night."

I slept little in that house. Whenever I took the Greyhound bus home on weekends, my parents wondered if I was on drugs, considering how many naps I would take throughout Saturday and Sunday.

At first Barry never gathered enough courage to follow through with his threats. He continued popping his knuckles and ring against my skull and calling me a little queer. I wasn't sure what a queer was, until Barry explained his insults: "You little faggot queer, wanting to kiss other boys and get at their dicks, what a little pussy queer." Logic pushed through the burgeoning tears around my eyes, asking, Isn't that what *you* want? I decided not to put this question to him. It could mean more than skull popping.

Sometime in late January of that year I woke up to a sound. I did not move. My eyelids opened. I felt that I was completely awake, that some strange, cool liquid had poured through me, lifting every muscle from sleep. Yet not one muscle budged, save those that dictated the movement of my eyeballs. Though I could see the outer edges of the bedroom window that showed, in the glow of a distant street-lamp, the snow-covered branches of an oak tree, I could not see the window's middle. It was obstructed by a stout, short figure that wore no clothes. My eyes followed the line of the body upward to the short mat of pitch black hair, blacker than mine. I could not see the color in the night. I just knew. I heard the breathing. It was shallow, both fearful and hungry. Then his lungs took in a long, slow breath, one which I thought meant the beginning of my consummate nightmare.

Somebody spoke. It was a hard voice, angry. Then he turned away. As he did, the shadow of his tiny erection flipped about, slapping the corner of my desk. He held in a grunt. I heard his naked feet upon the rug. Then he was gone.

The following morning, as he and I drove to school, he said nothing. Then, as I stared out the passenger-side window, watching people pull into McDonalds for breakfast, one of his knuckles slammed against the top of my skull. Others followed, interrupted only by his need to change the car's gears. He did not just use his knuckles; his whole arm came down and sideways, hitting me at a number of angles. The fury of punches did not end until the even pulse of fifth gear; nor did the words "You fucking faggot! Faggot! Goddammed FAGGOT!"

In that first year of high school I earned the reputation at Tennessee Catholic of being a very good little boy who was always willing to help out a teacher, the principal, or a student struggling with English or religion class. I got involved with the Key Club, a service organization that did volunteer work in the school. I also came to be known as religious.

When Barry drove us to school, I always ran from the parking lot to the building. "Where the hell you going?" he once asked. I turned quickly and told him that I wanted to attend the morning mass. He said nothing to this. I noticed his lack of mockery. I ran to the sanctuary, arriving just as Father Jackson, the school principal, began the rite.

I attended every morning mass. At two-thirty every afternoon, during study hall, I would ask the teacher if I could be excused. When she asked why, I mumbled that I wanted to go pray. The teacher smiled and allowed me to leave.

I did go to the chapel to pray. At two-thirty-five I prayed for the hour of three-fifteen. Actually I prayed for three twenty, when Barry would unlock the passenger side of his car and let me in. I did not pray to God for Divine Intervention, though that would have been nice. I had made an "A" in religion class, where I had learned to be above such petitions, learning that we are responsible for most of the events around us, that we could not always blame God's Will upon the incidents in our lives. It was up to us to live the good life, and thus change the course of events. I prayed to God that He help me do all the right and correct things so that Barry's wrath would be less that day. May God help me say the correct words to appease Barry, or perhaps know when to say no words at all. May God help me have the silent strength to withstand the knuckles. May God grant me the profound silence of tranquility and lack of movement if a stripped Barry were to visit my room after midnight.

Catholic religion class had taught me well. We were to be responsible for our actions. If we were not, then God would only shake His celestial head at us in an "I told you so" air. Not only had I honed into perfection my behavior around all adults, I also honed every movement I made. If I clicked my teeth a certain way, I noticed that Barry would forget about me in the car momentarily and stare out at a movie marquee. If I tapped my forehead twice before entering his car, Barry might not say anything to me, not even greet me. Perhaps the tapping of my knuckles upon my forehead was much like a symbolic sacrifice of his own knuckles biting through my hair into my skin. At night, if I clicked my teeth seven times (a holy number, according to religion class) and tapped my forehead seven times after making a sign of the cross both over my body as well as tiny crosses on my forehead, mouth, and chest, I would be protected from Barry the night visitor. An invisible shield would make the nude teenager turn away.

On one such two-thirty in the afternoon, as I left study hall, I heard an acquaintance named Beth Spellton ask for permission to go to the bathroom. I would have thought little of this, until I heard the chapel door open. She walked in. I was sitting on the left, three pews from the altar.

"Hi Tony," she greeted. "Am I bothering you?"

I looked up at her. Beth was my age, fourteen. She had long blonde hair and slightly sleepy eyes. She was thin, and I believe played on the girl's basketball team. I had always thought of her as nice, if I ever thought of her at all. When she greeted me in the chapel, the fact came to mind that she was one of the few girls in my class who I had not made love to in my masturbatory dreams. I did not know why, as she was not necessarily ugly. Beth was, however, very nice, more so than me, which in that freshman year of dodging knuckle blows with the silence of a perfect student, was quite a feat. I figured that anyone nicer and better behaved than myself would be no fun during a wet dream.

She sat down next to me once I said that she was not interrupting. Though wondering how I would get through my prayer rituals—including the decades of teeth clicking and forehead tapping—before the bell rang, I also welcomed the company.

"I noticed that you always leave study hall at two-thirty. The teacher always lets you do it. I guess I just got curious."

I smiled, embarrassed yet appreciative of her curiosity, that she actually found me worthy of it.

"So. You come down here to pray."

"Oh, yeah, kind of, I guess," I responded in the eloquence befitting a freshman. "Sometimes I just come here to sit. It's nice and quiet in here." I actually spoke the truth then. The quietude had always been comforting. A few times I had sought out God in this sanctuary, but all I got, until Beth's visit, was a profound silence.

"Yeah. Others have said that you're pretty religious." She used no tone of mockery. The words sounded almost respectful. It also surprised me that I was the subject of such gossip. "I heard a few teachers saying that you'll probably become a priest."

Her words struck me. The thought penetrated the folds of my brain as I saw images of the principal Father Jackson's life: his office; his home that stood to one side of the school; his 1978 Oldsmobile Delta 88 (the only thing changing being the year, every year); and the powerful yet caring authority he held over us all. Not a bad image, I thought. Such control over one's life could keep many a fear at bay.

"I've actually thought about becoming a nun," she said, then smiled with some embarrassment, "but I don't know. You can't get married or anything."

I knew her *anything* meant *fuck*. I lowered my head in understanding. "Yeah. That's a hard thing about it."

"So. What do you pray for when you're in here?" she asked.

It stopped me cold. I could not believe how much influence this fellow freshman was having upon the sparks of emotions that now split and cracked underneath my skin. Her mere presence in this, my moment of silent sanctuary, the time when I prepared for yet another evening in the Gilten household, with Barry wailing upon me while his mother drank wine and prepared dinner downstairs before her successful lawyer husband would come home and drink scotch while she poured herself a fourth goblet of chardonnay, shattered my nerves. I wanted to tell her. I wanted to tell this girl, to whom I had said more in this small conversation in the pew than I had said all year in the hallways, everything. How I prayed for strength so that I could withstand the upcoming evening. How I prayed that Mr. and Mrs. Gilten would not go out tonight to a church meeting or a dinner with friends, leaving me in that huge, West Knoxville house with Barry. How I clicked my teeth and tapped my forehead as mini-holocausts to the Almighty so that Barry would not visit me that night, and if he did, may I have the strength to endure. I wanted to tell her. I wanted to say all that so as to get a secret message across to her, one that she could take to some other authorities such as her parents who would then report it and then save me from another night.

But I said none of it. I did not, knowing without words that to stir the waters thusly meant to put the venerated Gilten family into question. Yet they would not be questioned, for they were the Giltens. Mr. Gilten's law practice had allowed him to give thousands of dollars to Tennessee Catholic all the four years that their only son attended. Mrs. Gilten always attended and coordinated the school fundraising events. They would not be questioned. But I would, most assuredly. I was but a half-white boy from a tiny hillbilly town in the eastern mountains. To speak meant to be sent back to Rakertown in shame and failure.

Though I remained silent, my eyes gave me away. I felt them sitting in their hot glisten.

"Tony? Are you all right?" Beth asked. Her voice trembled slightly, as if unready to take on a contemporary's tears.

"Oh, I'm fine," I said, quickly wiping my eyes. "I guess I just miss my parents." The lie pulled the tears back. The thought of my mother and father, they who had put me here, helped me to control the flow.

"Oh I can see why!" she exclaimed. Then she went on about how hard it must be to live away from home; and yet I seemed to be very happy; it must have been because I was so lucky to be living with such a wonderful family as the Giltens.

She touched my shoulder with a limp hand, smiled at me, then said goodbye and walked out, her curiosity satisfied. I knew she had to leave quickly, else the teacher would ask why she was spending so much time in the bathroom.

"I'll leave you be," she whispered, motioning toward the crucifix where a bloody Jesus dangled. I thanked her and smiled. In my head, saving words taught to me long ago both in San Francisco and Rakertown bubbled up as I watched Beth push the door open and leave. *Fuck you, girl*. But I knew that, in my dreams, I never would.

The bell rang. I jumped from the pew, genuflected, and ran out of the chapel. I collected my books in study hall, then ran to my locker. I cut through a block of students and bolted outside toward the parking lot, where Barry walked casually with a few of his senior friends. First I cursed, having had my afternoon ritual snapped by that girl, her blabbing curiosity taking away my rite of protection. As I crossed the school yard toward the cars, I rattled off the words that I would have said seven times in the quietude of the chapel, had not Beth interrupted me. As I muttered the holy refugee of words, I balanced my books in one hand so as to tap my forehead with the other, all the while clicking my teeth away, "Dear Lord, I ask for your strength, wisdom, Holy Spirit and love; may they burn in my heart so that I may be a sign of your life on earth. Please may I have your Holy Strength to endure the ride home, then the afternoon and evening, until I speak with you again before sleep. If I fail in endurance, may Your mercy be upon me . . ."

As Barry was the Giltens' only child and was graduating that year, Mr. and Mrs. Gilten had no more connection with the school. Some school officials feared this, knowing that it was possible Mr. Gilten would take his financial support elsewhere. It was the buzz of all the faculty and administration. Yet I feared nothing. What this meant for me was I could live with them no more. The word went out that I needed a place to stay. Hearing of my reputation as an upright young man, the Hartland family decided to take me in.

Through the first two years of high school, my mother called once a week, as she had done the night that I pulled a pocketknife blade over my skin. That night I wore a long sweater, one that pulled way over my wrists. Sweaters were appropriate. During the coal mine strikes, Mr. Hartland had been conscientious enough to turn down the thermostat and use less energy, thus putting in his part to ration fuel. Everyone wore sweaters. All winter Janice Lee, to my disappointment, wore huge warmup tops, which covered up her body. What was her body like? It was, objectively, quite skinny. Very tiny breasts, a child's butt. Yet I at the time did not see it that way. Once, two weeks before my suicide attempt, while pulling off her warmup sweaters, her shirt got caught between the sweater's folds. The action pulled the shirt's tail from her jeans. I saw a flash of her belly, white, thin, supple from her dance classes. A breath had shoved out of me at the time. "You okay?" she had asked. I had said that I was fine, saying nothing about the fact that I had just witnessed a carnal holiness.

"So you're feeling all right?" My mother asked, for the third time over the phone. I wondered if she could hear the lack of blood in my tongue.

"Yes, Mamá, I'm fine."

"You sound a little tired."

"Oh, I am tired, yes. But I'm fine. We just finished eating." I looked up at Mrs. Hartland, who smiled at me. She was putting away the dishes. "I always get a little sleepy after one of these great meals." Patronizing was, for me, a skill.

"That's good. But I bet that she can't cook *picadillo,* can she?"

Oh boy, I thought; here comes the list.

"Or *tortillas.* When was the last time you had *tortillas?*"

"Last month, when I visited home."

"That's right. You probably haven't had any *pupusas* either. I doubt Mrs. Hartland knows how to make those. How would you like some real *tamales* next weekend, for your birthday?"

"That sounds great."

"You don't sound too excited."

"Oh yes, Mamá. I'm excited. Really. That would be great."

"Well, I do want to celebrate your birthday, you know. Don't think I've forgotten that."

"I know." I knew too well that she had not forgotten. The weekly phone calls were constant reminders that though she had sent her son away to school, she had not forgotten him, and he needed to know that, needed to know that this was all for his own good, nobody else's.

Though the doctors who treated George Washington believed that they had bled the disease out of him, they did inevitably kill him. The draining of his blood had done nothing but leave a void where that living liquid was meant to be.

My own draining had made me sickly. It took some time for the heart to fill that void. The flu hit me one week later. Though my mother was disappointed that we would not be able to celebrate my birthday as she had planned, she took some consolation in the fact that she could nurse me back to health that weekend. As I emerged from the bus, coughing pieces of lung up, she looked at me and ushered me into her fifteen-year-old Oldsmobile. "Well, looks like we'll be slapping Vicks on you tonight."

I spent the weekend in bed. Mamá kept me through Tuesday, phoning Mrs. Hartland and advising her of my condition. "I'll get him back to classes by Wednesday morning," she said.

I took a fever. It was one of those high temperatures that made me see things. For some reason, my dreams became a nightmare of numbers, as if the computer programming in my brain spilled into fluid thought patterns. Small numbers multiplied into larger ones. Sleep was nothing but fitful. As always, whenever I suffered with fever, Mamá took cloths and soaked them in cool water, then rubbed down my chest and face. She whipped the cloth above me and snatched at the cool air before placing it against my hot skin. I could feel this. I could hear her talking lowly to me in Spanish. In the back, my father's angry voice cursed at the television, and at "That son of a bitch Carter, God damn peanut farmer who won't give the miners what they want so we can all get our asses back to work." That clinking, no doubt, was a glass filled with brown liquor and no ice, popping against the endtable next to the sofa. Mamá cooed in my ear as she tried to bring down the fever, forever whispering, smiling as she did so, snapping the coo only with a "Shut the hell up, Pete, for Christ's sake!" before returning to the soothing movements of a mother who wished to heal her child. I felt her cloth wipe against my shoulders and my legs, but I could see very little through the heat, could only see the numbers that multiplied before me, upon a backdrop of grey clouds, numbers slipping in and out of the folds of the clouds, and I wondered for a chance moment if the clouds were in fact my brain, and that my brain had jumped into overdrive to escape the burn. I could see only this. I could scarcely feel her cloth as it ran down my right arm and over my wrist. I could not see my mother whose voice popped slightly. I did feel a slight burn, sharper than the fever, as the cloth touched the wound. Then came the silence, a deep silence where a mother, whether she wants to or not, places her worst fears.

I had fallen in love with Janice Lee because of her goodness. I had not realized how much the previous year with Barry Gilten had played upon me. Once living in the Hartland house, a home that was surprisingly healthy, with fewer dysfunctional attributes than any other family I had met, I felt the barricade of well-constructed defenses slam and shatter around my feet. Their house became a sanctuary. In my first month with them I partly told Janice Lee about my year with Barry. I did not mention his nakedness over my bed, fearing that, somehow, this would shadow her thoughts about me rather than him (perhaps, she would think, I had *beckoned* him to come to my bed). She listened. She even wept. Then she hugged me and whispered, "This is your home, Tony. You're safe now." So adult, I had thought. Then again, she was a senior, two whole years older than I. The hug, and her listening, and her kindness, along with the sweet perfume that she splashed against her neck every morning, was her undoing. My heart plopped out of my chest. Through that winter it wriggled perpetually before her feet.

Her goodness toward me had transformed into her nightmare. I followed her in the school hallways. I stared at her at suppertime. After awhile I started looking for other problems in my life so that she would have to listen to me. When that didn't work, I made problems up.

Her kindness could not continue. She began to shut me out. She spent less time at home, dashing off in her car to a music or dance lesson or to a party with her senior friends. She avoided me at breakfast, dropping her head toward her bowl of cereal.

The day that I drew my pocketknife was the day that I had come to her with the truth. "I love you," I had confessed to her that afternoon of the third day of cancelled classes. "I can think of no one but you."

She, of course, did not love me. Time to die.

It was fortunate I had not tried to commit suicide in Rakertown. Otherwise I would have ended up very dead. Still, I had thought enough about it. Pulling the knife over my skin that cold February afternoon was not an act born out of pure spontaneity. A great deal of premeditation had been put into it. In Knoxville, with this upper middle class family, I had access to only a very sharp pocketknife. Back home I would have had a variety of artillery to choose from. Rakertown was smack in the middle of the Appalachian Mountains.

My father, born and raised there, also raised me with a variety of armaments, all of which I had learned to clean, load, fire, unload, carry, and maintain. I could have chosen from three different kinds of shotguns (twelve gauge for large openings, twenty gauge for tinier, more concentrated wounds, a double barrel for thoroughness), rifles (one sixteen millimeter, the other a musket loader that Dad had actually *made*) and pistols (Colt .45, and a handly little .22 which, with the right size bullet, could bring down a rabbit and cut a thin, clean wake right through my skull).

I was lucky. It would have been difficult, in that nanosecond between pulling the trigger and hearing the roar bellow down the barrel, to also have heard the distant voice which I can still hear *you don't want this*, that antithesis of Prufrock's limp soul, the original human who knows that he is all he's got. It screams through the gap, this is not what I meant at all, this is not it, at all. With the knife, the gap was mercifully large. With one of Dad's guns, no real gap at all. Pop. Too late.

Instead I had left myself merely with a reminder of self-mutilation, one that I covered up with a wristwatch for almost a decade before becoming slightly accustomed to its presence. I can still see it. That's the blessing and curse of olive skin: it leaves a history of wounds.

That fever from the flu had acquired for me another blessing: Due to the nightmare of numbers running like a chain hauled over the gunwale of my skull, I never really could care much about my mother seeing the scar. When I awoke from the fever, I was not sure if she had really seen it. Being the good, disquieted mother she was, she did not mention it. "Thank God," I whispered to myself, knowing that I had a chance of avoiding the third degree questions that she would barrel down upon me, ones that would whip up more embarrassment than fear. Explaining anything to her seemed an impossibility, though it all made sense to me: Yes, I had been extremely sad the past few months, but the slash over the wrist had woken me up. I was all right now.

That did not last long. My heart filled my body with the necessary pint that had slipped through the drain. In doing so, it filled me with that same melancholy. I wanted to show Janice Lee my wound, an offering to the goddess of my love. "Here. I did this for you."

March slipped into the rains of April. Dogwoods burst all throughout Knoxville. During the Dogwood Arts Festival, when parades and clowns and artists filled the streets of the city in the celebration of the state's flower, the Hartland family walked about, glancing at the artisan crafts and sideshow paintings. I dragged behind them, staring at the reminders of new love, the four-petaled blooms of spring. That fucking dogwood became my jester.

I no longer thanked God for surviving. It was the same God who would have condemned me to Hell had I died. I still, of course, believed in that God. Considering how little He would understand my reasons for wanting to die, and how ready he would have been to burn me forever, I preferred to keep my distance. A religious iconoclasm formed in me. I quit going to mass at school. When I had to attend, I scowled, pouted, and refused to pray. Prayer had done little to get Janice to fall in love with me. What good would it do in other circumstances?

My teeth clicking and forehead thumping, however, had become, in and of themselves, sacred. I could do no great act without them.

In May, Janice Lee graduated. My sophomore year ended. I was to be sent from the fast streets of Knoxville to the slow, backward-running roads of my hometown. I was to leave the Hartland home for good. I was to say goodbye to Janice Lee.

That first Saturday morning of summer, I did not get out of bed. My mother walked in. I had the covers over my head. She could not see me crying. She sat down on the bed's edge and began talking. She did not rattle on, surprisingly. I had expected her to fire questions at me: Why was I so sad all the time? Why didn't I want to get out of bed? Would I look for a job this summer? She asked none of that. Her voice was low, quiet and slow. Dad was not in the house. Carter had cut a deal with the coal miners. Dad and his friends had gone back to work in the strip mining that whittled down the valleys of Kentucky. Mamá and I were left alone in the house.

I knew that she knew. She figured out where my arm was underneath the cover and gently placed her hand right over my wrist. Though my wrist was down against the mattress, it almost jumped, as if the healed cut had wriggled. She spoke about getting me some help. I shivered at that. My worst nightmare was about to come: I was to be committed to some asylum or sent off to a psychologist for years of testing and evaluation. The only thing worse than burning in hell for taking your own life was to live in this life with the stigma among your schoolmates that you were a weak, spineless loony, three rungs lower than Benny Bitan, the lanky, horn-rimmed glasses pre-geek who actually carried a slide ruler in his back pocket and who loved to converse over the lunch table about binary operations. This was the seventies, for Chrissake. People carried calculators that could almost fit in your pocket. Red-faced digital watches could tell you the time with a mere push of that tiny, sharp button. It was no age to fail in socially.

"I've got an idea, *hijo*," she said to me. She rarely spoke to me in Spanish in those days. Mamá had kindly left my sluggish Spanish alone, knowing that living in East Tennessee was not necessarily the best way for a Latino kid to connect with his roots. Whenever she used a Spanish word with me, it was to show love. The moment she said *hijo*, I remembered a childhood scene, one that had been played over and over again with all the times that my mother did it: she would see me across the room from where she sat and would say to me, *"Veníte, mi corazón, mi'jito,"* and raise her arms to me, beckoning me to her. I would walk to her immediately, where she would take me up in those thin, strong arms and hold me on her lap, kissing my forehead and whispering Spanish rhymes into my ear. Spanish had always been associated with that lap and embrace, a transient Latino moment in a gringoized childhood.

"Let's go to San Francisco for the summer," she whispered to me. I caught my breath underneath the blanket. San Francisco? I thought. My birth-city . . . Why there? Then I heard her voice again, explaining the details of such a trip, how we could visit with Grandmamá Roselia, hang out with my aunt Felícita, spend some days seeing the sites and going out to restaurants. "You know how much Felícita likes to go out to eat." I heard the details; I also heard the tremor, the voice that rattled in her brown neck, tossing out words to a lost son.

She stopped speaking. I barely lifted up the blanket, peeked over, and looked at her. Below her careful smile and her glistening eyes she held, in her left hand, what I thought were two plane tickets.

Then she added, "I also thought it would be good if you spent some time with your Uncle Jack. That may be just the thing for you."

With that, more confusion sliced through my heaping depression. My eyebrow wrinkled up at that consideration: a summer with Uncle Jack. My mother's desperation had reached considerable levels.

Uncle Jack Villalobos came down to me both through legend and my own scant memories from childhood. I remember wrestling his thin yet brawny body when I was nine years old. He always quickly pinned me. I remember his wrists: he was an electrician, and his wrists were thick and taut with years of screwing bolts into wood and metal.

Though thin and shorter than most men, Uncle Jack's presence was known by everyone in the room. He combed his thick shock of black hair back perfectly. It had the look of one who has stared into a harsh wind. His face was undoubtedly Salvadoran. His skin was my grandmother's color, slightly lighter than my mother but still deep brown. His cheeks and nose revealed a slight indigenous ancestry. No doubt Nahuatl or Pipil Indians peppered the blood of his great grandparents. Jack usually was smiling, as if ready to laugh at any second, something which got on my mother's nerves. "Wipe that *jodido* grin off your face, little one!" she would say to him, even when he was a grown man. This only caused the grin to grow larger.

He had left El Salvador as a child. He and his two sisters had taken a bus from the old country all the way to San Francisco when Jack was a mere five years old and my aunt a baby. My grandparents had already made the trek north, having left the kids in Usulután to finish their school year. Mamá, a teenager, was expected to be like another parent to them, making sure that they behaved themselves throughout the trip to the new country. There the sibling pattern began: My mother would try to discipline him, and Jack would always grin at her reprimanding voice. According to family lore, even as a little boy he had that wild-ass tendency about him. The whole family believed he was destined to be fully *macho*.

I knew nothing of those early years. I remembered the Uncle Jack of my youth, when he would turn and stare at me with coffee eyes, smile and say "'Ey, *sobrino*, what's happenin', man?" Most times the "man" would be elongated into a "maaaaan" that seeped back into his throat as he approached me and offered me a handshake that mistook my fingers for a pair of vice grips.

His face was hard. It was softened only by the grin. Even then, "soft" would not be the appropriate word. The summer I spent with him, he was forty-nine years old. He at least appeared to be a mature man. Lines were making their way across his face. Crows' feet stretched away from the corners of his eyes. His nose, which seemed to emanate from the more Indian bloodline of my Salvadoran family, spread across his face, with two folding whips of skin that held back his cheeks and swooped down toward the corners of his mouth. Except for his thin, well-kept moustache, he was always clean shaven.

In the years after our summer together, he changed little. I have a photo of him back in my apartment bedroom in Knoxville. In the photo he's leaning upon the gravestone of my grandparents, Roselia and Juan Villalobos, Senior. It's a dark blue marble stone, with little oval photos of both my grandparents next to their names and their dates. Uncle Jack was sixty at the time. In the photo he has both elbows resting upon the stone. One of his thick hands grasps the opposing elbow. The other hand cannot be seen. He wears a thick, tight red sweater that shows his svelte build. Orchids and chrysanthamums lay upon the grave, hiding a few words on the stone about God. Behind Jack his black 1967 Mustang is parked. A thick tree and a fence stand behind the car. I can only see one of his legs, the other being hidden behind the stone. But I can tell that he's standing with his feet wide apart so as to lean against the stone and stare straight into the camera. He has no shit-eating smile, although the potential is there. He stares silently, straight at you, telling you without words *Nothing can fuck me, maaaan. Not death, not life, nada, cabrón.*

The fairly large photo now leans upon my dresser in the bedroom of my apartment in Knoxville. I wondered, while Julie and Bill dealt with shoving Bill's huge member into her, did they feel Uncle Jack's stare? Or perhaps Uncle Jack's potent eyes had been covered by Julie's flung panties. That would have made my relative happy, the moist smell of the panties blinding him to the disgrace of his cuckolded nephew.

Uncle Jack was a staple of storytelling during my childhood years. My mother and father recounted the tale of when he spent a summer away from San Francisco to live with us in East Tennessee. I was a baby at the time. Yet I can still imagine the event, as if the family recounting had transformed itself into one of my own memories.

Uncle Jack began visiting Mary Lou Harrison, a young lady from a farming family living over in Clinch Mountain. He learned the work habits of Mr. Harrison, her father, who spent his days in the fields.

Uncle Jack, the true extrovert, always liked to bring some friends with him. He seemed to make friends wherever he went. This day he brought in his East Tennessee buddies who respectfully knocked on the door of the Harrison house. Mary Lou's mother was not home. Mary Lou was happy to have visitors. The boys came in, bringing potables that were slightly illegal in that very dry county.

Daddy Harrison came home early from the fields. Fortunately for the boys, the old man's truck was one purchased a few decades earlier, and it let out a roar as it came toward the house. The boys ran out the door, blocking it for a moment. Uncle Jack tried to make it through the human clog in the doorframe, and seeing that as impossible, dove through the window. A shot broke the air, followed by an East Tennessee curse. Uncle Jack ignored it, but turned and saw Daddy Harrison next to his old truck, with the rifle up against his shoulder. "OH MAAAN!" Uncle Jack made it to the car, which all the local boys had already piled into.

They escaped. Uncle Jack, from the back seat of the convertible, sighed out and laughed. "That was a close one." He reached back to rub his shoulderblade that ached from the leap through the window. His fingers touched thick, warm liquid. The blood covered his palms and dripped down his wrist.

"Oh shit," and he passed out.

The boys got him to the hospital. The doctor said that it would be a major operation to take the bullet out from underneath his shoulderblade, but assured that it was in a position that would cause the young man no harm.

The incident had cut the summer short. Uncle Jack flew back home to San Francisco, to a mother who, while verbally berating him for getting into such trouble, also understood the difficulties of a poor, upright son such as hers who had fallen into hard times among mean, backward hillbilly folk.

It seems my grandmother would have caught on to the pattern. Years after his Appalachian bullet wound, Uncle Jack had stepped out onto Capp Street in San Francisco after having enjoyed a delicious lunch of *tamales* and beans prepared by his mother. He lit a cigarette while standing on the sidewalk, searched his pocket for his keys, then meandered toward his then-brand new 1967 Ford Mustang. After opening the door, he heard an engine that roared over the tops of the other autos on the street. Turning his head right, he stared down Capp Street and saw a large, white Chevrolet barreling toward him.

Wide eyed, Uncle Jack made a quick decision. It was obvious that the red haired woman in the Chevrolet was ready to slam her car into him and the Mustang, perhaps pinning him to it so as to watch him squirm. To jump into his car meant certain death. He leaped. His body landed on his car. He rolled to the other side just as the Chevrolet hooked itself onto the open door of the Mustang and ripped it from its hinges. The Chevrolet drove off, going about sixty miles an hour, the Mustang's door stuck to its grille.

Uncle Jack looked up from the sidewalk and over his car. They say he still had the cigarette dangling from his lips. My grandmother leaned out of a window from her Victorian home, looked down, and asked if he was all right.

"Yeah, Mamá, *estoy bien, estoy bien*. Damn." He still stared down the street, trying to remember the name of the young woman.

"Ay Dios, ¿qué puta quiere matar a mi'jito?" she asked. (Oh my God, who's the bitch who wants to kill my little son?) *"Y imirá vos tu pobre carro!"* And look at your poor car!

This was the uncle with whom my mother wanted me to spend the summer.

Four days after leaving Janice Hartland's home in Knoxville, Mamá and I took a Greyhound bus from East Tennessee to San Francisco. I was mistaken about the plane tickets in my mother's hand. They were two bus tickets. "It will be good for you to see the country. The one your father and I took a Harley Davidson on. And before interstates! It was rougher back then. You can handle a bus ride for a few days."

Nothing could go up against the cross-country motorbike legend. We boarded the bus at three o'clock on the Monday morning after my last day of school. On Thursday that same bus pulled into San Francisco. We had not stayed in any motels. We had not stayed on the interstate either. The bus had meandered off the main highway every two hours to pick up two or three people in each small town. Drunks, prostitutes, preachers, drag queens, nuns, blacks, whites, Asians and American Indians all boarded the vehicle. A three-year-old white girl who smelled like her last diaper had been changed long before we reached Texas fell in love with me and showed me that love by climbing over my chair and placing three wet suckers in my hair. Her mother demanded that I give each sucker back.

When we reached San Francisco in the early morning hours of a Thursday, my ankles had swollen to the size of tumors. It looked as if someone had wrapped skin-colored leather around my lower legs. My tennis shoes would not come off until I lay upon my bed in Abuelita's home and lifted my legs up, allowing the strange, built-up liquid to dissipate through my body. Neither the swelling nor the lack of bathing during the trip bothered my grandmother. She held me and whispered *"Ay, mi cipote, mi nietecito"* into my ear, holding me to her like a strayed refugee.

Doña Roselia Maravilla de Villalobos was more than just my grandmother. She was the matriarch of Capp Street and the surrounding avenues. Doña Roselia had immigrated to the United States the year before the end of World War II. During that year she worked as Rosie the Riveter, helping construct the navy ships that left San Francisco's harbor. After the war she found a job as a maid in a hotel. She worked that job in the evenings. In the mornings she made food for local folks who had to catch a quick lunch in a bag before they took off for work. As all of her neighbors were from Latin America, she made the appropriate food: tortillas, beans, rice, chicken and pork sautéed in tomato and onion sauces with *cilantro*. After awhile the demand became too much for one person. She hired two young women to help her. She bought a tortilla cutter and her own corn grinder. She discovered the process of *instantánea,* making the dried tortilla flour and selling it in bags so that women rushing home from work could make quick tortillas. This little discovery launched her corporation. The opening of Doña Roselia's Fine Latin Cuisine Company Inc. made sure that she would never need to worry about money again.

When Abuelita retired, my aunt Felícita took over the running of the business. After three decades of creating one of the largest corporations run by a woman—and a Latina woman at that—in

California, everyone was surprised that my grandmother would decide to return to maid work. She got a job at a local hotel called The Gentleman's Inn. Aunt Felícita made her cavils known.

"*Y, Mamá, ¿qué le pasa que ahora quiere ser una* maid *de nuevo?*" she asked. ("Why do you want to be a maid again?")

"*Hija, no me hablés como esos cipotes malcriados de la calle, que comen las dos lenguas a la vez.*" ("Girl, don't talk to me like those bad-mannered street kids, who eat both languages at once.")

My grandmother was a stickler for the traditional ways of speaking.

They fought for a long while. Grandmother finally refused to speak about the matter anymore, once she had said, "If I wish, I will clean shit in the shipyard latrines like I first did when I came to this blessed country."

Aunt Felícita could not live with this. So she bought the hotel from its two Hungarian-American brothers. She made Abuelita the owner. That way, Aunt Felícita could believe that her mother was merely cleaning one of her own houses.

Once Mamá and I arrived that summer, I listened to Abuela's cooing Spanish words, hearing the lilt and echo of my own mother who had taken me up into her arms and her lap in my childhood. They were, no surprise, the same voice. She let me go only to hug her oldest daughter. My mother dropped her bags onto the floor and let her mother take her into old, familiar arms that smelled of a fresh bath and an anonymous perfume, one worn by elderly ladies who tried to think little of old age.

Unlike my grandmother, my aunt did not have much fortitude to take on our four-day-old Greyhound smells. She came from the kitchen with a smile, but quickly showed me my room and the bathroom where I could immediately freshen up. I was glad to oblige.

After bathing and while putting on my clothes, I could hear the three women talking in the den room right next to my bedroom. They chatted in Spanish, so I could not understand everything they said. At one point my mother said something about my father Pete, which roused up a laugh from my grandmother. They chatted together like three friends who had not seen one another in a long time, yet would not let time and distance stop them from gathering the more important pieces of gossip. Then their voices turned low and serious as the Spanish whispered around my name, "Antonio." Then I heard the silences. I heard a *"No, no es posible."* I heard a mother weeping.

"Shit," I thought. I was about to prepare my hair, but I wanted to verify what they were saying. To prepare my hair meant blasting it with my long-mouthed blow dryer and flipping it back with a round brush for at least twenty minutes. Each day of my life those twenty minutes blocked out all other sounds, with only the loud, screaming hum of the blow dryer placing the hairs in perfect position as I stared into the mirror and played sculptor.

They talked more. Even though I could not understand them, I could tell from the changes in demeanor that they had gone from surprise to fear to immediate planning. My grandmother led the way. *"Ese nieto mío va a ver a la Chucharrona,"* she said. I knew that she held her right hand up level with her forehead, shaking it slightly as she always did whenever stating something angrily or with conviction. *"La Chucharrona le va a guiar, estoy segura de eso."* I had heard that word before, Chucharrona, but could not place where. I believed it to be a person. From the ending of the word, the person was probably a woman.

"Vaya pues, Mamá," my mother said. I knew that whenever Mamá said *vaya pues,* she was trying to shut her mother up. Whenever they spoke on the phone between San Francisco and Tennessee (which was about twice a week) and Mamá had to make supper for Dad or just wanted to go use the bathroom, she would say over and over again, *"Vaya pues, vaya pues, sí, vaya pues . . ."* Obviously Mamá did not agree with Abuelita's council. I did not know whether or not I would hear of the Chucharrona again.

The Holy Spirit of My Uncle's *Cojones*

"Pero quiero que él se quede un tiempo con Jack," my mother said.

The room got quiet. I don't know if their silence meant that they disagreed with my mother's idea of me staying with Uncle Jack for awhile, or if they were just dumbfounded by the idea. It seemed that they were more thinking of the ramifications, because at that point, both my grandmother and my aunt said, almost in unison, *"Vaya pues."* This was not used to put my mother off; they agreed.

It got too silent in the den. The women left the room. I opened my door slightly, just a crack, to watch my mother walk down the hallway to her own bedroom. No doubt she would now take a bath. My aunt followed behind, but she went on to the kitchen. I heard the one person left in the den, my grandmother, moving around. I quit the door and rested on my bed, looking out the window over Capp Street. My hair was just starting to dry. I knew it would be necessary to wet it again in order to perform the blow-drying ritual. Outside boys my age and color—some of them darker, others lighter— played soccer on a small field wedged between two buildings. A bus drove by on Capp Street. Mission Street was filled with traffic, but Capp was a smaller road that did not stay as busy. Following Eighteenth Street, I could see the traffic on Mission, as well as the food and clothing kiosks that lined the sidewalks. Stores ran along Eighteenth: a clock shop, a jeweler's, a couple of ethnic restaurants. It was surprising to see a small field where boys could play soccer just across the street, in this compacted section of the city. I could just hear the boys as they yelled and laughed toward one another, all in Spanish. They were less understandable than the three women who had been in the den, not because of the distance, but most undoubtedly because they spoke in a slang known internally to the group, used as a teenage, Latino code.

"Antonio," my grandmother's voice almost sang at my door. She did not knock.

"Oh." I got up from my bed and sat on its edge. I quickly gathered up courteous words from the corners of my brain, "*Sí,* uh, *pase adelante, por favor.*"

She entered. She smiled at me. She walked up to me, grabbed my face with both her hands, kissed me on the cheek, then held my skull like a globe. Her grip shook some of the water out of my wet hair.

"I so glad jyu are here, Antonio."

I smiled.

"Jyu, this is *tu casa*. Home. Always jyur home." She gestured to the entire Victorian house.

I thanked her with a mumbled *gracias*. I wondered if it meant I could wander about the entire building. But I knew that most every room in the building was occupied by renters.

Then my grandmother's hold on my skull turned even firmer. She almost squeezed spit from my lips.

"Jyu will see La Chucharrona," she said, her whisper turning sharp, as if to cut through steel. "La Chapina. She will help jyu. Help us. Yes!"

At first I did not move. My hands stretched out slightly to each side of my shoulders. Then I asked, my question puckering through my lips, "Who, who is the Chucharrona?"

"*La curandera. Una mayordoma.* She lives nearby. We will go, tonight!"

With that, she relaxed her grip on my face. She smiled, brought my head to her lips and kissed my forehead. Then she let go. She moved toward the door, turning only once to me, then raised one index finger up as she smiled serenely. "Tonight. Yes. Tonight."

My Uncle Jack was not to arrive until later that evening. When I asked where he was, all the women got quiet again. My aunt Felícita finally answered, "It's difficult to know, Tony. But he said he'll be here today. He's looking very forward to seeing you both."

At noon my aunt and grandmother fixed Mamá and me a welcome lunch. My grandmother had made a Salvadoran *picadillo*, beef that has been cooked in a crock pot all day before torn to soft pieces by hand, then mixed with fresh, sweet onions and peppermint. She knew it was one of my favorites. I watched as Abuelita, one of the richer Latin women in San Francisco, took tortilla flour from one of her own bags of *Instantánea* (which had her warm, smiling face painted on the side), mixed it with warm water, then shaped the ball through the movement of her hands and fingers, forming a perfectly round, flat tortilla.

I never learned that art. My mother and I have always relied upon a tortilla flattener. It is a simple device made out of two pieces of round wood hinged together. You place the ball of dough in the middle of the lower piece, cover it with the upper, then slam them together with a metal rod on top. It flattens the tortilla immediately.

My grandmother was the John Henry of tortilla making. In her own kitchen she had refused to ever use such a device. She could not compete with the speed of the tortilla flattener, but she could make them just as round and as thin as the flattener could. Although her entire corporation utilized machines throughout every part of the business, from the cooking of the dough to the packaging, at home she would not capitulate to the high technology of two boards hinged together. I was glad, though at the time I could not say why. There was something so very stable about watching her spread the dough into perfect round formations with her very palms.

The table was also covered with *pupusas*, beans, rice, dry Mexican goat cheeses bought on Mission Street, a small salad made out of cabbage, vinegar, fresh tomatoes and onions. My grandmother opened a beer for me. Then she turned to a large, sealed kettle and opened it, releasing a thick cloud of steam as well as the smell of a hundred-year-old recipe.

These were her Salvadoran tamales. If the instant tortilla flour was her launch into a successful corporation, these tamales were the next step into cullinary distinction and financial success. They were no ordinary tamales. Unlike Mexican tamales, which were composed of corn masa, pork, onions and spices; and unlike Nacatamales, the tamal of Nicaragua, which usually hid a large bone or thick shred of cartilage in order to fill the masa (According to my Aunt Felícita, "The most disgusting tamales on the face of the earth. Vile and not fit for dogs."), these Salvadoran delicacies held a variety of foods, ones that a consumer would not usually place in the same mouthful. Along with a pork and chicken mixture, the mound of masa also displayed eggs, potatoes, raisins, prunes, olives, and a sauce that held the entire entity together. To explain such a mix to a neophyte eater usually made their heads turn away. Yet the combination looked pleasing enough on the plate, much like a new, tiny planet upon which everything was edible. Then came the first bite, and that consumer would automatically be assimilated into the growing legion of fans.

The *Guanacotamales* (as they had been quickly nicknamed, after our people) had come from a recipe that an old Pipil Indian had supposedly given my grandmother back in the 1920s. About a dozen food corporations and several local Latino restauranteurs had tried to buy the recipe. Quaker, which had its own successful line of Latin foods, supposedly offered my grandmother's company four hundred thousand dollars for it. She refused. She guarded the secret of the ingredients as carefully as Coca-Cola guarded its own.

For the longest time Abuelita did not have the recipe written down. She even had the mass production of the tamales done in such a way that no employee could master the complete instructions. Only she and her daughters knew how to make the tamales from memory. Finally, after much persuasion from Aunt Felícita, grandmother banged out the recipe on a typewriter and placed it in the company's safe.

That afternoon in San Francisco, I ate the tamales first. Then I attacked the other foods. I ate more than I should have. Finally pulling away from the table, I slapped my belly. "Oh. *Delicioso*," I said, hoping that my weak endeavor in Spanish would make them happy.

It did. All three women clucked in the original tongue about little Tony, how he was trying to speak correctly. There was some scrap of hope.

"You sure you don't want more?" Aunt Felícita asked. "Here, one more *pupusa*."

"*No, gracias, tía*. I feel overweight already."

"Nonsense. Look at you. Thinner than I've ever seen you. Practically a little *flaquito*. *Y ¿qué?* Don't you eat well with those families in Knoxville?"

"Oh, fine. Not as good as this, of course."

"You need to eat more, *mi sobrino*," she continued, not really hearing me. "I mean, look at you. You hardly have any color, like somebody sucked the blood out of you."

It got quiet in the kitchen. I know I rolled my eyes. I quickly excused myself, leaving a mother and a grandmother to reprimand a loving auntie for her probing.

La Chucharrona, famous clairvoyant, had a bad cold. Nevertheless, she was known to be the wisest woman in the barrio. She had a wicked set of candles.

I was sleepy from the meal. I had also not wanted to leave my room that afternoon, taking into account my aunt's final remark upon my blood-drained demeanor. Best, I thought, to remain alone and hide my shame.

My grandmother walked into the bedroom as if nothing had happened at the lunch table. "Come. We go to La Chucharrona."

I put on a light jacket. Before leaving, I glanced into the kitchen. My mother and aunt were sitting at the table, sipping small shots of whiskey and smoking cigarettes. They spoke calmly. They did not seem upset by Aunt Felícita's *faux pas* nor by the fact that Abuelita was taking me to see the local witch doctor.

Abuelita and I walked out of the house onto Capp Street, took Eighteenth over to Mission and walked one more block toward San Carlos Street. There were fewer people out during the day. Many men and women were closing up their shops for the afternoon. Abuelita greeted a number of them along the way.

We came to San Carlos Street. Abuelita turned left and walked past a group of teenage boys. They stared at her as she approached. They wore their hair thick and combed back, no doubt kept there with well used blow dryers. I envied them their new polyester shirts with large, sharp collars opened wide over their necks, as well as the cigarettes that dangled from many of their lips. Abuelita stared straight into their group. *"Bueno, cipotes, ¿cómo les va?"* she said, asking them how they were. They all respectfully mumbled that they were fine. *"¿Y La Chucharrona?"*

The Holy Spirit of My Uncle's Cojones

I picked up from one of their responses that the elderly *curandera* was still home, that her grandson Chucho had just left her house.

Abuelita thanked them and turned to me. *"Veníte, vos,"* she said. I obeyed.

We walked toward another Victorian house, one not as well kept as my family's home. This building had yet to be refurbished. Three types of wallpaper peeled away from failing glue in the foyer. One of the tiny glass windows in the front door had been smashed, no doubt by a small projectile such as a ball from kids playing in the street. Dust and whispy cobwebs collected in the low corners.

Also unlike grandmother's home, there was no gate here to protect the residents from intruders. The broken-glass door was unlocked. Abuelita knew this, as she walked up and easily pushed it open. I followed her inside. Abuelita opened a second door to the first floor rooms and walked into a dark hallway. I followed, barely glancing up the stairs that led to the second floor, comparing the torn rug of the steps to the well-kept wood and carpeting of my family's house. No doubt Doña Roselia's Fine Latino Cuisine, Inc. had kept our home from going this route. Unlike my grandmother, who had lived her entire adult immigrant life in the same house on Capp Street, this was a house owned by a distant landlord who rarely saw his tenants, who collected rent, who kicked out late payers quickly.

La Chucharrona was one of the tenants. Supposedly she had been in this house for at least a hundred years, outliving seven landlords. She was old, much older than my own grandmother; or perhaps she just appeared that way. I remembered her from my childhood, when my family and I lived on Capp Street. As a kid I had accompanied my grandmother down into these rooms. I had never seen the elder in the marketplace on Mission Street nor in the churches of the area. La Chucharrona was not the same outside of this dark hallway that led to the one door at the end, the one that my grandmother now walked toward.

A white, unshaven drunk snored in one corner, his ski hat sliding off one side of his skull. Abuelita ignored him. She looked straight down the hallway. I walked beside her. We did not speak. Before we reached the door, an elderly voice from the other side muttered, *"Pasen adelante."* We obeyed.

At first I could see very little in the apartment, as it was even darker than the hallway. It was more than one room. This first room had no light at all, nor windows. I sensed that there was very little here, except for a large, metal crucifix that hung on a thick nail in one wall, before which grandmother blessed herself. I knew that Mary had to be around somewhere nearby. Sure enough, there she was, a small statue of the Blessed Virgin, standing on the floor in one corner. A black rosary dangled about her tiny blue shoulders.

We did not remain in this room. We followed the odors of pine needles and burning wax. I at first figured that the famed clairvoyant had cleaned her home with a great amount of pine cleaner. Yet this smell seemed fresher than a disinfectant. I stepped into the next room and felt the pine needles roll under my shoe. By the light of the dozens of candles lining the wall—the only light in the room—I could see that the floor was covered with pine needles. As we had gone deeper into the building, the appearance of so many candles actually seemed bright. I looked about. Another crucifix dangled on the wall, much smaller than the one in the first room. A large depiction of a white, blue-eyed Mary, with her heart sticking out of her chest while her eyes looked upward to the heavens, hung from a nail. To my right stood a table with the woman sitting behind the table. La Chucharrona's profile stared down at the tabletop. Her brown skin was much darker than anyone else's in the barrio. She had features that were purely indigenous. She wore a red blouse with white and blue embroidered figures around the neck. She wore a dress that reached below her skinny knees. The dress itself was multicolored, with greens and blues predominating.

Just below her, sitting on the floor and staring down at the pine needles, was a little boy. His black hair covered over his left eye. He said nothing, as if listening intently to the ostensible prayers that the old woman chanted above him.

Several objects stood upon the table, along with numerous candles. I could not see what was in the middle of the table, where La Chucharrona placed her sight, due to the unmoved troops of tiny books, plates, plastic and wood crosses, toy automobiles, miniature whiskey bottles and scattered boxes of cigarettes. Pine needles had also been tossed about the white plastic tablecloth. All was intrinsically Guatemalan, as if I had stepped through a door that had led me back to a neighboring old country. Her voice, which lifted up slowly and seemed to encircle the objects before her, also added to the scene, though she spoke in Spanish and not in an Indian tongue. She was reading something. Sometimes she had to clear her throat of phlegm.

". . . *y aunque las autoridades no han podido explicar el acontecimiento, muchos de los individuos del barrio Satélite de La Cuidad confirman que sí, el gran espíritu del cantor y bailador estadounidense* ELVIS PRESLEY *se ha aparecido aquí, dando conciertos breves a los ambulantes de la calle nocturna . . .*"

I was enraptured, overwhelmed, and not a little frightened, by the tone of her voice, the way it lifted from the table as she stared deeply, perhaps into tea leaves, perhaps into pine needles or the magic flickering of candles. I was not sure which until I moved slightly closer, following my grandmother, and saw that before La Chucharrona lay an open magazine, its slick pages shimmering from the light of the candles. A touched-up photo of a ghostly Elvis lifting himself over Mexico City appeared wide on both pages.

My grandmother greeted her by referring to the magazine, *"Acaba de llegar* La Voz?" she said. I remembered the name of that publication. Grandmother sent back copies to Mamá in Tennessee, so my mother could keep up with the latest important news (UFO sightings in Chiapas, Christ's appearance in San Salvador, woman gives birth to iguana in Tegucigalpa) from the old countries. Now, I supposed, it was Elvis giving concerts from the dead to the Mexicans.

La Chucharrona looked up from the table. She wore thick, small reading glasses that were perched on her nose, a half inch from her eyes. She smiled up at my grandmother, *"Ay, Rosi, ¿qué tal?"* They chatted to each other for a few minutes in Spanish. The little boy under the table—one of the *curandera's* grand or great grandchildren—shifted around. No doubt he was frustrated by our interruption of La Chucharrona reading the tabloid, wanting to know more about the apparition of Elvis' ghost in one of Mexico City's barrios.

My grandmother's demeanor changed slightly, and I heard my name within their Spanish phrases. Both elderly women looked at me. *"Salúdala, Antonio,"* My grandmother ordered me. I put out my hand. La Chucharrona grabbed it and shook it, smiling up at me.

"Un guapito, ¿sí? Pero bien débil, púchica. No se siente nada," she said to my grandmother while holding my hand. Her Spanish was different from my relatives'. It had a lilt to it that I would later understand to be Guatemalan. Though very clear, it was obvious that Spanish was her second tongue, that she no doubt felt more comfortable in her native Qua'chiqu'el. Then she looked straight up at me, her glasses magnifying her eyeballs.

"So you're having a little trouble walking through this life, yes?"

I was surprised at how clear her English was, better than my grandmother's. I did not respond to her readily. Then I heard the question once again, in my mind. It seemed too true; I wished to flee, to run through the doors of this cave of an apartment and into the streets of San Francisco, not stopping until I came to the Golden Gate, where I could jump.

The *curandera* did not allow any flight. She stood up, still holding my right hand. I looked down, not wanting to gaze into her eyes.

I stared at the five thin, silver necklaces that dangled low from her neck and fell between her wrinkled breasts. She did not look at me for the moment. Her eyes looked up as her right hand felt my palm, the back of my hand, then my wrist. I know I flinched. Then she looked at me. She looked straight at me and muttered something neither in English nor in Spanish; Qua'chiqu'el seemed her best way to whisper toward certain truths.

She did not let go for a long time, but kept her forefinger and middle finger upon my healed wound. The fingers' tips ran along its crease. At one point I could feel a fingernail touch it. I believed she could open it up again with that nail. It was strange, after four months of hiding the scar from the world, a wound of shame and adolescent fears, to have this old woman take the scar in her hand and almost fondle it. Yet she touched it not so much as if it were some enemy to my body, but as a lesion into something else: answers, perhaps. I could not tell from the way she looked at me.

La Chucharrona turned away and looked down at the boy. She said only one word: *"Pom."*

The boy immediately stood up and walked out of the room, his little black cowboy boots crunching over the pine needles. Less than one minute later he was back. He carried a small tin paint can that dangled from a rope hooked into two holes in its round top. He handed the receptacle to her.

Chucharrona took a large box of wooden matches from the table and lit one match, then held it to the can. I could see, from the match's glow, what was inside: a small pile of translucent objects— some of them fairly round and smooth, others more jagged, as if having been snapped off a larger object—glowed from the flame. After a few moments of touching the flame to the edges of the pieces, they ignited and tossed a puff of smoke into the air. The smell of burnt resin hit the insides of my nostrils. I wondered if one of the flames had fallen and had caught the pine needle on fire. More smoke lifted up from the paint can. She dropped the match into the can and walked about the room, carrying the burn to each corner. It took little time for the smoke to fill the room, though I did not feel that it would choke me. It had an acrid yet soothing texture to it. This I could not readily explain. But I did not cough.

La Chucharrona quietly ordered the boy in their native language. He stood again and walked to a shadowed area of the room. He reached up into the shadow and pulled something that made a fairly loud, metalic noise, like a rusty hook leaving a metal hole. Then he opened a window. It was still light enough outside to make this room seem like night. A few street sounds, a car's distant horn, the light scream of a playing child, pushed through the opening. Some of the smoke from the *pom* found the window and wafted through it.

I turned to my grandmother, who stood quietly beside me. She had a slight smile upon her face, as if approving of the familiar movements before her. I hesitatingly asked, "Why?" while pointing toward the open window.

She barely glanced at me. "Her prayers," she said, then she took her hands and gesticulated, moving them before her, making them act like the fumes themselves that left the room. "Smoke. Carries your prayers up to the heavens. Needs the window to get through."

Prayers, I thought. Fucking wonderful.

"If we did not open the window," La Chucharrona said, adding to my grandmother's answer, "the words would just stay in here. Everything would just stay here. And what good would that do?"

She then reached into the middle of her table. With so many objects upon its top, I could not see her hand or her forearm. I heard a soft clicking as she gathered up five cold, unlit candles that lay upon the table. She took them to the middle of the room, where the pine needles had been placed thickly upon the floor, so much so that I could not see the linoleum. She placed them upright in a diamond shape, with one in the middle.

My eyes had become accustomed to the darkness, enough to distinguish the colors of the candles. Unlike most of the other wax pillars in the room, which were all an off-white color, these five had distinguishing shades: one was red, its opposite was black; the third was white, and its opposite yellow. In the middle she had stuck a green candle. She lit them all.

She took the paint can and swirled it over the top of the candle-diamond. Then she knelt down and placed the can to one side. Remaining in the kneeling position, she turned, looked at me, and motioned for me to kneel down with her.

"Oh no, I'm fine, I'll just stand here and . . ."

My grandmother hit my back—near my left kidney—with a boney knuckle. I jerked forward. I was kneeling.

La Chucharrona took off her glasses and rubbed the space between her eyes. She then rubbed her whole face with her palms as if to rouse herself from the weariness of her head cold. Placing her palms upon her lap, she lowered her head and muttered in that Indian tongue. Then she looked straight at me.

"The day you cut yourself . . ." she said, too clearly for me to keep my eyes upon her. I looked down at the candles as she spoke. "That day, did you die?"

"What?"

"Did you die? You know. *Morir*. Did you?"

"No. Of course not. It was an accident, I . . ." I chortled, hoping to escape in laughter. This was all insane, I told myself. If it wasn't for my damn mother telling them, spilling the beans about my spilt blood, I wouldn't be here kneeling in front of an old quack from the mother countries. That was the truth, there was correctness in that term: mother countries, the mother of all countries. You could not escape the Mothers. "Look, I'm fine. It was just a mistake, I'm alive, I . . ."

"But something died in you, yes? Something had to. You wanted to kill it."

I said nothing, only looked at her.

"Perhaps you did kill it. That is good. As long as the dead part doesn't drag your living piece down with it." She turned slightly toward my grandmother while keeping her eyes on me. She spoke in Spanish. I could barely make out what she asked, something about what they (the women of my family, no doubt) were planning to do with me. Abuelita answered, but the only thing I understood was "Juan."

La Chucharrona raised an eyebrow and smiled slightly. She spoke again to me. "So you will be with your uncle?" Then she chuckled as she made to blow the candles between us out. *"Está bien. Es un buen plan. Con tal que no se muera en el proceso."*

"Es un riesgo, pues," my grandmother answered.

"Vale la pena," muttered the witch doctor as she puckered her lips to blow.

"Wait," I said, suddenly concerned about the flickering flames in front of me, as well as their Spanish conversation. "I don't understand . . . what is all this? This isn't prayer, it's something else. What have you just done?" I wanted to say "to me?" but didn't want to phrase it that way, afraid of how foolish it would make me look. I was not one to believe in voodoo, even if it had just been performed on me.

"Why, I just prayed for you."

"Yeah but . . . what are all these candles about?"

"Oh. The candles. Yes. They are everything." She knelt over and moved her hands to each one as she spoke. "The red and the black candles are the rising and the setting of the sun. Red for early morning, black for night. East and West. They are also the birth and death of God.

"The yellow candle is in the south. The white is in the north. They stand for the birth and death of Man."

She blew those four candles out, shielding the opposite side of the wick with her palm as she did so.

This made no sense to me. How could God die? And daily? I could understand the "man" part; we're all to die. I had almost passed that way not so long ago. But what the Hell did God's daily death mean?

"But the middle one . . ." I stopped her, pointing to the green candle that stood at the exact crossing of the life and death of humans and God. It still flickered light upon both our faces. "What is that?"

"That one?" She smiled as she bent forward. "That is you."

She blew it out. I watched as the thin smoke of me cut through the smoke of the *pom*, making its way toward the window.

My grandmother paid her with a twenty dollar bill. La Chucharrona took the money and thanked her. They chatted as she showed us the way to the door. La Chucharrona gave Abuelita the copy of *La Voz* so that Abuelita could catch up on dead Elvis doing "La Bamba."

Outside, the afternoon sun was still bright upon the city. We walked away from the *curandera's* dilapidated home. Here on the sidewalk, where boys played soccer on the street and where lighter-skinned Latinos drove home for the evening, the world took me and shamed me for being so frightened inside. I almost muttered about the stupidity of my people's ways. Yet I did not. No doubt Abuelita would have picked that up and translated it through her Spanish brain to rain down upon me the demand to never disrespect our heritage.

We walked home. My head was down, staring at the cement sidewalk under me. Abuelita said nothing. She bought us both some sweet bread from a kiosk on Mission Street. We stayed there so that she could talk with the middle-aged woman about any local gossip. I turned and looked down the street toward the house. I stared up at the second floor, at the window of my bedroom, where I longed to be with the door shut tight. Finally Abuelita said goodbye. So did I, barely muttering *adios* to the businesswoman.

In front of the house, Abuelita smiled a large, almost chuckling grin. *"Ay, mi hijo*, he ees home," she said as she stared at the eleven-year-old black 1967 Mustang that was parked in front of the house. We walked up the steps to her front door. She nervously jangled the keys and made her way through. *"Hace mucho tiempo, casi un mes . . ."* she muttered, which I could understand: it had been too much time for her, almost a month, since she had seen her only son.

We walked up the steps, then down the hall. Spanish come from the kitchen, my mother's voice, my aunt's, and that other sound, the gravel that juggled in the taut throat of a man. I turned the corner, still behind my grandmother. My heart shoved three lumps of blood into my throat. I clicked my teeth together, then followed up with a quick knocking of my knuckles against my forehead.

There, at the kitchen door, was the back of his body. His arms were crossed, which made his shoulders and lats wider. He wore a tight, light blue jean shirt. He also wore jean pants that covered the black of his leather boots. I could only see his thick black hair. Then my grandmother touched his shoulder. He turned and bent down to kiss her and take her up in thick arms. He hugged her tight, closing his eyes as he did so, whispering into her ear in Spanish, apologizing for being away for so long, that business had taken him out of town too much, but that now it was so good, so very good to be home.

Then he turned to me. His eyes opened. They opened wide. His mouth opened wide as he smiled. Yet he did not speak. His shirt opened enough for me to see the sharp crease between his breasts, made from either hard work or exercise or both. Then the gravel of his voice directed itself to me, "Ey, *sobrino*, Tony, man, Jesus Christ, you've grown up, man, you've grown up . . ."

That was all I heard and all I saw. I now saw the wall of the hallway and felt his right bicep plunging into my Adam's Apple. His left grip snatched my left wrist as he pulled my arm back to the side of his waist. My right fingers grabbed his forearm to keep him from choking me. It was not unlike trying to pull a thick root of an oak out of the ground. I know my eyes bulged from the pressure. This, I wanted to say, was much more than was called for. This most assuredly went against my rights, though at the moment I could not articulate what my rights were as a nephew. But he sure as hell moved too deeply into my comfort zone. I struggled against his entire body, which did not move, no matter how much I shifted. He growled words into my ear, laughing as he did so. Then the women laughed, all three of them, even my mother, while I fought against this familial conspiracy. I heard my grandmother half-heartedly ask him to let me go, don't hurt the poor boy, *hijo,* he's not as strong as you; but it was not much of an endeavor. Her only son kept me in that grip for what seemed to me a long afternoon, the first afternoon of a long summer.

I retreated to my room. The door was not thick enough.

"'Ey *sobrino*," Uncle Jack called to me. His knuckle battered against my door. I could not pretend to be asleep, as loud as that knuckle was. Sitting on the bed, my back to the wall, I invited him in. I forced a smile at him. He sat down on the edge of the bed. "How you doing man? You're looking pretty good. Shit, can you believe six years have passed. Last time I saw you, you were a little squirt, man! Now you're all grown up. Shit, I bet you still haven't had your first woman yet, have you, *sobrino?*" He slapped me against the side of my head. That hurt.

"Uh, no. Not yet, I guess."

"You *guess?* How you guess about a thing like that, man? Either you did or you didn't. Well, maybe if you're stone cold drunk you don't remember, yeah, I can understand that, but you too young to drink, right? So what you mean you guess?" He laughed.

His moustache separated slightly and curled up and around the laugh. He pulled a pack of cigarettes out of his blue shirt. The shirt itself was tight on him, showing the curve of his abdominal muscles. A lone gold chain pulled up from the shirt, almost tight around his neck. He offered me a cigarette. I declined. Then I wished I hadn't. I had never smoked before. I wanted to, dearly so, after having watched my father smoke all my life. Here, my uncle was offering me one. Yet I followed silent rules, ones that, when I still think about it, I'm not sure who put in my head.

"Yeah, it's good to see you, *sobrino*. Always good to see family." He blew out smoke. "You've grown up a lot. But you looking a little peaked, you know that? Aren't you eating right or something? Hey, they treating you right in that school you go to?"

"Oh yeah. I'm fine there."

"Your Mamá said something about you having some trouble over there." He sucked at his cigarette. I panicked. I placed my wrist down. He did not look at it. "What kind of trouble, man? Girl problems? Shit, that can be taken care of easy. Or is it some fucking *cheles* giving you the beef?"

I was confused. *"Cheles?* What's that?"

"Chele, you know, what you call them? White boys."

White boys, I thought. White. I had never really thought about it. What was I?

"Sometimes it's tough, you know. Gotta defend your skin when you least expect it. Shit, I had to fight my way out of a bunch of scraps when I was your age."

He began to tell me a few stories of how, when attending a city school in town as a kid, a gang of white teenagers surrounded him and threatened to skin him with their blades. He fought them all for half an hour, keeping their knives from his neck until the bell rang. I half heard it. I was giving thanks—to whom I don't know—that the women in my life had apparently not told my uncle anything about my winter endeavor.

"Yeah, so your A*buelita* she took me out of that school. Well, I think they were ready to kick me out. So Mamá sent me to a Catholic school over at the mission. I almost got religious there." He smiled at me. The cigarette smoke leaked through his teeth. "Damn, Sister María Elena had tits on her. That habit of hers lay on them like bedsheets."

I could only think of Sister McCartney back in Knoxville. But she had no breasts to speak of. Funny, to hear my uncle talk about a nun's breasts. I thought I was the only warped person in the world to think such thoughts.

"So what's your deal over there? Somebody leaning on you hard?" he asked.

"No. Nothing like that. Really, I'm not having any problems." I could hear my own voice for what it was. With Uncle Jack's Spanish-accented English that growled through the room, my own voice was soft, weak, and vaguely southern. "I mean, I was having some problems. But that's all over now."

"Sounds like women problems."

"Well . . . yeah, they were."

"Ah. Pussy's great, but it'll whip you from time to time." He sucked the last of the cigarette and flicked the butt out the open window. "So what was her name?"

"Janice."

"Janice. Nice name. So, did you get in the sack with her?"

I felt the heat of new tears push into the corners of my eyes. This, I knew, would not be acceptable. But his stark words about my heavenly queen who had rejected me were almost too much. I was both angry with him as well as ashamed at my own loss, my own inability to get the woman of my dreams. I looked down at the bed, trying to hide my eyes.

"What? Hey, Tony, you can't let a woman get you down, man," he slapped me on the shoulder again. Again, it hurt. "Shit. Let me tell you one thing: pussy is great, but it ain't worth losing your head over. I mean, unless you're in love or something. Then it ain't pussy. Then it's your woman. But then again, who wants *that* beef either?"

I said nothing. I still looked down at the bedspread, fighting to somehow suck the tears back into their ducts. I could not believe the position the women had put me into, that of having to spend time with my Neanderthal uncle. What did they expect me to do all summer with Jack? He was the stuff of dark, trashy myths, the exemplar of the bad life. He was Icarus long after the fall from the heavens, his head flopping around in the lake after his wings had burned off in the sun, and he saying, "What the fuck happened, man?" That was as far as his wisdom or intelligence went. He meant nothing to me. I had not seen him since I was ten years old, when we visited San Francisco for two weeks in the summer and he wrestled me down on the grass of grandmother's tiny back yard. I remember that time, those brawls. Back then I had fought back. Even when he had pinned my wrists down and shoved his knee into my abdomen, I would scream and push away at him, believing that I could break his steel electrician's grip and somehow conquer him, throwing him down on the ground and holding his shoulders to the grass. Naiveté allowed me to believe. And I remember Uncle Jack's face as I tried, that surprise in his eyes at the little runt of a nephew actually trying to pin down his uncle. Once I lifted my free leg up and pushed my foot into his groin area. He laughed as he tried to dodge the fatal blow. He did dodge it, but it also meant he had to lose the grip on my wrists. He rolled to one side. Instead of jumping up and bolting away from him to end the game, I had leapt on top of him and had flayed away, tearing and growling like a punk kid as he almost cried with laughter before pinning me down again. He had won, of course. Yet I had tried, fool that I was.

I had learned to be a fool no longer since those childhood days. Being sent away to school, to live with a family whose only enraged son wanted me to do something strange to his penis, taught me to be adroit, diplomatic, and not foolish. There was little reason for me to complain. Both the Giltens and the Hartlands were known as good, upright, wealthy Catholic families. They were so very different from my own. They were completely white, of course, unlike myself, a "half-white," which always gave me the self-impression of being half-baked or slightly stained. Though Uncle Jack's word for whites—cheles—was new to me, I also noticed that my family was not of the same purity of tone as were the Knoxville families. Those families were refined. They drank scotches from small, thick-glass tumblers. They smoked expensive cigarettes. They were on a first name basis with Father Jackson, the principal of the school. They had money. They did not yell at each other. They did not curse. Their children went to Tennessee Catholic, one of the best college prep schools in Knoxville. They were everything this cliché of a filthy mouthed, street-vocabularied Latino uncle of mine was not. After living away from home and sleeping in the homes of Knoxville's finest families, I had learned not to fight against such brute strength as that of Uncle Jack's.

Now I was to spend a few weeks of this summer with him. Did this mean working with him? If that was the case, I could see the point. I could use the money. But he was an electrician, and I could not imagine how I would be of any use to him. I resented all three of the women in the kitchen. My mother, grandmother, and aunt had made plans for my summer, but had not filled me in on the details. This, I knew, meant that they themselves did not know what the details were.

"Yeah, falling in love can be a real bitch," Uncle Jack said. He got a little quiet. "You gotta be careful when your balls swing in your heart."

He looked around, as if finding another subject to refer to. "Hey listen, I got some errands to do. Why don't you come with me? We can shoot the shit on what you'd like to do while you're here this summer. Your mom said something about getting you a job. I think we could do that, yeah. I've got a contract coming up in a few weeks at one of the hospitals here, stringing up some cable for a new lighting system. I could use a hand. But it's fucking hard work, *sobrino*. And I ain't in no hurry to get into it. I got some other stuff on the burner now, man. So come on, let's get out of here. We can do my errands, then maybe get a bite to eat or something."

I had no time to respond. My wish was to say, "No, that's all right, I don't want to put you out. I'll just stay here, stare out the window for the next ninety days until summer ends." Somehow those words did not come out. He walked to the bedroom door, opened it and walked out, reaching into his shirt pocket for another cigarette. He turned around.

"Come on, man," he said.

I obeyed. As I followed behind him, my mother walked down from the opposite end of the hall. She looked at me and smiled. "Where are you boys going?" she asked.

"I got some errands to run, *hermana*," said Uncle Jack. "Thought I'd take Tony with me, show him some of the city."

"Oh, that's a nice idea. Isn't that nice, Tony? You'll have fun."

Uncle Jack had already made his way down the stairs. I was at the top, staring into my mother's face, shaking my head negatively, waiting for her mother-authority to keep me here.

"Yeah," said Uncle Jack as he reached the door, "we'll be back before nightfall."

I spoke between my clenched teeth, "Mom, I do not want to go."

"You have a good time, honey." She kissed me on the cheek, not unlike Judas.

My eyes opened wide as I hissed *"Mamá!"*

"You want anything while we're out, sis?"

"No, Juan. Well, yes, get me some of that *queso de cabra.*"

"What, you making *pupusas* tonight?" Uncle Jack called up the steps. Mamá told him the menu as she grabbed my arm and turned me around toward the stairs. I half expected her to push me down them.

I descended. Once at the front door, I turned around and looked up the steps at my mother, who stood at the very top. She smiled at me her "Have a good time" smile, to which I responded with my "I hate my mother" scowl.

"Come on man," said Uncle Jack as he put on his sunglasses. "Let's see the sights."

It was the first time I took a good look at his car. The shiny black 1967 Mustang faced north. It looked recently washed. A tiny metal horse galloped right behind the front wheel. Jet air scoops cut into the metal behind the passenger door. Three-pronged bolt-like objects were locked upon each hubcap. The hood was huge, seemingly bigger than that of my mother's old LTD. Another silvery muscular steed raced across the front grille.

I got in the car. He turned the motor over, then revved it a couple of times to make the entire body rock before kicking the Mustang into drive. I heard the rolling of what sounded like tiny plastic maracas. I turned and looked at the back floorboard. Half a dozen medicine bottles clicked against one another. The car's interior smelled of burnt rope. The ashtray held a dry-vomit of cigarette butts. There were also some tiny wadded scraps of paper in the pile, like the off-white wings of insects. I looked up at two small yet furry white dice hanging from the rear view mirror. Yes, they were there. I looked back to see if a little ceramic doggie with its head bouncing up and down was standing on the back dash. It, thank God, was not. But a tiny playing card of a nude white woman with blonde hair, her breasts pushed out as if someone shoved their palms and fingers into the curve of her back, stuck out of an uneven crack that ran over the dashboard above the glove compartment. Uncle Jack shoved a cassette into the player. Just as he pushed it in I read the cassette's title. He had scratched "Los Lobos" on the cassette's side, his handwriting not unlike that of a primary schoolboy's. A song, *"El Cuchipe,"* vibrated the Mustang's walls. I turned to my Uncle Jack. He grinned at me while his eyes hid behind the wire-rimmed sunglasses. He said nothing to declare who he was. He didn't have to.

We took Mission Street south for several blocks. I kept up with the street names in order to place my attention upon anything else besides my uncle and his insidious conversations about women.

"So what's this Janet girl like?"

"Janice."

"Oh yeah. Janice. Seems like she's really got you in a sling, man."

"No. She doesn't have me in a sling." I spat my response, looking out the open window. I had to practically yell at Jack in order to keep the conversation above the wind pushing through the car and Los Lobos dancing all around us. I focused on a sign that said Highland Avenue. We passed it.

"I don't know. I get this feeling she stole your heart, man."

I looked over. Jack was barely smiling below his sunglasses. He had smoked a cigarette, had finished it, and now was chewing over a fresh piece of gum. He had offered me a piece, but I refused. He popped a bubble from time to time.

We passed under Richland Avenue and by St. Mary's Avenue before I responded. "So what if she did? That's over now."

"I see. So she's no longer in your life?"

"No."

"Good. Then that means you're a free man, man. You may make a score here in your hometown."

"This isn't my hometown. Rakertown is my home town." I said half heartedly. Claiming Rakertown as my own was not a priority in my life. Disagreeing with an adult, however, was.

"Yeah but you were born here, Tony," he said. "I remember the day you were born. Shit, your old man was so happy, he did a dance right in the hospital hallway. Some sort of hillbilly jig or something. Hey, how's your old man doing?"

"He's fine."

"Still in the mines, right?"

"Yeah."

I stared straight ahead at the next approaching street sign. I could feel my uncle's gaze on the side of my face.

"You don't like to talk much, do you?"

I hesitated, then said, "What's to say?"

We approached Bosworth Street. I figured he was planning to pass that too, considering the speed he was going. He veered right, making his wheels sing. The front of the car seemed too heavy to be able to make the sudden turn. Yet Jack handled the maneuver, squealing us into Bosworth. I grabbed the dashboard.

"Dang," I muttered as he pulled us straight into the road.

He laughed. "'Dang?' Jesus Christ, Tony. They've made you a real hillbilly boy, haven't they?" His gravelled accent screeched through a fake hillbilly one. "Shit. What's the matter with you, man? You forget your blood or something?"

"What are you talking about?"

"I don't know. You act . . . shit, like a fucking gringo that's just come down from the mountains."

The internal burn came on again, the hot tears made to fall. I looked away while letting go of the dashboard.

"I mean, come on, man. You don't speak any Spanish? You don't understand what this band's singing about?" He pointed to his cassette player.

The tears turned acrid inside. "No. Not much."

"I didn't think so. Then again, you're over there in Teyennasseeee." He laughed. "Not much *raza* over there man, I remember that. Fun place to play around in for awhile, but fuck if I want to live there."

We passed underneath a tunnel and took a couple of more turns. My eyes had blurred too much for me to see the street signs. I only saw, to my left, a street that was tucked between two blocks of fairly tall buildings. The name Castro caught my eye. I wondered if that were some Cuban barrio, especially with the multicolored lights hanging in windows and the young men who walked about in groups of two or three. Perhaps, I thought, they were refugees from the island. Even the tall blonde haired ones.

I tried to make conversation. "What's that place?"

"What, Castro Street? Naw man, you don't want to go there."

"Why not?"

"That's where the queers hang out, man. *Los maricones.* You know, homos and stuff."

We had slowed in the traffic, so I glanced at the street again. Two men held hands as they ambled down the sidewalk, looking into store windows.

"Yeah, they get together in there," Uncle Jack said. "I hear they got like Japanese public baths where they fuck each other up the ass, right there in front of everybody! Jesus Christ . . . I don't even like to think about it. I mean, I don't care what they do, that's their business. Just as long everybody's happy with it, know what I'm saying?" He shook his hand in the air while grinning. "But give me some real tits and wet pussy any day."

I wanted to bury myself into the black upholstery of his Mustang. I did not know what bothered me more, Uncle Jack's shallow references to women, or the thought of men shoving their penises up each other's asses. But I did think of Barry's shadow. Then I thought of what Jack had just said, about everybody being happy with it. I didn't know what to think of that.

"We're almost there, man."

"Where are we going?" I asked.

"To a friend of mine's house. His name's Chucho. He lives back in the Mission, but I got to go to Glen Canyon Park, meet a . . . a friend there."

I glanced at him, at his hesitancy.

We drove into the park. Uncle Jack pulled his Mustang into a parking lot beside a playground. Several children played upon swings and slides, watched by their mothers who stood in small groups and chatted. We sat silently in the car for several minutes. Jack smoked cigarettes. He didn't say a word, but looked into his rear view mirror every few seconds.

"So where's your friend?" I asked.

"He'll be here, man. We're a little early."

Five minutes later an old white, rusting car—what I thought was a Cadillac from my quick glance at it—pulled into the parking lot. It did not park next to us, but drove to the opposite side behind us. I turned my head to look at it.

"There they are," Jack said, opening the door. "You stay here." Then he grabbed the top of my skull in his palm and fingers like a basketball and turned my head forward, toward the park where the children were playing. "You keep your eyes on them mammas. Maybe you'll spot somebody who gets your crotch hot." He grinned, stepped out, and slammed the door.

He opened the Mustang's trunk. The hinges squeaked slightly. I turned my head just enough to look back. All I could see was the open trunk, which blocked my view of the white Cadillac. Through the passenger side rear view mirror I could see Jack's friend. He was a short, fat man with a black T-shirt and numerous gold chains dangling from his neck. He was Hispanic. He wore a cowboy hat. I heard Jack's voice, *"Eh Pepe, ¿qué tal, cabrón?"* They shook hands, going through three different moves before letting the other's fingers go. "So you got my packages, man?"

"Yeah, Jack, we got you set up for a while, *carnal.*" Pepe opened his trunk. I could barely make out two plastic garbage sacks the size of grocery bags. "Careful, grab them by the bottom. They're heavy."

"Yeah, not like last time, when your *patrón* fucked us with Styrofoam in the middle. You think he's messing with us again, putting bricks inside this time?"

"No man, I checked them before I took them. These are just what they were meant to be: rolled tight with the finest gold. They still trying to find out how that Styrofoam deal went through. But my *jefe,* Rata, he's trying to make it up to Gato. He got a cousin in the Mexican Police down in *la DF, carnal, y sabía donde los jefes escondían el mejor oro. Los chingados agarraban el mejor, sabes.*"

Breaking into Spanish, they lost me. But it sounded like an international business deal, protected by Mexican authorities.

"That's good, man. Because Chucho was pretty pissed with me, like that last time was my fault. I don't blame him though. Gato can breathe hard down your neck when he wants to."

"Yeah. Don't fuck with the cat, man." As Pepe said that, he grunted, as if lifting the sacks higher in the air. They landed in the trunk. Jack slammed the trunk closed. I saw him hand a small sack over to Pepe. They shook hands. Pepe walked back to his old Cadillac. Jack jumped back in beside me.

"Hey, cowboy," he said to me, somewhat nervously. "I'll take you to my best friend's house now, man. Chucho. Great guy. We've been *compas* since the crib."

The first time I met Enrique Osegueda, or Chucho, he was half running from the alleyway of his home to Jack's car. His voice ran ahead of him: "Jack, fuck, get the hell out of my driveway, man."

"Chucho, *carnal,* what's the matter?" Jack stuck his hand out the window to shake Chucho's hand. Chucho quickly took it, shook it, then looked down Valencia Street.

"I don't want your pickup, man."

"What the hell you mean you don't want my fucking pickup? I just paid *cinco mil* in cash, you can't . . ."

"Yeah, well you can keep it. It's yours. I don't trust anything Pepe sells anymore."

"Don't worry, Chucho. This stuff's good."

"Hey, don't blame Pepe for that last haul. It wasn't his fault. Something happened above him, with the Styrofoam trick."

"I don't care, man! Gato's on my ass. It wasn't just the Styrofoam. You know what that *hijo de puta* Pepe did to it? Mixed fucking oregano into it, man! And dried cilantro! One of Gato's boys reefed it, said it tasted like one of your mother's tamales gone bad."

(I would later learn that was an underhanded compliment. It was well known throughout the Hispanic community that El Gato was in search of my grandmother's recipe for the Guanacotamales. Rumor had it that he would end all other businesses he was managing and throw all his funds into the establishment of a competitive Latino food industry if he ever got his hands on that recipe.)

"Look, Pepe didn't do it," Jack said. I could see a vein in his neck. As he spoke, he pointed through the front windshield. His hand looked much like Abuelita's hand whenever she got angry, flinging itself back and forth while he spoke. "Somebody above Pepe fucked him and then ended up screwing us all."

"Yeah, well Gato's mad. I don't think he trusts anything from your channel now."

"I don't have a channel, man! I'm just helping out Pepe. Does Gato think I was in on it?" asked Jack, obviously concerned.

"No man, I didn't tell him your name. He just doesn't trust the connection with Rata. Says he wants to wait until Rata makes good, you know, makes up for the mistake. So I don't want to take what you got now."

"This shit's good!" Jack said, pointing back to the trunk.

"Yeah, well, I don't know . . ."

Both men got quiet. Jack sighed heavily.

"Hey, who's the *joven*?" asked Chucho, smiling through a change in subject.

"Oh, sorry. This is my nephew, Antonio. *Saluda a Chucho*, Tony."

I could understand that command: *Shake Chucho's hand, Tony.* It was an encoded formality that Abuelita Roselia had taught us all. I obeyed.

"From Tennessee, right? Well, welcome to San Francisco." Chucho actually smiled. "So what are you up to, Tony? Keeping your uncle company?"

I just grinned and shook my head slightly, not knowing what to say. Uncle Jack filled in the gap.

"He's gonna spend the summer with me, maybe learn some electrical skills, you know?"

"Hey that's great. That's great." Chucho's voice trailed, knowing he would need to return to the inevitable. "Look Jack, I'm sorry. I can't take this from you. Rata's just got a bad name with Gato now, you know? You'll have to get rid of this haul yourself."

"Yeah, fucking great, Chucho. I'll have a dozen fucking police dogs following my ass through the city." He turned the key.

"Man, don't leave angry, Juan . . ." That was the last thing I heard Chucho say. Jack pulled out of the driveway. He barely waved to his longtime friend before shoving the gear into drive.

Uncle Jack drove off without saying a word. He stared out at the road in front of him. The Mustang seemed to find its own way home.

I never was one to handle too much silence, especially when it's whipped up with tension. "So you and Chucho have been friends all your life?" I asked.

"What? Oh, yeah. Yeah. Since we were kids. Used to play soccer together all the time. We always made sure we got picked for the same team. Yeah, he's always been a good friend."

"Is he Salvadoran?"

"No. Mexican and Guatemalan, I think. At least, I know that his grandmother's Guatemalan. Old lady from that country. She's an

Indian, you know, the colored dresses and all? Good lady. Good friend of my mother's. They call her La Chucharrona."

"La Chuchar . . ." I squinted. "I met her. Abuelita took me to her."

"Oh yeah?" Jack smiled for the first time since leaving Chucho's house. "So what did she do to you?"

"I don't know . . . she lit some candles and said some stuff in some language, it wasn't Spanish. She said she prayed for me. It was kind of weird."

"Hey, be careful with that stuff, man," Jack admonished, as if concerned over my safety. "La Chucharrona's got some powerful shit on hand. The whole barrio goes to her for help. She can tell the future, and she can guess about your past. God knows what she said in her prayer about you.

"Yeah, she's really important around here. And her grandson's a good man," continued Jack. "Well, Chucho's a little chicken-shit sometimes. Doesn't always get things done right. But hell, we all got our quirks, right? Hey, you hungry? Let's get a hamburger."

He pulled into McDonalds. He ordered for us both. We sat outside around plastic picnic tables and ate. About the time we were finishing, Jack looked at me, a smile crawling over his face filled with french fries.

"Hey *sobrino*, you ever smoke any shit?"

I was not sure what that meant.

"You know. Grass. Weed. *Hierba magnífica*. Mary Jane."

I was starting to get an image in my head.

"You want some?"

Hours earlier I had turned down his cigarette and had regretted doing so. Now I had been offered *the* weed. I was not about to make the same mistake. Yet my heart pounded, shoving blood into my neck.

"Hell, what am I doing?" he said, laughing. "Shit, you're my sister's kid. I shouldn't be . . . but what the fuck, you're my nephew, man. You want some?"

"You mean right here? Can't we, you know, get in trouble?"

"Well, this ain't Tennessee. But yeah, you still got to watch your ass. Come on, get in the car."

Thus my introduction.

As I choked and spat on my first sucked breaths, Jack laughed. Then he stopped laughing. "No man, come on *sobrino*, suck it in, shit, this is the best Mexican gold you can buy."

And it was then that I learned how close my Uncle Jack was to Chucho's family. Twenty minutes into the first toke of my life, Jack told me of his encounter with Chucho's mother. "What a snatch, man. She was my first woman. It was crazy how it happened. She had sent Chucho down to the store nearby to buy us all some colas. Then the next thing I know, she's showing me her tits. Here I was younger than you. I must have been fifteen or so. She was almost twenty years older than me. She sits next to me on the couch and starts unbuttoning her shirt, then flicks that bra off. Before I know it, I'm up to my eyebrows in the nicest smelling breasts you could imagine. I didn't know what to do with them, so she taught me. Then I started to catch on, like a certain instinct, you know what I'm saying? Like some animal that immediately learns how to hunt."

Obviously this grass had no effect upon one's libido. I felt myself filling a corner of my jeans. After a few moments I started to panic, wondering if my erection would rip the zipper open.

"Then she took my head like a basketball and pushed it down. I didn't know that, while she had my head between her tits, she had wriggled out of her panties. She lifted up her dress. I saw the first tuft in my life. Then she opened up her thighs. I wasn't sure at first what she was doing. I mean, I knew where babies came from, and I had this idea that she wanted to shove me back up in there, you know, like have a baby in reverse? Hell I didn't know what was going on. But I figured out soon enough. She pinched my jaw open with her finger and thumb, which made my mouth open. Then she planted my lips right on her snatch. She bobbed my whole skull up and down with her palms."

My penis got confused. I had never heard of this before. All I knew was that was where a woman urinated from. "Gross!"

"What gross? You never had pussy before? It's the sweetest thing you've ever put in your mouth, *sobrino*."

I was not convinced. I shivered in the seat. "Doesn't she pee from there?"

"Yeah, man, but she wasn't peeing at the time. She was wet all right. Washed my whole face. I guess I at first had your reaction, you know, like 'Hey, what's going on, Mrs. Osegueda?' But once I got a taste of her, shit, I was like a dog licking the inside of a bowl."

The image of a woman's body fluids on a man's face (I of course replaced his face for mine) kept my libido confused. I choked again on the smoke.

Jack enjoyed this. He grinned. "Hey man, ain't nothing dirty about a beautiful woman. Or a woman you love. Not her snatch, her stomach, her armpits, nothing. She's clean everywhere. Shit, I've even licked a woman I really care for right up the ass."

I bent into myself, both wretching and laughing.

"I'm not shitting you, man. My wife Ricarda. Took my tongue right into her crack. She liked it. She screamed. Said she felt like a cat, getting a bath."

We both laughed. I looked over. Slight tears actually gathered in the corner of my uncle's eyes.

"Yeah, Chucho comes from good family. Delicious. Shit, I should be careful. He's my friend, man. It would kill him if he knew what his mother did to me. I still see her from time to time. She must be, oh, near seventy years old now. She just smiles at me." He turned and grinned at me, imitating that woman. "And I just smile right back."

We turned quiet. We had finished the reefer. I allowed my head to bob back and forth, while questions rolled in my mind: *Amazing, how the head can bob. Feel that? The head, it's bobbing, back and forth, back and forth.* It felt like someone had injected thick oil into my neck, so smooth, this bobbing, back and forth.

"What you doing, man, imitating a Jack in the Box?" he asked.

"No. Just feeling my head," I said.

"Oh. Yeah." He lit a cigarette, then held it between his index and ring fingers while staring out his window. "Yeah, Chucho's a good man. Shit, I shouldn't have left like that. Not good to leave your friends angry." He started the car. "We're going back to his place before we go home. I got to apologize for the way I acted back there." He almost mumbled the words.

Ten minutes later we drove back into the alleyway that led to Chucho's home. In front of us was parked a black Cadillac. It was not at all old, not like Pepe's beat up, white Caddy. This one shined. It also had a V-shaped antenna protruding from the trunk.

"Oh shit," mumbled my uncle.

"What's the matter?"

"Looks like Chucho's got visitors."

We both got out of the car. I followed Jack for a few feet, until he turned around to me. "You stay near the car. I'll go see where Chucho is." He walked away and toward the door of the old apartment house.

I did not go back into the car, but waited, leaning against the Mustang's warm hood. I still bobbed my head from time to time, fascinated by this simple movement. Then I heard a noise. It was a grunt, then a yelp, which came from around an inner corner of the alleyway. I turned and looked toward the corner. I could see nothing. I turned back. Jack had stepped into the unlocked door of Chucho's home. I could barely hear him calling his friend's name. I turned and walked toward the corner.

Once reaching it, I heard voices. "Chucho, why did you tell your pickup to get rid of that last haul? That was stupid. Very stupid."

I pushed up against the wall and carefully moved my right eye to the bricks' edge. There I saw two men bent over, holding Chucho's body down against a large, flat trash bin. One man looked Hispanic, with black hair and slightly tanned skin. The other appeared to be a gringo with blonde hair. Both wore polyester pants and shirts opened wide and deep from the neck down.

Chucho fought against them. Over to the left stood a third, older man with long, black, loose hair. He wore black. He wore black sunglasses. He wore gold around his neck. He held a black cat in his arms. He stroked the cat with a hand covered in rings.

El Gato.

Another fucking cliché, I thought.

This cliché was the one doing the talking. "You don't understand, Chucho. Rata called me, apologizing profusely about the *cilantro* hash recipe he sent me through you last time. Said it was meant for another dealer over in Sacramento, some lowlife who was trying to fuck him. The lowlife's *patrón* would have his little ass killed. But instead the haul was sent through you and your connections. So now I'm in the same position that the *patrón* in Sacramento would have been in. So Rata calls . . ." El Gato leaned into Chucho's face at this point. The cat panicked, squeezed by Gato's large arms. It jumped from the man's hands. Gato paid it no attention, but continued to breathe over Chucho's quaking face. "Rata calls and apologizes. But he knows I'm pissed. So to keep me from giving him a *chingazo,* he promises to deliver a special Christmas gift with this last haul. Now you've sent your man away with the haul. He's gonna sell the shit on the street and make money off of my stash. And what's worse, he'll get away with my fucking Christmas present!"

Gato stood erect again, his anger whipping up over Chucho and the two henchmen. I felt my legs buckle. For a moment the marijuana in my blood hoped to speak: *Wow, what a concept, your legs are wobbling, man, so very groovy.* My head shook the meditation away, especially when Gato nodded his own head to the blonde henchman. Blondie took a hand razor from his pocket, grabbed Chucho's right hand, and pushed the heavy blade into the space between his ring and pinky finger. Then the man's back got in my way as he pressed

Chucho's hand on the trash bin and pushed his weight down upon the blade.

Chucho's pinky flipped up into the air and over the man's shoulder. It landed on the asphalt. The cat jumped at it. Smelling the blood, it began to chew.

Chucho howled.

Then I heard the blade thunk through again. The ring finger flipped to one side and ricocheted off the brick wall behind them.

I meant to puke. The marijuana barely had a chance to whisper *Puke, what a concept,* when I retched. The Big Mac did not come up, though it wanted to.

The men in the alleyway, except Chucho, got quiet. Then I heard Gato say, "Shut up, sssshhhh. *Cállense.* Listen."

I bolted down the alleyway back to Jack's Mustang.

Jack had just walked out of Chucho's apartment. He looked confused, raising his shoulders up to me in an "I can't find him" fashion. He saw my face. Then he heard a few of my words concerning fingers flying in the air. He must have seen the men behind me. "Jesus Christ," he said. "Get in the car, man!"

We jumped in. He turned the key and shoved the Mustang into reverse. The blonde henchman slammed into the Mustang's hood. I remember yelping. Mine sounded like a little girl's voice. Jack jerked the car away, throwing Blondie onto the ground. He backed into the street without looking for traffic. Then he geared away.

"What the fuck happened back there?" my uncle asked me.

I sputtered about fingers flying, then about what the guy named Gato said to Chucho, something about presents being given to him from Rata, and that he wanted this haul. Spit fell from my lips.

"Presents? What presents . . . ?" Jack stared down the street. "Ah shit, Chucho! Chucho! Jesus Christ, *hijo de la gran puta* . . ." He rubbed his forehead with his left hand, then pulled his palm down over his face. "I can't fucking believe this. This is just hash, man, a little

Mexican gold. Why the hell is Gato suddenly playing Mafia with us all?"

I couldn't give him an answer, so of course I didn't. Rather, I spent the next five minutes running through rituals, clicking my teeth until my jaw ached and knocking a rhythmic pattern upon my skull with my left index knuckle.

We said nothing for a long while. I stared at the road ahead of us. It wasn't a road that I was familiar with. It was not one that we had taken today.

The sun moved low. It must have been near eight o'clock in the evening. "I wonder if Mom's going to bawl us out for being so late," I said. "Or Abuelita."

"Oh, you don't have to worry about that, *sobrino,*" he said, barely chuckling.

"What do you mean?" I asked, a tremor of understanding passing through me.

He didn't answer. He just took Interstate 280 East, then pulled into Highway 101, the Bayshore Freeway. We passed the International Airport. We drove through Burlingame, San Mateo, Redwood City. We left San Francisco far behind.

Part Three

After Uncle Jack's wake, I drove my parents and Aunt Felícita back to the house on Capp Street. For the first five minutes that we were in the Mercedes, no one spoke. Aunt Felícita looked out the window at the approaching night, her sunglasses still perched upon her nose. My mother and father sat quietly in the back. Sometimes I heard my mother's thick, smooth sigh that filled the car's interior.

"They did a good job on him, don't you think, Carmen?" Aunt Felícita asked my mother.

"Very good. He looked, you know, peaceful."

"Yeah," said my aunt. It quietly shocked me to hear her use that word instead of "yes." It meant she was caught up in her own thoughts. "It was a real blessing to be able to keep the casket open."

"This is true," Mamá responded.

"I mean, the fact that he just up and died, that his heart stopped. It's just incredible. The funeral home did not need to hide one scar. No slit on his neck, no bullet hole in his forehead, no car grille markings on his face. Nothing. He looks as perfect as if he were just sleeping." At this, she began to weep. She pulled a tissue from her small white purse, dabbed her eyes and cleaned her nose, carefully shoving the twisted tissue up each nostril with her forefinger.

"By the way, Tony, what did Chucho say to you?"

"He didn't say very much," I answered. Of the little he said, I did not care to share it with them. "He just came to, you know, pay his respects."

"Oh shit, Tony. Don't cover up for Chucho. What did he say?"

I told them, somewhat paraphrased, how Chucho had leaned over my uncle's cadaver and had thanked God for the gift of death while hoping that the tongues of Satan's hottest flames licked around Uncle Jack's testicles, *por los siglos de los siglos.*

In the rear view mirror I watched my dad's head shake slightly. Then a grin pulled over his lips as he looked out the window. No doubt he pondered over the Latinos' ways of expressing angst.

"You know," my mother said, "I wonder if it would be good if one of us went over and talked to Chucho."

Why did I suspect that the *one of us* would end up being me? "I don't know," I said. "Chucho was pretty angry. Enraged is the better word."

"Yes, but he talked with you, didn't he Tony?" asked Aunt Felícita. "We could see you from our chairs. He shook your hand. And you even introduced yourself, I could tell that. He remembered you. But he did not blame you."

"Right. Because I wasn't at fault in any way."

"But neither was your uncle! Yet Chucho is living with this rage, as you like to call it." Aunt Felícita looked at me while I drove. I did not need to turn right to acknowledge her sight falling upon the side of my face. "I don't think that's good. Juan would want peace with his childhood friend."

"Then why didn't he make peace before he died?" I asked. "That was his responsibility, not mine."

"I bet he wanted to make peace," my aunt said. "But he wasn't planning on having a heart attack."

I muttered out other excuses against speaking with Chucho. Aunt Felícita would not listen. She looked out the front windshield and calmly continued on with her words about peace, reconciliation, and harmony. She was becoming blatantly arrogant. My fingers, clasping the steering wheel, were sweating.

"Tony, this is the only life we've got. We've got to make the best of it. I just read in the *Reader's Digest* a long article on human relationships, and how disharmony can cause a great deal of pain and stress in a person's life. It's best to make peace with your neighbors, your relatives, your friends, before it's too late. Otherwise you live a life of anger and bitterness. That's what the article said. Now, your uncle was not bitter at all, no. But he was saddened once he lost his friendship with Chucho. I know all that other stuff that Jack did with Chucho's daughter and, well, the affair he had with Chucho's wife . . . but you remember your Uncle Jack." She stared at me again; this time I could feel her grin that meant to bless Jack's active penis with a smile of sisterly devotion. "He was a handsome, virile man. My God, look at him in the casket." She turned and spoke to her older sister, "Didn't he look tremendous, Carmen?"

"Oh yes. *Un gigante de hombre,*" my mother said.

"Exactly. Even death cannot take away that virility. Not for a while anyway. Did you see all those women in the funeral home? Chucho's daughter arrived after Chucho left. I watched her, she was weeping, *weeping* Tony, on the kneeler as she leaned over your Uncle Jack. He wasn't just good looking. He knew how to move women. That was his gift, you know. All those poor women, like Chucho's wife, no sex life at all. That's what happens in a lot of marriages nowadays, Tony." Aunt Felícita moved her arms about, gesticulating as she expanded her monologue. "All that passion and sex in the first year, then before you know it, you've got a husband who's growing a pot belly and who's sitting in front of the television with a beer in his hand. He'd rather watch that damned sports station than hop in bed with his wife. What's a woman to do? Well, the women around here just hoped that Juan Villalobos would notice their shadows in the bedroom windows."

Unbelievable, that I was listening to this. I did not know if they could hear the exasperated sighs that escaped my lungs every few moments. It had been years since I had seen Uncle Jack, and almost twenty years since that fateful summer in which I slipped so easily into my uncle's chauvinistic world. True, I had come to appreciate him in a real way after that summer. We had gone through too much together for me not to have been affected by the events of those few short weeks of '78. Still, there was something to be said about moving on, which I believed I had. Throughout the following years, I had gone to college and graduate school. I had traveled abroad, mostly in Central America, working among poor people. I had written reams of literature, trying to sort out stories and make sense out of personal and public histories. I had written about my heritage, my fellow Latinos, in a way that the reviewers called "poignant," "insightful," and "true." I had grown up. My Uncle Jack had not. Every time I got on the phone with him and heard that low, growling "'Ey maaaan, what's happening, *sobrino?*" I wanted to hang up. Six months ago I finally did hang up for the last time, saying goodbye in a pleasant manner but also closing away that part of my past, one which flew against all the teachings of a politically correct, progressive movement that had seeped into my bones throughout the eighties and early nineties. To speak of women as he did was not acceptable. To growl over the phone like that, well, it was just childish.

Now I was listening to Jack's sister, actually apologizing for and lauding his actions. I could not endure much more. "Aunt Felícita, Uncle Jack was a *mujeriego*. He slept with every woman he could. How can you uphold that?"

"Hey, nephew, your uncle did not force any of those women into bed. You need to know that. They hopped into the sheets willingly."

I drummed the steering wheel.

"Oh Tony, quit being so stiff," my aunt said. "I mean, well, okay, he was a bit of a womanizer. Yes, he did help to bring about a few divorces in this city, as well as back in the old country. And every country and state in between. But perhaps that was the best thing he could do. Divorce can be a blessing, you know. Some people are just afraid to make that move, thinking that other people will look down on them. So they stay together in an unhappy, sexless marriage. Then your Uncle Jack comes along and WHAM, there's a real reason to break up. There was always a reason to break up. But Jack helped them to get there. So in a way, you could say that he had a purpose in this life."

I sighed louder than my mother.

"Besides, I wasn't talking about your uncle's character. He was a good man. You can't really argue against that," she said, leaning toward me so as to make sure that her last statement sank into my brain. "I was talking about making peace with Chucho. I think that would be a good idea, so that your uncle can truly rest. To be at peace with your own blood is perhaps the most important . . . Why, that bitch, that BIG BITCH!"

Her sudden outburst frightened me. But I could see why she cursed. I had already turned the curve onto Capp Street and had seen the woman standing at the door of grandmother's old Victorian home. She was a few years older than I, but did not look it. She was ringing the doorbell as we approached the house. She was Felícita Villalobos, my Uncle Jack's only legal child. Jack had named her after our Aunt Felícita. So everyone called her "Little Felícita." Logically, my aunt became "Big Felícita."

The nicknames made little sense once you looked at both women. Little Felícita was big. Big Felícita was tiny. Little Felícita was bigger than her father and a good three inches taller than I was. She was also what some would call "big-boned," though I always thought that was a kind way of saying "overweight." There was a certain beauty about Little Felícita. She had the same dark skin color as her father, gorgeous thick black hair that fell all over her shoulders, and olive-shaped eyes that had a way of holding you in one position. Those eyes now darted about as she saw our Mercedes pulling up to the curb.

"How dare she show up at this house! How dare she appear in my sight!"

Aunt Felícita almost tore the leather off the Mercedes' dashboard. My father reached his hand from the back of the car and gently placed it on her shoulder, muttering, "Now now, girl, you just take it easy . . ." I thought that took incredible courage.

"She's on Capp Street! She's here!" my aunt continued. "What does she want? I know what she wants, the little whory *puta que se vale de la enfermedad de su propia sangre. ¡Ay, que se vaya al carajo!"* Her hand went up into the air of the car, whipping it up in true Villalobos fashion, taught to us all by my grandmamá.

I also stared down the street at my cousin. When I saw her face, just in that second before horror ran across her eyes and mouth, I saw the large beauty that I had fallen in love with when I was a child. She was the only root of incestuous thought I had ever had as a kid. Well, besides that of my Aunt Felícita, and that was much later, when I was in seminary.

Then the horror came, that of running into her namesake, her Aunt Felícita. After the horror came her own rage. As I pulled the car up into the driveway, her dark eyebrows knit toward each other and her mouth fixed into a scowl. She saw me, and a smile of nostalgia and happiness broke through, seeing a cousin after so many years. Then the rage returned. Her face contorted back and forth, confused by which emotional response would take control.

My mother admonished her sister, "Child, be good. Don't start arguing with her here on the street."

"*Hermana,* don't worry," my aunt growled. "I am like a serpent. I kill silently."

Ice shot up my spine.

We all stepped out of the car. A long history of rage and bitterness stepped back momentarily and allowed for cousins to at least greet each other. I hugged Little Felícita. I had to tiptoe to do this. She smiled, kissed me on the cheek. "How are you, Tony? Looking good, very good!"

"You too, *prima.* How is life treating you?"

"I can't complain."

"I'm sorry about your father." And that was the end of the niceties.

"Yes, I am too. I am also sorry that I cannot find him, even though I've called the house numerous times to find out which funeral home you stuck him in," she glanced toward our aunt, "but whenever I say 'hello' somebody hangs up."

My aunt responded, "It seems you would figure out that we would place him in the only decent funeral home in the city, La Colón. But then, you would have to actually care about your father and his family in order to figure that out."

Little and Big Felícitas stared at each other. Mamá stood to one side of them like a helpless referee. Dad, wise as he was, walked by us all, unlocked the door and ducked into the house. He turned to me and motioned me in with his finger. I took his silent advice.

He and I walked up the steps to the second floor. "I think I'll spend the rest of the night in the back of the house," he said to me.

"When was the last time they saw each other?" I asked.

"Oh, they accidentally run into each other from time to time. But that happened more when your grandmother was alive. Long before your grandmother died. Before Little Felícita made her Big Mistake."

Everyone knew what that mistake was. In my grandmother's last months, she had turned very sick and had to remain in bed most of her days. She had retired from the company three years earlier, handing over control of the corporation to her two daughters. She had also taken care of her Last Will and Testament, making sure that all of us would get a reasonable portion of her estate, depending upon our relationship to her. She was kind enough to give me ten thousand dollars, which, after taxes, I have kept in the bank since her death, afraid to touch it, pretending that I really didn't have it, believing that it would be best used at some vague, future date. I suppose she had left that amount to all the cousins, except Little Felícita.

In her younger years Little Felícita had worked in the family company as an office manager, but that did not last very long. She was deemed unfit for such responsibilities. That became apparent once Abuelita and Aunt Felícita noticed that files were missing, receipts were not being kept, messages were not being sent to the appropriate employees. A small swirl of chaos began to grow from Little

Felícita's corner of the company. My aunt did not wait for that swirl to grow into other areas of the business. She fired her niece.

This, of course, led to scandals that reverberated throughout the Villalobos world. Relatives from the old country were, according to Little Felícita, calling San Francisco, amazed at how cold-blooded Big Felícita had become. The younger Felícita told this to our grandmother as the elder lay in her bed, waiting for death to take her. The day of my cousin's Big Mistake came on a morning while La Chucharrona was also visiting Abuelita. The two old friends had been chatting all morning long. La Chucharrona had done a prayer for Abuelita, using a few lit candles placed on the endtables on each side of the bed. She was packing away her Guatemalan religious artifacts when Little Felícita walked into the room. La Chucharrona excused herself. My cousin sat down on the edge of the bed and held Abuelita's hand. Her weight pulled the mattress corner down. According to La Chucharrona, who stood in the hallway a long while, repacking her candles, Little Felícita spoke loudly to Abuelita, as if her hearing were part of the problem.

"So how are you feeling, Mami?"

"Oh, I am very tired, child. I wait for death to take me soon," my grandmother mumbled, her last bit of strength obviously fading.

"No no, Abuelita, that will not happen for a long time," said Little Felícita, smiling and almost laughing. "Why, I am sure you have another twenty years in you!"

"Don't be stupid, girl. I am very old, very old. I seek death . . ."

Again, her voice faded. Little Felícita continued to reassure her that all would be fine, that she would be walking down the steps to the marketplace in a few days. "But then again," Little Felícita said, "if anything were to go wrong . . . if it, you know, were your time, I'm sure you've taken care of everything, haven't you, Mami?"

Abuelita breathed out a sigh before turning her weak eyes directly upon her granddaughter. The weakness faded. "What do you mean, child?"

"Well," said Little Felícita, and she smiled shyly, looking down at the bedsheets, "my daddy explained to me that when you die, you will want me to be the one who gets this house as well as a good portion of the stocks in the company." Then she looked up at her grandmother.

According to Chucharrona, it got fairly quiet in the room. Abuelita closed her lips together. She did not move her head, but allowed her eyes to rotate toward the young woman.

"Yes," she said, "you will get your just share."

Little Felícita leaned over and kissed her grandmother on the forehead for the last time. She left. Chucharrona had ducked into a bathroom and had closed the door. She cracked the door open and watched as the young granddaughter walked out of the house.

"Chucharrona!" my grandmother's voice bellowed from the bedroom. Chucharrona walked to her. "Over there, in my dresser. Under the bras. My papers." Chucharrona retrieved them. Abuelita placed her small glasses upon her nose, near its tip. She asked her old friend to find a pen. Then she flipped through the numerous pages of the document before stopping and slashing the pen across three lines that referred to a specific granddaughter receiving ten thousand dollars. Over that she wrote, "To Felícita Villalobos, daughter of my only son: one dollar U.S." She signed the redaction, handed the document to Chucharrona, asked her to get it to her lawyer down the street on Mission, then lay her head down again on the pillow and closed her eyes.

I remembered this story in a flash while my father and I walked down the hallway to the kitchen. The thought of Chucharrona being the silent observer of that moment had always fascinated me; had she not been there, none of us would have known what had happened. She was a regular Tiresias, seeing everything important in the barrio.

Soon after I had flown into San Francisco for Uncle Jack's funeral, my mother had mentioned that La Chucharrona was still alive. I thought it would be a good idea to go visit her.

Dad now interrupted my thoughts. "Maybe you should duck out your window and see how it's going down there. We don't want anyone pushed off the steps again."

I agreed. I walked back to my room and quietly opened my window. The sun was already setting over San Francisco, but the city's movement had not followed suit. Still, I could hear the slicing voices of the three women below me, on the house's concrete front steps.

"I think you should leave," my aunt warned, staring up at the "little one."

"Why? You plan to throw me down these steps too?"

"No. Settling out of court for such things takes up too much of my time."

"Now listen, both of you," my mother intervened, "we shouldn't be fighting out here. Let's go inside and—"

"She's not coming in my house," said Big Felícita.

"It shouldn't be your house in the first place," said Little Felícita, staring down at her aunt.

"It never was yours, girl," said Big, "but you could have at least made a down payment on your own home if you hadn't talked to mother like you did on her deathbed."

"That stupid old witch told you all a lie!" screamed Little. "Who should you believe, some backward Indian *curandera* from Chichicastenango or one of your own blood?"

"Chucharrona is practically family, girl. You would understand that if you weren't so greedy."

"Oh sure, easy for you to say. Now that you're sitting in your own office of the richest Latino food company in California, you have no reason to worry! I still think it was probably *you* who had Abuelita change her will. You probably even forged her name!"

I had not been looking out the window. I had only listened as I crouched on my bed. Once Little Felícita said those last words, however, I could not hold back my curiosity. Obviously a scuffle had ensued, with only the words "Stop it girls! I'm too old for this!" coming from my mother. I peeked over the edge of the windowpane. Little Felícita had a good grip on Big Felícita's tiny neck, but Big Felícita reached forward and pushed her long thumbnails into Little's fat abdomen, forcing her to release her throat. My mother apparently rode them both, hoping they would let go of each other. They finally did.

"Little Felícita, go!" Mamá demanded, though her voice was more pleading than angry. "Your father is in the Colón. It's open until nine o'clock tonight."

Little Felícita fell back to the cement railing of the steps. She tossed her thick, black hair back. At the mention of her father, she began to weep. It was true crying. I could understand why. She and Uncle Jack had spoken little in the past few years, ever since the day that Little Felícita had spoken with Abuelita about inheriting the house and a portion of the business. Uncle Jack had been confused by the story. It hurt him both ways. He did not want to believe that his daughter was guilty of the accusations. Yet he could not go against his mother's will. Chucharrona's witness to that deathbed moment had allowed for certain familial truths to come to the fore.

I remembered earlier days, when I was a child, watching my cousin Felícita. At the same time that I felt a certain young lust for her, part of that lust was caught up in her teasing, manipulating ways. She actually flirted with my father, he an old man and she just a teenager. This had fascinated me as a child, seeing a girl of sixteen lifting up from her sunbathing as my father walked by, just to show him her large, brown breasts. My father had just shaken his head and had walked on. She had a way with me as well. She would get me to sneak into Abuelita's bedroom while she was asleep and steal two of her Lucky Strikes from the pack next to her bed. "Come on, little Tony," she would whisper into my ear. Her breath felt like a foggy tongue upon its inner folds. "You're smaller than I am, you can get in and out, and she won't even wake up." I, of course, obeyed.

I had never seen my cousin Felícita that summer eighteen years ago, when Mamá and I had visited and Uncle Jack whisked me away from San Francisco in the Mustang. But she had been there. Little Felícita had been involved in that story in such a way that was intrinsic, indelible, and catastrophic.

Now, however, was no time to think too much about those days. Those days had built into the bulging tension and rage of today. I listened and watched as Little Felícita backed down the steps of the house. My mother and Aunt Felícita watched her as she slowly moved toward her Volvo. They stared as she drove away from the home that had necessarily shunned her.

Mamá and Aunt Felícita stepped into the house and walked up the steps, talking lowly in Spanish about the incident, then sometimes breaking into English. "She actually thinks that I would push her down those stairs," Aunt Felícita grumbled. "That's crazy. Those are cement. These were the ones I flung her down. They've got carpeting on them. But then, that was a real problem for me, having to clean the blood stains out of a white rug. You know how hard that is to do?"

Aunt Felícita spoke to Mamá about that incident as if she had not been there. But Mamá had been there, of course. While Uncle Jack and I had driven away from San Francisco, escaping the finger-flipping blade of Gato's men, my mother had used all her will power to keep Aunt Felícita from killing her namesake.

The two sisters stood on the top stair. They were both weary, not so much from the climb up but from the encounter outside. I had already closed the window, but had not been able to escape my room and run back into the kitchen with Dad. Mamá turned and saw me. "*Hola mi'jito*. What are you up to?"

I moved toward my closet and pulled out one of Uncle Jack's old, light coats. As night was coming on, I figured I would need it. "I thought about taking a walk."

"You need to be careful. This isn't the same San Francisco of your childhood."

"I know. Actually, I thought about visiting La Chucharrona."

Aunt Felícita turned and looked at me. She smiled, cutting through the thoughts of her battle with Little Felícita. "Oh, that's a wonderful idea, Tony. She would love to see you. How good, that you would think of your elders like that. She is very old now. I wonder if she will remember you."

"Chucharrona remembers everything and everybody," said Mamá. "She would love to see you, Tony." Mamá smiled. I couldn't help but think that she was thankful that her son—though a bit of a milksop—had at least not turned into the likes of my manipulative cousin.

"And then you're going to see Chucho, *verdad?*" my aunt asked. "You know, make up with him for your uncle. Make peace."

Make peace, I thought. Between the living and the dead, while she still couldn't do it with her living niece. But I, of course, shook my head affirmatively as I moved toward the steps.

I had not forgotten where Chucharrona's home was. I always had a knack for remembering geographic positions of houses, buildings, streets, and the overall structure of a city, even if I had not visited it many times. I had forgotten, however, how I had necessarily walked eighteen years ago, when I had followed my grandmother down these same streets. Back then I had watched in shame as Abuelita talked with folks, offering salutations to the men who worked the kiosks, who sold *pupusas* and *tamales* and *burritos* for their living, and to the women who hawked various fabrics, rugs and adornments for the Latino home. Back then I could understand little of what they said.

Today I could understand everything. Still, I greeted no one. This was not my barrio, so even though I could speak the ordinary language of this street, I could not communicate in the way my Abuelita had. She, having lived here since the forties, walked by with a smile and a few minutes to spare for a short chat, leaving more than words at the kiosk, leaving another touchstone of history, of friendship.

I turned the corner and almost expected those street boys of 1978 to turn and look at me. No one was standing there, although a number of people walked up and down the sidewalk. I found Chucharrona's building. It looked as decrepit as it did back then. I glanced over to the other side of the street. A large sign had been staked into a pile of dirt there, in front of a barren field. The sign promised the quick arrival of a large grocery store named Ralph's. I knew that Chucharrona's home would probably not be standing here for very long. I hoped that she would at least have the chance to use the new Ralph's a few times before she either died or was asked to leave the premises.

Then I asked myself, Can La Chucharrona die? I could not remember how old she was, although she seemed extremely old when I last saw her. How many more landlords had she outlasted?

Down the street, among a cluster of buildings, my glance caught the blinking red, green, and white neon lights of an establishment that no doubt was either a pawn shop or strip show. As it was already dark, the lights blinked the tri-colored hue upon the other closing businesses around it. I paid it little attention as I entered Chucharrona's building.

The front door was not locked. There was no gate. I walked down the hallway that smelled of urine, something that I did not remember from last time. That was a sure sign that the conditions of her home had worsened. No doubt winos stumbled in here from time to time and pissed through their pants while sleeping off a long day. The hallway, of course, seemed shorter than it did eighteen years ago. Perhaps I had actually grown a few inches since then.

I knocked on the door. A radio played Cypress Hill, an old song from that Latino rap band's better days. It was not very loud. I knocked again. A man's voice yelled from the back. I could not tell if the yelp was Spanish or English. On the third knock the door opened. A young guy, perhaps in his twenties, with thick, unwashed curly hair and skin darker than mine opened the door. He looked at me with eyes not unlike a bulldog's that has just been rustled from sleep.

"*¿Qué pasó?*" he said to me.

"*Disculpe, es que busco a la Chucharrona . . .*"

"La Chucharrona? She ain't lived here in years. She gone man, down the street." He looked at me, up and down, quickly, then asked. "Who are you, man?"

"I'm a friend of the family's . . . Tony Villalobos."

"Villalobos? *Hijo de Mamá Roselia?*"

"No. *Nieto.*"

"Grandson? Really? Shit man, that's great," and he offered me his hand. "I'm Charlie. Charlie Vega."

We exchanged quick salutations. "Yeah, I remember your grandmother, man," he said. "She helped out my mother a few times, you know, gave us food from one of her stores. She was always helping people out around here, before the fucking Chinese started coming in, taking our homes away. All the *raza's* cutting out, going to Oakland or somewhere, man." He rubbed one sleepy eye with his left palm as he spoke. "So you looking for La Chucharrona? She's down the block, on the right. You can't miss her place."

I thanked him and shook his hand again. He smiled at me, a completely different person once I made the connection between my grandmother and myself. I had decided not to risk mentioning the death of my uncle, having no idea if this young man shared the same feelings for Jack as he did for Abuelita.

Back on the street I looked down at the cluster of buildings whose first floors glowed from the lights of the one establishment still open. I walked toward it. I muttered to myself, "Could this be it?"

It definitely was. Through the glare of the neon that ran from one corner of the large windows to the next, in the colors of the Mexican flag, was a decorative sign embroidered into a blue cloth stretched over a metal frame. *Mamá Chucharrona y Su Casa de Adivinación*. Mama Chucharrona's house of Clairvoyance. Along the bottom panes of the windows she had placed at least a hundred tiny trinkets, baubles, statuettes of the Blessed Virgin, of Christ, Chac Mool and even a Bolivian Pachamama. A fairly large Maximón from Guatemala stood alone in a corner, smoking a cigarette, with dollar bills stuck into his clothes. Little automobiles stood upon drawings of roads. Chucharrona had spread fake grass around the roads, with green plaster of Paris bulking up in the back to create hills. Dolls, everything from little Guatemalan cornhusk dolls to Barbies, sat alongside the cars' paths, looking down like giants. Matchsticks and their open boxes, tiny fake bottles of Coca Cola and Pepsi, a dusty bottle of unopened Corona Beer, a crucifix leaning up against the bottle, rosaries draping over hills and fences. Tiny national flags glued to toothpicks pierced the paper-maché terrain, all of their thick stripes composed of variations of blue and white, distinguishing the Central Americas. One stood somewhat alone, an eagle in its middle clawing at a serpent, with the same colors as those of the neon lighting. All of it looked like an amalgam of different Latino worlds piled together then sorted and placed into a strange neatness that stared out onto the street, the neon glow blessing them forever.

"She's done well for herself," I muttered while walking through the front door.

Inside a young Guatemalan girl of about fifteen looked up at me and smiled. She sat at a desk, reading a book. The desk itself had its own set of baubles. Soft marimba music played from a portable compact disc player behind her. She read a book that I had not seen in years: *Me llamo Rigoberta Menchú y así nació mi consciencia.* She wore indigenous dress, one of the many patterns of colors that would set her apart from the other tribes of her country.

"Hello. May I help you?" she said in perfect English.

"Yes, I'm looking for La Chucharrona. Is she busy now?"

"I believe she was just finishing her supper. Let me check. May I ask who is calling for her?"

I gave her my name, using, as I had with the young Chicano in the dilapidated home, my mother's maiden name. The girl did not show any sense of recognition regarding the name. She continued to smile as she walked away to tell her boss of the visitor.

Chucharrona's voice came from the back.

"Antonio está aquí? ¡Qué cosa, pero no hay nada de sorpresa!" Then the young woman returned to invite me into the back room.

"Antonio, the wandering son, coming back for his uncle's funeral, *iqué lindo!"* Chucharrona greeted me with a hug and a kiss on the cheek. Yes, she was much older than before. Yet she seemed renewed in her age. More wrinkles had sunk into her face and the white streaks had almost taken over all of her hair, but she did not move decrepitly. She wore new Indian clothing, so new that the colors of the clothes seemed sharp. The deep blues that offset the woven reds and golds looked as if they had never been worn. She wore jewelry upon both wrists, rings upon a number of fingers, and earrings. All of that jewelry looked handmade and from her old country. In the midst of all the newness of her business, among the wall hangings and paintings that decorated this inner sanctum, with the CD playing marimba music from all corners, stood the old table that had once stood back in the ramshackle house two blocks down. She had not gotten rid of that. I could tell it was the same from the chipped legs. Its top, however, had been newly decorated. A Guatemalan *huipil* blanketed it, with new statues and baubles carefully placed upon the cloth. In the middle of the table stood those five candles of various colors. They were now unlit. I looked about. This floor, just like the floor back in the old house, was covered in fresh pine needles.

"So how are you, child?" she said. Her Spanish had improved little through the years. Still, she chose to speak that language with me. She had obviously heard from my family that my Spanish had been *rescatado*, ransomed and salvaged from the inner folds of my childhood brain. "You have come back for your uncle, true?"

"Yes ma'am. We were at the Colón this afternoon."

She moved back to her chair behind the table. She invited me to sit down in another, softer chair to one side. Then she turned to the door and called to the girl, asking her in that indigenous language to do something. "You do like hot chocolate, don't you, Antonio?"

"Yes. Thank you."

"I went to visit your uncle earlier today. They did a good job on him. Then again, there was not much that they had to do. He was such a good-looking man all his life. He looks good in the box as well. It will take Death a while to strip him of his beauty."

The girl brought us hot chocolate and a plate of sweet breads. We ate and drank through our conversation. The chocolate was that perfect mixture, not too sweet, just enough sugar to take the cut out of the cacao. This, I knew, was much more than an offered drink. I knew how sacred chocolate was to Chucharrona and her folk. I drank it down respectfully.

She asked little of my life, such as where I was now living, what I was doing. These things were unimportant to her. "When was the last time you spoke with your uncle?" she asked.

"Oh, I think, about three or four months ago. Well, we didn't speak. I had sent him a short letter, just to, you know, tell him I was thinking about him."

"What were you thinking about him?"

"What? Oh, I don't know. He had been in my thoughts for some reason. I'm not sure."

Chucharrona looked at me. She shook her head as if absorbing a certain understanding. "And before then? When had you last spoken to him?"

"Oh gosh, over a year."

I naturally felt guilty for this confession. I wondered if Chucharrona were trying to point out my ways as the wandering boy, one who had committed the sin of not keeping up with family. Yet this had not been her purpose.

"Your uncle was in here just a few days ago. We talked a long while. I was not surprised that he died."

This struck me as odd. "Why? Did he act sick?"

She sat back and sighed. "In some ways, no. But inside, yes, I think so. He was feeling bad about my grandson Chucho. You know, the whole thing that happened long ago. And, well, your uncle also had a way of making Chucho's wife and her daughter happy." Chucharrona grinned as she sipped the chocolate. "So Chucho blamed Jack for their breakup. That was part of his sickness. But that wasn't all. Juan seemed saddened that he had no sons."

"No sons? Why was he sad about that?" I asked, thinking about that famous lineage of *hijos naturales*, bastard children that Uncle Jack had left all the way from San Francisco to somewhere in Ecuador.

"Your uncle was getting pretty old, Antonio. And you know that he abused the insides of his body, although it did not always appear that way on the outside. He drank fairly heavily for a while. By the time he left that habit behind, it had already done some of its damage."

"What do you think killed him? Heart attack?"

"I suppose that's what the doctors will say. But I just think he was ready to die. Especially after Ricarda passed away. She was his spark, you know."

Ricarda. Yet another name I had not heard in years. The mere mention of the woman's name was enough to swell my chest with unwelcome emotion.

I shook my head. "I don't understand all that, Doña Chucharrona. How could he just will himself to die? Nobody in their right mind wants to die."

Chucharrona turned away, studying the weave of the *huipil* upon her table. "I do not know. All I know is that he came in here, wanting me to light the candles." She motioned to the five candles with her lips.

I looked at all five: the red, the black, yellow, white and green. They stood in a diamond, with the green one in the middle. I remembered when she had done that blessing to me when I was sixteen, the day that she had snatched at my wrist and held my wound in her gnarled, brown fingers. All these years, whenever I thought of the tiny rite that she had made me go through, I had never understood it. The birth and death of man was easy enough. But the birth and death of God was something else.

I thought little of God these days. I had done some deconstructing of that celestial image, I thought. When my book had first come out, for some unexplainable reason I had believed that, due to my success, God was going to punish me. I was going to die of cancer, an aneurysm, or from an automobile wreck. The great success of entering the publishing world (a success that quickly was seen in its true light as insignificant, small, and financially nothing) had tossed me into a whirl of fear, anxiety, and worry over the future. Would I become successful as a writer? Would my book utterly fail in the market? Would I ever write again, or would I die in a plane crash or on the barrel end of a smoking shotgun?

It was inevitable that God would get caught up in the emotional equation. As I had been brought up in two God-fearing cultures— Appalachian and Latino, a double-whammy of lightning-wielding—I knew that God was out to get me. In order for that not to happen so readily, I started to get rid of him in my brain. It was a difficult yet somewhat helpful endeavor. I quit praying at night, shutting off the mantra of pleas that I had muttered since my childhood. Again, as in my teens, I quit attending church. I quit reading Catholic periodicals or any article that had to do with the Pope. A rosary that my mother had given me fell off the small bar in my apartment and into a crack between two partitions. I left it there.

As far as my intellect was concerned, God was out of my skull. I had barred the door. I still feared death, of course, and though God was outside the gate, I knew He could get in with a glance at the lock, shattering it to toss a quickie thunderbolt right at my loins. In order to defend myself against that, I still clicked my teeth and tapped my forehead. No need to give up everything. It became clear to me in these few short hours of being in San Francisco that, despite my having joined the seminary in college, lived in Central America through my twenties, and learned the discipline of writing daily, I had developed little new theology or philosophy throughout those years. Very little had really changed.

Now I stared at the unlit candles on Chucharrona's table and remembered the birth and death of God. That still seemed strange, coming from the lips of my Indian friend.

"Why did Uncle Jack—Juan—want you to light the candles, Doña Chucha?" I asked.

"Oh, he had done that numerous times throughout his life. He knew what they stood for. He knew." She shook her head, affirming her own orations. "Sometimes people come in here and ask me to light them and then tell them their future. They do not understand that the candles do not work that way. But then, they pay me pretty well, so I give them some ideas of their lives. Nothing surprising for me, once I hear where their lives have already been. To them, of course, it is inspiration. But your uncle, sometimes he just asked me to light them, and he wouldn't ask me any questions about the candles, whether or not they were 'saying' anything about him. He just wanted to hear the story again, about what the candles signified, the birth and death of man, the birth and death of God. You remember that?" She looked over at me.

"I do. But I never have understood it. I mean, how can God die and be born again?"

She chuckled. "How can He not?" She took a bite of sweet bread.

I was not sure what to say to that. "Do you think Uncle Jack wanted to make peace with your grandson before he died?"

"Oh, I think that would have been nice. Yes. Perhaps you're right. Juan wanted that. He felt bad that Chucho was so torn up and angry. But I don't know if you remember Chucho. He is a bit of a whiner."

Whiner, I thought. He lost two fingers and half a testicle. I, too, would whine.

"But perhaps your uncle and he will make peace someday soon."

"Where?" I asked, some of my cynicism leaking out, "and how? In heaven? With God?"

I had used the word *cielo*, which means "heaven," but it also means "sky."

"The sky?" and she laughed. "Why would they go into the sky to make peace?" She chuckled some more.

"I mean, isn't that where God is?"

"You are being stupid now. I do not know where God is." She looked down at the table again, studying it with a smile. "Oh. I see.

You are thinking in those terms. Yes. I remember, your Abuelita told me that you had spent a few years in the Catholic seminary, that you almost became a priest, yes . . . now it makes sense, the way you talk."

"The way I talk? What do you mean the way I talk?"

She did not answer me directly. "You believe in the God that lives in the sky, right?"

I looked straight at her, then waited about ten seconds before daring to answer. "I don't believe in any God at the moment."

"Ah. God is dead to you."

"Well, yes, I suppose you could say that." I tried to weave into her primitive ways of speaking.

"Yes. God is asleep."

"What?"

"Sleeping. God is asleep. He is dead."

The poor woman, I thought, would never make it in a creative writing class, the way she mixed her metaphors. "I just don't believe in God anymore."

"I see. You think that you have turned off that part of you." She grinned. I knew it was a mocking grin. "So God has died for the night in you."

I shook my head slightly, trying to make sense of it. I could not. She saw this in me. She turned, slowly grabbed a box of matches, and lit the five candles. She watched them flicker for a long moment. The silence between us became almost unbearable for me. I drank up most of my chocolate. I could only glance at her as she stared at the flames that licked against the perfect roundness of her calm eyes.

Then she spoke again, pinching out some of the candles. "You have passed over some roads that I do not know of, *hijo*," she said as her fingers pinched the yellow candle's flame. "It has been many years that you have been gone from here. I heard from your Abuelita that you went back to our countries for awhile. I was glad to hear that. By the way you speak Spanish now, I see that you walked at least fairly well there." She pinched the flame of the white candle. "Then you returned, and you wrote. I have seen your book. It is very thick. It is all in English, but I still have my copy. Your Abuelita gave it to me." She pinched the red candle. Only the black candle in the west and the green candle in the middle burned. "So now you find yourself, for one reason or another, with God sleeping in you. God is dead in you. He has yet to be born yet another time.

"This is all you, *hijo*. This is all you. Now my question is about this one," and she pointed to the green candle, its flame flickering over it. It was my candle. Me. "Is it burning, or not?" She barely glanced at me. Then she put her forefinger and thumb to her tongue and licked them before stretching them out to the green's flame. I wanted to stop her. I did not want her to snuff that fire out. I must have jerked, for she turned to me before squeezing the wick. She noticed my sudden movement. Then she grinned.

"Don't worry, child. They're only candles."

With that, she pinched it. The wisp of smoke leaked out from her closed fingers and rose slightly before dissipating. The only candle left burning was that black one, where God had fallen asleep, where God had died for the night.

Soon afterwards, La Chucharrona showed me to the door. I could barely finish my chocolate and sweet bread, due to her candle-scare on me. Out in the light of the front room, the fear diminished slightly. Reason crossed over my forehead, regarding the cultural anomalies of superstitions. Yet I realized that she had done some *adivinación* for me, without my having asked for one. Then again, I wondered why I had come to visit her in the first place. I thought the reason was for finding out about her grandson Chucho, but now I questioned that. Perhaps it had been for myself. I pulled out my wallet and asked her, "Doña Chucha, how much for the . . ."

She raised her hand, chuckling. "We found out nothing, son. For the moment. Don't worry about it. But oh, I almost forgot." She walked back into her room, then returned with a package in her hand. It was a brown paper package, wrapped tightly with masking tape. The mode of wrapping was very familiar. The package was large; her old fingers could not wrap completely around it. "Your uncle left this here when he visited me. He said he wanted you to have it."

"Me?" I took the package and looked at it. "But how would he know that I planned to come . . . I mean, how would he know that you could get it to me?"

"Sounds like you're surprised at yourself, ending up here for his funeral. But your uncle had not forgotten the past."

That sounded a bit harsh. I was almost angry with her, except that I knew she was right. I thanked her for the package, leaned over and kissed her on the cheek, then walked out.

"Come back and visit before you leave, child," she said. "I would love to see you again."

I said that I would try, then walked down the street. I walked quickly back to the house on Capp, made my way through the door and up the steps. Mamá, Tía Felícita, and Dad were all in the kitchen, having a drink. Dad barely sipped on half a beer, as his liver did not allow much room for alcohol. The two women drank straight whiskey out of tiny shot glasses. I knew that those glasses each would last them three hours. They sipped like hummingbirds.

"So did you see La Chucharrona?" asked my aunt, smiling.

"Oh yes, yes. Very nice visit."

"What about Chucho?"

"He wasn't there. I thought I would see him tomorrow. I'm pretty tired now, you know, from the long trip and all."

"Go on to bed, *hijo*," my mother said, smoking a cigarette. You've had a long day. Tomorrow we bury your uncle. It will be hectic. Perhaps you can see Chucho before the funeral."

I agreed, kissed the two women goodnight, touched my dad's shoulder, and left them. I heard my aunt commenting upon what a good young man I had turned out to be. "So mannerly, *de buena educación*. If he could just loosen up a bit."

That was precisely what I planned to do. I shut the door to my room. I opened the window a crack and tore into the package. Underneath the brown paper was plastic. I ripped it open. More plastic. Then a third layer. "He must have thought the dogs would sniff Chucharrona's house out," I whispered while tearing into the fourth layer. There, in two plastic, zipped packets, were the prizes: one ounce of bud, which made me smile, and a good handful of tightly wrapped, dried out mushrooms, which made me shake.

I opened the first bag. That smell, I had not experienced it in years. In all my years of living overseas, then of returning to the states to follow the life of a writer, I had never made any contacts, nor had I cared to, in order to buy the stuff. I did not want to get involved in the illegal trade. Besides, I was a runner, and smoking of any kind was not on my list of vices. But for some reason, at this moment, nothing sounded more attractive. That smell brought me back through those eighteen years. This grass, which could barely toss out an odor into this well kept, clean room, yanked me back into that summer, into the hot insides of that enclosed Mustang, driving through the days as if those days were the only thing we had ever cared to call our own.

The night my Uncle Jack drove us out of San Francisco, I panicked. Even through the haze of the marijuana that permeated me, fear still made itself known. When we had first left the city, I rattled demanding questions at him. "What are we doing?"

"We're getting out of town for awhile, *sobrino,*" he said, not looking at me, but staring directly at the road in front of him. He placed his wire-framed sunglasses on, covering the crows' feet on the edges of his eyes. He ran his fingers through his thick, black hair, the only nervous sign that I could spot. "It wouldn't be good for our health to stay in the city, know what I mean?"

"But where are we going?" I asked, my voice trembling. "Mom won't know where I am. She'll get worried, Uncle Jack!"

"Hey, don't worry about it Tony. We'll be calling her soon. Let's just get down the road a piece before we get on the phone."

"I don't get it. Why did those guys cut off Chucho's fingers? Oh God, that was sick, just sick . . ."

"Gato's playing hard soccer now, I guess. I don't know. It never was like that before. Grass is supposed to calm people down, take away the violence." He scrunched up his broad shoulders as he spoke, as if entering into some vague, badly stated philosophy on the values of weed. "But damn, Gato's gone to the edge. He must be watching too many Pacino movies or something."

I looked down the highway at the ending day. The sun was behind us, falling into the Pacific. "What about Mamá and Abuelita? What about Aunt Felícita? Will Gato come after them now?"

Uncle Jack grinned. "No. Gato won't dare touch your grandmother. He's been sweet talking her for years, trying to get that tamale recipe out of her. I don't think he'll hurt the family. He damn well better not. If he does, fuck, I'll lose a finger to him. But he'll lose his fucking balls to me."

"So how do you plan to take on Gato if he decides to play hard-ball and hurt Mamá and the others?" I asked. I was pissed by this time, and my young, sixteen-year-old voice revealed it.

"Well sometimes you just got to put your balls out there, *sobrino*, and show them who's man."

"Oh yeah. It's being a man, running away like this."

"No. I mean being a man. Even if another man's dick is bigger than yours, you make him believe differently."

"Oh yeah? How?" I crossed my thin arms over my chest.

"Like this." Uncle Jack rummaged for something underneath his car seat. I turned only slightly before that hard something pushed up against my forehead. My Uncle Jack had a very large handgun aimed at my skull.

I said nothing, though the breath left my body, along with a few tablespoons of urine that leaked into my pants.

"Look down that barrel, *sobrino*."

At first I did not obey, shaking too much to follow orders.

"You know, Tony, you've been a bit disrespectful in the few hours since I've seen you. I don't know, you've just been acting a little too big for your pants. That can be a deadly mistake. Your Abuelita and the whole fucking family like to tell stories about me. But did they also tell you how short a fuse I have?" He pulled back the hammer. I heard the very loud, steel click.

"Dang, Uncle Jack, I didn't mean anything . . . honest . . . I didn't mean to be disrespectful at all . . ." I probably mumbled a number of other words, though I cannot remember them. I do remember, how-ever, seeing images of how all this fell into place. My uncle was a drug runner. It was no surprise that he owned a gun, one that, in the scant glance I gave it, looked much larger than the little twenty-two pistols that my father owned. Jack worked with people who cut off other people's fingers. He no doubt had killed a few individuals in his life. He was most assuredly a psychotic, ready to kill his own nephew for smarting off.

"Listen, Tony, there's only two things that can keep me from wanting to rip a bullet through your head right now. One is I don't want to get my car messed up. This Mustang is practically my home. But I could take care of that easy. We could just pull over right here somewhere on the highway and take a little walk into the woods."

"Oh God, Jesus, Uncle Jack," and I started to weep. I couldn't control my face enough to click my teeth together. I didn't dare try to raise my knuckles to my forehead.

"Hold on son, just hold on. There's the other thing that keeps me from putting a bullet into your skull. Stick your finger down the barrel."

"What . . . ?"

"Do what I say! Stick your finger down the barrel."

I slowly obeyed, turning my head enough to look straight down into the blackness of that barrel. It was a large opening. I wondered if I could see the bullet's tip pointed straight at me. Then I stuck my finger in it.

Although the opening was sufficiently big, my finger did not go in. I pushed. A thick, fast sigh shoved itself through my lungs. My finger would not go in. It was not the blackness of a hollow barrel. There *was* no barrel. The tip was painted black, simulating an empty tube. The black facade felt like smooth, hard steel.

The gun was a fake.

Uncle Jack pulled off his sunglasses, stared at me, and laughed as loud as I had ever heard him laugh. "Man, *sobrino,* you should see yourself!"

My jaw quaked. My eyes felt ready to leave my skull. I think I said something like, "You fucking son of a fucking . . . God damn, Damn you . . . You, Uncle Jack . . . !"

He just laughed. He placed the gun on the seat and slapped the back of my head with his palm. That hurt. "I got this from a friend who works on a movie set. It's just a prop. Its hammer really works, so does the trigger. But it's just for holding and looking tough. Looks pretty real, doesn't it? You thought I was going to kill you, didn't you?"

"Well, yeah, I did! Damn you!"

"That's what I mean by making them believe your balls are bigger than theirs. If you can do that, then you're not pretending. Your balls *are* bigger!"

"You scared the shit out of me," I said, recognizing in my fear my own thick Southern accent. I felt warm tears collect and fall. I wiped them, forgetting shame for the moment. The pistol lay next to me. I picked it up. It was lighter than I imagined, as light as my father's weapons, ones that I was accustomed to handling. Or perhaps the hot adrenaline running through my body made everything momentarily light.

"Hey, Tony, listen, I would never hurt you," he said, hitting me in the shoulder. The pain seemed to carry with it an enigmatic sense of *cariño*. "You're blood, man. You're blood. Shit, sometimes family is all we got, right?"

I nodded my head, agreeing with anything he said. I waited to listen to more of his words, just to make sure that he was not in truth some psychopath whose emotions and moods switched every few minutes. After awhile I could calculate that his bravado with the fake pistol was just that. He lit another cigarette, offering me one. I took it. I choked at first, but the hit of nicotine then actually felt good. It cut through the logjam of fear in my chest.

"Listen, we'll call your mom soon, I promise. I just want to get down the road as far as possible. Why don't you take it easy? You hungry? We'll pull over and get a bite to eat later. There's some bags of chips in the back seat, if you want."

I was famished. The grass, followed by the dissipating fear of my uncle wanting to assassinate me, made for an appetite. I looked back. Uncle Jack had a cardboard box filled with small bags of chips, pretzels, and crackers. I grabbed several bags and tossed them onto the front seat.

"There's an icebox back there with sodas too, man,"

We ate the junk food and swallowed down the colas. Jack pulled out the *Los Lobos* cassette and shoved in Bo Diddley. I watched the sun leave the rearview passenger mirror. With Bo's growl asking me "Tell me now, who do you love," I fell asleep.

Several hours later Uncle Jack slowed the Mustang down. I woke up and glanced over at his lit dashboard. The tank was on empty. He pulled off Interstate Five. In the blast of his headlights I saw a sign, DEVIL'S DEN, TEN MILES. I could see no town. Only the low glow of a lone truck stop.

"Let's get some grub," he said, looking for a place to park. "But we'll call home first."

I stayed in the car as he walked to the public phone. He called. I heard him say, "Collect from Juan." He turned, smiled at me, put a thumb up in the air, then looked back at the phone's rotary dial. He grinned at the rotary as he spoke. He shuffled, Bo Diddley's rhythm in his head, and moved from the ball of one foot to the next. I could hear his voice only slightly muffled with the glass door of the phone booth. "Hey, Carmen, *hermana,* how you doing, honey? No, we're fine, really, we're fine. Fine. We just decided to take a little trip, you know? Men getting together, wanting to do a little fishing . . . No, Carmen, there's no trouble, really. No trouble at all. It's just so good to be with your son and . . . I promise you, we're fine. He's fine. Wait a minute . . ." He motioned for me to come to the phone.

I got out of the car and walked over. He was still smiling at the rotary dial. "Talk to your Mamá, tell her everything's fine."

Then, because he had pulled his ear slightly away from the receiver, I heard Mamá's voice saying ". . . Chucho's in the hospital. They put him on tranquilizers, but they say he was still screaming that he got cut in his, in his pee-pee . . ."

"What?" Uncle Jack turned back to the phone. "What did you say, sister? What? Fuck! That fucking Gato. That motherfucking Gato . . ."

I could not hear my mother admonish her little brother for his words. I could only see Chucho, his fingers flying, then imagining his penis bouncing off a wall, with a cat approaching it, and that's just about all I wanted to imagine. My legs pinched together.

"Listen, you listen to me, Carmen," my uncle demanded, though his voice tried to be as soft as possible to his older sister. "We're fine. I promise you, we're okay. But if a guy named Gato calls you, don't stay on the phone with him. You just tell him the truth. Tell him you don't know where the hell I am. And just act calm when you talk with him."

I heard my mother's telephone voice say, "Oh my God, Juan, what is going on?"

Uncle Jack talked with her a while longer, until she could obviously not take it anymore. "Okay Carmen, just calm down. Calm down, honey. I promise you I'll take care of your son. Hell, he's my nephew, right? What? I don't know where we'll go . . . What do you mean about Ricarda? Why do you think I want to go running off to her? That is not true, *hermana,* I don't *always* run to her when I'm in trouble. Listen. Carmen, Carmen, please honey, don't cry, just . . . why don't you sit down, have a drink, get Felícita on the phone."

Jack and his younger sister spoke. He was not as patronizing with her. I suppose it was because she was younger. They talked about his daughter, Little Felícita.

"What? Why would I know what she was doing in the company? Hell, she never talks to me about her business . . . No, I didn't tell her to try to get her job back! I know she was screwing up in there, no need for me to defend her for that. No way I'm getting between her and Mamá . . . Yeah? Maybe she's dating one of your employees, I don't know . . . Yeah, hang on just a second . . ." He turned to me.

"Your aunt wants to talk with you."

He walked over to the car, reached into the back, grabbed a San Francisco 49ers jacket and put it on.

I took the phone. "Hello?" I said, quite meekly.

"Tony, what's going on? Where are you?"

"I don't know, I think we're somewhere . . ."

"Shit! Don't tell them where we are!" Uncle Jack turned, holding his palms up in the air to show them to me.

"I don't know," I said.

"Are you all right, Tony?" she asked.

"Yes, yes, ma'am."

"You're sure?"

"Well, not exactly."

I heard my mother's voice in the background. "Let me talk with him." She got on the phone.

"Antonio. Son, where are you?" Her voice pleaded.

"Hi, Mamá, I'm not sure." Then my voice cracked, and I started to cry.

"Oh, *hijo* . . ." And she started to cry. Then I heard her turn to her sister, "He's crying, Felícita . . ."

"Oh fuck," Uncle Jack mumbled. He lit a cigarette. "Tony, don't cry over the phone, for Christ's sake. They'll think we're in trouble or something."

"Well, we *are* in trouble!" I turned to him, my eyes undoubtedly glistening.

He shut up.

"Tony, you listen to me," Mamá continued, her tears sucking back into her throat. She had that way, the ability to be quickly strong. "Whatever happens, whatever you do, don't get away from your Uncle Jack. Stay right next to him."

"I will." I was not sure why she asked this of me. After all, it was because of him that we were in this mess.

She explained. "Your Uncle Jack has a way of getting into trouble. But the strangest thing about him, he's got some angel or somebody watching over him. He never gets too badly hurt. Oh, maybe a bullet in his back, but he still gets out of the situation. Stay next to him. I mean right next to him. Then you'll be protected too."

Latino superstitious advice over long distance. I had nothing to say to this.

Soon we hung up. I cried some more, then wiped my face before leaving the phone booth. Uncle Jack was leaning against his Mustang. His hands were in the pockets of the 49ers jacket. He looked at me. His eyes were somewhat soft, as if trying to ignore, for my sake, my sadness.

"Well, hey," he said, "you hungry?"

Truck drivers meandered in and out of the diner. They were all shapes and sizes, some of the men older, others perhaps in their twenties. Only a few were women, and they looked as worn and ready for coffee and cigarettes and an unmoving stool as any of the men. The air stood stagnant with years of burnt cigarettes. The only movement—and salvation—of that air came from the kitchen, where thick chunks of meat—hamburger, steaks, ham, chicken, some fish— sizzled on a grill. Those smells wafted through the swinging doors like a silent, gum-chewing beckoning, a redolent siren for the weary roadmen.

We sat in a booth that was covered in red plastic upholstery. Surprisingly, I saw no rips in the plastic. The truck stop seemed fairly well kept. A white waitress with red hair and with a tiny nameplate over her left breast that said "Bertha" approached us. She took our orders. I glanced at her cautiously, at her mid to late thirties body, her thick makeup that tried to cover a string of weary nightshifts, her smile that seemed sincere enough. Uncle Jack, however, looked straight at her. He called her "honey" as he ordered. He asked about the eggs, how the cook liked to fix them. He said he loved the coffee, that she must have accidentally stuck her finger into it, it tasted so sweet. He mentioned how good the food smelled, and that he was one very hungry man, smiling at her and looking straight into her eyes as he talked. I could not believe his blatancy. And I could not believe how she responded. She smiled at him, then placed the edge of her order board on her hip, resting her palms on the opposite edge.

"So you want your eggs scrambled, with hot sauce?" she asked him.

"Oh honey, that sounds just right."

She scribbled, then, without looking at him, quietly murmured, "Well, maybe you'd like to try a couple of sunny side up next time through."

He said nothing. He just looked at her and grinned.

She walked away. Jack sipped his coffee. I looked at him, my head down slightly, but my eyes angry and righteous.

"What's the matter?" he asked.

"I can't believe this. We just fled San Francisco for our lives. We just called home, my Mamá is worried sick, and you're making passes at a waitress."

"Yeah. What about it? And hey, I'm not making passes at her. I'm just making her feel good."

"What's the difference?"

"Plenty of difference." He lit a cigarette. "What, you think I want to jump in bed with every woman I see?"

I did not answer, though I opened my eyes wider, as if to say, "And do you?"

"Look, I'm a bit more careful than that." He strained slightly to look around me and toward the waitress booth. "She *is* a pretty good looking piece, I gotta admit . . . but take her, for instance, what's her name . . ."

"Bertha."

146

"Right. Bertha. Nice girl. Looks like she cares for herself, you know, watches her weight, wears some makeup. But she also works hard. Probably been working in this shithole since dawn. Maybe she's got some kids at home, but no old man. She's the one bringing in the bacon. Maybe a little lonely. So I come along, and I just appreciate her beauty." He opened his hands to the air as he settled back into the plastic upholstered booth. The cigarette was pinched deep between his middle and forefingers. "I make her feel, for just a few minutes, like she's special. Because she is. What's the matter with that?"

"So you don't want to get in the sack with her?"

"Hey, I didn't say that. I could make her happy that way too, *seguro que sí.*"

I rolled my eyes.

"Hey, who asked you to come around and be so high-and-mighty, *sobrino?* Or haven't you had your first piece of ass yet?"

I turned my head away, unable to control a smile.

"Oh, so that's it. I got me a little Virgin Tony on my hands. I'll be damned. How old are you? Sixteen? Damn, we got to get to work on you."

"No, I don't want it."

"What the hell you mean you don't want it? You're a man now, aren't you? Every man wants . . . unless, of course . . ."

"Hey! I'm not queer," I said. The word *queer* seemed quite queer coming out of my mouth. I was not one to use such language. I would have usually said *homosexual*, the appropriate, intellectual term. I suppose this was an endeavor to reach down to my uncle's level. "I like women. I was in love, you know . . ."

"Oh yeah. That's right. You left your heart in East Tennessee. What was her name? Jennine, Janet . . ."

"Janice. Janice Lee." It seemed strange to say that name after a few days of mourning her absence, of considering, once again, some sort of death, a final escape from the pain of her rejection. Now, running from Uncle Jack's drug cohorts, survival had kicked in quite conveniently. Her name skimming over my tongue did not have the same sting.

"Yeah. Janice. Pretty name. I bet she was a pretty girl. You know what you need in order to forget about her? Another pretty girl. But one who will smile down on you as she mounts your naked ass." He bent down over the table and grinned.

I once again grinned uncontrollably and almost laughed. It was the inescapable giggles of a teenager, that intrinsic shame of being placed in one of the multitudinous embarrassing situations that older relatives always placed us in. Then again, I had to admit that none of my other family members could create such moments of embarrassment as could this uncle before me.

The thought of losing my virginity was of some interest to me, but I tried to move the conversation other ways. "So what did Aunt Felícita say about my cousin Felícita?"

"What? Oh, the phone call. Yeah. My daughter's just probably getting into more shit, I don't know. Your aunt said she was hanging around the company, flirting with one of the workers on the second floor. Big Felícita didn't want to confront her. You know how well they get along. So she just let her hang around. But your aunt was asking me what Little Felícita's up to, like I know what my daughter is doing with her life. Shit, she's a grown woman now. Bigger than me. She's gotta fend for herself. I never knew that all this shit would be hitting the fan when I named her after my sister . . ."

I could tell that he was not happy talking about this. I could understand why. He had been placed in the rather uncomfortable position of defending either his daughter and her capricious ways or his sister.

I asked another question to steer the conversation away from Little Felícita "Who is Ricarda?" I asked, lifting up my glass of cola.

"She's a friend." He drank his coffee. His eyes darted about the truckstop diner.

"A friend? Sounds like she's more than that."

"Well, yeah. She was my wife."

"Your wife?"

"Yeah." He sipped more coffee.

"Is that little Felícita's mother?"

"No. No way. Little Felícita's mom is a woman named Sherrie, a gringa who I was married to back in the fifties.

"I never heard of Sherrie."

"Yeah, well, she and I divorced after six months. But she was pregnant with Felícita. She gave the girl over to Mamá to raise."

Whoever the Gringa Sherrie was, Little Felícita had come out taking on more of the Villalobos appearance: dark brown skin, jet black hair. But maybe Sherrie had been a tall, stout woman, which would explain Little Felícita's height, the way she towered over us all. "I didn't know that about my cousin."

He said nothing, only smoked and glanced over at our waitress, hoping to give her a smile across the floor.

I kept asking questions. "So this woman Ricarda, I don't think I ever knew her either. Would Ricarda be my aunt?"

"Yeah, I guess so. Right. Your aunt."

"So are we going to go see her?" I asked.

"Well, yeah, I think so."

And given the conversation he had with my mother, this now verified that we were indeed in trouble. Still, I asked, "Why?"

"Hey, she's my *compañera*. Or was, at least. She's good people. Real good."

He said nothing about her looks, her age, her weight, her breasts, the wetness of her thighs. This seemed peculiar.

"So yeah, we're going to see her. Hey, maybe there I can get you hooked up with a girl. Someone who will take your *huevos* and slowly bake them in her soft hands."

No matter how much my mind turned sour with his sexual references, my loins had a way of listening to his imagery. Being baked in soft hands made me leap up against my jeans again.

In a few minutes Bertha brought our food to us. Uncle Jack smiled at her. She stopped a moment and smiled back. She also gave him an extra napkin and even placed it on his lap for him. Then she walked away. The leaping against my jeans got stronger through that vicarious moment. Then Uncle Jack turned to his meal of steak and eggs, hot sauce, potato cakes, and tomato slices.

He was halfway through the meal when I asked him, "And where does my aunt Ricarda live?"

"Just south of a town called Tecate."

"Oh. Where is that, near Los Angeles?" I took a bite from my hamburger.

"No. Farther south. Down in Mexico."

I choked. I think it was on a pickle.

We drove about two more hours on Highway Five before Uncle Jack pulled the Mustang off the interstate and toward the outskirts of a small town called Lebec. A few other signs displayed information on the Los Padres National Forest, along with a number of parks and recreation areas. Uncle Jack headed straight toward a small motel where the VACANCY sign still burned neon red. A bigger sign read "Tejon Motel" in plain white neon.

"This'll do for the night," he said. "Tomorrow we'll get up early. We can be across the border before evening. L.A.'s always a shit to get through, but I bet we can make it."

"Is my Aunt Ricarda expecting you at any time?" I asked, sarcasm dripping from my words.

"Oh, always." He laughed as he opened the door to the room.

The first thing I noticed was the smell. It was not necessarily unpleasant, nor was it attractive. This was one of those family-owned businesses in which the children of the owners probably cleaned the rooms. They left the quarters with a waft of pine detergent and bleach. At least, I thought, it was disinfected. I looked outside. The few people who were staying in other rooms looked middle age to older, folks who had spent the day exploring the nearby national forest and who were ready for a decent night's sleep.

"We don't have much in the way of luggage. Except for the shit in the trunk. I think I better bring that in," he said, walking back out the door. A few moments later I heard the trunk close. He walked back in, holding what I had barely seen earlier that day in the slight reflection of the passenger mirror. They were two large, full, black plastic garbage bags.

"I, uh, I suppose you know what this is," he said to me.

"I've got an idea."

"Yeah, well, you've got to keep quiet about this," he said. "I could get in a lot of trouble. So could you, just being in the room with it."

"So you're a drug runner," I said, righteousness pushing my words forward.

"I'm no drug runner," he said. "I just sell from time to time, you know, like a side business. And, actually, I haven't done this in a long time. This was just a special favor for my friend Rata, to be the point man."

"That's a drug peddler."

"Oh come on, kid, don't get high and mighty with me. What, you think I'm an even lower life than what you first thought?"

I sidestepped the question and asked the obvious, "But isn't this illegal?"

"Yeah, it's illegal. Barely. But yeah, you could have your ass in jail for possession. And this is a shitload of shit. Must be pretty good, too, according to what you heard Gato say. Sounds like he wanted to have his paws around this order quick. Hey, wait a minute, didn't you say he said something about a special gift or something like that?"

"He mentioned something about a Christmas present."

"Yeah, well maybe this ain't what I thought it is," Jack opened one of the two bags. He looked in. I looked over his shoulder. A certain thrill jumped over my self-righteousness as I peeked. The bag was filled with dozens of smaller paper bags, all of them tightly wrapped, with masking tape crossing over their middles.

Uncle Jack studied the bags. "Yeah, this is a big haul, but it's not like he had already paid for it. Why'd he be wanting to cut Chucho up for this?" Jack stuck his hand down into the bag and tossed a number of smaller packets onto the bed.

"Hey, is that door locked?" I went to check. It was. I returned, just as Jack said, "Yeah. I think we got something here," and he pulled out a larger packet that was distinct from the others. Its paper was colored white, not brown, like the rest. "Let's see what we got, now," he said, carefully pulling the packet apart, not wanting to tear up the contents. He chuckled. "So I guess this is the little Christmas gift."

He pulled out a soft, spongy looking article, much like a large, broken button on a stem. "This looks pretty good," he said. "I wonder where he got it?"

"What is it?"

Jack looked at me. "This? This is a mushroom. Kind of like peyote."

I didn't understand that word. "What do you do with it?"

"You eat it."

"Oh. Is it good?"

"No. Tastes like cow shit. But it ain't the taste you're looking for."

"What are you looking for?"

Jack chuckled again. "The trip of your life."

"Really? More than marijuana?" I said, obviously enthused. I looked about the motel room, seeing that it was probably much safer than where I had experienced my first high.

"Shit, marijuana and this stuff is like comparing apples and tequila. You don't do this stuff unless under adult supervision."

"Well, you're around," I suggested.

"Listen to this! The high and mighty preacher here now wants to get ripped on mushrooms. Pretty quick change, *sobrino.*"

I just shrugged my shoulders.

"Still, I don't see why this shit would get Gato so riled. I mean, he doesn't use *any* drugs. He's as clean as a whistle. Just sells it for the money. It's not like he'd make a big haul here. There's only a few hundred dollars of mushrooms here."

Jack studied the large bag, then looked at the package of mushrooms again. He shook his head, confused. "This shit ain't worth somebody losing their fingers or balls for. Maybe Gato's just gone off the deep end . . ."

"You think this marijuana is pretty good?" I said, my tongue still getting used to saying 'marijuana' on a regular basis.

"I'm sure of it. You want to try some?"

So we did. He rolled a joint up dexterously, as cleanly as my father could roll a regular cigarette ("Your old man taught me how to roll a cigarette. Did you know that?"). We smoked the entire fag. I experienced my neck once again. We talked. I remember feeling very close to my Uncle Jack, then very far from him, at the same time. I would feel a certain emotion, one that promised to swallow me. It would be gone in a breath. Sexual urges began in my groin but ended up in my armpit before floating away with my body odor and burning up in the light bulb of the desk lamp. Uncle Jack turned on the radio to a local station. Neil Diamond sang. "Oh man, Neil!" cried out my uncle. I thought he was joking. He was not. "Shit man, this guy sings from the heart . . ." I shook my head; Los Lobos and Diamond did not compute. Then I shook my head again, and of course it all computed. Neil Diamond, no doubt, had recently given birth to the new L.A. sound of Los Lobos.

We turned on the television and watched Carson. We both laughed at different times. Uncle Jack had become dexterous enough in the smoking of grass to know when to laugh at the appropriate moments. I laughed between the show and the commercials, when the screen turned black. Nothing could be more witty. Jack walked out to the Mustang and brought in the box of snack food. We shoved the chips between our lips. Sometimes I could not remember opening my mouth to the food. Crumbs fell to my chest. I wiped them off, waiting for them to float away from me like tiny astronauts leaving the main ship.

"Man, I'm gonna turn in. It's been a long day." He walked by me, touching me on the shoulder. "You stay up as long as you want, *sobrino.*" He fell to his bed. It took a while for snores to come pouring out of his open mouth.

I looked past Johnny Carson toward the two black bags. Though my mind had floated through the second buzz of my life, it still latched onto a goal. I quietly stood up, walked behind Carson, and reached down into the open bag. There, on top, was the open white paper package. Uncle Jack had rewrapped and tied the inside plastic. It took me five minutes to open it, all the time trying to make no noise.

My fingers pushed down into the open bag and touched the tops of the large, soft buttons. I grabbed one. I raised it up from the bag. Carson was talking with John Travolta's younger brother, who had just recently made his way into Hollywood. It sounded like a failed interview. I looked at the mushroom.

I raised the button to my lips.

A wave of grass passed over my sight, almost like an endearing caveat. Perhaps mixing the two could prove harmful. I had no idea. As far as I was concerned, the chemical mix could detonate my body.

I placed the button in my shirt pocket, then closed up the bag as carefully as possible. Then I went to bed. I thought about Janice Lee. I thought about the day I watched her take off her sweatshirt, and how the act had pulled up her T-shirt. I focused upon the whiteness of her thin abdomen, the two lines of muscles that I had been allowed to see. I saw the sweatshirt whip off her head, and she looked at me, smiling innocently, not knowing that I had caught a glimpse of her skin. Then I thought of Uncle Jack and that waitress Bertha, how he had told her, through so many words and so much well-placed eyesight, how beautiful she was, how becoming and attractive she was to him, how he would touch her until she was satisfied. I realized that his silent signals were no different from my signals that night when I watched Janice Lee pull her sweatshirt off, when no doubt my eyes said to her, "You are Beauty itself." Now, as Janice saw my eyes, she smiled, for she knew that I worshipped her like no other. She swooped over me as a wind whipped off her shirt, showing me the perfection of her small breasts. How interesting, in this dream I could see the real Janice. No doubt this smoked substance had a way of bringing realities together, through time, through distance . . . whatever. It did not matter, not as her naked chest pushed against the mushroom of my shirt pocket, not as she pulled my pants away before dropping her head down to me, wrapping her brown hair around my buttocks while her lips found me and clutched me and pulled me down a slick hole, into the thick brilliance of neon lights, until I ceased to exist, a match swallowed by the sea.

The following morning I woke to a grunting noise. It was rhythmic. I opened my eyes. My head still undulated slightly from last night's smoke. The patterned groans came from the foot of my bed. I raised my head from the pillow and looked down, my sight still glazed. Uncle Jack's head lifted up and above the footboard, looked at me with a grimace, then disappeared. It appeared again, this time his eyes barely opened through the squint.

"Morning, *sobrino*," he said, and his head lowered again, out of my sight.

"What are you doing?" I asked. Though it became obvious.

He did not answer directly. I could barely hear him grunting out a set of numbers. His hands were behind his head.

I got out of bed, scratching the sides of my abdomen. I walked to the bathroom to pee. When I came back, he was still doing situps.

"How many of those do you do?" I asked.

He finally ended the set, blowing a blast out of his mouth. "Three hundred. In two sets."

"Wow."

He flipped over on his stomach and began doing pushups. I counted to fifty before he ended. "How many of those?" I asked.

"*Tres cientos también, hombre,*" he grunted, smiling.

My torpid monolingual mind worked the words into English. "Three hundred? Dang." My complete admiration was summed up in that word. "Do you do this every morning?"

He spoke to me as he finished up the final set of pushups. "Oh, yeah. Been doing them for years. I begin every day this way. I feel funny if I don't. Like my day's not complete. Somedays I'll run too, but not very far. Maybe just do a mile or so. It's something."

He finished his last set of pushups, then stood up. I glanced at him, careful to not let him see my eyes falling onto his body. His forty-nine-year old chest sucked in air, expanding like a solid chamber. He had little or no extra fat around his waist. He whipped off his shirt while walking toward the bathroom. I saw the muscles of his stomach. Truly, he had been following his exercise routine for a while. His brown skin rippled above and around his navel. As he disappeared around the door to take a bath, I lifted up my own shirt and looked at my soft, placid abdomen, its off-whiteness, its lack of any real form. Unlike my uncle's torso, which displayed an array of angles, curves, a few scars (knife fights?), and a skin that appeared rough hewn, mine had but one shape: a slightly rounded horizon, a plane that didn't even stretch, but merely existed, between my chest and waistline.

Though he did not catch me examining my own body, he spoke to me about it while brushing his teeth with his forefinger. "Gotta buy a toothbrush today. But then, Ricarda's got one for me. You're gonna need one. Hey, do you do any exercises?"

"No, not really."

"You should, you know. Good for your heart. Good for everything."

"Yeah. I guess."

"Here, let me show you," he washed his mouth out. "Sometimes all you need is a little outside influence, you know, like a coach. Get on the ground."

"No, that's all right, I don't think that I . . ."

"Come on, you'd like to get in better shape, wouldn't you?"

His voice was actually somewhat endearing, with an edge of sandpaper to it. I could sense a passable father in the words.

"Well, yeah, I suppose so."

"Good. That's the first step. Self motivation. Get on the ground with me here. Now put your hands to both sides of your chest, right even with your titties. Your elbows are up, straight up. Then you push, like this," and he did a smooth pushup without the least bit of exertion. Without his shirt on, I could see the string of muscles ripple under his round, solid breasts, as well as the curves of his shoulders.

I tried to do one. He coached me, "No Tony, don't arch your back. Look. Keep your back completely straight. Otherwise the pushup doesn't do shit. See? Look at my back . . ."

He worked with me through a set of ten. I grunted and strained to raise my body off the ground. He yelled at me all through the set, even as he did the set in front of me. His face was directly in front of mine. We looked like two four-legged land animals greeting each other, only that my body contorted side to side, twisting its way through the pushups, while he leisurely pushed his body up, then slowly lowered it down before me, talking all the way. I screamed as I pushed myself through the final one. Then I collapsed onto the floor.

"Great. That's great. Your first set of ten. Now some situps."

I groaned. "No, I don't think I can do it . . ."

"Come on, get your feet underneath the bed."

He coaxed me through a set of twenty. My stomach felt as if someone had shoved a hotplate into it. The last two took at least a minute to complete.

"There," he said, still breathing easily. "That's all there is to it."

"I don't think I can do that every day."

"Don't say that. That's where the trick is. It doesn't mean shit unless you do it every day. I'm telling you, Tony, do it for a week, or maybe two weeks, and after that, you'll be so used to doing it, you'll feel funny if you miss a morning."

"What do you mean 'funny?'"

"I don't know . . . funny. Like something's missing in your life. It's just that you get so used to doing it, you don't feel right when you miss. You feel bad about yourself."

"Like a discipline."

"Exactly." He smiled at me and slapped my shoulder, then pointed his index finger at me. "Discipline. You got the right word. You got to be disciplined."

That word seemed strange coming out of his mouth. Out of all the images of my uncle, both those that I had seen with my own eyes as well as the images created from the family legends, to be disciplined or diligent in anything was not one of them.

He showered. He was cleaned and ready for the day in ten minutes. I then took over the bathroom. This morning was going to be a trick, considering that I did not have a blow dryer. I took a bath, looking down at my newly worked-over muscles, noticing very little difference except for the red blotches over my chest where I had done my first real pushups since a gym class long ago. After my shower I stood before the small bathroom mirror, wiped it down with my towel, combed my hair, then tried to place the hairs in perfect position without the help of a blow dryer. It proved difficult. I had to use Uncle Jack's only comb, which he had quickly shoved through his hair after his bath, grooming the hair back with a mere ten quick swoops before tossing the comb to the side of the sink and entering the day. I pulled it through my hair, then pulled it through again, then again and again. This was not usually a time when I thought about things. Getting one's hair in perfect position for the day took concentration, a certain dedication, and a desire to survive in the world of teenage appearances. This morning, however, raced through me in all its truth: we were on the run. I was far from either of my parents. My dad was working his ass off in some coal shaft in Kentucky. Mom was in San Francisco, wondering why the hell her son and her brother had run off together. And I was with her brother, my famed uncle, because I had witnessed some Mexican guy slice off various pieces of a family friend. The marijuana buzz that I had awoken with was completely gone, no doubt due to that strenuous set of exercises that I had just been put through.

"Hey Tony, what the hell, man? What's with the hair?" He leaned against the open bathroom door. "Come on, hurry up. We gotta get some breakfast. Long drive ahead of us."

"Yeah, I was wondering, Uncle Jack, about this trip . . ."

"What about it?" He looked over the bed for his pack of cigarettes.

"Well, don't you think we should go back?"

"Go back?" He laughed. "You crazy? You saw what Gato did to Chucho back there. Ain't no way we're going back to that now."

"Then what are we going to do?" A fear rattled my legs, the thought of being on the run for the rest of my life, when I had high school to finish. "I mean, we've got to get back sometime."

"We'll go back. Just not now. We got to see what's gonna happen." He lit a cigarette, then looked around for the car keys. He glanced over at the garbage bags of illegal produce. "I gotta put that shit in the car. You hang here a second." He left with both bags in his hands.

I watched through a window as he crossed over the small parking lot, opened the trunk of his Mustang, dropped the two bags in, then closed the trunk, as easy as loading dirty laundry. He walked back to the room without looking any other way.

"Yeah, but," I said the moment he walked back into the room, "Mom could be worried about me, you know? And what about all that, that marijuana we're carrying around? We could get in a lot of trouble for that, couldn't we?"

"You don't think I know that? Look, Tony, I appreciate your concern," he sounded a little bit sarcastic, "but I believe I'm better equipped to think out our problem here. You're a little out of your territory, if you know what I mean. What we got to do is head to your Aunt Ricarda's for a little while, wait it out and see what happens."

"But what do you think will happen?"

"I told you, I'm not sure yet. Come on, *cabrón*, quit your worrying. Damn, I didn't know my sister's kid turned out to be such a whiner."

He pushed me slightly, slapping me on the back as he moved me through the door. I said nothing, not wanting to add to the "whiner" image. That word singed up against me with a heated shame. Shame turned to anger. I didn't want to talk with him.

"You hungry?" he asked. "I saw a breakfast place just a few blocks down from here."

"No." But it was a lie. I was famished. I had heard that marijuana gave one an appetite. My stomach roared. Again, I thought, the physical workout must have added to it. But I was not about to let him know how much I wished to sit down at a table. I had no desire to sit with him, not after his mean remark.

He paid for the motel room. We drove to the breakfast restaurant, one of those places that is not known for its hamburgers nor its evening meals, but which puts out a great morning feed of eggs, bacon, sausage, pancakes, hash browns, oatmeal, coffee, milk, and juice. I ordered each of those foods.

"Damn, boy. For a kid who's not hungry, you can put it away." He chuckled. "Too bad they don't have any grits here, huh?"

Though he laughed at his own remark about Appalachian food, I did not. I plowed into the meal. I tried to ignore him. He at first did not seem to notice. He ate his meal slowly, then smoked a cigarette and looked out the window. He rested his arm up over the booth's chair. "Yeah, we should make it over the border by this afternoon," he muttered.

That thought made me shudder. "Don't we need passports or something?"

"Naw, not to get into Mexico. If you're a U.S. citizen, all you need is a driver's license or some other form of identification. You got yours, don't you?"

I at first thought about lying, saying that I had no I.D. whatsoever, hoping to trick him into staying in this country and inevitably returning to San Francisco. But I knew that one tiny object such as an I.D. was not going to keep him from following his half-formed plans. Besides, I had just got my driver's license a few months ago, something to be proud of. I nodded my head affirmatively. Then I asked him, "Are you a U.S. citizen?"

"Fuck yes, I am!" He stared directly at me. "What, you think I'm some fucking wetback, just getting into this country? I was a citizen long before you were born, *sobrino*. I came here when I was five years old. My mother got our citizenship taken care of by the time I was nine. This is my country, man," he pointed down toward the floor and the North American earth under it.

I realized that I had touched a sore spot, though I could not figure out what the origin of that spot was. "What about El Salvador?" I asked. "Isn't that your country too?"

"Oh, yeah. According to Salvador it is. The U.S. don't like it if you carry dual citizenship. But I still got my Salvadoran passport. So does your mother. And my sister and mother. We all are still Salvadorans. But we're Americans too."

He took a drag from his cigarette. "Yeah, I was in Salvador just last year. You know, visiting some family there. My Uncle Chico still lives in the capital. He's got a big family now. You got a mountain of cousins over there. Chico's an old man now, but he's still got some energy to him. He was a revolutionary, you know."

"No, I didn't know that." I had heard the name Chico before, but did not remember who that great uncle of mine was.

"Yeah. He fought with some bunch of guerrillas back in the twenties or thirties. He still talks about it. There was some big killing that went on, when I was just a kid. I don't remember any of it, except, well yeah, I remember that my mom and me and your mom had to hide out in the corn field one night. I can still see the corn stalks all around me, and I can hear Mamá telling me to be quiet, not to make any sounds. We just crouched there all night long, trying not to move around. Then I heard a bunch of gun blasts, you know, like a pa pa pa pa pa, one after another. That's all I remember."

He got quiet. He had my attention. I slowed down in my eating to wait for another part of the story. But nothing came. "So you don't know what happened?" I asked.

"No. I asked my mom about it when I grew up. But she didn't want to talk much about it. 'Those are the old days in the old country,' she'd say to me. 'Better to live in the new days.' I think she's right. There's no country like this one," he said, again pointing, this time out the window toward that American world. "You can't beat the U.S. of A."

I was not anti-American. But I did not care to hear patriotic enthusiasm. Such babble turned off my teenage attention quickly. Nothing was more embarrassing than an enthusiastic adult.

"Hey, don't you agree?" he said, catching my silent protest.

"Oh sure. Yeah. Whatever."

"Shit," he said. "You're like any other kid. You don't know how good you got it."

Again, another slam. I cleared my throat and finished my meal. A few minutes later I tried for one final conciliatory, well-placed patronizing tone. "So you still like being a Salvadoran citizen, as well as a U.S. citizen?"

"That's my blood, man. I'm *guanaco* to the core. But I'm also American. I'm both. That's what makes me so strong, man." He made two fists and bulked up the muscles of his arms and shoulders, smiling. "You don't fuck with a Salvadoran American."

I could not resist, as the opening had been made too wide. "Then if nobody, uh, fucks with a Salvadoran American, why are we running away from Gato and his boys?"

"I told you, we're not running away, Tony." He leaned into the table. His grin was completely gone. Only his eyes, those deep-set, hot eyes, remained the same. "But sometimes you got to pull back and look at your situation before you make a decision. That's what we're doing."

"So we're really in a bad situation, aren't we?" I asked.

"Why do you say that?"

"Well, we're going pretty far away in order to look at our situation. I mean, going to Mexico is really taking a big step back."

At first he said nothing, but worked over a cuticle of his fingernail with his teeth. Then he glanced out the window, checking his Mustang, no doubt verifying that the trunk had not flown open to show the world our stash. "Yeah, well you could say it's a pretty big situation. Yeah."

"Can we cross the border with all that marijuana?"

"Sh, quiet, Tony. Jesus, don't tell the whole world."

"Oh. Sorry." I lowered my head along with my voice. "So what about those bags?"

"You're right. We'll need to drop them off somewhere before we cross over. I don't want to take a chance with the Mexican *chota*. They'll cut your nuts off if they want to."

"I still don't understand why we're going to Mexico, Uncle Jack." I tried to talk in a way that showed confusion and curiosity, rather than fear. "I mean, there are a thousand places to hide out right here in California. We could get a hotel somewhere for a while. Shit," I lowered my voice again, "if we sold some of your stuff, we could stay in a *nice* hotel. You know, one with swimming pools, movies on the television."

"Now who's the lawbreaker?" he asked, smiling. "I don't get you, Tony. One minute you're preachy and scared shitless about my stash, the next minute you want to sell it and live high on the hog." He put out his cigarette. "I guess that's what it means to be a kid."

It did not sound acrid nor attacking. It almost sounded as if, for a transient moment, he could figure out his teenage nephew.

"Look, we're going to Mexico because that's where Ricarda is. It's a good place to hide. Gato has no idea where she lives. And for me, her place is just a good spot to return to once in a while."

I looked straight at him. "She was your wife?"

He said nothing, but just shook his head as he lit another cigarette.

"But you all are divorced."

"Yeah."

"Why'd you divorce?"

"Hey, why does anybody divorce today? Sometimes things just don't work out. We fought a lot. We went through a rough time together . . . then we got divorced, and we became better friends. Who could argue with that?"

I had heard other familial gossip. The facts were that Uncle Jack slept around too much. I did not remember my aunt Ricarda, but I always thought his promiscuity would be the breakdown of his marriage. I thought of that chain of cousins that I supposedly had from northern California all the way down to Ecuador. What woman could put up with that?

"Ricarda's good people. Some of the best. My mother likes her. Not that that matters, of course," he said. "But Mamá does like her."

"So do you and she still keep in touch?"

"Oh yeah. Quite a bit."

"And do you . . . do you . . ."

"Still fuck her?" He stabbed out the cigarette. I could tell it would be his final smoke at this table. "Damn right I do. She and I get it on all the time. The earth genuflects when we make love," he said, quickly making the sign of the cross on his forehead, abdomen, and shoulders. He smiled. "Come on. We're losing daylight."

Three hours later I craved movement. I had quietly calculated the facts about the past four days. Since my mother and I had left Rakertown, Tennessee, I had spent eighty six hours in vehicles, and only ten standing up or sitting down in one place. I looked down from time to time to see if my ankles had swollen again. I also needed a bathroom. Uncle Jack, however, did not plan to stop until we passed through San Diego. We had already driven around the vast sprawl of Los Angeles. I stared at the city for the hour-long passage around its suburban edge. Jack had no intention of passing straight through it. "That place is fucked up, man," he said. "Nothing like San Francisco. Man. San Francisco is like a chunk of heaven that's fallen out of the sky, while this place is nothing but a garbage heap."

I didn't know where his editorials were coming from. I knew L.A. to be the place of Hollywood, where all my favorite movies had been made. I hoped that he would have changed his mind at some point, deciding to be a grown-up with his young nephew and take me to some sights such as Paramount Studios, Disneyland, anything. There was no chance of that. He was as out of touch with Hollywood's reality as he was with any of the newest music that I and all my teenage compatriots were listening to. A few times he let me pick a station on the car radio. It only took two minutes of the Brothers Gibb singing the rousing falsetto to "Staying Alive" for my uncle to react.

"What is this shit, man? Who are those women screaming their lungs out?"

I informed him that they were men.

"MEN? Shit. Somebody cut their nuts off?"

I told him that they just happened to be the number one music group in the country, no doubt in the world. The Gibbs were the very heart of the disco movement over the planet.

"Disco? You listen to disco? That's faggot music, *sobrino*. You got to be kidding, my nephew listens to queer music," and he laughed for five miles.

Instead of changing the channel, he allowed me to listen to my music. But the Gibbs began to lose their momentum with Uncle Jack sticking his left arm out the window, imitating my hero and mentor John Travolta in his famous jutting stance. Then he started singing, shoving his Chicano-accented voice through a mean falsetto. I switched to another station. Steve Martin warbled his song "King Tut," singing about Tut being buried with a donkey, how Tut was a great honkey; that Tut was born in Arizona but he had moved to Babylonia. I found this to be the highest essence of comedy and music blended together. Yet I knew it would not withstand my uncle's caustic mockery and turned off the radio.

"Hey man, come on. You can listen to the music."

"I don't want to listen to it. You go ahead," I said, looking out the window, my arms crossed over my chest. "Turn on your damn wolf music."

"Hey, they're called Los Lobos. They're a great band, man. They got heart. They're new on the block. I once heard them play in a small bar in San Jose, and I thought, shit, this band's gonna go big. Well, maybe not as big as your disco kings," he said as he turned the radio back on, "but this is their first album. It's great."

He plugged the cassette in. As we drove around San Diego, Los Lobos sang songs that I could not understand at all. All of the songs were in Spanish, something about a thing called a *cuchipe*, something else about an iguana, and a slew of other words and phrases that, no matter how many times Uncle Jack flipped over the cassette and played the other side, I could not decipher. I scrunched down into the upholstery and tried to push myself through the car and onto the street. It was not possible. San Diego's sprawl disappeared behind us, yet another city that I would not know, not the way my uncle made for his destination.

He took a two lane road south. More signs were written in Spanish. At one point I wondered if we had already crossed over into Mexico. Yet there were reminders that we were still in California. Plenty of signs were still in English, and a few gringos walked the streets and drove cars. Yet the farther we drove, through tiny towns named Jamul, Dulzura, and Potrero, the songs bashing out of Uncle Jack's rattling stereo player became more fitting. I looked out at the dark-skinned people, dark like my mother, others different shades of lightness and brown, most all of them with black hair, some older men with streaks of white, who sat on benches and chatted with one another, their legs crossed leisurely as they watched me and the rest of the world go by. Women spoke and laughed over a piece of gossip. Children kicked soccerballs or cheap, plastic balls over dusty parks. With the windows down, and between Lobos songs, I could hear them yelling, *"¡Ya es tu turno. Dame la pelota, pues, me toca a mí!"*

I brushed my hair back over my head. I knew that my hair had not withstood any of the day, lacking in spray, gaining in dust and sweat. Yet I was tired, and for a brief moment my hair did not matter. There was no one from my school here who would see me. As far as I could see, there were no teenagers around here who were worthy of my concern. I stared out at this world that was gradually becoming more and more Latino, less and less a place where people like the Bee Gees and myself would feel comfortable. There were places in the world, I realized, where the Bee Gees did not reign. There were corners of the world that could strip me of the last slivers of control.

In the town of Potrero, Uncle Jack drove directly to a small garage. Two men worked under car hoods. The sign to the place was in Spanish, though it looked vaguely English: "Reparaciones de carros Jorge," then underneath, "Yo fixo todito." Being able to read this sign gave me hope. Perhaps I was not as far from my Latino roots as my family considered me to be.

"Hey Jorge, *que pasó*, man?" my uncle shouted into the garage.

"*Nada*, Jack, what's happening?" Jorge raised his head from the hood and grinned. His small moustache crawled over his upper lip. He cleaned his hand of oil as best he could, then offered it to Jack. They shook hands hard, the "power shake" of all good Chicanos.

My uncle explained, "Hey, *cabrón*, I gotta go on the other side *por algunos días*. You know, *visitar a mi* lady, see how she's doing."

This sounded strange to me. I had heard Jack speak with Abuelita before. He always spoke pure Spanish with her.

"*Ricarda anduvo acá* a couple of days ago, man," answered Jorge. "She was asking about you."

"Yeah? *¿Quería verme?*"

"She just sounded more, you know, curious. '*No has visto a Jack?*' she asked, like she was surprised you haven't been around much."

"No, I've been *ocupado*. Hey, here's my *sobrino, Jorge. Salúdalo*, Tony."

Jorge smiled at me, offering me a warm handshake. He seemed kind all over. "How you doing, Tony? Good to meet you." He said not one word to me in Spanish. I supposed, sadly, that he could see the strain of gringo in me. I knew that sight many times dictated which language people used.

"Yeah so, Jorge, could I leave my 'Stang here for awhile? I don't want the *chota* looking at it, *queriendo joderme, ¿sabes?*"

"*Está bien, hombre*, just park it in back, *al lado de mi casa*. But *deja a mi mujer en paz, ¿entiendes?*" admonished Jorge, trying to look mean.

"Hey, *cabrón*, your lady is *muy fina para un hombre como yo*."

"You got that right, *compa*."

They both laughed.

We parked the car and left Jorge's place. "You always leave it here?" I asked.

"Usually. That's a Mustang, man. You know how many people want to get their hands on it? But Jorge's cool, he'll take care of it. He won't even let his kids get near it."

"But what about the bags?" I asked.

"Why else you think Jorge wants to keep the car? He knows he'll have a prize from me once we come back."

"You didn't bring any prize with you, did you?" I asked, hoping that he had.

"Shit no, man. I ain't getting caught by the border patrol. Some guys do it, but not me. Besides, I can get fixed up on the other side if I want. I got friends there who'll take care of me. But no way I'm getting in trouble with the patrol. Shit, I ain't crazy."

"What . . . what happens if you were to get caught with, with some marijuana?"

"Why, you got some on you?"

"Not at all," I said, not lying.

"Well, on this side, you could get a fine, or maybe a few days in a local jail, along with a record. But on the other side, the *chota* will fuck you until your ass is blood red. They'll do what they want, throw your dick in jail, interrogate you, make you practically disappear. You won't be heard from again. And that's just for weed. You get caught with something bigger, and, well, I don't want to think about it."

The mushroom burned against the underside of my nipple.

Uncle Jack kept talking, "No. No reason to take such chances. Hey, I want to live."

Just toss the thing on the street, I told myself, *just flick it over into the bushes.* But I did not listen to that. I am not sure why. Part of it was wanting to, at some point, experience this piece of fungus that even my Uncle Jack would not allow. That, in itself, said a great deal. The man without moral borders telling me, his innocent nephew, not to do something was to be the greatest demonstration of teenage rebellion that I could imagine. I had quietly planned to consume the button sometime during our trip, perhaps later at night, when the world slept, so I could experience the journey that Jack so obviously respected and, in some ways, feared. It was just one mushroom, so it undoubtedly could not do much to me. I pictured it as a quiet, short trip, a sort of quick dip into that unknown, forbidden world. I was sure that it would have been akin to drinking maybe half a six pack of Dad's beers. That would have been something. I hated to part with the little piece of fungus.

I also feared to. I knew that he would see me stick my fingers in my pocket and toss it to one side. Then he would question me. He would become like any other adult, breathing down my throat, asking me what I was up to. I would, for lack of better phrases, get in trouble. So the mushroom stayed in my pocket.

"How are we going to cross the border, Uncle Jack?"

"By bus. There are buses about every hour or so. We should be at Ricarda's house in a couple of hours."

He sounded excited. I was afraid to speak, knowing my cramped voice would give me away. I thought about going into a bathroom and sneaking the mushroom into my wallet. It would get squashed, but at least it would be well hidden. Then again, if the border guards wanted my identification, and I pulled my wallet out, and the piece flipped out along with my driver's license . . . then I thought about using my underwear . . .

"Come on. There's a bus leaving now." Uncle Jack ran to a window at the dilapidated terminal building and bought two tickets. I had to jog to keep up with him. I thought the rush would take care of my predicament and toss the mushroom out of my pocket. It didn't. I boarded with the button still resting in my shirt.

Uncle Jack had acted as if the bus was ready to leave immediately. It was not. We got a seat together. The bus driver waited until the aisle between the seats filled with standing passengers. Half an hour later the bus pulled away, the roar of its engine dragging its weight forward.

I started clicking my teeth and knocking my forehead with my knuckles. I must have done it for a long while.

"What are you doing, *sobrino,* playing baseball?"

"What?" I stopped in mid-teeth clicking.

"All this shit," he waved his hand around his head while moving his jaw from side to side. "What is all that? You look nervous."

"Oh it's just . . . nothing."

Though he stared at me, either concerned or disgruntled, he said nothing.

I saw a sign to Tecate. Uncle Jack had mentioned earlier that Ricarda lived south of that town. Then another sign, regarding Mexico, waited for us. It was about to happen. I was about to cross the border. I was about to get caught. I was to die within the next few days, with Mexican policemen grinning over me as they cut off my testicles. I imagined Gato and his men, and Chucho's fingers flying. It was more than enough to transfer such memories to imagination.

We approached the border. A man dressed in a white shirt with an open collar and jean pants greeted the bus driver through the driver's open window. They spoke little. The white shirted man looked down the bus at us. He waved the bus on.

We were in Mexico.

A breath rushed out of me.

Uncle Jack glanced at me. "What's the matter with you?"

"Nothing. I've just . . . never crossed the border before."

"Oh. Yeah. This is Mexico. *Bienvenidos."* He grinned at me. Then he surprised me. He ran his fingers roughly through my hair.

In Tecate we had to board another bus that took us south along Highway 3. I had stared at the landscape for awhile, comparing it to the dry desert land we had just left on the other side of the border. There were no real differences. Borders, I learned, did nothing to the earth. I also quickly turned sleepy. I woke when Uncle Jack poked me and said, "Hey. Wake up. Time to get off."

I looked outside, but saw no town, no city, not even a village. Nothing but a few dry rolling hills, scraggly bushes that grew every few feet apart from one another, and a slight wind.

"Where are we?" I asked.

"Close to Ricarda's house. Come on."

I followed him, but not very willingly.

We lowered from the bus. It drove off, leaving a fat tail of dust.

"There's nothing out here," I said.

"No, not here. But just over that hill about a mile is Macizo. It's a little village. Come on."

I looked at him as he turned toward the hill. "We've got to *walk*?" I said.

"Yeah. What's the matter? It's just a mile."

A mile. A *mile*.

He walked up the hill. I stood about thirty seconds, shook my head, then followed him.

"Aren't there any roads to this place?"

"Yeah, but the bus doesn't go that way. At least, not the bus we took. We could have taken another bus straight to Macizo, but it wouldn't have left Tecate until sometime tonight. This way we'll get there a lot sooner."

I did not understand this logic at all. Yet I had not been given a choice. I followed.

Twenty minutes later we walked toward a group of adobe buildings. I looked at them as if staring through a haze of mirages. It was not my image of an oasis. The buildings stood haphazardly, strewn along one dirt road that ran through the middle of what my uncle called a town. As it was after lunch, few people appeared. We were the only two individuals who walked underneath the afternoon sun. I supposed that everyone was taking a siesta. I heard a radio playing

Mexican music, yet nothing like the songs that I for the past twenty-four hours had been forced to memorize.

We entered the boundaries of the village. Uncle Jack crossed the road and headed straight toward a specific building that had a sign dangling above its door: *"Refrescos."* He walked ahead of me, his black boots kicking up tiny clouds of dust. *"'Ey, ¿Dónde está mi corazón?"* he belted out before reaching the house.

"No hay corazón aquí, pendejo, porque un corazón que espera a Juan Villalobos es un corazón tronchado."

Uncle Jack laughed at the loud, mean words that emanated from the store. It was a woman's voice. I understood nothing of what she had said. But I could hear the acid of rancor.

I caught up with him. "What did she say?"

Jack had his hands on his small hips. "Oh, it's her way of saying she loves me. 'Ey honey, *vuelvo a verte, no me niegues así."*

"Te niego hasta el carajo," said the voice.

"She doesn't sound happy to see you," I said. I looked into the door. It was dark, almost as if night had, in the middle of this hot, blinding day, penetrated the insides of the adobe. The sun that forced beads of sweat from me even while I was standing still could not reach inside.

"It's our way of greeting each other," he said. He sounded a little nervous, as if unsure himself as to the sincerity of the woman's curses. He walked a little closer.

Then the woman appeared. She moved through the inside darkness and stood in the middle of the door, her arms crossed over her chest. I could still see her chest. It was round and full. Her hips underneath the light blue skirt and white apron were solid, a little wide from her thirty-five years of life and hard labor. Yet she stood in a poise that obviously worked for Jack. He took another step forward, murmuring a few words like *"querida," "mi* honey," *"mi corazón,"* almost like a trainer approaching a capricious Doberman.

The woman's right leg then crossed in front of her left. She leaned against the doorway, her arms still crossed. A lock of thick black hair fell over to one side of her face. It looked sensual. I do not know why, but that lock pulled at something in me. She was a beautiful woman, even in her hardness, with the slight crow's feet beside her eyes.

"*Solo vengo a verte, querida,*" he said.

"*Sí. Y ¿cuántas putas has jodido en el camino?*"

"*No hay nadie que me atrape el corazón tal como tú.*"

"*Ay, pﬀﬀ.*"

This did not look good. He was obviously trying to woo her. She was not falling for it. Yet he still approached her, cooing at her with each step, saying words that sometimes I could decipher, others which lost me completely. I thought he planned to walk as closely as possible before grabbing her from behind to keep her from biting him. Yet he continued to walk until he was on the first wooden step of the three steps that stood underneath her door. As he placed his boot on the second step, the woman released her arms from her crosshold, lifted one arm up, then brought it down, so quickly that neither Uncle Jack nor I were ready for it. I had no time to shut my eyes. Jack had no time to dodge the blow. Her tightly closed fist struck him broadside against his head. His face flipped toward me. I could see his eyes begin a roll, like two marbles. His open mouth said nothing. Then her fist, which had swooped down below his skull, opened up and straightened like a thin bat as her arm reversed and slammed the back of her hand against the other side of his face. His crossed eyes disappeared from my sight.

Then she stopped. She lowered her combat arm. She stared at him while he shook his skull. I almost shut my eyes, afraid as to what he or she would do next. But neither lifted a finger to hurt the other. Jack merely reached forward, shoved his hand between her left arm and waist, took hold of her pelvis and pulled her to him. Suddenly she was on the same step as he, her arms around his neck and her mouth opening wide to his. They kissed, moving their skulls back and forth, sometimes pulling away so that their lips could suck into the other's again and their tongues could probe deeper.

I had to wait. Two minutes passed, longer than the time it took me to ask myself what the hell was going on, why did she strike him only to practically make love with him here on the street? I cleared my throat. It didn't get their attention. I shifted my shoes in the dust. They didn't hear this. Finally they came up for air, staring at each other with silent, knowing smiles. Uncle Jack turned to me.

"Hey, this is your Aunt Ricarda. *Salúdala,* Tony."

My aunt, Ricarda Guerra, lived in the back rooms of her small store in the tiny village of Macizo. She had lived there, supposedly, ever since their divorce. I never understood what brought her to this side of the border or to this little town. Neither Uncle Jack nor Aunt Ricarda gave me any explanation of their life together. I had to pick up what information I could from their conversations (which were mostly in Spanish) and from some of the memorabilia that hung on her walls. A few photos dangled from nails, with a number of them having Jack's smiling face somewhere in them. I sat on a soft couch in the shadowy back room. My aunt bent down and smiled at me. "*¿Quieres una bebida?*" she asked. I smiled at her. I was weary from the mile-long hike, but I did glance at her stretched shirt, at those perfect, brown curves. I understood the word *bebida*. She was offering me a drink.

"*Sí,* uh, *un Coca Cola, por favor.*"

"*Ah, habla un poco de español,*" she said, approvingly, to my uncle.

He laughed with a certain acid as he responded, "*Nah. Es puro pocho, pues.*"

I knew that word, *pocho.* As others in my family had, from time to time, called me that, my curiosity made me look up the word one day in a Spanish-English dictionary. *Pocho* meant a dried out, hollowed log; a piece of putrefying fruit; and a Latin American who did not speak Spanish. Uncle Jack flung the word about with added mockery. I suppose this was one of his many ways of toughening me up.

"*Ay Juan, no digas eso de tu sangre,*" she admonished him.

"*Bueno pues, es la verdad.*"

"*Sí, pero es un joven . . .*"

Their bickering did not last long. Uncle Jack grabbed her as she walked by to get my cola. She screeched, then fell into his lap. He placed his cool beer down upon the counter next to where he sat, forced her higher into his lap, and whispered into her ear. She shoved her elbow into his ribs. It was not a fake blow. Jack responded to it, his breath heaving out of his mouth. *"Déjame servir a tu sobrino, cabrón,"* she said, walking away and toward the refrigerator in the front store. When she returned, she held a frosty bottle of cola in her hand. She placed a glass upside down and over its mouth before walking up to me. Smiling again while handing me the drink, she whispered slightly, "Anything you want here, you make yourself at home to it." It was perfect English in a rolling Spanish accent. It shocked me.

"Thank you," I finally said.

She winked at me before turning away. I could not tell if it had been a sexual gesture, or one of a certain maternal nature. Then I thought, sometimes a young man was not able to distinguish the two, especially in my family of women. Then again, it did not seem necessary to distinguish.

She walked away, kissed Uncle Jack on the cheek, then turned toward another room. I heard her picking up some pans. I glanced through the open door and saw her light a match and place it over a gas stove. She placed a thick, iron pan over it, then got to work on a meal.

Jack looked at me, smiling. "That's right, *sobrino*. You make yourself at home here. Your aunt Ricarda will treat you right. She's the best. You smell that? She's cooking *chorizo*. Damn, I'm hungry. You?"

"Yeah, I could eat."

"Damn right. Hey, maybe you want to get cleaned up. You want to take a shower? It's outside in the back yard." He motioned for me to follow him. We walked passed the kitchen where Aunt Ricarda was stirring the *chorizo* in a thin layer of oil while also flipping tortillas on an iron plate. We walked out to a large back yard. A rickety fence that stood just above my shoulders separated it from the neighboring houses' yards. Though there was no grass growing in the area, the dirt itself looked as if it had been recently swept. The ground actually looked clean. There was other foliage to take the place of a grassy yard. A few trees stood alongside the fence, and a number of bushes had been planted next to them, breaking up the dull brown look of the fence itself.

Over in the far right corner grew several plants of various colors, some of their leaves thick and wide, looking as if they had just been recently watered. The entire back yard looked well kept and clean, and that corner stood out as a multicolored burst of energy, a neatly tended garden of flowers, stems, leaves, and blooms.

"What's that over there?" I asked, pointing to the arrangement of flowers.

"What? Oh, that's nothing, just a little flower garden of your aunt's. Here's the shower over here," said Uncle Jack, walking me to the left side of the yard. "It only puts out cold water, but in this heat it feels great." I looked at the square cement and block cubicle. A lone metal pipe arched just above the wall. He pulled back the cloth curtain. It was simple enough: shower head, one switch, and a drain in the cement floor.

"I'll get you some soap and shampoo from the front," he said. "Over here is where you can dress." He motioned to an open area of the yard, right next to the shower. A small mirror hung from a drooping nail that had been forced into the cement wall. I looked around, realizing that I would be dressing right out in the open. He caught my look and smiled. "Don't worry. Nobody will see you, except maybe the neighbors. Hey, you need some other clothes. I'm sure these stink to high heaven, just like mine. Ricarda's got some of my clothes in her bedroom. I'll put some jeans and a shirt over here." He pointed to a wooden bench.

I thanked him. He walked away and toward the kitchen. I took my wallet and the mushroom from my pockets, folded the billfold over the dry fungus, and placed them both on one end of the bench. I ducked behind the cloth curtain and shed my clothes, tossing them through the curtain and onto the wooden bench. At first I cringed when thinking about turning on the water. After that first splash, Uncle Jack's words proved correct. It was delicious. The water hitting me seemed to run through my skin and drench my very insides, cleansing the dust from the road off my chest, abdomen, my liver, stomach, heart. The coolness slapped against my dried out thoughts, waking the memory of Aunt Ricarda's expanded shirt, and making for a healthy erection. Getting a hard-on while taking a cold shower was the epitome of a teenager's prurience. I was proud.

"Here, I've got some jeans and a shirt for you, plus some underwear," my uncle called from the other side of the curtain. I turned away instinctively, afraid that he would open up the curtain and see me. "There's a towel too, son," he added. "I'll put your old clothes in your room. Ricarda will wash them tomorrow."

At first I panicked, then remembered that I had folded the mushroom in my wallet. I looked through the curtain and saw that he left my wallet alone. I thanked him, then watched him walk away. I watched him until he disappeared behind the kitchen door. I was confused, but thankful.

Halfway through my shower I wished I had done some of the exercises he had shown me early that morning. I promised myself to do them the following day, perhaps falling into the same discipline that he had taught himself. I rinsed, then peeked through the curtain. No one stood outside. The yard was vacant. I looked at the bench. Alongside the clothes lay a neatly folded towel. My old, dirty clothes were gone.

I grabbed the towel. It smelled clean and no doubt had been dried by hanging on a line. It even unfolded stiffly. I wrapped it around my waist, then tried to slap away my erection. I stepped outside, put on the underwear and jeans, then buttoned the shirt up. It was a jean shirt, much like the one that he was wearing today.

After putting on clean socks and my tennis shoes, I approached the mirror. A thick-bristled brush lay on a wooden shelf. I took it in my hand, hesitated a moment, then thought that considering how well kept everything else was (the clothes, the towel, the bleached-out floor of the shower), my aunt's brush no doubt was just as clean. I brushed my hair back, regretting the absence of a blow dryer. Then I looked at myself in the mirror. I had combed my hair straight back, hoping that it would hold in that position until it dried. In doing so, I had combed it in the same style as that of my uncle's. My thick black hair stayed in that position with no help from a dryer. I knew it would not remain that way for long, but for the moment it looked perfect. I looked at the jean shirt in the mirror, then unbuttoned one buttom lower from my neck, just like he did. I sucked in a breath. I forced my stomach into a fake hardness. After placing my wallet in these jeans and the mushroom button in my shirt pocket, I walked to the kitchen.

No one was there. The flames of the stove had been extinguished. On the table two plates had been half eaten, along with two half-consumed beers. One full plate of food was set before a chair. I took this to be mine. I heard no movement in the house, and thought that perhaps they were out somewhere, or that Aunt Ricarda was tending to a customer up front while Uncle Jack walked about the streets. I was about to walk up front and check, when the smell and the appearance of a full plate beckoned me to sit down. I scooped up *chorizo* and egg with sautéed onion onto one half-folded tortilla and shoved it into my mouth. The drip of grease from the meat closed over my tongue. I barely stopped to glance at a small pile of Mexican magazines, most of them back copies of *La Voz*. I flipped through one as I slowed into the second half of my meal.

The sun was setting. It was strangely quiet in the house. There was only one lightbulb hanging in this half-closed kitchen, and it was not on. The sun's last rays pushed through the wide cracks in the wall, making a few shadows of the open boards on the opposite side. The shadows crossed over a calendar that displayed a well-formed blonde white woman wearing a bathing suit. Why, I wondered, would my aunt have such a poster up on her kitchen wall?

Then I heard a noise. It came from the front of the house, or somewhere in the middle.

I finished my meal, wiped my face with a cloth napkin, then stood and walked to the door. It was even darker there, though I could still see the shapes of the small table in the hall, the wooden chairs in the room where Ricarda had first served me a cola, and the panes of the glassless windows. I walked through the hall and toward the front, expecting to see my aunt tending to some customers. The front doors were closed. The crossbeam had been placed over the door, acting as a wooden lock. She had closed shop for the day. This was not where the sound came from.

Then I heard it again. It sounded strange, yet terribly familiar. It copied, gutturally, all the sounds that I had imagined with all the girls I had loved before (in my head). I, of course, followed it, stiffening immediately as I did.

I turned a corner. Looking up, I noticed that the stucco walls inside the house did not reach all the way up to the ceiling. If I stood on a chair, I would be able to peek over the top of the walls and see the other side. I did not do this, of course. I followed the sounds, one of his followed by one of hers, then one of his again. Then hers. I got as close to it as I could, then came up to a wall.

The door to this room was closed. I could see the glow of lights from the crack below the wooden entrance. Yet unlike other doors and walls in this home, such as the ones outside in the outdoor kitchen or the curtain that barely kept one's privacy within the shower, this door was solid. No way of seeing through a tiny crack. So naturally, I had to resort to the chair idea.

Just behind me was a wooden one. As the grunting moved like waves of heat through the bedroom, I carefully picked the chair directly up from its four legs and moved it to this wall. It took a good minute to place it down evenly upon the floor. Even I didn't hear the legs touching the ground. It took me a full three minutes to get up on it. Then I looked slowly over the edge and used only one eye to gaze down.

A lone table lamp burned to one side. I first saw a huge tub of water big enough for a man to fit in. Then I followed a recent splash of water toward a used towel that lay upon the floor. I saw the jeans, the shirt, the dress, underwear, bra, shoes, socks. Then I saw the bed. Then I saw her.

She was glorious. It was not only her completely uncovered chest that snatched up my eyes, nor the curve of her abdomen that took me. It was the way in which her brown arms pushed against the pillows, as if some invisible being held them there while sitting atop her, making her strain to lift them up. As I watched, her breasts filled before me, her very nipples stood up like two tiny—then, after awhile, not so tiny—erections. I had never seen, nor imagined, this before. But even her arms punching against the pillows was not what wrapped me in fascination. It was her face. That face which had lowered down to me, smiling and whispering in clear English to make myself at home, now writhed as if in a strange pain, only to smile while her tongue licked out and sought something. As if knowing this, a rugged brown arm pushed out from under the one thin blanket and rubbed up against her abdomen, breasts, and neck, and found that tongue. Ricarda pulled his finger in with her lips and sucked it hard.

My legs buckled. I thought I would tip the chair over, then give myself away by slamming the two legs back down. I composed myself and looked again. The sheet had been flipped off. My uncle's head bobbed inside her thighs. I sucked in a breath, then covered my mouth with my hands, afraid that my loss of control over my body would give me away. It did not. Jack lifted up, flipped her around and massaged her back and her buttocks, then lowered his head down to the crack of her round, brown ass while flicking his tongue and, Jesus! I almost cried out, no way! No way! I thought he was bullshitting me in the car, talking about sticking his tongue down there. But there he went. And then she went, obviously, the way she started balling the pillow inside her fist and barely muffling a scream. For a moment I thought it was over. But he didn't give her much time to come down from her own yelps. He flipped her once more onto her back, lifted up her butt with his forearms, opened his mouth wide and clamped his lips onto her sex. He held her pelvis suspended. Still, her waist, thighs, and pelvis shoved and pivoted for five uncontrollable minutes, wiping his face with herself, until she yelped again, until her voice melted and cooed.

My legs ached.

A few seconds later he lay upon the bed. He placed her on top, holding her directly over him. His hard shaft disappeared under her. My lungs responded to this, especially as she rocked up and down on him, her hair flipping about. He held his hands on her breasts, then her calves, then her waist, sometimes smiling, sometimes cringing. He kept his sounds low, staring straight at her as he pumped.

Then his eyes darted. His gaze rose up through the air of the room and slapped up against my eyes. They held there for two complete pumps, burning into my voyeurism. Then his eyes turned away and focused upon her once more.

I at first did not move, frozen in the fact of being caught. A few seconds later I lowered from the chair, placed the chair where it had been, and ran. I did not know where to run to. I passed a room where a small lamp was burning. Inside I saw my dirty clothes, hanging over another wooden chair. This was no doubt meant to be my room.

I walked inside and closed the door. "Oh shit," I muttered, "He's gonna kill me, he's gonna be mad as hell . . ." Then I thought about how he reacted. Instead of jumping up from the bed screaming and telling his woman to cover herself and hide away from my half-hidden eyes before bolting out the door while wrestling on his jeans so as to beat the shit out of me, he just kept going. He did not break any stride. I started to wonder if he had seen me. Then I knew that, there was no doubt, our eyes had connected. He had seen me all right. He just didn't let me get in the way. Still, I couldn't help but think he would pay me back later, maybe in just a few moments, after they finished.

But they would not finish just yet. Their sounds died down in about twenty minutes. Then they started up again. The whole house seemed to get louder this time. It ended. Then a third match began. I had to close my eyes tight from either fear of his reprisal or angst over the fact that this vicarious experience was ripping my nuts apart. I thought of masturbating, maybe doing it three times in a row, but I did not know when he might come walking through the door. Yet blowing my rocks out seemed the healthiest thing to do. If only I had something to blow into, some tissue paper, toilet paper, maybe a soft newspaper or paper bag. I lay on the bed and thought about it, thought about them, thought and rethought about Ricarda's round body and her writhing, the way she clenched his finger between her lips, the way her arms pressed against the bed. I raised my own fingers over my jeans and the jean shirt, touching myself through my clothes, rousing up the miniscule shots of electricity just underneath my skin, hoping that my imagination, as overwhelming as it was becoming, would somehow explode into this reality and produce a perfect copy of Ricarda on top of me. My fingers seemed to follow their own course, over my abdomen and my chest. Then my fingers felt the large mushroom button in my pocket.

So I thought about it. I remembered that, though I could get all hornied up while smoking the grass the night previously, I could also just turn my thoughts slightly another way, and my body's responses would follow. I could go from a deep-set libido to an all encompassing wonder of the hotel's panelling in a half second. To eat this mushroom possibly meant to escape the anguish that I now found myself in, hearing and remembering the graphic moments of a perfect, repetitive fuck that was happening mere feet from me. It would also have the extra perk of taking me on a unique, unexplored ride.

It was nighttime. No doubt my aunt and uncle would fall asleep in each other's naked arms. So I ate the button.

The taste, I could most appropriately say, was like shit. Dried up shit. The texture was that of a spongy fungus, which my father had always taught me never to eat while hiking through the forests. I almost spat the thing out, but decided to withstand the taste until my saliva broke it down into wet crumbs, ones that could more readily be swallowed.

I lay down and waited. Nothing happened for a number of minutes, perhaps ten. Then something did happen, but it was not in my body. Outside I could hear them talking. They were not whispering, they spoke like a happy couple. Uncle Jack was saying something in Spanish: *"Ya es su hora."* It's his time. She was not disagreeing, she just didn't sound like she wanted to do anything else at the moment. Her voice was relaxed, satisfied. His was still feisty, but not for himself. Their talk sounded as if they had come to some agreement.

Then her bedroom door opened. I panicked, knowing he would come my way to punish me for peeping over the wall. But he did not. He left the house. I heard the wooden beam get lifted off the front door. Half an hour later he returned. I almost forgot about eating the mushroom, except for the shit taste that still stuck to my gums. He rapped on the door. "'Ey, *sobrino*, you there?" He sounded friendly enough.

"Come on in," I muttered, hoping to make my voice sound relaxed, calm, and hip.

He opened the door. He had his pants on. His shirt was draped over his shoulders. I could see the curve of his hard chest through the unbuttoned clothing. "Hey, Tony. Taking it easy?"

"Yeah, just a little," I smiled, then cringed, waiting for him to slam the door open and bring his heavy finger down to my nose with an enraged, bilingual reprimand.

"Good. It's been a long day. But listen," and he turned and looked down the hallway for a second before continuing, "your Aunt Ricarda and I got a surprise for you."

"Oh? What's that?" I asked, sitting up slightly from the bed. I wondered if it were a real surprise, or a trick to get me back for looking at them. He had probably told her that I had peeked over the wall. Yet she had not sounded embarrassed.

"Oh, I think it's something you'll like." He opened the door a little wider. He was still smiling. Yet I heard no trickery in his voice.

"Well what is it?" I asked, laughing with some embarrassment mixed with curiosity.

Jack looked down at the floor for a scant second, then raised his large, dark eyes to me. "Time to lose it, *sobrino*."

"Lose what?"

He laughed, shook his head, then walked away from the door. "I'll be right back," he said.

Then I knew. I panicked more than ever, trying to wipe the taste of the mushroom from my mouth. I thought about vomiting. Yet that was too late. The mushroom was gone, absorbed into my very tissue. This I knew, for the door that he had just closed began to expand, then contract, its very wood breathing before me.

Uncle Jack's and Aunt Ricarda's surprise was named Sara. She was in her early twenties. She had long brown hair that fell over her neck and shoulders like a thick blanket of silk. She had deep brown eyes, and she smiled a lot. She spoke in Spanish, which I thought I understood, though I didn't. She called me Antonio. Sometimes it seemed that she was right on top of me, other times I felt that a great chasm had been placed between our bodies. She unfortunately had walked into my room a good half hour after I noticed that the door started to breathe. The above features were the last shreds of factual data, or what I had known to be factual data, that I could fold into my brain. Then came the breathing sensations. When my lungs filled up, so did the door's lungs, along with the walls and the expanding bed. She spoke as she undressed. I watched her clothes fall to one side of the bed. If I focused upon them, I could make them stand up and flap like giant butterfly wings before flying out the slightly open window into the stars that barely shown into my room, stars that I knew were billions of light years away. I thought about how light I felt, and if I pondered it too much I would float through the crack in that window and flip into the air of this little town and through the silent gaps of the galaxy, so I decided not to think about that. I focused upon her. In the moment she brought her thick lips to mine, I thought, "I will break the buzz," knowing that the power of my almighty penis was known to break through anything. It only recently broke through the beating of a cold shower. It was invincible. So when her lips touched mine, I felt its magnitude expand in my pants, and I knew that it, my very own beloved member, would save me from this mistake, the error of eating a hallucinogenic fungus right before losing my virginity. I knew how the body worked. I had read two tomes of *The Joy of Sex* while visiting Knoxville's public library. I knew that the hormones in a teenage boy were not unlike the very flames of hell that flashed uncontrollably through a youth's body. Thus I had full confidence in my balls, knowing how they would shake the rest of my muscles and bones from the oncoming buzz of the mushroom. The fungus was no match for my horniness, especially as she unbuttoned my shirt and ran her thin fingers over my chest while continuing to slowly, thickly kiss me. Then her fingers ran down my soft abdomen toward my belt-line and I thought, this is it, this is what I have dreamt of for so long, ever since my first orgasm from the time I masturbated into my mother's old, thick brown furry bedspread, the one that I always had had my eye on all through eighth grade, though I wasn't sure why, until that fateful evening when my parents had been out and I decided to watch "All in the Family" naked, lying upon that blanket under which I had placed a pile of pillows. As I watched Archie Bunker call his son-in-law a meathead and his wife a dingbat, I waited until Archie's daughter walked into the room before moving my hips over the covered blanket, and low and behold look what happened! Just what's happening now, only then the blanket invited my prick deeper into it, the fur enveloped my shaft and pulled me in and before I knew it something down there, all through my pelvis and thighs, shook. Just like it's shaking now, only now, as I shake, I see this woman named Sara above who speaks in another language, one that is deeply familiar, yet unrecognizable. Yet she speaks, she speaks, and I wonder what she's saying, if she's admiring my young, sixteen year old flesh, if she's talking about possibilities, how she would perhaps like to run away with me. Or perhaps she's just reciting recipes. The thought of recipes causes me to turn flaccid; just like the grass yesterday, a mere thought can take it all away, take me somewhere else, plunging a distance between us, so even though she's sitting right on top of my pelvis, I feel as if a chasm has fallen between Sara and me. I reach up to touch her, help her take her blouse off, her bra, yet my fingers do not follow complete orders, for they are experiencing the air of the chasm. She laughs, and the laugh echoes, bouncing off the stucco walls of this room, bouncing over the open space between the wall and the ceiling, to where no doubt my aunt and uncle are listening on the other side; perhaps that is their payback, to hear me in my first time. I think of him, what he did to that sexy aunt, how he did it. I look up at Sara's nakedness. There she is, fully nude, sitting on my jeans and rocking, calling up everything in me. There are two breasts hanging down. I reach up and squeeze them in my palms, knowing that such an act is correct, even in this new reality, even as the nipple of one squeezes between my thumb and forefinger and looks at the other nipple and asks, "What time is it? When do we get off?" Talking breasts, what a concept. Then I think more of what he did, how he lowered his head down, so I take her by her hips and try to lift her. *"Ooh, qué cosa,"* she says as I try to lift her up over my face. She laughs again, while accepting this. I stare straight into it, there, where the arch of her inner thighs spreads to my right and left below the tuft, into that certain darkness, a darkness not unlike the one that I experienced in that momentary flight between the stars upon the back of her winged clothes. I lift my face up to it. Yet that darkness is as deep and as infinite as the sky, something I did not know. It pulls me into its field, where I float momentarily, confused, thinking, where will this take me? Where am I going? Then I realize, I am going back into the womb, I will be sucked into this woman's vagina where I will smack up against her cervix before wriggling through its tiny hole where I will swim into her uterus (I know these words from anatomy class; I made a B+ in it). There I will be shrunk and stuck to the wall of her womb, where I will be made to begin it all again, all this life, walking through it one more time, only this time with the knowledge, the knowledge . . . what knowledge? That knowledge. That one. In Sara's darkness, I see a figure. What is it? It is short, stout, nude. It is male, with hair blacker than mine. It turns as if to leave the uterus, and the shadow of his tiny erection cuts through the very darkness of this womb. I reach up to touch my forehead with my knuckles, but here, such repetitive prayers mean nothing. I am alone with him and his adolescent laugh. I scream, but just as the scream leaps from my mouth, Sara's infinite darkness swallows me up, closing tight her labia behind me, leaving me forgotten to that world out there, leaving me alone, in here, with him.

When I opened my eyes, I saw rays of sunlight. The sun was already hot. A bird sang, telling me it was morning. My eyelids blinked to the cracked open window. I raised my head to my surroundings. This was still my room in Aunt Ricarda's house. I was clothed only with my jeans. I looked down toward my loins. Then I looked around again. Sara was not next to me. I was alone.

I shook my head with my eyes closed, then opened them and looked at the room. The door did not breathe. It was closed and unmoving. Nor did the walls fluctuate.

I shook my head again. "Jesus, what a nightmare." Yet I knew those words were not adequate. A nightmare was a dream, a transient, subconscious fright. This had not been a nightmare. As far as I was concerned, the door, last night, had breathed. I looked at it, then stood up from the bed and approached the door, touching its inanimate wood. It did not move. I was sure it had last night, as I was sure that I had been sucked into that woman's vagina and had spent the night inside her sexual organs. I could not remember exactly everything after that, though I did remember screaming.

I walked out. Down the hallway, toward the kitchen. At the table my uncle sat, drinking a cup of coffee and smoking. He had already showered, I could tell by the sweep of his wet hair. I also knew that he had no doubt gone through his morning ritual of exercises. Aunt Ricarda was not around.

"Hey, *sobrino*. Come on in. Let me get you some coffee." He smiled at me. It was, for lack of a better word, endearing.

I sat down at the table. He poured me a cup. I reached for the sugar and the tiny pot of cream. I knew that he was staring at me as he sat down to my left. "How you feeling today?" he finally asked.

"I'm fine. I think."

"What happened last night, man?"

"I'm not sure, I . . ." I hesitated, not knowing which way to go, whether or not to confess about my eating the mushroom. Yet I knew it was inevitable that I would confess. I obviously had acted in such a way that gave me up. "Can you, tell me what happened . . . what I did?"

"Shit, man, your aunt and I were sitting in here, drinking a beer, while you and Sara were going at it. Well, supposedly going at it. Then we heard you screaming, and you just wouldn't stop. We ran in. Sara was in one corner of the room, shivering and putting on her clothes. You were on top of the bed, staring like you had seen a fucking monster or something, man. I had to hold you down onto the bed, and I kept talking to you, telling you it's okay, it's okay. Your aunt took Sara home. The girl was pretty shook up, said that you freaked out right in the middle of it. So I kept talking to you until you calmed down some. But I stayed up with you, because you were muttering something about some guy named Barry, Barry, then you'd start screaming again."

I was dumping sugar into my coffee when he said the name. My facial muscles punched my tear ducts.

"Man, let me ask you . . . Did you sneak some of that mushroom yesterday?"

I confessed that I did. Then I started to cry.

"Hey, Tony. Don't worry about it, son. Listen, I ain't going to chew your ass off for that. Hell, I've done enough stuff myself. Who am I to get down on you? Don't cry, Tony, come on." He slapped me on the shoulder. It hurt.

"The only thing is, eating mushrooms isn't something you should do alone. That stuff's all right, but you need some, what you call it?

Supervision, yeah. Somebody who knows how to use it. Otherwise you're tripping out by yourself, and it can get wild, like I guess it did with you last night. It won't kill you or anything, unless you get in a car and start driving around, or if you got a gun in the house. Then it could be really dangerous." He chuckled slightly. He sounded glad that he had not lost me.

"So, who's this Barry character?" he asked again, and again tears fell out from the corners of my eyes.

I remained silent. He waited a long minute before saying anything. "Seems like this Barry guy really fucked with you somehow. What, some asshole at school?"

It was then that I told him. I told him more than I told Janice. I told him everything, how Barry would beat me, how he would walk into my room naked, how I would lie there, hoping, praying to God that he would not touch me, asking God what to do if he did. I stared forward at the table as the words and the story dribbled from my mouth. Tears streamed down my face. Snot blocked my nostrils. Then I went all the way, figuring, what the hell? All my other relatives knew about the knife wound. I wept uncontrollably. He shifted in his seat upon hearing that news. I cleaned my nose with my sleeve, then barely glanced at him with my ruined face. He did not interrupt me once. He waited at least one full minute after my final words before commenting.

"So this fucker tried to rape you?" he finally said. "And you had to live with this bastard? Oh shit, man," and he turned his face away, then turned back to me. "Your mother doesn't know any of this? They send you to a school away from home, for you to get sexually molested? God damn that shit, man . . ."

He turned away again. He stood up and walked to the stove for more coffee. As he passed me by, he put his hand on my shoulder, squeezing it, then patting it. When he came back, he broke from his silence, as if a thought had come to him. "You want to cut this guy, Tony?"

"What?" I asked, through sniffles.

"Cut him. You want to hurt this Barry fucker?"

"I don't know . . . why?"

"I'll drive to Tennessee with you tonight, man. We'll go right up to his house, walk right by his fucking lawyer dad and slice the boy's dick off."

I mumbled that, no, I didn't think that was a good idea.

"Well you got to do something, man. This guy tried to take something from you."

"Yeah, but he didn't, he didn't do it."

"You sure?"

"Yes, I'm sure!" I was defensive. "I remember he, he walked away. I was praying. Somebody said something, and he walked away."

"What do you mean somebody said something?"

"Just that. I don't know. Maybe he said something . . . or maybe I did. I don't remember. But I do know that he left my room. Then he beat the shit out of me the next day."

Jack said nothing at first, studying what I had just said. "Fine. He didn't touch you. But he still fucked with your skull."

"What do you mean?"

"Just that. Here you were, trying to love a woman last night, and this guy was waiting for you on the other end. In your head. It's not the mushroom's fault that you went nuts last night. That was Barry's fault. The mushroom just made everything real."

I still did not understand.

Jack looked down at the dirt floor of the kitchen, then looked back up at me. "That button you ate last night, Tony, it tripped you. You went places. I know what it's like. It's not like alcohol, which just makes you drunk. And it's not grass either. Grass relaxes you out, makes you feel easy," he held his hands out. "Mushrooms show you shit that you may not know is there."

By the way he responded to my facial expressions, he knew that I still did not understand. He was right. I had never heard him speak this way before. It was as if my Uncle Jack, the man known for the essence of a highly hedonistic life, had taken on someone else's vocabulary, as well as a certain understanding of psychology.

"Look, what I'm saying is this," he said. "You just 'fessed up to me about this guy Barry. And you say you don't want to take out anything on him, you don't want to do any sort of revenge. That's cool, I can respect that. But you got to do something about him still fucking you. Up here," he popped his skull with the tip of his index finger several times. "You got to get him out of here."

"How do I do that?" I asked, still sniffling.

"We can do it, Tony," he said, leaning in slightly. "I've got a friend just outside of town who can help you."

"Yeah? Who's that?"

"His name's Chicolino. He's a friend of the family's. Well, a distant friend. He was married to La Chucharrona, you remember her?"

I thought about the name, then remembered that it was the old woman who had prayed for me with the multicolored candles a few days ago. Great, I thought, even my damned uncle is going religious on me. I must have rolled my eyes.

"Hey, what's that look? You don't even know what I'm proposing, man. What's the matter with La Chucharrona?"

"Nothing, it's just that . . . she prayed over me the other day, before I saw you."

"Oh. With the candles? That's not really praying, Tony. It's a form of, well, it's like an *adivinación*. You know, kind of telling the future, but not really."

"She was talking about God, and man . . . something about men dying and God dying . . . I don't know, Uncle Jack. I'm not much for praying now."

"I'm not talking about praying, Tony!" He laughed. "I'm talking about getting ripped."

"What?" I looked at him.

"Yeah. Chicolino's got some stuff like that mushroom you ate."

"No, Uncle Jack, I'll never eat that stuff again!" I pushed the chair back slightly.

"I think you better. If you don't, the mushroom that's in you will work the shit out of you again."

"What, what do you mean?" I tightened in the chair.

"I mean that you had just enough to show you your friend Barry. But you didn't really rip through. You just went nuts. It took me two hours to calm you down, man. You've got to finish it. Chicolino can help you do that."

I continued to tell him that I would never again, as long as I lived, eat any form of mushroom. The experience of last night was worse than any roller coaster ride, any falling off a high tower, any jumping into a lake from a high diving board.

Uncle Jack let me finish my complaints. Then he stood up. "Come on. Chicolino's house is a good five miles away. I'll tell Ricarda that we'll be home tomorrow." With that, he slapped me on the back. It hurt again. The pain itself told me that I had little choice in the matter.

Don Chicolino wore white pants, a white cotton shirt, and no shoes. His hair was completely white. His skin was a deep brown, like hardwood. His clothes were old, well worn and washed hundreds of times. He also wore an off-white hat. I could not help but think of a Mexican Mark Twain, without a tie, with the collar open wide over his dark brown collarbone and his thin, barrel chest. He looked a hundred years old. I was wrong on two accounts. Later Uncle Jack told me that Chicolino was Guatemalan, not Mexican; and he was one hundred and two years old.

Uncle Jack and Don Chicolino embraced. The old man chuckled as my large uncle enveloped him with a hug. They spoke, but I did not try to decipher their Spanish. My uncle had just forced me to walk what he said was a five mile hike, what I figured was more like fifteen.

Though it had been morning when we left Ricarda's store, the days' heat had already begun. I had sweat through my shirt and jeans. I regretted my last look at Aunt Ricarda. She had offered me a cola from her store, which I did not accept, as I had just eaten breakfast. She kissed me on the cheek and whispered *"Cuídate"* into my ear, then a harsher, almost threatening *"Cuídalo a él"* to my uncle, who only mumbled back to her, *"Ya, ya."* I could tell she was concerned for me. I could not discern whether it was for what had happened last night or for what was about to happen to me today.

"Tony, this is Don Chicolino. *Salúdalo."* I obeyed, forcing a smile over my sweating face. The old man's hand in mine felt like a large, warm, dried out prune stuffed with mahogany. He obviously felt the sweat in my palm, for he made a comment about it, something about a young horse like me not being able to handle the heat.

The two men spoke several more minutes as Don Chicolino invited us into his shack of a house. The roof was made of tin. The walls were adobe, which I hoped would help cool the house down. But that tin roof, I knew, would leave us cooking.

Surprisingly, the inside of the one-room house was much cooler than the outside. The low ceiling, built of wood, separated us from the baking tin above. That, along with the thick, old, crumbling walls of adobe, helped to create an arid, cool room. The old man motioned to me to take a wooden chair. I looked around. The dark walls were mostly bare, except for an animal skull that hung from a nail on one wall. I figured it was a steer, judging from its horns. Very little filled the house except three chairs, an old, dusty table, the skull, and the necessary appliances for cooking. An old Coleman stove, well-used, sat in one corner of another tiny table. A coffee pot sat on top of it. Don Chicolino lit the stove and covered the flames with a pot. As he and Uncle Jack spoke, the water boiled. The old man dropped spoonfuls of instant coffee into three old, stained cups. He poured the water, then dumped sugar into each cup before handing them to us. Don Chicolino did little talking. It was Uncle Jack who had moved their conversation from that of light chatting outside about the weather and how long it had been since he had last visited here to the reason for our coming today. I heard a few of the words regarding my situation. *"Un joven . . . jodió a mi sobrino . . ."* I could not understand all, though I knew it meant something like "Some other teen has fucked up my nephew." I could not help but think that Jack was telling him the story in its entirety. Don Chicolino did not seem shocked. He shook his head from time to time, listening, saying only, *"Ya . . . sí . . . mmm hhmmm . . . Ay . . ."* Uncle Jack and I sat on the same side of the table, while Don Chicolino sat opposite us. He never interrupted. He did not speak until Uncle Jack finished the tale.

"Entonces, ¿busca a Mescalito, pues?"

"No, no creo . . . no está preparado para Mescalito."

"Por eso, no le quieres dar peyote."

"No."

"Entonces, ¿para qué los hongos?"

"Para que pueda enfrentar al pendejo que anda en su corazón. No puede vivir ahora. Se cortó su muñeca luego, pues . . ."

I was not sure what Jack said, but I did see him quietly make a quick movement of his left index finger slicing over his right wrist. Goddamn, I thought; I couldn't tell anybody in my family anything without them, within minutes, having to tell somebody else. Now even this old Indian man, who I barely knew, would know that I was some sort of loony, having tried to commit suicide.

"Ya pues," said Chicolino. *"Quería tranquilizarse. Que lástima. Pero sí, los hongos, con tal que tú estés a su lado, Juan."*

"Sí, voy yo. Sin comerlos. Me quedo con él."

"Vaya pues." With that, the old man stood up quickly from the table, much more quickly than I thought possible for an elder his age. He walked to a far corner of the room. He had his back to us, so I could not see what he was doing. He looked as if he were filling up a bag with small objects.

Uncle Jack and I watched him. Sometimes Jack would look down at the dirt floor, as if being reverent in some way.

I finally asked, "What did you two talk about?" Then quickly added, "You told him everything, didn't you?"

"Of course."

"Why did you do that?"

"Hey, Tony, you want to get out of this, don't you?"

"I can get out of it fine without any help from a witch doctor."

"Tony, you watch your mouth." He hit my back. "Don Chicolino is one of the wisest men I know. He's taught me a lot about life."

"Yeah? Like what?" Then I mumbled, but still loud enough, "Like how to get high all the time? Seems that's all you know how to do."

At first he said nothing. I braced my body for another paternal blow. Yet he did not hit me. I could, however, feel that steely stare slamming up against my head. Then he turned and said to Don Chicolino, *"Con su permiso, Don Chicolino, tengo que hablar con este malcriado un momentito."*

"Vaya pues," said the old man. He didn't even turn around.

Uncle Jack grabbed the full of my upper arm. "Hey, what's up?" I asked. He lifted me from the table. He locked my soft arm in his grip as easily as if snatching up a large screwdriver during one of his electrical jobs. He walked me outside. Out in the heat of the beating sun, he pushed me away, then released me. I complained with grunts and a few words, but with little else. I turned. It felt as if he were on top of me. He placed his open hand on my chest and shoved me. Although it looked as if he had used little force, his movement knocked me down to the ground.

"Uncle Jack! Come on!" I said, trying to get up.

He took my shoulder in his grip and flung me. I landed five feet away from where he stood. "Jesus, dang! What's going on, man? I didn't mean anything."

He approached me. I tried to get up again. Again he shoved me, his body barely moving, mine flying back and down. I landed on my buttocks.

"Look, I know how you think of me, *sobrino,"* he said, staring down straight into my face. I could not see his so well, as the sun hit him from behind. "You think I'm some stupid Spic who doesn't know shit about things. Your Mamá sends you to some high-brow Catholic prep school where they teach you how to act decently, how to get ready for a better life, how to get into college. You've also been living with some high-class rich folks, who don't care much for people like me. They'd prefer to teach little fucking halfbreeds like yourself how to cut out the *raza* in you and act like some damned gringo all the time."

I did not know where this was coming from. As far as I was concerned, I had done nothing in the past seventy-two hours to deserve all these reprimands. It was I who had practically been kidnapped and forced to flee San Francisco, I who had not seen my mother in the past three days due to my uncle's drug selling, I who had to witness some Mexican Mafia guy cut off another man's fingers. I wanted to say all this. I wanted to say that I didn't know what the hell he was talking about and that he had no right to beat me up like he now prepared to do. Yet I did not, perhaps for fear of being beaten harder, knowing that he could leave me in pieces if he wanted. Or perhaps because what he said, those crude words concerning him, and me, of how I thought of him, of where I lived and what I studied and who the people were who formed me back in Knoxville, sounded familiar.

"You can't even speak Spanish, Tony. Shit. You act as if you're ashamed of your own heritage." He stopped for a moment, still standing over me. As he paused, I wanted to say that it was not my fault that I could not speak Spanish. None of this was my fault. But I thought he was planning to shove his boot into my ribs, so I kept quiet.

"Tony, I don't really give a shit what you think of me, because I live my life the way I want to live it. You can think the worst of me, or Ricarda. You can think she's some kind of whore and that I'm nothing but a fucking pimp. I don't care. But don't be believing what others say to you about your *raza*, man." He spoke this quietly, and without forcing out the word, *raza*. He spoke it as if he saw that it was something in me, as natural as blood or bone; yet something dried out my blood, my bone.

He squatted next to me. His face was but a few inches from mine. I could tell, the way he looked at me, that he was not going to hit me anymore. "There's some things about your heritage that you should remember. Respect for your elders. And I'm one of them. You don't smart off with me. And that old man in there," he pointed to the house, "has more in this life than you may ever have. You think he's just an old man, worthless. Fuck you. That old man, if you listened to him, could teach you how to live. And you, *sobrino*, ain't living. You're fucking half dead, as far as I can see."

It was becoming preachy. Yet I listened, afraid not to. It also seemed, in all its pain, much like the punches that he gave me from time to time, the slaps against my head, the hits upon my arm or back, painful and paternal. I was sixteen. As much as I abhorred and was embarrassed by the adults in my life, something in me craved that certain paternal dolor.

"Now those folks in that ritzy private school of yours, they're teaching you how to get ahead in life and all. Fine. But all the while, they're also planning to shove a big dick up your ass. You know that's what Barry was planning to do, don't you? Did he ever do it?"

"No!"

"You sure? You sure he didn't bend you over and spread your little cheeks wide and try to split you open with his prick?"

"NO! He didn't do that! Goddammit Uncle Jack!"

"You know, I'm not sure about that. Too scared to stand up to him, you just lay there in your bed too frightened to say anything, because who's going to listen to a dirty little halfbreed like yourself?"

I started to cry. Yet this did not make him stop.

"Shit, man. I bet it did happen. I bet old Barry, knowing you wouldn't say a word, got the chance to shove his shaft into your ass and ride you like a donkey."

My fist balled up on its own. It flew through the air. Its flight, however, was blind. Looking back, I don't know if I had aimed for his face or his stomach. Either way, it landed, not exactly squarely, against the edge of his chest. Yet it was enough contact to give him some pain. Then I leapt from the ground. I jumped him, knocking him down with my weight. I flayed at him. I flung my arms wildly, knowing that they, like old, dried bamboo reeds, were no match for the thick tautness of his own limbs. Yet he did not hit back. He only used his arms to deflect the blows, knocking them to one side and another. I could see, on the other side of the fray of our four arms, his face and his closed lips, barely smiling. I did not care. The smile only kept me going, as well as fed the heat of words that shot from my mouth, "You stupid old fucker, son of a bitch, bastard, God damn mother fuckin' son of a bitch . . ." Not one curse word in Spanish, of course. These curses flew out with a certain Southern, Appalachian lilt. I knew this by Uncle Jack's response. He almost looked shaken, as if the Appalachian slurs reminded him of the day he flew through the window of Mary Lou Harrison's Lynch Mountain home while her father raised his rifle and took aim. Seeing that other side of me, my *other* heritage, no doubt sent a certain chill through him, one based in his own history. Those mountain folk could get kind of crazy.

I exhausted myself. He gripped my arms. He held them up as if to balance me. I breathed in chunks of air. His breath fell heavy as well. We almost breathed in unison, sucking in the hot air of the day.

About ten yards from us, at the tiny house's door, Don Chicolino stepped out. He held a pile of spongy buttons and stems in one hand and a small glass half filled with water in the other. He looked at us after having watched us for a few minutes, respecting our space and our brawl. Once we both looked up at him, he smiled.

"*¿Listo?*" he asked.

Chicolino handed the materials to Uncle Jack. Then Jack walked me away from the house to the bank of a drying creek. A few trees stood around the creekbed, dry as firewood. Yet they offered some shade, especially as the day waned. Even in this desert of land, where I expected snakes and lizards to slither out from under round stones, cool air was possible, as was a little water.

"What do I do?"

"You just eat it. Eat it all. You can drink some water, but not much. You don't want to have too much water in your stomach with them."

"What's going to happen?" My voice trembled.

"I'm not sure."

"Will it be like last night? When I was with Sara?"

"I doubt it."

"How do you know?"

"No one was with you when you ate it. You did it alone. Your mind wandered alone."

"Yeah, but, who's going to be with me now?"

"I'm here, *sobrino*."

"But I don't get it . . . how is you being here going to help me when I get, you know, buzzed?"

"It's not a buzz, Tony. You're getting it confused with smoking grass or drinking. It's not the same thing."

"Yeah, but I saw some crazy things, like the door to my room, it was, well . . . it looked strange . . ."

He laughed. "Some things look strange. But they're real."

I did not know what to make of this. Of course the door had not breathed last night, nor had I really been sucked up into Sara's vagina. But it was true—it all seemed, even in retrospect, real.

"I'll be here, Tony. Don't be scared."

He gestured for me to sit down on a rock. I did. He motioned for me to eat. I obeyed. I ate one after another, until all the mushrooms were gone. I had to drink enough water to get the taste off my tongue.

He sat down in front of me and lit a cigarette. "You want one?" he offered me the pack.

"Won't it mess me up with this?" I motioned to my stomach.

"I don't think so. It's just a cigarette."

I took one. I smoked it. I had sneaked cigarettes before from my parents, so I had some practice in the art of nicotine hits. I felt the nicotine run into my heart, making it beat faster. Though I at first confused it with the first beats of the mushrooms, I soon distinguished them as familiar, from the times I smoked the Pall Malls in the back of the house in Rakertown.

"Uncle Jack?"

"Yeah?"

"I'm sorry."

"About what?"

"About getting mad back there." I motioned to where we had fought. "About, you know . . . disrespecting you and him," motioning toward the old man's home.

"Oh. That's fine." He changed the subject. "Hey, you sure scared the shit out of Sara last night."

"Oh yeah? What did she think?" I grinned, embarrassed.

"When we walked in she was rushing to get her clothes on. She was going on about how you just went nuts on her."

"I hope I didn't hurt her."

"Nah."

"Did I . . . did . . ."

"What? Did you fuck her?"

"Well, yeah."

"Nope."

"No?"

"I don't think you got that far."

I didn't tell him how far I thought I had gotten, that of planting a home in her uterine wall. "So you mean I didn't, uh . . . lose it?"

"No man. Not last night. Another time, maybe."

"Oh." I looked around. I was not sure whether or not to be disappointed or relieved. "Hey, listen, you think I could, you know . . ."

He chuckled. "Yeah, I'm sure we could arrange something."

"Is Sara a, you know . . . a prostitute?"

Jack took a deep drag. He looked at me. "I suppose if I said 'yeah,' then you'd think a certain way about her."

"Well, I don't want to think bad of her."

"Yeah, but you would. You know, prostitution is the oldest profession. I don't know why anybody thinks bad about it. Shit, it's legal in Nevada. Sara's not really a prostitute in that sense, though. She's a friend of the family's."

"And she just wanted to go to bed with me?"

"Well, I don't know about that. Maybe. But after last night, I don't know."

"I didn't mean to scare her. I wish I could tell her I'm sorry."

"Don't worry about it, Tony."

He got quiet for awhile. So did I. I was listening for something, though there were few noises in this desert. A couple of birds chirped in a nearby tree. I could hear the trickle of the tiny creek below us. The stone was beginning to bite into my buttocks. The sun was going down, thank God; the heat, along with the day's burst of emotions, including the physical fight with my uncle, had just about worn the last of my strength away. I figured that we would spend the night here with the old man. The water trickle grew a bit louder. With the coming of night, perhaps more water would flow through the area. Just beyond the trickle I heard someone's voice, something about hiding a bottle. It was Mamá's voice. I looked over to the other side of the creekbank. Several stones, large ones like the stone I sat on, rested upon the bank. They did not move. Nor did they speak. Well, maybe that one over there, nearest the water.

"Jack. Uncle Jack. I think it's starting."

Jack put out his second cigarette. I could hear his voice nearby, but it seemed less real than the one speaking over there, about hiding a bottle. I knew what that phrase meant. Mamá was hiding the whiskey before Dad came home. It was her usual action. He would come home, not find it, and say nothing, knowing that she had hid it. He'd just go out and buy another one. Then I heard Uncle Jack's voice again, muffled, as if he spoke through a pillow. He said something about my high school. He asked me, what was the name of the family I had lived with? I told him, the Hartlands. What was their kid's name? I said, Janice, for God's sake, Janice. No, no, not her (so sad, that he negated her, just as she was crossing over that desert hill and walking my way), the other family, the other kid, the bastard *pendejo* who tried to get you. Barry, I said. Barry. That's right, I heard his diminishing voice repeat, Barry. Go find Barry.

I turned. A figure walked toward both Uncle Jack and me. I could not see the person due to the shadow of the setting sun. Yet I jumped from my stone and stood, poised, yet trembling. *"Ay Dios, me cree mal,"* said the old man's voice. Uncle Jack greeted the figure. Both their bodies were in shadows now, both up against the dying sun. The day was dying all around me. As they spoke to each other in Spanish, I looked about. The day was leaving me alone. Darkness made to take the earth. I turned again to the two men. Don Chicolino placed tall candles down on the ground. They frightened me. Yet he did not place them in the same positions as had La Chucharrona the other day, when she had told me about the births and deaths of God and man, that lousy witchcraft mumbo jumbo that had momentarily frightened me until I had walked out onto the San Francisco street and its light of day. Chicolino placed these white candles in a cluster.

"Para que no se pierda en el camino," he said to Uncle Jack. My uncle smiled and thanked him, then turned to me and said, through the growing chasm between us, "These are so you don't get lost along the way."

I did not understand. Was I to take a walk? There were no other lights around, save for the wax cluster to my right and the appearing stars above. I walked toward the creekbank. As I did, the horizon of the bank snuffed the candles from my sight. Except for the stars, darkness absorbed everything. Yes, it looked like the insides of Sara's womb. Yes, I was there again. I waited. I do not know how long it took, but he came. He came. There he stood. I lay myself upon the ground. I could feel the stones against my head and my shoulders, my backside and calves. Why did I decide to lie down? Was it true, what my uncle had said, that I had allowed it all to happen? At that, I screamed. I screamed one of the many curses taught me by my father. I flung the words at the figure just as I flung a stone that stood to my left. I jumped up, yet stood in my position as if to defend this tiny square of Mexican desert. The darkness had swallowed the rock. I did not hear it land upon the earth. I heard nothing now, not even the trickle of the creek, which was only three feet from me. That chasm, which had separated me from Sara the previous night, which now separated me from Uncle Jack and Don Chicolino, had also swallowed the creekbed as well as the birds. Now there was nothing. The backdrop of the world vanished as I held my hand up to my face, seeing only it, seeing my fingers move. I saw another memory approach, that moment when the knuckles reigned down upon me, when his screams belted over me, calling me a faggot, a faggot. With that memory I saw him turn away, his tiny erection cutting through the darkness of this place. He turned quickly away from me, as if he had seen or had heard something, as if he had been stopped, stopped by that one tiny voice that I could now hear so very clearly, growled through the lips of one who feigned sleep, Leave me the fuck alone. Goddamn you. Leave me alone.

That voice had been mine. Mine only.

He now turned away. Yet I knew that the following day his reign of knuckles would come down on my head. Now, however, this was all mine. I could make all things real. I could ride reality like an untied bull, even if for only a passing moment. So I did. As he turned away to disappear, I dove into that darkness, ran up and over a rocky hill, and caught up to him. Someone yelped behind me, but I ignored him. I snatched Barry by his neck and turned him around. Before he could raise a fist to me, I threw him down. The fall punched air from his lungs. Before he could get up I raised a large stone in both my hands. He unfolded and tried to decide between crawling away or attacking me. In that moment of indecision I brought the rock down. His head cracked open three ways, the cracks meeting where the rock had hit.

That voice came from behind again, "Jesus, Tony, don't run off like that . . ." Then Jack must have seen Barry's body. "Oh God, *hijo de la gran chingada* . . ." He walked away. I did not. I stayed over Barry and watched him ooze.

The candles had burned all the way down, leaving only a half-inch stub against the ground. I could see them, directly in front of my face. Each candle still burned. There were seven of them. At first I felt nothing. Then I felt the earth. I felt the stones biting into my body, over my stomach, my chest, the front of my legs. I tasted dirt in my mouth. Something hard scratched itself against another object. Then came the aroma of a newly lit cigarette. Still, I did not move. I stared at the candles for what seemed like an hour. One of them melted completely away, its wet wax falling over a tiny pile of rocks and coagulating under them. Its entire wick had burned into a tiny thread of ash.

"You okay, *sobrino?*"

I turned. The sun was barely rising. For a scant moment I confused the six remaining candles with the one sun. At first I thought that I remembered nothing, that I had slept through the whole experience. Then I shook my head and remembered how I had come over the horizon of the creekbank, back toward the lit candles, when they were still tall, before running off again to leap into the darkness, to dive into the night before it closed, regardless of whether or not the candles would be there to beckon me back. Fuck the candles. Fuck the stones. I had dived directly into the darkness. I had been there all this time.

"You hungry?" he asked.

I said that, momentarily, I was not. I stood up from the stones, but did not brush the dirt from my clothes. I felt as if my body were still deciding whether or not to be back here, shuddering as it walked this closely to such supposedly real things as stones, the candles, the burn of my uncle's cigarette.

"I bet Don Chicolino will have some breakfast going for us," he said.

It was then that I started to brush the dust from my shirt. Uncle Jack offered me a cigarette. I declined, thanking him. Then I changed my mind. He lit one for me, handing it to me from where he sat. He stood up from his rock, looked at the candles as if ready to put the rest out, then turned away, deciding to let them burn off as had the first. He walked away from the creek's horizon, away from the trees, toward the old man's house on the other side of the hill. I followed him. As I walked, my body shook slightly, not a shiver, but rather a rehabitating. Then I stopped. I stared at Uncle Jack's back without seeing it.

"Damn. That's why he went away," I said.

Uncle Jack turned around, the cigarette in his mouth. "What?"

"Why he went away. He didn't do it to me."

He stood, saying nothing, allowing silence to move between us. Then he asked. "Why?"

"Because I told him to leave me the fuck alone. It was my voice. I don't know . . . I guess I thought I was just whispering prayers to myself."

Uncle Jack did not move from his spot. He placed his hands in his pockets. Then he asked, "So it was your own mouth that saved your ass?"

"My own mouth, I guess. But he still whaled on my head the following day."

"Yeah, but he didn't rape you. You defended yourself."

"I guess that's right." I paused a second, then asked, "What did you see me do last night?"

Jack pulled the cigarette from his lips. "You stayed here a long time, lying down, standing up, talking. Then at one point you took off running. I almost lost you. You went over that hill. Then I really thought you were a goner, when you killed the rattler."

"The what?"

"That rattlesnake. On the other side of the hill. Big old bastard. You flattened it out with a rock before it could bite you. I couldn't believe it. I thought you were a goner for sure. You want to go see it?"

After a moment of thought I shook my head. "No. I don't need to see it."

"So after that I led you back here. You've been on the ground, mumbling, since then. You feel all right now? You want to head back?"

"Yeah. Yeah, I'm ready."

Jack turned away and walked toward the little house. His wide shoulders seemed to expand as he walked, as if becoming thick, dark wings. Smoke rose from Chicolino's house. I could smell hot grease, tortillas, and coffee that permeated the wide open air of this desert, as if turning the very stones into food. I walked toward the odors.

Uncle Jack and I returned to Ricarda's house later that morning. I thanked Don Chicolino, knowing I would probably never see him again. I hugged him. He grinned a large, yellow-toothed smile and gently slapped me on the back. *"Que te vaya bien, joven,"* he wished me. Uncle Jack paid him for his services. How much, I have no idea. They also said goodbye with an embrace.

After Don Chicolino's breakfast, I felt more prepared to make the trek back to Ricarda's home. Still, the five miles over a desert terrain exhausted me. I did not complain. The past twenty-four hours had been too important in my life to complain about insignificant things, such as hiking five miles in the heat. I felt even more cleansed when we arrived. Ricarda smiled at me, as if seeing something different in my mere appearance. Perhaps it was my own smile. Perhaps Uncle Jack had whispered something to her about my well-being. Either way, she welcomed me with a strong embrace, crunching me up against her body. I was too tired to fully appreciate that. I just let my hot, sweaty body be enveloped by her cool one.

I bathed. Afterwards Aunt Ricarda had a lunch of beans, rice, chicken, tortillas, cream, hot sauce, and beer waiting for us. Uncle Jack suggested that we drink either colas or water before putting down the beer.

"That sun has sucked a lot of water out of us. Best way to get a headache and a quick hangover is to drink alcohol after sweating so much."

I followed his advice. We both drank a number of glasses of water with our meal. Aunt Ricarda put the beers away, to keep them cool for the evening.

After the meal, I slept. My siesta that day most undoubtedly lasted longer than any other person's of the village. Yet I was not surprised by my weariness. According to Uncle Jack, I had been up all night. After a full twenty-four hours without sleep, along with a ten-mile hike and an immeasurable journey through my skull while out in that desert, it was no wonder my body dropped off to sleep, not waking until the sun made its way west.

When I awoke, I found Uncle Jack and Aunt Ricarda sitting in wooden chairs just in front of the house, looking out at the day, greeting passersby on the street. Sometimes Jack would offer someone a beer from Ricarda's store, himself paying for it by dropping a dollar bill into her cigar changebox. When I stepped outside with them, Ricarda went in and found another chair for me. She brought me a beer. *"Aquí, ten,"* she said, smiling. I drank it down easily. I glanced up at her. Strange, I thought, that though she obviously spoke perfect English, she would not speak in that language with me now. Nor did she point out the fact that I could understand little of our mother tongue. Rather, she spoke to me easily in Spanish, as if it were not important whether or not I understood. She was going to communicate with me as intimately as possible, in her own words. Somehow it seemed to be her greatest form of acceptance.

Still, her own form of affirmation did little to take away my anger and shame over my monolingualism. Like a good, rebellious teenager, I had shown disdain for my culture and a lack of interest in learning anything about it. Yet the truth was obvious: it was embarrassing to be Latino and not understand what everyone around me was saying. I watched my uncle as he greeted folks on the street, talking with those who stopped to chat with the well-known visitor. Men who had obviously just come in from work, their hands drooped to their sides with a used machete dangling from their fingers, their shirts stained with the day of labor, talked easily with my uncle. They smiled at him, cajoling and joking about an old story. Jack introduced me as his nephew, always reminding me to greet the newcomer. Then they would fall deeper into their chit chat, leaving me behind in my ignorance.

I drank my beer and thought about the past couple of days. I thought about the hallucinogenic experience that I had dropped into yesterday. As my uncle had said, it was not like getting high on grass. Nor was it like drinking this beer, which now made my head swim slightly. The mushrooms had made such things as talking stones real and had turned rattlesnakes into enemies I could kill. They had also made the reliving of the days and nights in the Gilten home as real as if I were living them for the first time. Yet the memories had come on with more clarity; the words *Leave me the fuck alone, God damn you, leave me alone* that came from my lips were like balm to my aching soul. The fact that I had actually defended myself with the harsh curse taught me by my father woke me from an enigmatic guilt that I had, up to this point, not understood—a guilt that somehow I had played a role in Barry's malice, that I had brought it on. I had brought nothing on. It was no wonder that he brought his knuckles down upon me the following day, screaming at me as he did. I understood. The understanding brought on a certain peace.

Nonetheless, the understanding along with the memories of his attacks raised a certain rage within me as well. That bastard beat me all during my freshman year. He couldn't fuck me, so he hammered my head when his parents weren't looking. I swallowed several gulps of my beer, remembering that, during the mushroom experience, I had busted his skull open. I had murdered Barry. I was not always sure how to feel about that. Remorse did not come to mind. Watching him ooze was very satisfactory. The fact that I had actually killed something—the rattlesnake—with the same stone also made me happy. There was something salvific in knowing that I was capable of such a kill. Thus the reason I didn't cross over the hill the following morning to see the dead snake: I didn't want that animal to ruin the kill in my brain. Barry still lived somewhere in Knoxville. But in my head, he was as dead as that split-open rattler.

The mushrooms revealed a certain me. This town, my aunt and uncle, revealed another side of me. I watched Jack as he chatted with men who made their ways toward their homes and families. I listened to that language which once beat up against me in shame, that now swirled around me in invitation.

We spent the next week in Macizo before I finally called my mother back in San Francisco, a phone call that would have Uncle Jack and me running from the little village and making our way across California. In the mornings, I immediately lifted from the bed and hit the floor doing pushups. Though they hurt, I forced myself to do three sets of fifteen. I also did the situps, fifty altogether. If I could have seen myself in a mirror while doing them, I'm sure I would have appeared like some panicking snake with its tail caught underneath the bed, forcing myself to lift my upper torso, almost screaming as the unused muscles in my stomach crunched together. In the other room, I could hear my uncle as he ripped through his sets, his smooth, even breathing moving him through the daily discipline.

I bought a dusty little notebook from Ricarda's store, found a pencil, and wrote out a list of Spanish words. Ricarda had an old English-Spanish dictionary in the house. I looked up the words and jotted down the translations. Throughout the day I carried the notebook with me. Whenever sitting in Ricarda's store and listening to buyers' conversations with her, I would write down as many words as I could, then look them up later. It did not take long to fill up five pages. Being a student, memorization was something that I did not find daunting. I memorized fifty words every night before joining my uncle and aunt in the kitchen for a beer and a snack. I would use the words that I had just learned on them, placing the verbs and nouns into the conversation like adornments, hoping that I would not only impress them, but that I would also be using the words correctly. I had some difficulties forcing some of the words into the dinner conversation. Someone that day had come into Ricarda's store complaining about her visit to the doctor. So when I started talking about *llagas podridas* (rotting ulcers) and *infecciones de sangre* (blood infections) during supper, my uncle had a hard time complimenting me on my studies. "Damn, Tony, why you talking about that over dinner?" Yet my aunt chuckled, slapped Jack on the arm, and reprimanded him for dousing my enthusiasm with cold water. I took my energy from her. Her eyes would look upon me while she smiled, telling me *qué lindo, mi sobrino quiere aprender el español, qué maravilloso*. They were enough to make me go back to my room and memorize another list. Sometimes I wondered if I did it just for Ricarda. Each time the memory of her writhing nakedness crossed my thoughts, I studied another set of ten words. It was good discipline.

I became attached to my little notebook. After a few days, it was already becoming ragged with use. The pencil marks where I would make notes around a certain word worked their way alongside the margins. *Bochorno,* for instance, could mean "sultry weather," but it could also stand for "embarrassment." I had to remember in what context the visitor to the store was speaking, reminding myself, had it been a hot day? I would remember how the person had wiped their forehead with their forefinger, then had flicked the finger against her middle finger, snapping the air with her demonstration of how hot the day was. I remembered my mother doing that numerous times whenever talking about hot foods, troublesome times, or good-looking men. I wrote notes about such linguistic and cultural actions all through the margins, filling the pages with lists and notations. If not in my hand, the book was always in my back pocket.

I also used the back of the notebook for a journal. One night I wrote down the entire experience of the past days. I began with our bus trip into California from east Tennessee. I wrote about seeing my grandmother and aunt Felícita for the first time after many years. I wrote about Chucharrona, her candles, and their meaning. I tried not to rush to get to the points about meeting Chucho, then later, watching his fingers fly in the air. Though I had not seen it, I wrote that they had also cut off his testicles. It was mostly journalistic, the whole trip south through California into this Mexican town. I even wrote about the marijuana and the mushrooms, daringly. This journal was mine, something that my mother and father and all others in the family needed to respect. This was my privacy. I was sixteen years old. Boldness and audacity concerning my privacy were at the helm of my thoughts, so much so that they superceded any concerns over some-one reading about my illegal escapades. In my mind I dared my mother to touch my journal.

Which brought me around to thinking about my mother. I had not seen her all this week. We had had no contact. Even in the midst of my silent demands concerning my privacy, I missed her. I also wor-ried, knowing that she was concerned over my safety. The more I thought of it, the more I was surprised that she had not demanded more of Uncle Jack, telling him, perhaps, to bring me back to the house and drop me off before fleeing the city. Why had she allowed him to take me with him? Then again, why was it that Mamá had thought of me spending my summer with Uncle Jack? I knew that it was her way of healing the invisible wound in my head, the one reflected by the gash in my wrist. Yet when we first arrived, I had interpreted her idea to be that of spending work days with him, learn-ing about electrical jobs, changing old wiring in buildings, putting in electrical ballasts, and climbing telephone poles. In my mother's mind, my time with Uncle Jack was to be a way of forgetting about the psychological pain inflicted in Knoxville.

I shuffled through the pages of my new journal and quickly read what I had written. I had referred to those pains back in Knoxville. But not once did I write the name Janice Lee. According to this written account, she did not exist. In ten days I had seemingly forgotten about her. In these few days, in one night of tromping through the desert on a mushroom trip, I had looked the past two years straight in the face. Something had happened. Some things were now very clear.

Yet now I missed my mother. I longed to talk with her. Again I wondered how long Uncle Jack planned for us to stay here with Aunt Ricarda. My comfort level over being away from my family was beginning to wane. Yet Uncle Jack seemed purely at home here. I saw no sign of his movement toward departure. I wondered if I should help motivate him in some way.

I closed my journal and shoved it into my back pocket. Walking outside in the late afternoon of Macizo, I looked around Ricarda's back yard to find him. He stood in the very back of the *sitio*, his back to me. His hands were in his pockets, making his elbows protrude slightly on each side. He was looking down into the corner of multi-colored flowers that grew in the right-hand side of the yard.

I approached him. He did not move. I stood to his right, just behind him, waiting for him to recognize my presence. He finally did. He turned and glanced at me, still keeping his fingers shoved into his jean pants.

"Oh. Hey Tony."

"Hey. What's up?"

"Oh, nothing, nothing." He turned around, barely glancing at me as he appeared to make his way back to the house. "Just spacing out a little, you know?" Then he stopped, as if deciding that going back to the house was not what he wanted.

I decided to be more direct. "What is this place, Uncle Jack?" I pointed to the flowers.

"It's just a flower bed that your aunt planted, kind of like a memorial." His voice trailed. He scratched the back of his head, looking down at the flowers. Seeing his eyes, I wondered if he forced his gaze into a hardness, as if in opening his lids wider, he would keep something back. "It's one of my kids. He died, several years ago."

"Kid? You had a child who died?"

"Yeah. Yeah, I did." He shook his head slightly up and down, cocking his jaw open, jutting it forward. "Just a little kid, three years old."

"Three? God, I'm sorry, Uncle Jack." He said nothing. I turned, bent down, and looked at the flowers. A wooden cross had been shoved into the ground, hidden among the blooms. On the marker had been carved the words "Juan Jr. Villalobos." There were no dates.

Without thinking about how harsh the words would be, I muttered, "He was a boy."

In the swirl of family legends, many that dealt with Uncle Jack's libertine ways, I recalled one story in particular which professed that Jack had spread his seed from San Francisco to Ecuador. Supposedly he had children in several countries. I did not know if this were true or not. Yet I had also heard another twist to the myth. Uncle Jack had no sons. All of his children were girls. Then, from behind me, Uncle Jack confirmed the legends.

"Yeah. He was my son. My only son."

I heard a crack in his voice. I did not know whether or not to stand back up and look at him. Then he cleared his throat harshly. I heard him spit. It seemed like a cue, permission, for me to turn around.

"I'm really sorry, Uncle Jack."

"I don't mean to say anything bad about little girls, you know. Hell, I love my daughter. I've got two. Little Felícita and Silvia, who lives in Mexico City. Silvia's all grown up and has kids of her own. Then there's Felícita, of course. They're both my girls. I love them, even when Little Felícita pulls her tricks."

Only two. I was almost disappointed that the legends were not true. But it did not seem very important at the time.

"And shit, it's not like he died yesterday. It was over ten, twelve years ago. He would have been fourteen or fifteen now, I guess."

"What did he die of?"

"Got sick."

"He got sick?" My incredulity was obvious. When you get sick, you take medicine, you rest, you get over the ailment.

Jack heard the disbelief in my voice, and knew where it came from. "Yeah, well, here, it's not like back in the States. Sometimes, when you get sick here, you die. He had some sort of spinal disease. I wasn't around at the time. I was working up north of San Francisco somewhere. Ricarda was from here, and she didn't want to leave the area. So she stayed here while I worked. I sent money to her to live off of. When I called home and she told me how sick Juan Jr. was, I told her to get him to a hospital. She did, but the doctors said it was too late. Something about meningitis in his brain, I don't know. But he died.

"I guess that's why we started fighting so much after that. Blaming each other for losing him. So we got divorced. Crazy. I divorce the one woman I truly love, only to come back every once in awhile to hop in bed with her."

I glanced over at him. In the dying sun, I could see a glisten of moisture around his eyes. I shifted from one foot to another, not sure what to say. Again I said, "I'm sorry."

"Yeah, well like I said, he died a long time ago. I usually don't think about him much. But he's been on my mind this week."

I at first did not hear that. "What about Little Felícita? Did she know her, uh, half brother?"

"Felícita? She knew about him, but never met him. Your grand-mamá raised her in San Francisco. Felícita never came to Mexico until she was an adult, and that was just for a vacation. That's why she's so fucking spoiled." He shook his head. "Ah, she's a good kid, I guess. But she's used to getting her way. She may be as dark as I am. But she's more gringo than you are."

I said nothing, letting the insult slide. This did not seem the time to defend my Latino-ness. I was also too curious about a number of questions regarding my family's stories. I had just learned that I had a dead cousin, whose body was buried before me. He was the only male cousin I knew of. He had died over a decade ago. Had he lived, he would have been near my age. He would have lived here in

Macizo, far away from my worlds of San Francisco and east Tennessee. He would have spoken only Spanish. He would have been dark skinned. His name would have been Juan. He would have seen his father from time to time, learning, no doubt, about the legends. Yet he would have been the son. What effect would those legends have had upon the boy? Then again, would the legends have existed, if this child had existed? Perhaps the boy would have kept the father home more.

Then his statement seeped into me. I, in my selfish curiosity, had not been able to comprehend many things. "Why have you been thinking about him so much?" I asked.

Jack smiled, barely turning his eyes toward me. He said the obvious. "Well, having you around reminds me that he would have been your age or so. A little younger. It's just kind of amazing, seeing you in your life, thinking about him, where he would have been." He then quickly added, "But Jesus, seeing how you turned out, shit, I don't know."

"What do you mean how I turned out?"

"Oh, just a little half-assed virgin, talking about open sores at the dinner table."

He shoved me. I caught myself before falling. Then I attacked. He merely moved his stout arms before him, knocking me to one side and to the ground. He laughed as my back hit hard against the dirt. Then I whimpered slightly, which brought him closer to me with a "Oh Jesus, Tony, I didn't mean to hurt you. Don't be a crybaby. Here."

He offered me a hand, which I took and pulled as hard as I could, lifting him from his stand and forcing him to the ground. He laughed as I jumped on him. We rolled. He pinned me once again, so easily that I screamed for him to get off my damned back, "You're gonna break it!" He did release me, thinking the game was over, until I scissor-kicked his shins. That brought him down.

"'Ey, *sobrino*, you little fucker!" he growled, which meant it really *did* hurt, which made me proud. So even when he shoved me hard, almost wanting to make his shove a blow, wanting to inflict some pain, I laughed, knowing that I had given him a slight challenge, even if it was momentary. He lunged at me, practically sitting on me as I tried to raise my legs up and snatch his neck from behind. We fought and laughed, giggling as we made the other one feel some pain. An evening wind blew over us and through the thick leaves and flowers of that lovely memorial, causing them to wave toward us, rubbing their foliage together like whispers.

Later that night he knocked on my door and dropped his head through the crack. I first saw the Band-Aid that Aunt Ricarda had placed on his forehead from our little brawl. He grinned at me. "What's going on, *sobrino?*"

I placed the *La Voz* magazine down, the one that I was trying with all my might to read. I had filled six more pages in my journal with vocabulary words. My hope was to have them all memorized before morning.

"Oh, nothing. I was just writing about how I beat the shit out of you today."

"Really?" He laughed. "Well, you got a visitor here, who wants to see you."

"A visitor?" I stood up from the bed and sat on its edge. The way he smiled, I had no idea. Then I knew. Darned if Mom hadn't looked us up, perhaps even called us somehow, and made her way down here. My smile spread over my face, only to drift away as Uncle Jack opened the door wider. It wasn't my mother. It was Sara. So my disappointment was not necessarily tremendous.

"Oh, uh, *hola*."

"*Hola*," she said timidly.

Jack closed the door behind her, leaving my head with a multitude of questions. Why is she here? Did he pay her to return? How much did he pay her? Did she get paid last time? I shook slightly. She sat next to me on the bed. She talked to me as if I spoke fluently. I understood a few things, especially when she talked about how afraid she had been the other night. I think she thought that I had suffered an epileptic seizure. Then she mentioned Aunt Ricarda, and used the words *"Ella me explicó,"* which I took to be, "Your auntie explained everything." I wondered what Ricarda had explained. Whatever it was, I was grateful that the explanation had gotten the young woman to return.

Sara raised her fingertips to the Band-Aid that Aunt Ricarda had placed upon my own face as well, on my left cheek, just in front of my ear.

"¿Qué pasó?" she asked, touching it.

I wanted to tell her something about how I had to fend off an attacker, but knew that lies would not befit me in my limited Spanish. *"Jugar,"* I said, *"Tío Juan y* me, uh, *y yo."*

"Ay," she responded, softly chuckling, *"ese hombre es pura fiera."*

Then she kissed my cheek. She moved silently and kissed my lips. She moved quietly and shed me of my clothes, my magazine, my journal filled with words and a new discipline. I looked up at the wall that did not reach all the way to the ceiling, expecting to see both my uncle's and aunt's eyes up there, watching gleefully. Then I turned away from that gap, realizing I couldn't give a damn. Not as Sara cooed to me in the only language she knew, a language that pricked at my skin, that opened and closed over me with a thick tongue and warm inner thighs.

Half an hour after Sara left, I rose from the bed. I think I was still smiling. After putting on my pants and shirt, then trying in vain to comb my hair into place, I walked to the kitchen to look for food.

Jack sat at the table, drinking a beer and reading a three-day-old newspaper. He barely glanced up at me. "How's it going?"

"Fine," I said, barely stifling a laugh. I sat down.

"You hungry?"

"Yeah, I could use something to eat."

"There's some *postre* in the refrigerator, and some beer."

I took both. I grinned at the large piece of cake.

"Look at you. Like a damned cat. How do I know what happened in there, *sobrino?* I didn't hear one noise. What'd you all do, play cards or something?"

"No, man. Come on."

He laughed. I expected him to ask me questions over my most recent experience. I hoped he would, like a curious colleague wanting to know the details. But he did not. He left my moment alone. In retrospect, I was glad, knowing that whatever details I would have told him would be nothing in comparison to his lifetime of rolls.

He quickly moved the subject elsewhere. "Hey, listen, I've been thinking about when we should go back."

"Yeah?"

"Yeah. I got a hunch that Gato's cooled off some by now. But I'm not sure. It bothers me, what he did to Chucho. I just fucking can't believe that, cutting off the man's nuts. I mean, I thought that had been a regular delivery, maybe a little bit bigger than usual, but still, it's just grass. The way Gato's acting, you'd think we were running heroin or something, or that cocaine shit they're starting to get into more from Colombia. But now he's acting like some damn mafia guy. That's just not like him."

"You talk like you know him pretty well."

"Are you kidding? Gato's from the Mission, just like me. We grew up together. He's a few years younger than me. He got into the market way before we did, or I did. So, he's got a handful of money now. I knew how that money changed him. Everyone knew. He used to come to my house as a kid and eat tamales with Mamá. He'd eat more than anybody. Once I saw him eat thirteen tamales in one sitting. The rest of us kids just sat there, staring at him with our mouths open. And my mother was just more than happy to feed them to him. *'Ay, que comilón!'* she'd say, handing him another plate. Mamá always liked Gato as a kid. But then he got caught up in this drug running way too much."

"So you've known Gato all your life," I said.

"Yeah. We all know one another from the Mission. It's a small world. So when you see somebody get messed up, like Gato did, it's kind of sad. Shit, makes me want to never get involved in that stuff again."

He sounded serious about it. I found it interesting how Uncle Jack distinguished between Gato's obviously well-developed business and his own peripheral participation in selling the weed.

"Why did you get involved in the first place?"

"Oh, I don't know. It's fast money. And you always get a little bit of bud on the side. It's not like I'm dealing in it all the time, Tony. I work for a living, you know. I'm an electrician. That's a good job. I don't know. Once Rata asked me to do him the favor of delivering some shit, and he said he'd pay me five hundred bucks to do it. So I said sure. After that he asked me a few more times, said he could trust me more than most people, because I was older. Shit. I think it was because he was dicking my daughter."

"Who? Felícita?"

"Yeah. She and Rata were in it pretty serious for awhile. I thought they were going to get married. But she started dating some gringo in Berkeley, then Rata wasn't good enough for her anymore."

Uncle Jack tossed out this family gossip as if it were so much known information. Whenever he spoke about his daughter, his words did not necessarily smack of paternal care.

"I guess Rata kind of saw me as his father-in-law or something. But then *he* got way deep in the business. Now I don't even see him, just his henchmen, like that guy we picked the bags up from in the park. Shit, Rata's a hell of a lot younger than me, but he just sees me as one of his runners. To hell with that. These young punks get a fist-ful of *billetes* in their hands, they think they own the world. And it's because of the damned drug selling. Look here, in the paper. Three people were killed in Mexico City the other day for supposedly dealing in cocaine. I tell you, I'm getting out of this shit. No more favors for nobody."

He sounded fairly committed to this new promise. I hoped he would not be so committed to it that he would give up smoking it.

"So what do you think," I asked, "about going back to San Francisco?"

"I think we should head back soon. That little bastard Gato needs to calm down some. I think I need to tell him that. Yeah."

It was the first time that I heard some hesitation in his voice when referring to putting someone in their place. I was sure that the image of Chucho's flying testicle had something to do with it.

"Yeah, and I need to get you back to your mom. I'm sure she's worried about you. And your grandmother will have my head in a sack if I don't get you back. What do you think?"

"I think, well . . . sure, Uncle Jack. I'm ready to go. I mean, I like it here. Aunt Ricarda's really nice and all."

"Yeah, she's the best, isn't she?"

"Yeah. I hope I can come back someday and visit her again."

"She'd like that. Maybe by the time you come back you'll be speaking Spanish like a Mexican." He grinned. "So why don't you go into town and call your mother from the local public phone? They'll ring the number for you. Here, take this," he pulled a wad of bills from his pocket. "That'll pay for the call. Talk to your mom and tell her that we'll be home in the next couple of days or so. Tell her everything's okay, you're fine, I'm fine, but don't tell her where you are. And *don't* tell her anything about our visit with Don Chicolino. Shit, that gets out, they'll never let me see you again."

"Okay, Uncle Jack."

"While you're out, why don't you get us some beer? Your aunt ran out in the store." He tossed me another wad of cash.

A few minutes later I walked away from Aunt Ricarda's store and down the street. Several lights were still on throughout the village. Radios played in a number of houses. A few homes had televisions. I could hear one man cursing at his set while banging on its side. I walked the five blocks up to the local telephone company, where a small line of people waited their turn to make a call. Like almost every person in El Macizo, Ricarda did not have her own phone. Most people, whenever it was necessary to call someone outside of town, made their way to the phone company's office, where an operator dialed up the number for them, taking their money after they hung up.

I had no idea how long I would talk on the phone. It could be a long time. Then again, there was little I was allowed to tell my mother, except that I was fine, that Uncle Jack was okay, and that she didn't need to know where we were. Still, I longed to hear her voice. Taking a place in line, I thought about those weekly phone calls I received from Mamá from Rakertown, while I lived in Knoxville. Sometimes they were not as welcomed as she wanted them to be. Even in long distance I took on the role as teen, feeling embarrassed whenever my parent would call to dote and reprimand me through the line. Now, however, due to the forced separation as well as the dangerous situation that we had left behind in San Francisco, I longed to hear her. Childhood flashed through me, of her calling me to her, *"Vente, mi corazón,"* while waving her beckoning arms to me, pulling me into her lap and singing directly into my ear, *"Dormite niñito, cabeza de ayote."*

While not ever wanting such a moment to escape my thoughts and fly about a roomful of people my same age, it was one that I valued. I looked down the row of people, watching as each person left the wooden phone booths, allowing another person in.

I handed the phone number, scratched out on a piece of paper, to the operator. He nodded and dialed it in. A bell went off in the third booth. *"Número tres, por favor,"* the operator said, pointing it out to me. I thanked him. I closed the booth door quickly behind me as a smile stretched over my face. I unhooked the receiver. "Hello? Hello?" A buzz pushed into my ear. It was still ringing. Perhaps, I thought, they were out for the night. But why would they go out? They should be home, worrying about me.

Finally, on the sixth ring, they picked up. *"Bueno?"*

It was a man's voice. I opened my mouth, but nothing came out. They had said *Bueno,* instead of Hello, a common Latino form of answering the phone. Then that voice, the deep voice of a man. My confusion kept me silent.

"Hello?" said the voice, as if noticing my confusion, thinking that I could be a monolingual gringo.

"Hello, yes, is Carmen McCaugh there, please?"

"Who is this calling?" he asked. Then I knew who he was.

"Oh, shit . . ." my voice squeaked.

"Hello?" said the man. "Hello? Who wants to speak with Carmen McCaugh?"

Behind him I heard the voices of the three women in my life, all of them speaking on top of the other, bantering back and forth in both English and Spanish.

The voice asked me, "Is this Tony McCaugh calling?"

I opened my mouth, but the wind hung in my throat, as if physically caught there.

"This is Tony, isn't it, Tony?"

"Yes . . ."

"Tony, son. We've been waiting for you to call. We've been here, what, three days now?" I could hear his lips leave the phone, as if asking one of his thugs to verify that figure. "Yeah. Three days. I mean, I can't complain. Your grandmother has kept me well fed and all. But if you know me, you know I like to get out once in awhile."

Still I said nothing. I heard the meow of a cat that lifted up to his receiver. I thought I felt hot liquid in my pants.

"Listen, Tony. Don't think I've done anything wrong here. I promise you, your family is fine. Your mom is okay. We're just visiting, isn't that right, boys? Just paying a nice visit to your grandmamá's house. We're just waiting for you and that uncle of yours to come home."

At first I tried not to say it. But an anger that hid underneath my fear forced itself out of my throat, "You cut Chucho's fingers off . . . I saw you . . ."

"Listen, that was my mistake. I thought that Chucho was holding out on me, you understand, son? 'Ey? But then I saw you and your uncle, and I realized that I had made a mistake. And then you all took off. That was not a wise thing to do, Tony. I was just coming for my pickup. It's a very special pickup, and I don't want to lose it."

He allowed for that to seep into my silence. Then I heard my grandmother's voice raise above the two voices of my mother and aunt, "*¡Este malcriado nos ha secuestrado!*" I could imagine her hand up in the air, shaking back and forth like a thick whip.

"*No, Doña Rosie, no hacemos tal cosa, sólo queremos recoger lo que es mío,*" he explained to her, taking his lips away again from the phone.

"*¡Ay, y al pensar que te alimenté tanto cuando fuiste cipote, sinvergüenza!*"

"*Vaya pues, Doña Roselia, vaya pues* . . . Jeez, your grandmother can get pretty dramatic, huh Tony?"

I hung up the phone.

I ran out of the office. Someone yelled at me to come back. The operator asked for the payment. I threw him all the cash in my pockets. He protested softly, saying, I'm sure that it was way too much. But I was already gone.

I ran all the way to Aunt Ricarda's house and spilled out the whole story. Uncle Jack stood up from his chair. He slammed a large fist on the table. His beer, my empty plate of *postre*, the fork, a vase of flowers, and my beer all toppled as if knocked dead by the blow. He cursed. He did so in both languages. He muttered about his beloved mother, then sent Gato to hell with tongues of fire licking around his scrotum. He knocked the chair down while walking to Aunt Ricarda's bedroom. He woke her up and told her. She jumped up, dressed, ran to the neighbor's house and asked the man of the house to drive both Uncle Jack and me to the border. Within ten minutes, I was kissing my aunt Ricarda goodbye. She hugged me, wishing me back to her home someday.

We left. An hour later we were at the border. Half an hour after that we were at Jorge's garage. Uncle Jack banged on a window and woke his friend up. "Hey, ¿qué pasa, man?" Jorge said. Jack demanded the keys. He explained in quick, Spanglish phrases what had happened, that a *pendejo* named Gato had *secuestrado* all the women in our family, and that his nephew and he were on their way to *cortar los cojones* off the *chingado*. "Oh man, *cabrón. ¡Cuidado!*"

Not forgetting Jorge's hospitality, Uncle Jack opened the trunk of the Mustang, shoved his hand through the closed plastic of one bag, then ripped out a fistful of grass. He shoved it down one pocket of Jorge's robe. Then we got in. I could barely hear Jorge's words, "*Que les vaya bien*, man!" over the squeal of the tires.

I thought the Mustang's engine would explode. I also worried about cops. Neither occurred. This, I thought, was just a little short of a miracle. I once glanced over to see the speedometer. It was beyond ninety. Knowing how much illegal vegetation we had in the trunk, I knew that we were destined to spend the rest of our lives, from this night on, in prison.

Uncle Jack seemed to sense this fear, or perhaps felt the concern himself. After an hour of dodging other late night cars that appeared parked on the interstate, he found a speed that was closer to the limit.

"That motherfucking Gato . . . he's gone way too far. No wonder no one wants him back in the barrio . . ."

Along with my fear, I had also shed some tears. I had never needed to deal with my mother being kidnapped before. I played, over and over again, the words that both Gato and the women in my life had said over the phone. One fact that gave me some relief was the way the women spoke. They chatted as they always had, especially when they held some juicy gossip to share. Then my grandmother, no doubt standing up and yelling something about this bad, bad boy Gato holding them for ransom, showed me that, even though captured, Doña Roselia had some control of the situation. Gato's voice toward her was very conciliatory. She still held motherly authority over him.

Yet the facts were before us, beyond the long stretch of road. They were being held as hostages. Gato meant to put this fear into me and Uncle Jack, knowing that it would be the only way to get us back, the only way for him to get his hands on the packages of grass.

"What the fuck's so special about this grass?" Uncle Jack asked rhetorically. With that question, he lifted his foot off the accelerator and pushed down on the brake. We skidded to a stop. He parked the

Mustang underneath a tall streetlight, one of many that lined this stretch of highway. He walked to the back of the car and opened its trunk.

"What the hell more is there here than grass and mushrooms?" He almost shoved his head into one bag. I hoped he would not do that too long, fearing that the smell itself would affect his brain, buzzing him out of his rage. I knew his rage was going to be necessary soon.

"Tony. Open that other bag, start looking through it."

I had to pull the plastic bag to the edge of the trunk so that the streetlight would hit it. I saw wrapped packages of dried green herb, along with one that he had torn open for Jorge. I shoved my hands through the packages, knocking them from side to side. I found another white package, which I could barely distinguish from the brown ones. I turned it over, looking at it. It was just like the one we had found in the hotel room previously. No doubt it was filled with mushrooms. Yet something else was taped to its bottom: an envelope.

While Uncle Jack rummaged through his bag, cursing about not knowing what in the world would be so important as to make a man go to such extremes, I carefully tore the envelope from the taping, opened it, and pulled out the contents. It was one page of words. I pulled back from the trunk slightly and held the paper up to the streetlight. The words were typed in Spanish. I could also see, from its shape, that it was not a letter. It began with a list of words that covered the first third of the paper. Then the rest of the page held paragraphs. I read the first paragraph, as best I could, out loud: *"Lo importante de la carne es que la mezcla de la gallina con el cerdo se hace más jugosa la masa . . . pero hay que quitar la espuma mientras se cuece la carne . . ."*

Uncle Jack stopped rummaging the moment he heard my words. He lifted his head up too fast. His skull slammed against the trunk lid. He turned to me. "Give me that," he spat out as he snatched the piece of paper from my hand. I stood next to him and read the paper over his shoulder. I had ignored the list of words above, but looked at them now as he murmured aloud: *huevos cocidos, una docena por cada cien; tres limones por cada gallina y cada cerdo; tres cajas de ciruelas; dos cajas de pasas.* Then I knew. I knew about the same time he mumbled out the truth.

"Damn. This is my Mamá's *recipe*," he said.

He lowered the paper from his face. He looked at me without seeing me. "Gato's always wanted this. Rata accidentally fucked him with the last batch of grass. So Rata wants to make up to Gato and get him what he's always wanted. Mamá's recipe for the tamales . . . But how did Rata get this?"

He still held the recipe up in his hand as he tied the bags closed again and slammed down the trunk lid. Then he gave me the paper. "Hang onto this, Tony. Let's get going."

I barely had time to fold it up and tuck it into my back pocket. We were gone within seconds, the speedometer once again touching ninety from time to time.

The sun was barely rising over San Francisco when we drove into the city. Jack slowed down and found streets familiar to him, weaving his way toward the Mission District.

"What's our plan?" I asked.

"What you mean, *plan*?" he responded. I noticed that, during this trip, he began cutting even more words out of his sentences.

"How are we going to get them out of there? I mean, just showing up isn't going to do anything. We should have a plan."

"Here's the plan, *sobrino*. I'm going to walk in and tell those motherfuckers to get the fuck out of my mother's house or I'll kill every one of them with my bare hands. That's the plan."

I wanted to argue that I saw a few holes in the plan. I could also imagine a few holes in us. More concretely, I could see us limbless before noon.

"I want you to stay downstairs, Tony. Don't come up. I'll deal with these *pendejos* alone."

"But Uncle Jack, what if they get, you know, crazy or something? I think we should call the cops."

"Right. Call the cops, with thirty pounds of grass in the back, along with mushrooms. Who you think they'll haul away? Then Gato will still have control of my family. *Ni modo. Voy a chingar a ese pendejo ya.*"

He seemed to have forgotten that, though I had taken on serious study of the mother tongue, I was still a ways from fluency. For him, expressing it in Spanish took on more meaning. It also seemed to prepare him for the confrontation.

The streets were fairly desolate. Then I remembered, it was Sunday morning. Few people would be out at this time of day. He had hopped off Highway 280 and was down Mission Street within seconds. He turned into Capp Street, which was narrower, with cars parked all alongside the road. He did not slow down until he could see his mother's house. Even then, his tires screeched as he jerked right and parked before the garage door. I closed my eyes, thinking we were about to go through the door without opening it. But this was Abuelita's house; Jack's anger still could not be enough for him to cause that much damage.

"Tony. Go open the door." He handed me a set of house keys. I walked out, opened the garage door, flipping it up and barely moving out of the way as he pulled the Mustang in. He motioned for me to close it.

I turned. Uncle Jack was gone. The door that opened to the first floor swayed back and forth. At the end of the long hallway was another open door. It showed my grandmother's back yard in all its landscaped splendor. He had decided to take the back stairs, ones that would bring him up to the back door of the kitchen.

I did not obey his command of staying in the garage. Yet I did not make my way through the bottom of the house in the same way he did. I walked quietly, not wanting to make noise here on this cement floor. I then made it to the back yard and looked up. Uncle Jack had already opened the kitchen door. It swayed slightly. I could hear voices. I made my way carefully up the steps. The voices were intimate, between a mother and a son.

"Ay, Juan, por fin regresaste vos. Pensé que te olvidaste de mí." Abuelita's voice sounded as if it were ready to crack with the onslaught of tears.

"Nunca, Mamá, nunca me olvido de usted. Dígame, ¿dónde están esos sinvergüenzas?"

"Están roncando en tu cuarto, Juan." Her voice turned acrid, losing all tears. Then I heard others, in the front of the house. They were approaching.

"Mamá, mejor salir ya. Antes de que se despierten."

"¡Yo no me muevo de mi casa, hijo! Esos malcriados son los que deben salir."

From the top stair I watched as my aunt Felícita walked in, tying a white robe around her. "Juan! You're home! Where's Tony?"

"He's downstairs, he's fine, sister," he smiled, hugging her.

I was about to stand up and run into the kitchen. Then I saw that man, dressed in black, his clothes looking as if he had slept in them for days, walk into the kitchen. He was followed by two other men. They were all familiar. One was Hispanic, with his long black hair falling over his shoulders. The other was the blonde-haired gringo. Both stumbled behind Gato, as if they had been roused from sleep too quickly. The gringo rubbed his eyes and sniffed slightly before looking up and seeing Jack. Then his eyes opened wider, as if knowing that he had to get to work.

I ducked my head down below the top steps of the back porch. I positioned myself behind a post so as to sneak one eye around it.

"So you've come home, Jack," Gato said. "Glad to have you back."

Jack stood up from his mother's side. His hands dangled in the air beside his thin waist. It looked as if he were ready to pluck two invisible guns from their holsters.

"Get the fuck out of my mother's house," he said. "You're trespassing."

"Jack, I don't think you're the one who should be giving the orders. Look, I just came to pick up my packages. Hand them over, and we'll be gone."

"Sure, Gato. I'll give you the packages. But you're not going to get the fucking recipe."

My mother walked in, scratching through her mop of hair and asking "What's going on?" She then saw Jack and asked for me.

No one noticed Mamá. My aunt Felícita said, "Recipe?" She looked over at Gato. Then she looked at Jack.

My Abuelita, who understood most all English (though she refused to speak it), said, *"¡La receta! ¡Me secuestra por la jodida receta! ¡Ay, este ingrato!"*

Then my mother said, "But Jack doesn't have the recipe, Gato. What are you talking about, boy?"

"I think Jack knows what I'm talking about," answered Gato. "Don't you Jack?"

"How did you know about the recipe?" asked Uncle Jack. "How did Rata get ahold of it?"

"Maybe that's something you should ask Rata about. Or better yet, your daughter."

The whole room turned silent after a collective sucking in of breath from the three women. Aunt Felícita muttered through clenched teeth, "Ooh, that little *puta*. Stealing from her own family . . . So that's why she was hanging around the business . . . ooh, that big BITCH."

Uncle Jack said nothing. Still, this news of Little Felícita being involved stopped him momentarily, until he said, "Get the fuck out of this house."

They bantered back and forth for a moment, each demanding their desires from the other: Get out of the house, Give me the recipe. Then Gato whistled slightly while looking at the gringo. The gringo approached Jack. He was larger and taller than my uncle.

"Come on, Jack, just show us where the stuff is," he said calmly, as if not wanting to use full strength against my uncle so early in the morning, before a cup of coffee.

Suddenly the gringo was much shorter than my uncle. Jack's boot that shot up from the floor into the gringo's groin had much to do with that, as did Jack's fist slamming down between the blonde's ear and shoulder. I heard the crunch in the tuck of his neck. Jack's back expanded, the muscles unfolding like a cobra's. The gringo stayed on the ground. My mother screamed. My grandmother yelped out a curse, *"¡Hijo de la gran puta!"* Then Gato signaled the Hispanic bodyguard forward. He obeyed, unsheathing a long razorblade from its handle. My aunt screamed. Jack lowered his head and raised his arms to the height of his shoulders, bracing himself.

I ran down the steps. I could see nothing, though I could hear the struggle of two men knocking down kitchen furniture. A glass shattered. A male voice yelped. It sounded too much like my uncle's. I shuddered as I made my way toward the basement. There, next to the Mustang, I stood, unmoved, trying to make decisions, while the yelping grew louder, followed by a man's scream.

As I still had the keys to the house, I opened the front door of the first floor. It let me into the foyer. I jangled through the keys to find the one that would let me into the door that led to the front steps of my grandmother's apartment. I had a difficult time finding it, as none of them seemed to fit. I held my wrist with one hand to keep the other hand from shaking so much. Finally I found the key and opened the door. I walked quickly but quietly up the steps. Upon reaching the third to the top step, I stopped, looked over the horizon of that final stair, down the wooden floors of the empty hallway. No one was there. I hesitated for a moment that was, no doubt, too long. I glanced over at my grandmother's bedroom, at the telephone that stood on a table next to her bed. I thought about it. Then I shook my head, muttering to myself no, no, not with thousands of dollars of grass downstairs, in my uncle's car, which would get him carted off to jail, leaving Gato and his men to terrorize my family for the recipe.

I walked down the hallway, then pushed myself against the wall so that they could not see nor hear me approaching. Once near the kitchen, I could see the back of Gato's head. He did all the talking now. I saw why: though I could not see my uncle, I could hear him breathing heavily, moaning. A large smattering of blood sprayed grandmamá's white wall and stove. Grandmamá moved between cries and murmurs, both admonishing and pleading. But Gato did the real talking.

"You see, Jack, we're serious about this. I'm tired of having to wait all fucking week for you to finally show your cowardly ass in the Mission again. So give me the fucking recipe."

Jack's breathy voice muttered, "Fuck you."

"All right, Jack. You asked for it." I saw his head turn slightly, as if giving an order to the Hispanic thug.

I sucked in a large breath, hoping the breath would clean away any fears that would keep me from doing what I was about to do. Then I looked at the blood upon the wall, knowing it was my uncle's. This sunk deeply into me. Not in fear, but in a certain anger, that one of my own had been hurt. And I had learned, this week, that he indeed was one of my own.

I stepped away from the wall, stepped directly behind Gato, and raised my uncle's large handgun up to his head. Then I waited for a silent moment so as to pull back the hammer. Its click could be heard throughout the kitchen.

Gato turned. He was looking, or thought he was looking, down my barrel. I saw what I needed to see in his eyes: the onslaught of fear. He tried to conceal it, but it had already escaped his vision. It was enough to feed my rage and my actions.

"Leave my uncle alone."

Gato seemed confused by my words. I was not sure why. I said them clearly enough. As I continued speaking, I began to understand. "You all better leave my family alone, or I'll be more than happy to blow the livin' shit out of your boss' skull. You got me?"

The Hispanic, who was towering over my wounded uncle, looked more confused than Gato. "*¿Qué dijo?*" he asked.

Gato explained to him what I had said. Then he smiled at me. "You're Tony, right? Listen Tony, you don't want to shoot anybody with that thing . . ."

I acted without thought. My hand lifted high. I slammed the gun butt down, right on top of Gato's balding head.

He fell against the wall. As he stumbled I shoved my whole body up against his. I locked my thighs up against him. I held his neck with my left hand, then shoved the barrel between his teeth, forcing his mouth open. I looked around the room.

"Let me tell you all something," I began, feeling a smile come across my face. I am still not sure where it came from. "This ain't my idea of being good visitors. Now your bossman here, what's your name, mister? Gato? Don't that mean 'cat?' Well listen here, boys. You're gonna have cat brains all over this fuckin' wall if you make another move."

I could not understand how my father's voice was punching out of my mouth. All I knew was that I was angry, and my brain snatched around for the most powerful voice it could find at the time. Considering that my Spanish voice was still quite fledgling, my head found the best equivalent.

The gringo was standing up about this time. He was a gringo: he spoke white-like, Californian English. He had a pistol in a small holster on his waist. Yet he did not look ready to reach for it yet. "Watch out, man, Jeez! He's fucking crazy, man! Be careful with him!" He spoke to the Hispanic who still wielded the razor blade. It seems that the Hispanic could understand the gringo's English. He just couldn't understand my Appalachian. The gringo continued, "Haven't you seen *Deliverance*, man? These people will do anything to you!"

Gato was still in my grip. I knew that he might overpower me in a second if I was not careful. So I inflicted a little more pain, shoving the barrel just a little deeper, scraping it up against a molar. "Now listen. I want you all to get the hell out of this house. But before you do, kindly hand me that blade and you, asshole, your gun."

They obeyed. My uncle groaned as the Hispanic let go of his shoulder and slid the bloody razor over the table. I turned. My mother was staring at me in a way that I had never seen her stare at me before. I could not tell if it was gratitude or awe or fear or all of the above.

Gato, at this point, whimpered. He tried to form words around the gun barrel. I think he was saying something about the recipe, all he wanted was the recipe, so he could go legit. I paid little attention to it. I reached over toward the table. I tried not to show it, but a certain sense of salvation pumped under my skin once I had the real gun in my grip. I felt no hesitancy in holding it. Coming from east Tennessee, I had been raised by my father to handle armaments. Again, my father's heritage came through twice in one day. I kept the fake gun inside Gato's mouth and pointed the real gun at the two henchmen. "Back away from my family."

They followed the order. My mother and aunt moved toward Jack. Abuelita was crying, looking out the window. She searched for something. I soon figured out what she sought. There was Uncle Jack's bloodied hand, the stub where a pinky finger had been.

"Oh fuck," I muttered, "you cut my uncle's finger off, you moth-erfucking bastards!" I pushed the barrel deeper into Gato, no doubt choking him, perhaps even damaging his esophagus. He cried as he gagged. I tired of this. I pulled the barrel from his mouth, forced him toward a chair, then held both guns up in the air of the kitchen. "Get out of here."

"*¡Espérense!*" It was my Abuelita, ordering them to wait. I turned. Most everybody else did too. She stepped forward. She rattled off something to Gato, forcing her angry voice through her tears. Gato spoke back, his voice quivering. He turned out to be much more a coward than I had thought. He and my Abuelita spoke back and forth. My aunt interrupted them, "*¡No, Mamá no se la puede dar!*"

"*Yo puedo hacer lo que me da la gana, hija. Hijo, ¿dónde está la rec-eta?*"

"*Tony la tiene,*" murmured Uncle Jack.

Abuelita turned to me. "Antonio. Geeve the *receta* to heem."

"What?"

"*La receta ¡La receta!* Geeve eet to Gato."

My aunt quickly explained. "They made a deal. Mamá made Gato promise that if she gives him the recipe, he will never bother the fam-ily again. He said he promised."

I looked at him. He sat below me, staring up at me, perhaps afraid that I would make him squeal like a pig. I leaned down slightly, not able to resist one last bit. I held both guns up to his face and smiled again. "So. You promise?" I asked, rousing up my father's voice as best as I could.

"Oh yeah, Tony. No problem. On the soul of my mother, I will never bother your family again."

I pushed the fake gun under my belt and worked the paper out of my back pocket. I handed it to him. He unfolded it, making sure that he was getting the real thing. He smiled through his fear. "This is it, man. This is it. The recipe. Los Guanacotamales. Yeah." He made to stand up. I did not allow that.

"You stick with me, Cat," I said, lifting his fat arm with my free hand. I held the real gun to his head, and allowed his henchmen to pass. We all walked down the hall. They walked down the steps. Before they stepped through the door, I said, "Hey Cat!" Then I shot the gringo's pistol twice. The report slammed up against my palm. They stumbled through the door. I wanted to shoot more, but looked up at the two bullet holes in the ceiling. I knew I was already in trouble with Abuelita for that. The door slammed closed. They were gone.

I sucked in a large amount of air, then fell back on the floor. When the women in my life ran around the corner, they hovered over me, looking for bullet holes in my body. They stopped looking, then reprimanded me once I started laughing uncontrollably.

Not all the women in my life ran to my aid. Abuelita had stayed in the kitchen. My wounded uncle held his hand up as his mother wrapped a white dish towel around the stub. He said nothing as she whispered to him how he would be all right. "*Yo te cuido, vos, sos mi cipote, mi único, y esos te han hecho esta malicia.*" She wept as she cared for him. He did not weep. He did not speak. He only stared into a vacuum that the rest of us could not see.

Part Four

I excitedly opened the packet that La Chucharrona had given me. An ounce of bud was a good amount, but there was no safe way to carry it on the plane ride back home to Knoxville, after my uncle's funeral. I would worry about that later. For now the problem was how to smoke it. Uncle Jack had left no receptacle for me. He hadn't even packed any papers inside the packet. I was on my own. I could almost hear my uncle's voice in the silence of the room, reprimanding me: *Jesus, son. Get off your ass and do something about it.*

One alternative would be to forget the marijuana and just eat a couple of the mushrooms. "No, I'm not ready for that," I said to the empty room. I almost felt the need to click my teeth together and knock my forehead with that thought, remembering the drop into another reality that night in the Mexican desert.

Someone knocked on the door. I closed up the packet and invited the person to come in. It was my father.

"Hey Dad."

"Hey there, son. Want to see my plane?"

His voice was asking for something. The plane was his center of joy these days. Perhaps, I thought, the loss of his brother-in-law was touching something in him.

"Sure." I shoved the package into my jacket pocket and followed him. We walked down the steps to the first floor of the old house, turned and walked through the door that I had quietly stepped through eighteen years ago, wielding a fake gun in my hand, preparing myself to take on a group of thugs. Dad opened the door to the garage and flicked on the light. It was nighttime now. No sunlight shown through the tiny windows of the garage door. Dad hit another switch. Flourescent lamps burned above us.

My father had taken over this garage for the past several months. It was impeccable. All the tools were placed on one long table or hung on nails in a large sheet of masonite. The cement floor had recently been swept. Even the odor of epoxy that hung in the air smelled crisp and clean, a reminder that work was done here on a regular basis.

The old flourescent bulbs flickered slightly over the two vehicles that stood in the garage. Uncle Jack's 1967 black Mustang was parked deep in the room, farther from Capp Street, closer to the door that led to the landscaped back yard. A small smile flickered over my lips. I turned away from the car in order to follow my father, who walked around the second vehicle: his airplane.

The ultralight was in five large pieces. The fuselage filled the middle area of the garage. The two wings hung on four hooks that dangled down from wires tied to the ceiling. They had been recently painted. The back tail fins leaned against a wall. The motor stood on two-by-four wooden blocks, looking similar to a lunar module.

"I just put a coat of primer on the wings last week, and painted them yesterday. I got this motor a couple of weeks ago. It's used, but it's been rebuilt. It's in good shape. I got a good deal on it. Brand new motors are expensive as hell."

"Is this the cockpit?" I asked, pointing to the open front of the fuselage.

"Yeah."

"Where's the door?"

"You don't use a door. I'll show you how you get in." Dad grinned as he explained the plane's intricacies. I knew how much joy building this craft gave him. It was scarcely a vicarious understanding of his happiness. I had never been interested in flying. I had a hard enough time getting on a jet, let alone crawling into something as small as this, a seemingly balsa-wood contraption that could barely keep the pilot from crunching through the floor to his five hundred foot plunge to the earth.

I stood to one side as he showed me how to board the craft. Dad lifted up his right leg, bending his knee in order to dip his foot into the one-person seat. His foot did not touch upon the floor of the plane, but went through a large hole in the floor until his shoe met the cement of the garage. Then he balanced himself on that right foot in order to lift his left foot up and follow suit. He stood up straight from the garage floor, with this fuselage surrounding him.

"Then you sit down, you see," he explained, carefully placing himself upon the cushioned chair.

"That's really great, Dad. But why do you do it that way? Why the hole?"

"Because I'd put my foot through the cloth of the fuselage if I didn't have that hole. It's so thin and light, it couldn't hold my weight. This chair, however, is bolted into the aluminum frame."

"But what do you do when you're flying? Couldn't you fall out of it, through that hole?"

He grinned. "I've got that one figured out too." He pulled his feet into the plane, shoving his knees against his chest. Then he reached down and flipped a lid over the hole. He placed his feet upon the lid. "See? No way to fall out."

I congratulated him upon his ingenuity. Yet his creativity was no surprise. He had invented, constructed, taken apart, and reconstructed such things all his life. According to family lore, he supposedly had built a self-oiler onto his Harley Davidson in 1948, long before self-oilers had been invented. He had broken down a 1946 Luscombe airplane at least three times in my life, only to build it back again each time. As a child I watched him overhaul an ancient outboard motor that someone had given him. Since we did not own a boat, he built one. It was big enough for Mom, Dad, and me to sleep in during summer outings. He could build and take apart anything.

None of his talents had seeped into my genes. I was lucky to be able to change the oil in my Honda in less than an hour and a half.

Dad reached down underneath the seat and pulled out a helmet. It was an old San Francisco 49ers football helmet that he had found in a dumpster somewhere in town. He had cleaned it up, though he had done nothing about the scratches all over the shell. It was obviously not a real helmet from the city's football team, but a remake of the originals, perhaps sold in toy stores for adolescents. He had lined it with Styrofoam. It had no face guard. Either he had found it without the guard, or had taken it off himself. He had also added something that no football player would need: goggles. These were strapped completely around the helmet, the elastic cutting over the number 49. He pulled the large goggles down from the helmet and strapped them over his face. The black-rimmed eye pieces were deep enough to reach behind the helmet's rim and suck tight around his eyes. He turned and looked at me, an old man of seventy six years, staring through the thick lenses that made him appear slightly crosseyed. Then he turned and looked at the joystick and the scant meters on the tiny dashboard.

"Time for takeoff," he said. He reached down and found a twist of tobacco in his shirt pocket. He ripped off a piece with his teeth and adroitly placed it in his cheek.

"You look ready to go," I said. I leaned upon the fuselage.

"Oh, yeah. I just need to get all these pieces together. But I can't do that here. I've got to take it in pieces out into a field outside of town. I'll put it together there and fly it. But I've got to test it a few times, you know, just taxi around a little bit."

"Where do you hope to do this?" I asked.

"Your aunt's got some land out beyond Daly City somewhere. It's a field that nobody's using."

He reached down again near his feet and lifted up an open tin can. It still had the label wrapped around it, Doña Roselia's Home-Style Refried Beans. He hooked his lower lip to the tin's edge and spat. "I'd like to think I can get this baby in the air before you go back to Tennessee."

"You better do it quick, then," I said. "I plan to be flying out of here Monday morning."

"Why so soon?" he asked. I could see, even through the large goggles, his eyebrows knitting slightly, perturbed at my quick departure.

"I've got to work on Monday, Dad. I've got a night class."

"Can't your students miss a day or so? Shit, we'll be burying your uncle tomorrow. You leave like that, you'll have a couple of sad women on your hands. Or maybe I should say that you'd be leaving *me* with a couple of sad sacks."

He was looking for excuses. "We'll see. Maybe you can get this thing flying by Sunday afternoon."

Dad looked down at the dashboard. He studied the lining of the walls, ones that he had carefully placed together with epoxy, bolts, and primer. He seemed to be silently asking the vehicle if it was ready.

"Maybe," he finally said.

As he worked himself out of the fuselage, opening the floor hatch and carefully lifting his legs over the cockpit's wall, I meandered over to his clean table. I noticed, among the well kept tools and paint cans, his smoking paraphernalia: an ash tray, two lighters, and two tiny books of papers.

There was the solution to one of my problems.

Yet it also carried its own obstacle. I did not know how to roll a cigarette. I had watched my father do it numerous times, making a perfect smoke. I had once tried to do it, just to see if I could. I had placed too much tobacco on the paper and had wrapped it too loosely. I had also slapped too much saliva on its edge. The soaked tobacco had dribbled out of both sides. It had been a complete failure. Before me now were the necessary papers. All I needed was the skill.

I turned around as Dad crawled out of the seat. A slow movement of conversation could get him to roll one for me; perhaps he wouldn't even know what he was rolling.

"Hey Dad, are these cigarette papers?"

"Yeah." He walked over without taking off the helmet or the goggles.

"That's a real trick, isn't it? To roll your own cigarette."

"Not really. Once you get the knack of it, it's not."

"I bet you save a lot of money rolling your own."

"Maybe. Hell, I don't know. I rolled them when I first began smoking, when I was six. I've smoked storebought sometimes. But I just got in the habit of making my own."

I hesitated a moment before I asked, "Could you teach me how to do it?"

"What? Roll a fag? I didn't know you smoked. Or did you also get a package from your uncle?"

I looked at him. He grinned, his eyes sparkling behind those goggles.

"You got a package from Uncle Jack too?" I asked.

"Yeah." He lowered his head while pulling the goggles off. Still, he did not take the Forty Niners helmet off just yet. "Kind of a going away present, I guess."

"So, have you . . . have you smoked, uh, you know . . ."

"Weed? Shit son, I'm seventy-six years old. I've probably done a lot of things you haven't gotten around to. Your uncle and I go back a long way, Tony." He then pulled off the helmet. The Styrofoam had made square impressions on the skin of his bald head.

"You want to toke a joint?" he asked.

It seemed strange, hearing such language coming from my geriatric Appalachian father. Obviously he had been around my uncle long enough to learn it. He walked away.

"But not down here," he said. "I only smoke when I've got the door open, and then I step out on the sidewalk. Too many fumes in here, could blow up the house."

I followed him upstairs. We went into my room.

Ten minutes later my father dexterously poured a line of dried green foliage upon the plane of thin, white paper.

"The trick of rolling a cigarette is to make sure the tobacco is tight enough to keep it from burning up in your face, but not so tight that you can't suck any air through it. The problem with this stuff is it's not cut like tobacco. Prince Albert in a can is made to lie real even over a paper. But this here weed, well, it's raw and hasn't been processed. So it's a little trickier. Then, when you go to close the fag, you don't lick it up and down like an ice cream cone. You just take your tongue right along the edge like this . . . see? Then you roll it up until it closes." He held the cigarette up vertically, pinched between his thumb and forefinger. "That there's the perfect joint, son."

A little less than an hour later we both agreed that the death-gift my uncle, his brother-in-law, had left us was indeed of high quality. Then again, I was not one whose word could be taken as solid. I had smoked little grass in my life. All I knew was this stuff worked.

Dad and I lay on our stomachs on the bed. We looked out the half-open window to Capp Street. A number of people walked by in the night.

"Shit, I wouldn't want to be out there this time of night," he said. "It's not like in the old days. There's gangs all over the place. Then again, I guess it's not as bad here, in the Mission. All those rich folks are moving in, taking over the place."

My mind followed another meandering path of conversation. "When did you see Uncle Jack last, Dad?"

"The morning before he died. He and I had a cup of coffee together."

"How was he?"

Dad looked down at the bedspread, then lifted his eyes up to the city again. "He was acting kind of strange the past couple of weeks. I can't help but think he knew something was going to happen. Maybe he was feeling sick. You know, his heart. Then again, Jack really wasn't the same ever since Ricarda died."

Again, the mere mention of her name shoved sadness, and perhaps a little guilt, into me. I had heard through the family network that Ricarda had suffered from uterine cancer for two months before her death. Jack had been with her in the end. She remained in the little village of Macizo once a doctor in Tijuana told her it was malignant. Jack had begged her to go to the States for further diagnosis, but she refused. That did not seem strange to me, knowing her for the few days that I had been in her home.

After re-learning Spanish, I had written her a long letter expressing my gratitude for her role in the rescuing of my heritage. She had written back a short note, apologizing for her lack of writing skills and hoping that all was well with me. Her grammar and spelling were those of a primary schoolgirl. Knowing how difficult it was for her to express herself on paper made me ache to see her once again, to eat at her table and speak with her in full Spanish conversations. I never took the opportunity. Many consequential events had taken hold of my life. Then death had taken hold of hers. I had sent a letter of condolence to Uncle Jack. He had called back, thanking me. Still, it had lacked the potency of being present.

Dad's voice pulled me from my nostalgic guilt. "He talked about you a couple of times."

"Yeah? What did he say?"

"He was wondering how you were doing over in Tennessee. I think he wanted to see you. Said he'd lost touch with you about six months ago."

Actually it was I who had lost touch with Uncle Jack. He had sent me a postcard from somewhere in Mexico. When he had returned from that trip, he had called me. "Tony, *que pasó*, man? What's going on?" I remembered that I was not ready to get into a conversation with him at the moment. I was in the midst of working on a manuscript. He had called in the morning, and though it was almost noon my time, I was still in the painstaking process of forming a new book that failed utterly before it got to my laser printer. I had spoken little with him. Now, as I lay on a bed next to my father, the both of us gazing through a haze toward the skyline, I realized that guilt was an entity too tremendous for even a good high to remedy.

Dad interrupted my jumping thoughts. "You know, I'm surprised you and he didn't keep more in touch, considering you had saved his life and all."

In my mind I repeated what I had said to Chucho at the funeral. Uncle Jack had been the one to save me. Back then, he had shown me the way. Since then I had slipped back into the spiritually moribund, a chronic, pathetic confusion in which one allows himself to be afraid of plane flights, who stands by while a woman cuckolds him, who approaches the computer with fear rather than imagination. What had caused this slippage? Then again, was it a slipping back at all? Or better said, was it just a loss, pure and simple? Eighteen years ago I had stuck a fake pistol into Gato's mouth and made him believe that I had the capacity to shoot him. I had, as my Uncle would have phrased it, made him believe my dick was bigger than his. Now, at age thirty-four, I cowered before the world, bending before the weight of a Confederate nose-picker who breezed the chassis of his pickup up my ass and drinking myself into an escape from a jet's possible fall.

"Your uncle talked quite a bit about that summer. I'm not sure what was getting into him. Well, maybe I do. He said he wasn't feeling well, like he was having acid indigestion, heartburn, something like that. None of us thought he was having heart problems. He talked about Chucho too. Said he wished that Chucho would get over what happened. You know, try to live with what they lost, just like your uncle was able to do."

"Yeah, but Uncle Jack didn't lose as much as Chucho did, Dad."

"What do you mean?" He looked at me.

"Well, it's one thing to lose your fingers. I mean, that's bad enough. I was there both times. I saw what that bastard did to Chucho and Uncle Jack. But to lose your testicles! That's a much greater loss, don't you think?"

"Who lost their testicles?" My father seemed to be baiting me.

"Chucho, of course! Gato had them cut off."

Dad laughed. I asked him why. He answered me with more laughter.

"Come on Dad, what's so fucking funny? You wouldn't be laughing if it had been you who lost his nuts."

He probably heard the testiness of my words, and finally answered me. "Chucho didn't lose his balls, Tony. Gato never touched them."

"What?"

"You heard me."

I stared down at the bedspread. "But I thought that he had gotten castrated . . . that's what they said . . ."

"That's what *Chucho* said."

"Why would he say a thing like that if it wasn't true?"

"Because Chucho, spiritually, has no balls." Dad chuckled.

I laughed too, knowing how few times in my father's life he had referred to the mystical.

"Chucho could never satisfy his wife. So his wife Amelia opened herself up to your uncle. Jack and she were hopping in the sack long before Chucho lost his fingers. Amelia told Jack that Chucho couldn't even get a hard-on anymore. But it wasn't because that Cat guy cut his nuts off. He just couldn't perform anymore in bed, I guess. But your uncle still could. So Chucho got cuckolded.

"That day was just a mess. Before Gato had shown up, Chucho had gotten your uncle mad, you remember? Yeah, your mom says you were there. So you and your uncle took off. Chucho went in and told Amelia that Jack had left mad. Then they got in a fight. Amelia, all pissed off, let it out that she was fucking your uncle. Then she took off. Chucho fell apart. Then Gato came and cut his fingers off. He really had a bad day that day."

I know my jaw hung open. "I knew about Jack and Amelia. But you're saying that Chucho learned about them that same afternoon?"

Dad nodded his head. "Yep. So he lost it in the hospital. Just kind of went nuts. After he got out, he kept that rumor going, saying that he had lost 'more than his fingers' to Gato. If you ever talk to him, you'll notice that he'll never say 'Gato cut my nuts off.' He just makes you think that happened. I guess that's his way of not having to take responsibility for having a limp dick. It's also his way of blaming your uncle for everything."

"But that's crazy," I said. "He blames Gato, but he's never forgiven Uncle Jack. Why?"

"Don't ask me. I've been married to your mother for forty-nine years. That doesn't mean I understand everything about her people."

I looked out the window. "Does everybody but me know that Chucho's got his penis intact?"

"I suppose so. For awhile there everybody believed it. But then Gato, after he got out of prison for poisoning all those people, started telling it differently. He got born again, you know, joined one of those crazy religions. He started repenting for all his sins. Once he got in the middle of the park over there across from Mission and started preaching about the Lord and shit. He talked about his bad ways with drugs and gangs and stuff. He asked God for forgiveness, as well as the pardon of all the people around here. 'But I ask forgiveness for the sins I *committed*,' he said, 'not for things I didn't do.' He just looked right at Chucho, who was in the crowd. That's when things started to clear up a little."

"So, Chucho blames Uncle Jack for his impotence. Jack died with Chucho hating him."

"Yep."

"That's nuts."

"I'd say so." Dad rubbed his forehead, as if to keep a certain sensibility intact so as to continue on in the conversation. "Chucho's one of those men who blames the world for his own fears."

That statement did not get lost in my high. It settled right on my brain's ability to reason.

I got quiet. He filled the silent gap with another subject. "I think I'll try to get that plane in the air on Sunday. That way you'll get to see it fly before you go home."

I looked over at him. "That sounds great."

He got up, stretched, and walked to the door. "I better get to bed. Your mother will wonder if I'm getting drunk somewhere or sleeping with another woman. Goodnight, son."

I wished him goodnight. He disappeared behind the door. I stared at the door as if wishing it would breathe. It did not. This was only marijuana, nothing more. I glanced at the package, now sitting on the bedtable. I saw the top of the mushroom pile. "Not tonight," I said aloud, pulling the sheets off the bed and shedding my clothes. "Maybe not ever." I lay down, barely looking out at the night before closing my eyes to the swirl.

Then I realized the concept of hunger. Not that I was hungry. I just realized the concept. I put on my pants and made my way through the dark house. A light left the kitchen and fell out upon the hallway floor. I turned the corner and saw my father as he pulled various foods out of the refrigerator: leftover tortillas, cheese, cola, peanut butter, jelly, fake crabmeat, mayonnaise, pecan pie, milk, bread, margarine, beans, ice cream.

He turned to me. "Hey. You hungry?"

I wanted to tell him that, no, I just realized the concept of hunger. Instead I sat at the table. So did he. We ate from each and every container.

The following morning, three hours before Uncle Jack's funeral, I rose from bed and prepared for a morning run. It was before seven o'clock on a Saturday. I hoped the traffic on the neighborhood roads would be light.

The morning sunshine helped to clear my head from the previous night's toke with my father. It could not clear, however, the guilt that built up within me, one planted by Dad when he mentioned that my uncle was asking for me days before his death. The fact that I had not been thinking of him at all, until I had received the phone call from Mamá telling me he was dead, did not help matters. Since that call, and since arriving in San Francisco, that summer of long ago roused itself in me, playing before me shards of moments that collected into a solid mass of memory, one which proved powerful enough to break through two decades.

The days following that distant morning, when I had chased Gato and his henchmen out of my grandmother's house, rattled down into a certain quietude. My uncle had lost one of his fingers. During the fight, the Hispanic, having become accustomed to taking people's appendages off, found Uncle Jack's arm, held it, and pressed the razor underneath the knuckle while I had been downstairs, frantically looking underneath the Mustang's seats for the fake pistol. After Gato and his men fled, we spent the rest of the day looking for the finger while Jack rested in a nearby hospital. Abuelita had seen the finger fly out the open door of the kitchen. According to her, it had bounced off the railing and had either dropped into the back yard or sailed over to the neighbor's grass. We never found it. No doubt one of the neighbor's legion of cats had taken it away. The doctors ended up sewing Jack's wound closed. They asked him what had happened, who had done this to him, would he like for them to call the police? He did not respond. He would do nothing against Gato, holding to the pact that Gato and my grandmother had made.

That same day Aunt Felícita pressed charges against Little Felícita. She quickly found out what had happened by demanding the truth from the young male employee named Harold with whom Little Felícita flirted. Harold thought that Little Felícita actually loved him. They had made out a number of times in the back storage room of the office. She had finally promised to make love to him, right there, in the back closet, if he would only go to a bathroom and buy a condom. It was nearly five o'clock, so most all the other employees on the floor had gone home. He was the last one to leave the building, and had been trusted to close up and lock the offices, including closing the main safe. Knowing that the company's restrooms for some strange reason had no condom vending machines, Harold ran down the block to a nearby gas station. He ran back up into the offices, smiling, pulling the newly bought merchandise from his pocket. Little Felícita smiled back at him.

"Perhaps another time, Harold," she had said, blatantly folding a piece of paper and tucking it into her purse. "I just remembered, I have another appointment." She left him.

He cursed her teasing ways as he closed up the office and turned off the lights, not ending the string of words until he noticed that the safe had already been closed and locked.

Aunt Felícita placed that piece of information alongside a phone call to a local bank where she had a good friend who was able to whisper to her facts concerning certain people's financial situations. My aunt learned that Little Felícita had recently deposited five thousand dollars into her savings account. The only person Aunt Felícita knew who had such on-hand cash (besides herself) was Rata, Little Felícita's old ex. But Aunt Felícita knew she could never link Rata to this break-in. She could, however, threaten Harold with a firing if he did not testify to what had happened. Though it was not enough to prosecute her, it was sufficient to have Little Felícita picked up by the cops and thrown in jail for the night.

While Uncle Jack lay in a hospital bed, receiving blood transfusions, Mamá, Aunt Felícita, Abuelita and I visited Little Felícita in jail. She stood on the other side of the bars, screaming through curses about her innocence. Her long, thick black hair jostled off her skull, bouncing over her shoulders. She looked down at all of us, that's how tall she was.

Aunt Felícita was bold enough to walk closer to the bars. "Little Felícita, You big shit. You sold the family recipe to a drug dealer. You sold the secret of the Guanacotamales. The *Guanacotamales!*"

I thought she meant to punch Little Felícita through the bars. The two women stood and verbally fought each other for awhile. The guards did not get involved.

As the two Felícitas screamed at each other, Abuelita was talking into my mother's ear. My mother finally cut through the screaming with a solid, calm voice, *"Mamá dice que no va a* press charges."

Both Felícitas turned and looked at Abuelita. Both said, "What?"

"Mamá's not going to press charges."

We all turned and looked at Abuelita. She only stood there, saying nothing for a long while. Finally she said, and my mother translated for me, "I cannot believe that my own granddaughter would do this. I cannot believe it. I want her free."

My aunt turned and stared at her mother with eyes that metamorphosed into white hot stone. She walked out of the local jailhouse. We followed behind her. Abuelita and Mamá talked to each other, back and forth, speaking in Spanish. I understood nothing, neither inside nor outside of the language. Perhaps, I thought, the family is the tie that binds, as well as forgives.

"No te preocupés, hija," Abuelita said to Mamá, *"todos van a recibir lo que merecen."*

It was not long before we all learned what she had meant, that all would get what they deserved. Halfway through the summer, a commercial played over a local Spanish radio station, announcing a new tamale on the market called Gato's Tamale Delights. We had heard, before the commercial, that Gato had recently left his fledgling drug industry behind and had invested all his money into new equipment—industrial size dough kneaders, huge stoves, pots, pans, rental of a kitchen (which he had planned to buy later), and employees. He had failed to report the new business to the Food and Drug Administration, as well as the Food Safety Board. They, however, would soon learn of him.

Two days after the commercial, fifty-five people checked into hospitals complaining of gastrointestinal inflammation. Most all of them were from the Mission District. All of them had bought and had eaten Gato's new tamales. One of them, a man in his late eighties, died. The police found Gato. He was charged and convicted with involuntary manslaughter as well as failure to report his new business to the proper institutions. He was given ten years in prison.

Later we learned how this happened. It was no mistake on his part. He had followed Abuelita's instructions to perfection, even the part that said, "*Deje que la gallina se quede en la salsa de tomate y de mayonasa y dentro de un cuarto caliente por cuarenta y ocho horas, para que absorba todos los sabores de la salsa.*" Let the chicken sit in its tomato-mayonnaise sauce for forty-eight hours, exposed in a warm room, so that it absorbs all the flavors of the sauce. Gato was a drug runner, not a cook. He knew nothing of salmonella.

When the authorities asked Abuelita about this, she shrugged her shoulders and told them that the piece of paper was not her recipe. "My tamales don't have a drop of mayonnaise in them!" she insisted. "And who would be stupid enough to leave chicken out in the heat for two days?" She invited the authorities to dissect one of her tamales in order to verify the absence of mayonnaise. They felt no need to. They left Abuelita's home, satisfied that Gato had just screwed up on his own.

Later that night, gathered around the kitchen table, we talked about the recent events. Abuelita stayed silent. Finally I asked her, "Abuelita, excuse me, but where *is* the recipe?" She answered by smiling at me and tapping her forehead with her fingertip.

We all figured that Abuelita just did not want to believe that Little Felícita was involved in the plot. This perturbed some of us. Yet we only had to wait a few more years, when Abuelita was on her deathbed, for her to make one final decision, one that would give Little Felícita—as my Aunt put it—her final just rewards. It was my grandmother's slashing of her name in the will and of giving Little Felícita only one dollar after Abuela's death that excommunicated my cousin from the Villalobos clan.

Uncle Jack came home the day after he lost his finger. Abuelita made sure he remained in bed. He made sure that a bottle of Early Times always stood nearby. He swallowed straight from the bottle while staring at a television set on the other side of the room. He also popped a number of painkillers that the doctors had prescribed him. Once, when we walked in, we saw that he was not sleeping, but had passed out. My mother took that opportunity to hide both the bottle away as well as the medicine. "Maybe, if he feels some of the pain, it will wake him up, remind him that he's still alive."

I was not sure what she meant by this. Of course he was alive. Gato's men had not killed him. Yet after a few days, I had to wonder if my mother was talking about another kind of death. Or perhaps a dark form of anger. I felt he pointed the silent anger at me.

Whenever I walked into his bedroom, Uncle Jack would barely look at me. He only stared at the television while Donahue talked to celibate transvestites. I tried to get a conversation going, to no avail.

Once, while searching for something to talk about, I said, "Maybe we should call Aunt Ricarda. She may want to come up and visit you." It was one of the few times he answered. He almost jumped down my throat, cursing at me, demanding that I make no mention of this to Ricarda. I promised I would not, although I wanted to ask how he planned to hide it from her. I said nothing, while he retreated into a cold distance from me.

I spent the rest of the summer working in my Abuelita's company. I cleaned the huge pots that the tamales were made in every day, along with various other cooking utensils that the workers used. I had to go among three rooms to make sure that everything was cleaned. In this way I learned that Abuelita's recipe had three general levels to it. One room of employees worked with the meat itself. They quartered fifty pounds of stewing hens and pork loins a day, cooking them in vats of water filled with various spices. After this, the rest of the process necessarily fell into a process in which no one knew what the other did. The boiled meat was taken to another room where workers tore it apart and added seventeen spices to it. Meanwhile, the broth was carried to a third room, where the *masa harina* would be added to make a thick batter. This batter was cooked at high temperatures and stirred with mechanical whipping spoons that I would later dismantle and spray with hot water before running them through a huge dishwasher. I started to see how the guanaco-tamales were made, though I did not have all the ingredients down. I also saw that the batches were made fresh. One thousand new tamales went out daily. This was not a large amount, considering how many thousands of tortillas and millions of cans of refried beans and hundreds of thousands of bags of prepared corn meal went out from the factory each week. But the tamales were meant to be sold in small quantities in the local San Francisco area. They were the delicacy of Doña Roselia's enterprise.

I worked six hours a day, which gave me time to enjoy most of the afternoons and all of the evenings. I forced myself into the habit of exercising every day, doing the pushups and situps that Uncle Jack had taught me, as well as running around the block of Capp Street five times. I went to movies every week. My aunt took me to a number of discos, where I learned how to shove my pointed finger up into the air just like Mr. Travolta. Aunt Felícita bought me three suits that summer: white, brown, and black. They were all three-pieced, with wide collars, no ties, and slight bell bottoms in the pants. She went all out, purchasing for me the best in polyester shirts. She also bought me a pair of leather boots, which I took to wearing all the time. I could see how the boots helped motivate guys into a constant, strutting walk, like Travolta. *Strut* became a silent, important word for me. Aunt Felícita even bought me a new hair dryer, a huge gun with three settings and a cannonlike barrel. I was in heaven.

I kept my journal on me all day, sticking it in the back pocket of my jeans. During work hours in Abuelita's company I would pull it out periodically and jot down a word that someone on the floor had just used. Most everyone there was Latino, either Mexican, Guatemalan, Salvadoran, or Honduran. At work, for six hours a day, Spanish swirled around me. I tried to use the newly memorized words with them, which made a few laugh. *"¡Oye, el pocho nos quiere platicar!"* Then another admonished the one who seemed to ridicule me, *"Cuidáte vos. Es el nieto de la jefa. No querés encachimbarte."* I did not care what they said. I kept tossing the words at them, forcing them to deal with me. They did, sometimes with a cruelty that I could not understand. I shut my eyes of pride. If I stuttered a mouthful of words to one young man, trying to talk about how all the big spoons from the *masa* mixer could not fit all at once into the dishwasher, he would turn and rattle thirty seconds of pure Salvadoran idioms at me, while the rest of them laughed. At the moment I resented them. Later I would thank them, as their refusal to treat me with gentle gloves made me persist in the search for my childhood's lost language.

Two weeks after he lost his finger, Uncle Jack bolted through the door of his room and walked down the hallway. Jack wore his jeans and jean shirt. He shoved a cigarette between his lips. He barely looked at me. I glanced down at his bandaged hand. He turned and made his way to the stairs.

"Where are you going?" I asked.

"What's it to you?"

At first I stuttered. Then I chose not to stutter. "I was just asking. It's the first time you've left your room."

"I'm feeling better." He turned and made his way down three steps.

"Are you going to see Chucho?" I blurted out, hoping my stab at truth hit the mark.

"What about it?" He did not turn around to look at me.

"I want to go too."

"No you don't."

"Yes I do!" I hopped down the stairs.

He turned and put the index finger of his left hand in my face. "Stay home, *sobrino*. I got some shit to clear up."

"Yeah, and so do I. I mean, I want to be there in case . . ."

"In case what? You think you're going to protect me or something?"

I would not have put it that way, but I suppose that was what I had planned to do. Actually, what I had wanted to do was merely be by my uncle's side. Since the incident with Gato, I had yearned to spend time with him. The days in Macizo had somehow been lost to the two weeks of enraged, silent mourning over his finger. I wanted back the time that he had given me while at Ricarda's house. I wanted ed to be with him. I was, however, not about to tell him that.

"Well, yeah," I finally answered him.

He rolled his eyes. "I don't need your protection."

I waited until he almost reached the door at the bottom of the stairs before saying, "You certainly needed it two weeks ago, when that hoodlum was ready to carve you up."

"He fucking *did* carve me up!" Uncle Jack held up the wounded hand. Then he jerked up three steps before catching himself. The sudden exertion was not kind to his body, which was still weak from blood loss. "Look, I had told you to stay downstairs in the basement. You disobeyed me, man! And where the fuck did you get an idea like that, waving a fake gun in Gato's face? Who the fuck gave you Samson's balls, 'ey? That was a stupid thing to do!"

"Stupid? You're calling me stupid?" I laughed hard as my breath caught itself, afraid yet angry. My voice trembled with both emotions. "So this is why you've been pissed off at me for two weeks. You were the one who just ran into the house without any weapon. You stormed in, threatening to break them apart with your bare hands. You weren't even thinking, Uncle Jack! You could have gotten killed."

"Hey, that's the kind of action that men like Gato understand. But you walk in with a Hollywood shooter and start mouthing off like some Appalachian hillbilly, Jesus Christ! That was too big of a risk, Tony. You show a fake gun, they could have plugged us all with real guns. I ran in without any weapon. That way I knew they wouldn't pull a pistol on me."

"But they would have cut you up, either way."

"Better me than my mother." He stood face to face with me now, his boots on the step just below mine. "Better they cut me than cut my sisters, your aunt and your mother, Tony."

"So that's what it is. You sacrificed yourself." I kept my eyes directly before his.

"Whatever. But you almost got us all killed, kid."

"I was trying to keep them from hurting you." I hoped this would reach into something soft in him.

I was at first not sure if it did, for he turned away. So I tried another tactic. "Hey, if you're the sacrificial lamb, then why are you moping about it? You chose to do that, *tío*. Why do you now have to wear a long face all the time?"

He veered and focused upon my use of the Spanish word for Uncle. "So now you're suddenly from *La Raza*, 'ey Tony? Now you've decided to be Latino." He laughed. It was a stab of mockery, anything to bring me down.

"A la chingada contigo," I said to him (I had studied that phrase just that morning).

"Hey, you watch your mouth, punk. You don't talk like that to your elders."

"I still don't see why you hate me now. All I wanted to do was help you!"

He said nothing. I heard him breathe. He walked through the door, down the hall, and into the garage. I followed him. I walked to the other side of the Mustang and got in. He just shook his head while shoving the keys into the ignition.

When he pulled out, the bottles of old pills on the back floor-board rattled again, tiny maracas calling to him. He reached back, then stopped. My mother's hiding of the other pain killers and the whiskey had kept his body clean for two weeks, enough to give him the choice. Looking at me, he listened as the rattle of pills came to a rest. "Ah, fuck it," he said, leaving them alone.

At Chucho's house, Uncle Jack slowed. He got out of the car carefully, still weak from blood loss. I followed behind him. He called out to Chucho's apartment. No one answered. Finally a woman stuck her head out of a window. Jack smiled at her, then asked where her husband was. She clicked her tongue while saying, "He's in bed, of course. Won't get up for anybody."

Just then Chucho proved her wrong. He pushed through the front door and stood on the porch step. The way he looked, I thought he was prepared to pull a weapon on Uncle Jack. He did not. He only stared, trembling slightly while speaking. He said the same words over and over again: "You've taken everything from me, man, everything." I interpreted this to mean what I would believe for eighteen years, until my father set me straight. Because of my uncle, Chucho had supposedly lost his testicles. Then Chucho turned and slammed the door closed.

Uncle Jack looked up at Chucho's wife. *"¿Se enteró de nosotros?"* he asked, and she nodded in affirmation. *"Enterarse,"* I remembered, meant something like "to find out." Jack shook his head. He stared at the door as if hoping his old friend would come out again to say something else. But Chucho did not. Those were the last words spoken between them, and would remain the final words until the day Chucho stood next to me and over my uncle's corpse, whispering the long-held curses of bitterness, of loss.

We drove home. The sun was setting. In front of the house, Jack parked the car. He looked over the steering wheel and down the road, not really seeing anything of Capp Street.

After a long, silent moment he said to me, "Listen, *sobrino*, I'm sorry about blowing up earlier. I'm just not in my right head these days, know what I'm saying?"

I nodded.

He chuckled sardonically. "Looks like I've lost a good friend. Don't want to lose my nephew."

He stared a long while at the sidewalk before speaking. "You just don't know what shit's going to happen."

Then he turned to me, his eyes giving me a sideways glance. "Yeah, I'm sorry about getting pissed. You were just trying to do the right thing, I guess. And hell, who knows what the right thing is in moments like that?" He then looked down at his right hand and the white bandage that criss-crossed it. "Funny. I look at this hand and feel like I've lost everything. I've never been hurt like this before. I've been shot, but the bullet didn't take anything away from me. It left me whole. But this . . . this means that I've lost something. I can lose stuff. I could have died. Could have lost that." He stared long at the place where his pinky once had been. "But I didn't. I didn't die, because of you." He gave me a direct look. "That did take some balls of steel to do what you did, you know that?" He reached over and grabbed my skull with his left hand, the one with all the fingers; he rattled my head back and forth. It hurt. I grinned. "Yeah. I think you're going to be all right, son."

After a long pause he asked, "Hey, you want to get stoned?" Then he answered himself before I could, "Nah. I don't feel like it myself."

I was not necessarily disappointed.

"But what about a bite to eat? We could get some hamburgers and a couple of beers, go over to Golden Gate Park. It's pretty over there this time of day."

I agreed. He told me to go inside and inform the women that we wouldn't be home until later, that we were planning to eat out. I did, then I returned to the car, with my mother and aunt following right behind me. Mamá stared hard at Uncle Jack while Aunt Felícita reminded us both of what happened the last time we went out for hamburgers, that they didn't want to get another phone call from Mexico, "and you *cipotes* better be back before night, *¡Dios mío como estos malcriados nos tratan!*" My mother nodded her head in agreement while looking at me. I smiled at her. I hoped my gesture would also thank her for what she had done this summer, taking me away from the eastern hills of Tennessee in order to save my very body here, in San Francisco, with the refilling of familial blood.

We bought three hamburgers apiece. We also bought two large cartons of fries and giant colas. Uncle Jack drove to the west end of Golden Gate Park so we could enjoy the sun setting into the Pacific Ocean. He pointed out numerous women who were either running or walking their dogs or kissing their lovers under trees. He commented upon various angles of their beauty. I grunted in agreement while polishing off the hamburgers. We sat on a bench and leaned upon the picnic table, sipping colas through straws and watching the beauty of women go by. He tested me on my Spanish. I surprised him with my studies, having at this point memorized a good five hundred words. I showed him my journal. "Hey, that's great, man. But you know what you got to do in order to really get into the language? You got to go back across the border, live there awhile. That way the language has a chance to seep into you." I quietly agreed, tucking that idea away, with the hope of resurrecting it sometime soon.

Our backs were to the night and our faces to the ending day. We stared until the Pacific completely swallowed the sun.

"Well," he said, still staring at the sea, his words falling from his lips, "we better get home to the women."

By mid August Mamá and I prepared to leave San Francisco. After little persuasion, she decided to buy us two plane tickets. "I suppose we both got our fill of the country on that bus, don't you think?"

In a week I was to start my junior year in high school. My mind was far away from the first days of class, though Mamá had once again arranged a living situation for me. I was to live with a family whose father was a teacher at Tennessee Catholic. There were no other teenagers in the house. The parents did have a nine-year-old son, but that suited me fine. I did not want to deal with another person near my age: neither a sadistic, sexually repressed teen or a pretty young woman with whom I would struggle to keep myself out of love. Still, it meant another year of living away from home. I knew my mother fretted over that. She grew angry sometimes, a way of channeling her sadness. She finally confessed to me, two days before our plane trip home, "I just hate to let you go again." She wept. I wanted to weep, but did not. I had grown strong this summer. I would not fall apart as I had fallen apart before. Besides, at this point, the only life I recognized was that of living away from home. Yet I did promise her that I would let no *pendejo* at the school *joderme*. She smiled at my curses, taking stock in my conviction. It was a true conviction: Whatever awaited me in the new household or in the halls of the school, I would let no fucker bring me down.

Uncle Jack, Aunt Felícita, and Abuelita took us to the airport. My grandmother smothered me in kisses and Spanish phrases, half of which I could readily understand. Aunt Felícita thanked me for working in the company. I thanked her for giving me the employment. I left San Francisco with seven hundred dollars in my pocket.

Uncle Jack grinned at me behind his sunglasses. He took them off and stared straight into my eyes. Taking my left hand with his five-fingered one, he shook it as one man shakes another. He barely nodded his head in approval. "Don't you forget how much fun we had in Mexico, ¿*me oyes?*"

"*Nunca,*" I answered. "*Me acuerdo de todo.*"

He laughed, then slapped me on the back. It hurt. I grinned, like a teenager, uncontrollably.

I took our carry-on while Mamá took her purse. We boarded. I could see my family through the window of the plane and the window of the public watchtower. My grandmother and aunt stood on each side of my uncle. There he stood, his thumbs behind his belt, his stature the same as ever, making the world believe that he was whole, and in so doing, telling no lie. They waved at our plane. Mamá and I waved back. Then my uncle tossed his arm around his mother and kissed her on the cheek. No doubt he was chiding her about the tears she spilt over her departing daughter and grandson. Aunt Felícita poked Uncle Jack in his ribs, obviously telling him to leave their poor mother alone. He then grabbed her by the neck. She struggled, trying to keep her well kept hair from being mussed by his thick arm.

My mother wept quietly as well. I looked at her. She smiled at me. "*Bueno pues, vamos a la casa.*"

"*Sí. Vamos, Mamá.*"

She patted my hand with her own. I suppose she wept for her son as well, happy she had lost nothing of him, had in fact, gained something more.

Part Five

A handful of people, perhaps twenty-five in all, gathered in the funeral service at the Funeraria Colón. There was a priest, but few people paid him much attention before he began the Catholic service. We spent time taking photographs. Aunt Felícita handed me her camera. "There's a whole roll. Use it up." She stood and approached the coffin. She and Mamá stood at each end, Mamá at Uncle Jack's head, Aunt Felícita at his feet. Then they switched places. "Stand on a chair, Tony," my aunt directed. "That way you'll get a better shot of your uncle."

Then they made Dad get in two pictures. "I don't want my picture taken with a dead man, Carmen. That's too god damn weird," he whispered. My mother looked him straight in the eye without saying a word. He obeyed. As I aimed the lense at them—my mother, aunt, and Dad all gathered at Jack's head, with Aunt Felícita placing her outspread fingers upon Jack's chest—I heard my father mutter, "You all have the damnedest customs."

My work was not over as a photographer. Most every woman in the crowd had brought a camera. They asked that I remain on the chair while they posed next to Uncle Jack's head. I heard behind me a Latina explaining the custom to a young gringa. She was the same blonde woman who wore blue yesterday and who now wore black. She still had really, *really* nice breasts.

"Oh gosh, I didn't know about this," she said. "I didn't bring any camera!" The gringa then asked the Latina, "Could you please let me use your camera? I'll pay you twenty-five dollars for the shot."

In the procession, about a dozen cars followed the hearse. Behind our Mercedes was a lavender 1970 Cadillac that had been overhauled into a low-rider by one of La Chucharrona's grandchildren. It was the same grandson who had sat at her feet the first time she lit the candles for me, eighteen years ago. He must have been twenty-three now. He drove the vehicle without making it hop, while Chucharrona sat in the back, holding a small leather bag in her hands.

In the cemetery the priest moved through the service with his eyes turned mostly to his book. Afterwards he shook my hand, then the hands of my mother, aunt, and father. He exited through an opening in the small crowd of women, then stood behind them. He was one of the few men who gathered around the hole in the ground.

Chucho was not here. This angered me. Yet I realized that, had he shown up, he might have done something inappropriate, such as spit into the grave or, after everyone left, urinating upon it. Now knowing that he had not lost his testicles to Gato's blade, I had little respect for the man. I remembered the days following the incident, how my uncle had stared at his own hand in amazement and sadness, knowing that he had lost a part of himself, that he indeed could lose a great deal in this life. Then I remembered that photo in my apartment back in Knoxville, the one of him leaning over his parents' tombstone, staring straight into the camera, with no fear of either life or death. That photo had been taken years after the loss of his finger. He had regained his fearlessness. Perhaps it had even become stronger, knowing how great the risks were, yet still willing to live with them. Chucho, on the other hand, had decided to live behind a strange lie, willing to have the world believe that he had lost his physical manhood rather than tell the truth about his cuckoldry. I did not fully understand why or how Chucho could live that way, except to take stock in his grandmother's opinion that he was just a whiner. I too would have called him a name, had I not felt my own life drawing dangerously close to his.

I put thoughts of Chucho away to watch my family walk up to the grave and drop palmfuls of clay into the hole. I did the same. Within twenty minutes the grave diggers had the hole filled, using a backhoe to do most of the heavy work. Then we all stood back as the priest walked away, shaking his head as La Chucharrona approached the grave. His face demonstrated a sense of resignation. No doubt she had followed his rituals up on other occasions. He was driving away before La Chucharrona pulled the candles out of her leather bag and planted them into the loose earth. She lit each one, first the red, then the black, followed by the yellow and the white, lighting the middle green one last. The day cooperated. There was no wind. The midday sun shined into every crack and turn of leaf and grass in the rolling hills of the cemetery. It was truly a magnificent day, crisp air, few clouds, stillness. There were no shadows. It was a day in which I could imagine my uncle barely smiling as he turned about and looked for the most beautiful woman in the area, ready to compliment her ways and demeanor. If there are souls, no doubt he was standing among us now, amidst the handful of women who had attended the funeral and the procession. Perhaps they wept now for feeling the only wind of his spirit licking over the curves of their thighs and filling their inner folds.

After lighting the candles, Chucharrona stood and took a step back. She muttered a few words in her own language of Q'achiq'el. Then she walked away, leaving the candles to burn down to their nubs, a final gift to her friend. I noticed that she too was weeping. No matter what she knew about this life and any other lives afterward, she still walked within our existence. Uncle Jack would no longer come by her office and ask her for divinations, nor would he kid her about her beauty even at the age of one hundred and twenty. No doubt she would miss his youthful, chiding ways.

Before we left, I realized that I had not gotten the opportunity to have someone take a picture of me with Uncle Jack. It was too late now. He was under the dirt. I had missed something. I thought about that photo in my bedroom back in Knoxville, of Uncle Jack leaning over the tombstone of his parents, staring straight at me. It was then that I wept. I had my sunglasses on, but the tears streamed and collected upon the dark lenses before brimming over the edge of the wire frames. I felt something in my body, like a giant invisible hand that shook within, reach forward toward the grave in one last chance to hold onto something. The fact that I had not had a picture taken with his body and that he was now buried told me the only truth of this day: He was dead. He was dead.

While we were driving out of the cemetery, a small car came in from an opposite entrance. I recognized the driver, then glanced over at my mother and aunt. They did not notice, as they were busy cleaning the tears from their eyes and wiping mascara with the corners of facial tissues. It was just as well. As I turned the wheel and looked toward the opening of the cemetery, Little Felícita unfolded out of her car and stood alongside the filled grave of her father. In the distance I could not see if she was weeping. No doubt she was. It had never become fully clear to me what form Uncle Jack's relationship with his daughter took. She had sinned one too many times in the minds of the family. Even Uncle Jack couldn't support her ways. Still, she was my cousin. I wanted to turn around and stand by her side for a moment. I felt those hot waves of childhood, from the moments when she whispered into my ear. She had a way with another's body. No doubt she was her father's daughter. Perhaps, I pondered, that would be a saving grace. Yet, much like Chucho's spineless inability to reconcile with my uncle, there was little that I or anyone could do to rectify the maelstrom of history left in the wake of Little Felícita's actions. I drove away, distinguishing between the things that I could control with those that I could not. There was some tranquility in recognizing such limitations.

That afternoon we were exhausted. My father retired to his and Mamá's bedroom and picked up a book, only to fall asleep after a few minutes of reading. Mamá and Aunt Felícita had fixed something for all of us to eat, then left the dishes in the sink to be cleaned later in the evening. The finality of funerals, I have noticed, has this effect upon the survivors. Such close proximity to another's death puts a strain upon the body, forcing it to retreat for awhile into the thick folds of human sleep.

I too retired to my room. I picked up the English Literature anthology that I had brought, along with the shallow goal of preparing for the following week of classes. The thought of returning to Knoxville and teaching English to a roomful of well intentioned but barely interested students wearied me as much as did Death. I dropped the heavy, onion-skinned anthology to the floor and stared up at the ceiling, then fell asleep for an hour.

In the evening we dined together. I ate lightly. My aunt did not understand why I wanted to drink only water. I told her that I just was not in the mood to have any alcohol. She shook her head in affirmation, seeing my abstention from drink to be some form of personal homage to her brother. She did not ask me whether or not I had dealt with the issue of Chucho's reconciliation. Perhaps she had come to the same conclusion that I had earlier in the day, that we were not able to fix unmendable bridges.

Though I had consumed no alcohol, it was not due to homage to the dead. I had planned on joining the dead later on in the evening. I didn't want other substances ruining the trek. I had no idea what form of dreaming I would take. Still, I opened myself to it.

While the rest of the house settled down for the evening, I wished them all goodnight. "Be ready for tomorrow, son," my father said. "We'll go out to that field and put the plane together." I told him I looked forward to it. As I walked away from the living room, I could hear my mother admonish Dad for his desire to fly a homemade plane and no doubt quickly join his brother-in-law in the grave. He mumbled something back to her. Their bickering made me grin. Yet I also had a certain nervousness about Dad's desire to take that plane up. It was good that I was going to do what I had planned to do early in the evening, so as to be fairly awake tomorrow, in case of an emergency.

I ate three mushrooms, sipping down three small gulps of water with each piece of fungus. They hadn't changed in taste. Pure horse-shit. Then I sat back in the sofa chair and waited.

Outside someone beeped a car horn. People walked down the streets, heading to shows, cinemas, bars, nightclubs, restaurants. The sun had yet to set. I stood up from the chair and walked to the bed, then lay upon it, staring out the window. A few boys rode expensive black skates on the sidewalk, jumping over the curb, twisting around, then jumping back up on the cement walk. It seemed so dangerous; any moment they could fall and crack something, their head, a wrist, a knee. Yet they danced with a grace that seemed inherent, a gift that would lift them up the moment they fell, keeping them from mussing one hair on their head. I knew that was not true. Any one of the boys could slip and accidentally slide underneath the fender of a passing car. They could catch a wheel on the curb, which would fling them downward, smashing their face into cement. It could be all over with-in the minute. That was what made the skating beautiful, what made their moves utter grace: how near they danced to invisible graves.

Looking about the room showed me that nothing had happened yet. It was still a room. I was still me. Yet the mere consuming of the mushrooms made me think about things differently. Indeed, the knowledge of the upcoming twists in my mind's perception of the world had a way of affecting me even before engaging that new vision. An intense pause enveloped me. There was a fear involved. No one stood by me to make sure I did not hurt myself. That was the only real concern. I believed that this trip would not be like the one in Mexico at Don Chicolino's home. There, a great entity of pure fear, which took on the form of Barry, had waited for me in the darkness of that desert's night. Barry no longer haunted me. He was long dead in the desert. Yet there were other things that haunted me these days: Julie and her cuckolding grip upon me through Bill. The fear of flying back home. The upcoming classes that I hated to teach. The truck-driving, tobacco-spitting Confederate who would be waiting for me the moment I stepped off the plane. The writing, the lack of writing.

Yet they were not the issues. I knew that. They were much like Chucho's lie over his castration. His balls remained physically intact, but Chucho was indeed emasculated. There was nothing I could do for that poor half-man. Yet perhaps it was not too late for me. The Confederate would probably not be waiting for me on the other side of the mushrooms, nor would Bill's Redwood Forest penis. Yet it was certain that the ride would be as ravaging as the one I had been pulled into eighteen years ago. I hoped to guide the ride slightly, if that were anywhere near possible. Then I smiled as the possibilities became real, as the closed door expanded and the room took on breath and blood. The perfect sounds of the skaters' wheels on Capp Street zipped through my skull as I stared at the growing darkness of my bedroom. Then I heard the growl, the low, human purr of that voice which sounded ready to laugh. "Borderless," I said to the room. "*Sin fronteras. No hay murallas entre la vida y la muerte.*"

'*Ey*, said the growl, *my sobrino's Spanish whips it up good. Can you make love to a woman in Spanish?* I grinned. "I can fucking do anything." *Big words, Tony. Especially for a guy who's been clicking his teeth and knocking his knuckles on his forehead again, right? Knock that shit out, son. Prove yourself. A man's dick is only as big as his life.* Though I did not fully understand that, I laughed as I stood up and approached the low purr of the darkness.

The following morning we all drove out to the large field that my aunt owned in Daly City. I drove Mamá and Aunt Felícita in the Mercedes. Dad had hooked his trailer full of plane parts to a small truck and followed behind us. The trailer was an old U-Haul receptacle. The fuselage stuck out of the open back door.

While Dad and I took wrenches to the vehicle, bolting tight the wings, tail section, and motor to the fuselage, my mother and aunt made a picnic spread underneath the shade of a tree. It took us a little over an hour to construct the plane. After we finished, I looked over at the women. They both wore large sunglasses. My mother was dressed in jeans and a cotton shirt. My aunt wore a pure white jumper outfit. Both of them drank beers and ate *pupusas* that they had prepared earlier in the day.

Dad stepped back from the machine. "Looks like it's ready."

It was a beautiful craft. Looking much like a model of a regular plane, the Ultralight stood ready for flight. The red stripes down its middle matched perfectly the stripes on the wings and tail. He had also painted black lines alongside the red, which brought out the distinction from the white background.

"Now the question is, are you ready?" I asked.

Dad looked down at the ground, then backed up. He wiped sweat from his forehead. Both of us were tired from working. "I hope so," he finally answered.

We decided to partake of the picnic before he took off. Much of the food was already cold, but we ate everything. Mamá and Aunt Felícita had packed *pupusas,* beans, rice, *picadillo* meat, salad, fruit, beer, wine, and pieces of *postre* for dessert. When I commented on the spread, how delicious it was, my mother was quick to answer, "If it's your last supper, might as well make it a good one."

Dad did not respond to her comment. He just looked out over the field, probably checking to see if too much wind swept the area. No doubt he was also gazing into the day to make sure he had a final picture of it in case anything happened.

After eating, Dad took a nap. Mamá read a book. Aunt Felícita watched a show on her portable television set. I lay down, but did not sleep. I thought about my mother's phrase concerning this airplane and Dad's desire to fly it, that it was his *ataúd con alas,* his winged coffin. That frightened me less than before.

The Holy Spirit of My Uncle's Cojones

Half an hour later Dad awoke, rubbed his face, donned his Forty Niners helmet, and walked to the plane. He stepped in, pushing his feet through the trap door and placing them upon firm ground. Then he sat down and closed the floor hatch. He asked me to flip the propellor. It started on the third twist. I stepped back as he taxied away from where I stood. "Oh God," I murmured, "I hope he gets back down on the ground." Then I wanted to erase that prayer. Obviously he would inevitably get back on the ground. The question was, in what shape? There was no need to pray for such matters beyond my control. As far as I knew, it was beyond God's control. The only one who had any hint of manipulation of the present situation was the man who now placed the huge goggles over his eyes.

He turned to me, gave me a thumb's up, looked down the stretch of grass, and did nothing. I waited, wondering if perhaps he was making sure the engine was warmed up. But it was not that. He was just staring at the pathless ground before him. He remained in that position for more than two minutes, while I stared at the Forty-Nine on his head. I thought that he would, at any second, cut off the engine and choose to step out of the cockpit. Then he glanced down, snatched the stick in his hands, and left the earth.

We watched as he first carefully circled the area. The low buzz of the Ultralight was the only thing we could hear. Then he became more emboldened. He banked enough for me to see his wrinkled face that did not smile. Still, it was obvious he was enjoying all this. He flew over the treeline behind Mamá and Aunt Felícita, disappearing from our sight, only to reappear to our left. He did that three times. Each time we heard his distance in the diminishing of the motor's buzz. When the buzz grew stronger, we had to guess from which angle he would arrive.

On the third time, he aimed toward a taller set of tree tops. It was obvious from our position that he was too low. His wheels were heading straight for the tips of the large oaks. Then we all knew, this was it, this was where it ended. Both Mamá and Aunt Felícita stood at the same time as they watched his fuselage dip under the treeline. I braced myself, ready to run toward the base of the trees and search for his body in the downed, shattered plane.

"Oh shit, pull up, pull it up," my mother muttered. Her throat filled with tears. Then she yelped, "That son of a bitch!" as Dad pulled the stick back and leapt up and over the treeline, just like the boys in the neighborhood who gracefully jumped from the street to the sidewalk, just missing the dangerous curb.

I laughed so hard I thought a muscle had pulled in my stomach. My mother scolded me, so I walked to her side and hugged her, knowing that her tears would still come. Yet in a few moments she would be both grateful and angry, approaching his plane with both curses and thanksgiving rolling over her tongue. As I ran to the perfectly landed plane, my geriatric father slowly peeled the goggles and lifted the gold helmet off his head. He wiped the sweat from his face and grinned a tobacco-stained, toothy grin at us. We welcomed him back to an earth that I knew he loved even more for his buzzing flight as a successful Icarus.

"Your uncle never forgot about you, Tony," my mother said, her head lowering slightly to the kitchen table while her eyes rose toward me, not unlike a rib shot coming from underneath.

I said nothing, allowing for the necessary guilt trip.

"He left you something in his will."

My mother sat opposite me. My aunt sat between us, to my right. We all drank coffee on this Sunday afternoon, just a few hours after my father's flight. Dad, having celebrated his success in the air with half a beer and a few chapters of a novel, now lay upon the couch in the den, sleeping peacefully. The women took this time to talk business.

"You know, Tony," she continued, "Juan had received the same inheritance from your grandmother that we all had. But he had no desire to be part of the business. He never wanted to work there. He had managed not to spend his entire inheritance before dying. So he left most everything to his . . . his daughter." She barely glanced over at Aunt Felícita. My aunt did not even flinch. She did hate her niece, but she also had no qualms with her brother leaving most everything to her.

"He left some gifts of cash to other folks as well. He left you ten thousand dollars."

I know my eyes opened wide. I looked at them both. Both smiled at me, pleased and perhaps not a little proud that they had been able to rouse such a physical response from me.

"That's incredibly generous," I said. "I didn't know he had that kind of money."

"Well, he wouldn't have, if he had not let me invest it for him," Aunt Felícita said. "Little Felícita will inherit the bonds and the stocks, plus most of the cash. You will get the ten grand. It will take awhile for it to get through probate, but once it does, we'll make sure you get it."

I was already recalculating some plans that had been gathering in my head the past weekend. I already owned ten thousand dollars, given to me by my grandmother. I had not touched it, always seeing it as a nest egg of sorts for whatever vague possibilities would await me in the future. Now, with this news, I had twenty thousand. That amount of money, knowing my own way of living, would be enough to keep me alive for almost two years without having to work.

"There's also one other thing," my mother said, interrupting my thoughts. "He wanted you to have his car."

Again, my eyes burst through any possible façade of stoicism. "The Mustang?"

"Yes. That's what it is, isn't it, *hermana?*" my mother asked Aunt Felícita. She had never been good with the specific makes of automobiles.

"I get the Mustang . . ."

"Now, if you don't want it," Mamá continued, "I can understand. It will be difficult to take care of such an old car. If you would like, we can sell it for you here . . ."

"No, no. Don't sell it. I'll take it."

"Oh. All right. But what do you plan to do? Have it shipped to you in Knoxville?"

"No. I'll drive it."

"What do you mean you'll drive it?"

"Just that. I'll cancel my flight. I'll drive home tomorrow." Neither said anything to me. "Is that all right? Can I take it that quickly? Or should I wait until the courts deal with the will?"

Aunt Felícita answered, "It's not yours until the will goes through probate. But then again, we'll know you've got it. If there are any questions asked, just call us. And don't get caught by the cops for speeding."

I smiled and promised her that I would be careful.

My mother looked straight at me. "I don't understand. You said you were in a hurry to get back to your classes."

"I'm going to quit teaching."

Again, I caught them off guard. I was winning the game of 'who can surprise who the most.'

I tried to explain. "I'm not sure what my plans are. But I'm thinking about quitting my teaching jobs. Maybe keep one of them, just for a little spending money. But I'm tired of working my ass off and not having any time to write."

Both of them nodded their heads in affirmation and understanding. They knew how much writing meant to me. They had employed local women in the barrio to pray novenas for my success as a novelist. They had no problem in a man's decision to quit working in order to follow a passion, as long as he threw his entire heart into the attaining of the goal. I knew that was the way of my family, the motto of many a Salvadoran: It doesn't matter what you do, as long as you do it, as my grandmother had said, with all your loins.

"You think the car will make it that far?" my mother asked her sister.

"Juan was always working on it. I think he had the engine overhauled. It's more beautiful now than it was ten years ago."

"But it's an antique. I wonder if it will hold up on the road . . ."

I interjected, "I'll go down with Dad and look at it. He'll be able to tell me if it's ready for a cross-country road trip."

It was settled. I would take the Mustang with me tomorrow. I called the airport and cancelled my flight due to a sickness. I would get little money back. I did not care. I called Knoxville for the first time that weekend. The phone rang three times before Julie answered it. My heart pushed too much blood into my throat when I heard her say hello.

"Hey. It's me."

"Oh. Hey Tony. How's it going over there?"

"Fine. You?"

"Oh, you know. Same old stuff." I could almost hear her smile, that beautiful, pearly, perfect smile. "Studying my ass off and playing tennis."

"I see. You play with Bill this weekend?" I did not specifically say 'play tennis.'

"Yeah. Bill and me against Tommy and Jessica. We played a lot of doubles. We're eating dinner now together."

I thought I had heard forks clicking against plates, for more than just one person. Sure, I thought, all of them having a fine dinner in my apartment, no doubt drinking my wine and eating my cheese. No doubt satiating themselves at my table before fucking each other on my bed, my couch, my kitchen table.

"So how was the funeral?"

"Oh, about what you'd expect." I desired to share not one word with her about this weekend, nor about what had happened both inside my brain as well as outside, in this old community of mine, in this *barrio* that had been the first home of my life. "Listen, I just called to tell you that I won't be coming in tomorrow. I'll probably stay here a few more days . . . and I'll be flying in on Thursday night or so."

I turned and looked toward the kitchen. Mamá was looking at me, confused, knowing that just a few moments ago I was planning to drive the Mustang home. I held up a hand to her in an "I'll explain later" fashion, also known as the "I'm lying to my girlfriend" gesture.

"Oh really?" Julie could not hide all the glee in her voice. "Well, you know, that may be a good idea. To be with your family during this time of mourning."

"Yes," I said, faking myself into her false concern. "You know, that's just what I was thinking. So I'll give you a call once I know when my flight's leaving on Thursday or Friday, okay?"

I also asked if she would be so kind as to call the universities and tell them that a family emergency had occurred over the weekend, and that I would not be teaching classes until perhaps Friday night. I would deal with whatever repercussions would be awaiting me. I doubted that there would be many, knowing that the students of my once a week classes would not mind a break from reading and lectures. She agreed, wished me well, and hung up. I could imagine her on the other end turning to her guests, telling them the good news, that the old man wasn't going to be back in town all week. I could imagine them shouting with joy while ripping their tennis skirts and shorts off right then and there, ignoring the spaghetti and garlic bread in order to jump on one another's bodies in a fit of celebratory coitus. Then I ground my imagination away into an angry planning. Three days, I thought, it'll take three days to get to Knoxville. I told her Thursday or Friday, four and five days from now. Surprise surprise.

Dad woke up about an hour later. I told him of my plan. He was immediately and happily jealous. He gladly checked out the Mustang. We walked into the garage. Dad opened the hood and looked all through the engine with a bright mechanic's spotlight beside his head.

"Jack really took care of this car," he said. "He had the engine rebuilt just about a year ago. It's in beautiful shape. Look, he even cleaned it periodically, see?" He shone the light for me. I could see our reflection in some of the metal. We could not find one grease stain. I wondered if I would be so good to this machine.

"You better take good care of it," Dad said, as if reading my thoughts. "It's an antique. Worth a lot of money. You treat her right, she'll take care of you on the road."

He looked at the belts (all new) and the tires (only a year old, bought when the engine was rebuilt). I opened the driver's door and sat inside. Uncle Jack had the seats reupholstered in black leather. He had had cruise control installed. Although the dashboard looked the same, the dash itself was new. I remembered the crack in it eighteen years ago, where Jack had shoved in a playing card of a nude *gringa*. No such cracks nor card were there now. Nor were there any huge dice hanging from the rear view mirror. The radio had also changed, dramatically. No longer was there a cassette player in the dash. He had replaced it with a compact disc player. I looked down to the compartment that had held the cassettes almost two decades ago. It was filled with CDs. Right in front was a thick CD box titled "Just Another Band from East L.A." Los Lobos.

I knew I would have to check the entire car to make sure there was no grass planted on it anywhere. That would have been an enjoyable perk to the gift, but I didn't want to get caught with it on the highway. I had decided to give my packet to Dad for his own use. This weekend had been a one-shot deal, and I was not ready to have either the mushrooms or the marijuana a part of my daily life.

I would try to leave as early as possible, perhaps before sunrise. A certain thrill pushed itself through me with that thought. Before I got out of the car, I leaned over and opened the glove compartment to see if there were any necessary ownership papers in there. I looked in it, and grinned a big grin.

The only regret I had about making this trip was that I was making it too fast. Given any other situation, I would have enjoyed taking a slow, leisurely passage through the United States, avoiding the interstates to drive on the quiet, two-lane highways that would have taken me into the various worlds of the nation. That was not to be the case this time around. Perhaps, I thought, this Mustang and I would make that sort of meandering trip in the future.

For now I took Interstate 5 through California, then hooked onto Highway 58 until it connected me to Interstate 40 East. I stayed on 40 all the way to Tennessee, cutting through Arizona, New Mexico, Texas, Oklahoma, and Arkansas. The weather remained warm, with no rain for the three days of travel. I drove twelve hours a day, stopping for meals and bathroom breaks, making sure that I checked into hotels around six at night so as to have a full night's sleep. It also allowed me to throw off the dregs of long-distance driving by running four miles around the hotel before jumping into the pool. In the mornings I would do pushups and situps, bathe, eat a quick bite, grab some coffee and hit the road. I listened to two hours of news on public radio before shoving in Los Lobos and cranking the volume high.

It gave me time to think and not to think. The past few days had done something to me, yet I could not completely explain to myself what had happened. At first I thought it was just the mushrooms. As Uncle Jack once said, they have a way of showing a person what's really happening in the world. It may seem like a strange trip, with breathing doors and talking breasts, but within all that, there are some truths to be found. Perhaps. Yet I also wondered if it was the fact that I had returned to the barrio of my childhood, the neighborhood where I had been reminded, in my teenage years, of who I was. That was a time when I studied Spanish furiously. The sophomore year before that summer I was making a "C" in Spanish class. In my junior year, not only was I making an "A," I was embarrassing Sister

Mary Kay with my apt accent and fairly decent flow that triumphed over her Georgian lilt. Before my sixteenth year the monolingual, white, southern world had taught me to forget my other side. It was not that culture's fault. There were just no reminders in Tennessee for a Latino youth to see himself in.

I had spent my twenties searching for Latinos to live with. I had lived years in Central America and Mexico. I had hung out with Latino migrant farm workers in Alabama. Then I got a novel published and followed the university road, where the ascetic life of an adjunct professor filled my days, leaving no time to write, to stop, to eat and enjoy a *sobremesa* with someone who understands what *sobremesa* means. It was no wonder that my life had turned into mere existence before my uncle's death.

I arrived in Nashville around noon on Wednesday. I was making better timing than I had calculated. I ate lunch in the state capital, then checked into a hotel. I had paced myself on the road since Monday morning, but the days were catching up with me. I wanted to be fresh for the encounter that awaited me three hours down the road.

At the hotel I sprinted a couple of miles, jumped into the pool, then took a shower. By the time I finished it was late afternoon. I hoped to show up at my apartment around seven o'clock that evening. There was no science to this, only history. I usually taught class between six and nine, which gave Julie and Bill time to toss each other around in my bed. Figuring that most people were creatures of habit, I hoped this to be the case tonight.

In the parking lot of my apartment complex I opened the glove compartment, emptied its contents into my duffel bag, closed the bag and got out. I locked up the Mustang and walked in, jingling the keys in my hand. At the door I jingled them some more, holding them in the air and shaking them before inserting the house key. It was fair, I thought, at this point to give as much warning as possible. Opening the door more loudly than usual, I shouted into the apartment, "I'm hooome!"

The Holy Spirit of My Uncle's *Cojones*

I heard a scuffling. I looked down the hallway. The door to my bedroom quickly closed but did not shut, thus making no slamming noise. The scuffling continued. What luck, I thought.

I walked to the kitchen, opened the refrigerator and pulled out a beer. I drank a small sip from it before turning around to Julie. She was wrapped in a towel, holding it to her with both hands.

"Tony. Tony! You're home!" She smiled, but did not move from there.

"Yeah, I got in earlier than I thought. My plane left at a good time. I thought I'd surprise you." I smiled at her, an endearing, husbandly smile. "Hey, aren't you going to welcome me back?" I asked, holding my arms wide to her.

She smiled again, cocked her head to one side in an "of course, dear," fashion, and walked to me. She hugged me carefully. I could smell Bill on her. Fresh.

"Were you just going to hop in the shower?" I asked.

"Yes. That's right."

"Good. I could use a shower myself."

She half protested, saying that I should perhaps lie down and rest on the couch in the living room (she said that twice) while she cleaned up, for no doubt I was tired from the plane flight.

"On the contrary, *mi amor,* I'm wide awake. It must have been those days away from you."

I moved her to the bathroom. She muttered some half-eaten words about having to tell me something, perhaps a last ditch effort to spill it all out and hope for my mercy. Knowing how I had acted before San Francisco, I could not fault her for this. She probably believed that she would get an easy, understanding response from a boyfriend who had acted like a patient waiting for a spinal donation. I did not give her the chance. I kissed her. At first she stiffened. I pushed into her mouth. She opened. I reached under her towel. She jerked. I reached behind and pushed my middle finger into the crack of her buttocks before moving on down and toward her slightly wet labia, no doubt still warm from whatever was going on before I arrived. She loosened slightly in my grip.

"You get in the shower. I'll follow right behind you."

"Tony, listen, I think it'd be good if we talked . . ."

"Sounds great. We'll talk in the shower." I smiled and walked out of the bathroom toward my bedroom. She protested, saying loudly, like a warning, "What are you going to do *in the bedroom?*" to which I answered that I just wanted to get these stinking clothes off.

I quickly looked about the bedroom, searching for anything that would help with my plan. There, on the bed's side table, they lay. In the midst of the scuffling, they had forgotten to snatch up the car keys to Bill's Land Rover. I grabbed them, brought them into the bathroom and hid them in the medicine cabinet. Julie had obeyed me. She was in the shower. Through the glass I could see that her forehead was leaning against the wall. Perhaps she wished to push through that wall. I opened the door and got behind her.

I worked her over with the soap. I cleaned every inch of her body, from her neck to her ankles. I soaped her everywhere, massaging her skin, hoping to loosen her even more as well as clean off any remnant of the other who no doubt hid somewhere in the bedroom. It seemed to work. I smelled no Bill on her, and she smiled at me, a real, though quick smile of certain satisfaction. Then another look came over her face, that of scarcely concealed panic. I kissed her as if telling her to worry about nothing. She looked at me confused. Perhaps she wondered if I knew and that, instead of reacting like either an enraged, violent boyfriend or a weak, cuckolded one, I was actually turned on by the idea of another man mounting her. God knows what she thought at that moment. I thought of little else but her body.

We barely toweled down before I pulled her into the bedroom and lay her upon her stomach. I massaged her back, lumbar, legs, feet, and finally buttocks. At first she said nothing, making no noise whatsoever. I had my doubts that this was going to work. I wondered, was it more than she being bored with me? Did I repulse her? Finally, she did grunt slightly, after a full twenty minutes of the body massage.

"That feels good," she muttered.

Those words saved me from falling into complete self-doubt. I massaged her scalp with my fingertips, then her neck. Again, I took my time. I had to give Bill credit; he kept completely quiet, wherever he was. I ran my tongue slowly over her tanned back, down into the lumbar, then over each cheek. I continued licking down the back of her thighs and over her calves. I did not stop until I heard a soft, purring breath leave her. Then I lifted my head up, stuck my tongue straight out and slowly pushed it in.

She yelped. We had never done this before. I followed my uncle's wisdom, that there is nothing dirty about a beautiful woman, that she is lovely unto her ass.

"Tony. Wait a minute . . ." But I really don't think she meant that. I could tell by the way she pivoted slightly and spread her cheeks with her own fingertips. Besides, I would not stay in there forever. I ran my tongue down while pushing her left leg to one side. This, too, had not been done before between us. As far as I knew, Bill relied mostly upon his large member for physical responses. Julie had, as far as I could tell, not enjoyed the opportunity to have her sex treated like a ripe peach. She seemed open to this simile. She lifted her pelvis, allowing me passage. I carefully clasped her with my lips. She rocked with me in a lovely rhythm for about three or four minutes before a moan—not at all like that of her backhand shot—shoved out of her chest. Then she spoke, using both my name and God's in the same broken phrase, which did a world of good for my character building.

Out of the closet I heard another moan, but it was not a vicarious one to Julie's. It escaped before the person could stop it from leaving his mouth and the closed closet door.

"What was that?" I said.

Julie said it was nothing. She snatched my head with her fingers and pulled my lips to hers.

I reached over to the bed table and pulled a condom from the drawer. I slapped it on quickly, as things were about to end. I was barely in her when I came, which was another good thing for my self-confidence. I had not nearly pre-ejaculated since my mid twenties.

We lay together for about five minutes. She suddenly stiffened again, as if remembering. "You, uh, you want to go out or something?" she asked.

"Why?"

"Oh, I don't know. If you're hungry."

I smiled. "No. I'm not hungry. But we can go out."

"Great. Where do you want to go?" she asked.

I did not answer her right off. I stood up and pulled my thick black robe from the closet. I didn't even bother to peek in and see him crouched in there. Then I collected her clothes from the floor, opened the drawer to her set of clothes, gathered them all in my arms, walked to the glass door of the bedroom's small balcony and tossed the clothes off the edge. I returned. She had barely seen me act. Her eyes grew wide over the bedsheets. She didn't say anything until I grabbed all her hanging clothes from the closet, walked to the balcony, and threw them off the side.

"What are you *doing?*"

"I'm not doing anything. You're moving out."

"What? What?"

As she screamed, I reached down into the final dresser drawer for her T-shirts. My Sandinista shirt was on top. I picked it up and put it on top of the dresser before grabbing up all the T-shirts and throwing them through the balcony door.

She bolted up from the bed, flung off the sheets, and ran to the glass door. She crouched to one side, making sure that no one at the pool just below my third storey balcony saw her. Then she screamed some more, calling me crazy, stupid, lunatic, all laced with a few choice curses. Then again, perhaps they were not choice. She was too angry to be able to choose anything. She started beating my chest.

Then she aimed for my testicles. I ducked away, then moved toward my duffel bag.

"Look," I said, "you're trespassing. This is my apartment. I pay the rent here. You and your friend in the closet shouldn't be in here."

With that said, the man in the closet jerked. His knee or elbow popped the closet door.

"You're fucking crazy!" She stopped yelling once I pulled out Uncle Jack's gun from the duffel bag. I didn't aim it at her. I just let it dangle from my fingertips, beside my hip. She stared at it for ten long seconds, her eyes growing wider.

"Get out, Julie."

She obeyed. She walked across the bedroom, down the hallway and to the front door. She reached for a towel that was on the floor. "Uh-uh. That's mine," I said, pointing casually at the towel with the gun. She jumped, opened the door, and sprinted out. Half a minute later I heard the half-breaths, half-gasps, full yelps of the people at the pool.

I lay down on my bed and crossed my ankles in a relaxed position. Pulling my black robe over my chest, I pointed the gun at the closet. In the silence of the bedroom, I pulled back the hammer. The steely click cut through the room's air.

"All right, Bill. Come on out."

He did. He was naked, so he only at first showed me his head. Then he saw the barrel of my fake gun pointed directly at his face.

"Jesus!" He stood up, popping his head against the metal bar where Julie's clothes had hitherto hung. He stood right in front of me. Yes, it was big. Very big. Seeing its size, I wondered if Julie had made her grunting noises due to pleasure or lack of room. I did not let its magnitude make me flinch. I merely pointed my barrel directly at it.

"God, Tony, please, for God's sake!" he squealed. "I know this all looks bad, man, but please, it's not worth you killing me! Julie's not worth that!"

I had hoped that, while she quickly dressed herself down on the ground next to the pool, she had heard his scream through the open balcony door. I let him plead a few seconds more.

"Okay, Bill. Just leave, all right?"

He gathered his clothes from the closet. "Oh, but before you go, toss those things, will you?" I motioned to the balcony with my gun.

He looked at the balcony, then at me, then at the gun. Then he obeyed. He threw them all out. I suppose he hoped that the keys to his Land Rover were in his pants pockets, for he ran from my apartment as soon as he let the clothes go.

I walked to my bathroom and pulled the keys out of the medicine cabinet. Walking to the glass door, I could hear Julie's voice as she pitched curses up to my balcony. I walked out, my robe still on, and stared down at all the kids and parents and a few older folks who stared from poolside at me, then at Julie, who was now dressed, then at Bill, who struggled to get his pants on. I noticed one older woman pull her sunglasses down and give Bill a good stare. Then she glanced up at me, as if to thank me.

I said nothing to Julie's retorts, nor to her threats of somehow suing me or calling the cops. I had this sense that she had very little on me. As she called me names that made mothers run to their children to cup their ears while also yelling at Julie to shut her filthy mouth, I lifted the keys in my palm and flung them far and wide. They arched above the multitude and splashed into the deep end of the pool.

The closed balcony door was enough to muffle her voice. I walked to my kitchen. There I called the house on Capp Street and told my aunt that I had arrived safely. Mamá got on the phone. We had a nice conversation about my trip. She hoped that I would come back to San Francisco someday soon. *"No hay duda,"* I said. "I wouldn't mind getting back there myself." I also talked with Dad. While talking with Mamá, we flipped into Spanish easily. While talking with Dad, I flowed into a certain southern lilt: "You have fun with your plane, you hear?" The two seemed inextricable and very much at home with each other.

After hanging up, I looked for something to eat. I was in the mood for tortillas. There, behind all of Julie's plastic vessels of left-over Chinese food, tofu, pizza slices, salad, and yogurt with sprinkles, was my old bag of *masa harina*. It was my grandmother's brand. There was Abuelita, smiling approvingly at me from the label. I made a batch of tortillas, opened a can of refried beans, sautéed some chick-en breast strips. There were no jalapeños in the house. I would have to shop the following day.

I slept a most peaceful sleep.

The following morning I rose early. Making sure the phone's recorder was on and its volume down, I flipped on the computer at my desk. The coffee steamed to one side of the screen. The sun rose over Knoxville in front of me, tossing a golden glint off the side of the old World's Fair Golden Ball. I looked over the town of Knoxville, not seeing it at all. I doubt that I would see it for very long. I hoped to be looking over another skyline in the next few months. I knew I would have to write myself there.

The sun moved a good twenty minutes over the morning. Yet I did not panic. This was not writer's block. That big dick was gone. This was something else. This was the silence that I as a writer walked through with my hands slightly out, feeling the very air of the darkness. Within the solitude stood a raw energy that waited for me. Then, with the assurance of one who has witnessed an incident, or at least, has created an incident in his mind, my fingers placed them-selves upon the keys and rattled out a title.

The Holy Spirit of My Uncle's Cojones
By Antonio McCaugh Villalobos

Then I began to write.